*It was a time when gods walked the eart
of land, but for the very existence of hun........,
formidable warriors stood against an evil greater than any the earth had
ever seen. But evil is not an honorable foe. Betrayed by someone they
trusted, the warriors were cursed, one by one, tossed into the maelstrom of
time, imprisoned in stone, their freedom resting on nearly impossible condi-
tions. Alone of the five, their leader, the sorcerer Nicodemus, was left free.
His curse? To know that his fellow warriors remained trapped forever out
of his reach, condemned to an eternity of searching for their stone prisons
and the keys to their freedom.*

DAMIAN

*Damian Stephanos, warrior and lover, who bedded the Amazon queen
but refused to take the battlefield by her side . . . you shall remain locked
in stone until a woman warrior shall sacrifice her own blood, calling you
forth to fight for her cause.*

Look what people are saying about D. B. Reynolds's latest *Vampires in America. . . .*

"This series is at the top of my list for fabulous Paranormal Romance with plenty of action, thrills and hot sexy Vampires. No sparkles here but plenty of charisma."

—La Deetda Reads

"I am loving the direction that Reynolds is taking with the series and it's absolutely one of my favorites and one that I highly recommend to vampire romance lovers."

—The BookChick Blog

"Captivating and brimming with brilliance, Christian is yet another defining addition to the ever-evolving world of Vampires in America created by D. B. Reynolds."

—K T Book Reviews on CHRISTIAN

"Did I mention that the sizzling sex factor in this book is reaching the combustible stage? It is a wonder my Kindle didn't burn up."

—La Deetda Reads on DECEPTION

"It's the brilliance of her characters and the staying power of the world she has created that always keeps me coming back for more."

—KT Book Reviews on DECEPTION

D. B. Reynolds
Vampires in America

Damian

The Stone Warriors
Book 1

by

D. B. Reynolds

ImaJinn Books

This is a work of fiction. Names, characters, places and incidents are either the products of the author's imagination or are used fictitiously. Any resemblance to actual persons (living or dead), events or locations is entirely coincidental.

ImaJinn Books
PO BOX 300921
Memphis, TN 38130
Print ISBN: 978-1-61194-703-8

ImaJinn Books is an Imprint of BelleBooks, Inc.

ImaJinn Books was founded by Linda Kichline.

We at ImaJinn Books enjoy hearing from readers. Visit our websites
ImaJinnBooks.com
BelleBooks.com
BellBridgeBooks.com

10 9 8 7 6 5 4 3 2 1

Cover design: Debra Dixon
Interior design: Hank Smith
Photo/Art credits:
Man (manipulated) © Pawelsierakowski | Dreamstime.com
Background (manipulated) © Susan McKivergan
Baroque illustration (manipulated) © Rainbowchaser | Dreamstime.com

:Ldsf:01:

Dedication

For Roman, the heart and soul of every hero I've ever written.

Love you forever.

Chapter One

Somewhere in the American Midwest, Present Day

CASSANDRA LEWIS raced down the deserted street, her booted feet slapping on the wet pavement. Gripping her right arm hard, to hold back the dripping blood, she dared a glance over her shoulder. There was no one in sight, but all she could hear were the echoing howls of the hounds on her tail. She swerved to the building on her right, stumbling over the short step up to the sidewalk as she went directly to the big plate glass window. Wincing, she lifted her gun and fired a single shot. A crystal snowflake of cracks spread outward from the small hole. Stepping back, she aimed a hard kick at the weakened pane and broke it inward, before leaving a bloody handprint on the shattered glass, hoping to mislead the hounds and give her an extra few minutes. It wasn't much, but it was all she could do.

She ran across the street, stepped up to the security keypad on the Kalman building, and entered the code she'd paid the daytime guard for just a few days ago. The lock buzzed and she opened the door, entering quickly and closing it behind her. The Kalman was an institution of sorts, a five-story building that had once been the center of the financial district. The big banks had all moved to the new high rises downtown, taking most of the smaller businesses with them. But, as with all of the other buildings in this part of town, the Kalman had been repurposed. Some had been converted to light industry, others now housed a growing number of the city's burgeoning wholesale fabric suppliers, while the Kalman itself had been divided into separate office suites which were leased mostly by lawyers and other young professionals who couldn't yet afford the high rents that went along with high-rise buildings downtown.

For Casey's purposes tonight, the Kalman was perfect. The building's occupants had all gone home long ago, it had an elevator that went all the way to the roof, and it was close enough to its neighbors that she might be able to make her escape over the rooftops, high above the pursuing hounds.

She ran into the elevator and punched the button for the roof, leaning wearily against the back wall, scowling at her reflection in the polished doors. She was dressed all in black—combat boots and fatigues, her T-shirt torn and bloodied over her wounded shoulder, exposing the gory proof that she'd been shot. She swallowed hard at the sight. She'd seen injuries before, had even seen bullet wounds. But never on herself. She forced herself to stop staring, to take stock of her situation. She popped the magazine on her 9mm Glock. Five rounds left and one in the pipe. Not nearly enough, especially not shooting with her left—off—hand.

She reached automatically for the spare mag in the right-hand pocket of her black fatigues and closed her eyes in pain as the movement jarred her injured shoulder. *Christ, that hurt!* She'd never been shot before, and now she was pretty sure she'd been shot twice. After the first bullet, it had been simply all pain, all the time. She couldn't really tell if that second shot had actually hit her or just skimmed by.

As the fourth floor lit up on the indicator, she dropped the nearly empty magazine into her left pocket and inserted the new one with a hard slap that made her breath catch in her throat. That gave her thirty-four rounds, and it still wasn't going to be enough. Not against what was chasing her. Hellhounds. She hadn't expected that. Fuck, she hadn't expected any real resistance tonight, much less a magical defense worthy of a full-on sorcerer. It took serious power to call up a pair of hellhounds, and it made her wonder if her enemy tonight was more than some random magic user.

The Talisman—the thing in her backpack that had started all of this—could be a powerful weapon, one that a sorcerer like . . . she hesitated even to think his name. But damn, Sotiris would love to get his hands on the Talisman. Was that what was happening here? Had their ultimate enemy been behind this all along? Sotiris was possibly the most powerful sorcerer left on earth, and unfortunately, he was just as evil as he was powerful. Keeping artifacts like the Talisman away from *him* was a big part of why her boss, Nick Katsaros, and the rest of the FBI had her hunting them down in the first place.

The elevator doors opened on the roof to a slap of cold, damp air and the baying of the hounds. Did they sound closer? Shit.

Ducking outside, she made a dash for the big air-conditioning unit and hunkered down in its shadow until she was sure the roof was empty. This was her last chance. She had to make it work.

With the Glock in her left hand, she slung her backpack over her right shoulder, ignoring the stab of pain. It might have made more sense to dump the heavy pack, but it was the Talisman that made all of this mess worthwhile. She'd abandon her gun before she'd leave behind that damn pack.

She rushed across the roof and peered over the front edge of the building, bracing her bloody hand on the Kalman Guardian, a statue of a half-naked warrior standing guard with a knife at his hip and a huge sword gripped before him. The statue was a landmark, reputed to be a few centuries old. The warrior it depicted was supposedly life-sized, assuming the man was about six and a half feet tall and built like a fucking god.

Leaning forward to scan the street back the way she'd come, she gripped the statue's thick arm. Grit slid beneath her fingers to mix with her forced to watch the world go by without so much as the sun's heat penetrating his stone prison, this agony was as joyous as the light of Elysium.

His lungs expanded with the first breath of oxygen he'd drawn since that long-ago moment on an ancient battlefield. So unexpected was the feeling that it shocked him at first, terrified him. It felt as if he was being ripped apart, his body unable to cope with the awakening of his flesh after all this time.

And then came the pounding of his heart, so loud that he strained to turn around, to see what enormous beast was coming upon him from behind.

Fingers which had long rested around his sword now gripped it properly, the ridges and grooves as familiar to him as if they were part of his own hand. He lowered his gaze . . . and his eyes opened to the world around him. Not the inhuman, unblinking eyes of stone, which were all the world had seen of him for centuries untold, the eyes with which he'd been forced to watch as time went by around him. These were his true eyes, and he wanted to weep.

But there was no time for womanly emotion. He was a warrior, and he'd been called to battle by the female, who was enough of a warrior herself that her blood had broken the curse. Wounded, but still fighting, courageous and strong. She'd freed him from this endless prison. He was honor-bound to help her.

He tried to turn, to search the roof for her. But his muscles were still sluggish and awkward. It infuriated him. He'd been the greatest fighter of his time, his prowess on the battlefield unlike any other. And now that he was needed again, he creaked like an old woman. He forced himself to move, feeling fresh warmth seeping into his muscle and sinew, fresh awareness flooding his mind. He was nearly overwhelmed with sensory input, everything so much more vivid than during his long imprisonment, trapped in stone. The damp air that stank of the filth that humans took for granted as the price of civilization, the distant sound of sirens, the roar of a plane overhead and—he frowned—the baying of hellhounds? He'd not heard that sound in thousands of years, not since before he'd been cursed.

He stepped down from the pedestal that had been his home, turning just in time to see the woman drop over the back of the building. He took two steps in her direction and heard her cry of pain, a sound even louder to his ears than the thumping of his own heart. He ran to the edge of the roof, shedding stone with every step, leaning over to peer downward just in time to hear her defiant snarl. He'd seen her break the glass across the street, seen her leave a smear of her blood. But her ploy had failed. The hellhounds raced to the Kalman, creeping in shadow along the side of the building, waiting for her as she climbed out of the big metal bin. The two beasts crouched, one on either side of her, their gruesome mouths dripping saliva while their eyes gleamed with the fire of hell itself. She drew her weapon, but he could see the pain it cost her.

He didn't know what cause she fought for so determinedly, but she was going to die if he didn't help her. He lifted his blade, exulting in the weight of it after so long. Anticipation raced through his bloodstream, energizing his muscles, shattering the last of the stone that surrounded him. Leaning over, he grabbed the rope she'd left behind and leapt off the roof after her.

CASEY BIT BACK her cry as knives of agony stabbed through her wounded shoulder, seeming to travel in waves down her arm and over her back, tightening her muscles into spasms that only added to her pain. She struggled to breathe through the dust and dirt that filled the air of the overflowing dumpster after her fall, waiting for the throbbing to ease up enough for her to think. But the nightmare that had become her life tonight wasn't going to grant her even that.

Grabbing the edge of the metal container, she rolled out onto the hard asphalt only to find the nightmare hiding in the shadows, waiting for her. Damn, but they'd figured that misdirect out quickly. *Note to self—hellhounds weren't totally stupid.*

She put the dumpster at her back and drew the Glock with her left hand, still gripping the strap of the backpack with her right, grateful for the rough weave that soaked up the blood without getting slick and unmanageable. She huffed a silent breath, thinking that this was what her life had come to, gratitude for a blood-soaked strap that still worked.

A soft growl had her spinning in a crouch to find one of the hounds eyeing her hungrily. She'd no sooner clocked his position than the other one showed himself, prowling out of the darkness, lips pulled back in a snarl that bared terrifying fangs below a pair of red-drenched eyes.

She waited for them to come to her. The blood leaking from her shoulder should be drawing them like a magnet, sending a signal to their tiny brains that their prey was wounded, vulnerable. But they didn't move from their watchful crouches, and Casey realized something. Every instinct was telling them to attack and kill, but whoever was running them was holding them back. It was because of the Talisman. It was not only valuable, but unstable.

She didn't know what would set it off, and she'd bet her enemies didn't either. It could be triggered by something as ordinary as a stray bullet or a deep graze from a hound's fang. And once triggered, it would emit an electronic pulse that could wreak havoc on today's technological society. The death and destruction could be terrible. And it would take a power much greater than she possessed to shut it down.

Its potentially disastrous nature was why she'd been sent to retrieve the thing. Her boss, Nick Katsaros, ran a team that was funded by the FBI and existed solely to find and retrieve the various magical artifacts scattered throughout the world. Magic and the FBI might seem an odd fit, but it frequently made her life a lot easier. Like when she needed to slip weapons through customs or reassure the local law enforcement that it was perfectly okay for her to engage in the breaking and entering of a private home or institution, or even the occasional gunfight, like tonight.

Casey was only one of Nick's hunters, but she'd been with him long enough and had proved herself often enough, that he trusted her to go after the really significant pieces. Especially the ones with unknown magic. But someone had dropped the ball on this mission, because the background information they had on the collector was simply wrong. Shit. Hellhounds?

And now she was crouched in an alley, with the deadly artifact that she'd stolen suddenly acting as her best defense against the very people she'd stolen it from. How fucked up was that?

Her pursuers came into view behind the hounds, nothing but flashes of movement as they kept to the shadows and doorways, mindful of her weapon. Casey scooted back a few feet until she was mostly hidden behind the dumpster. They might not want to shoot, but that didn't mean they wouldn't. Especially if one of them thought he was a sharpshooter and decided to go for a headshot. She leaned out from the dumpster's cover and sighted down the alley, waiting for one of her enemies to show his face. They couldn't shoot her, for fear of hitting the Talisman, but she sure as hell could shoot them.

Someone moved out of the shadows, scurrying for the next cover. Casey quickly lined up her shot with both hands, and pulled the trigger. The man's head exploded like a bloody melon, and he dropped to the ground. It was always best to go for a headshot when dealing with magic users. Too many of them could recover from even the most severe wound to their body. But no one could survive a hollow point to the brain, and she was a very good shot.

Down the alley, one of her pursuers swore violently. "Just slide over the pack with the device," a voice called. "We don't care about you."

Casey didn't waste the energy it would take to voice her skepticism. They probably wouldn't shoot her once she got rid of the backpack— they'd loose the hounds. The two beasts remained totally focused on her, snarling non-stop, their powerful muscles bunched as they fought their handler's control, waiting for the release they knew instinctively would come. The freedom to attack and kill their prey. Oh, yeah, and then *feed*.

Someone else scurried down the alley, and she fired off another shot, hitting the brick wall where her target had been only seconds earlier. Damn. She couldn't afford to waste ammo. Although, for a moment, she actually wondered why not. She didn't see any resolution of this stand-off that didn't include her dead body. She might as well take as many of them with her as she could.

That didn't include the hounds, unfortunately. To some, they might seem the obvious target. They weren't protected, weren't hiding in the shadows, or huddling behind a filthy garbage dumpster. The problem was that the hounds hunted in pairs, and she could only shoot one at a time. And once she shot the first one—assuming she managed a kill shot, which was no guarantee, since their skulls were like rock—the other would go a little nuts, breaking whatever hold his handler had on him, and freeing him to kill whoever struck his fancy. As the one who'd killed his partner, she'd be the first target. She wouldn't be the only one, which she might have taken some comfort in, if she'd really thought there was no hope of survival. But she wasn't ready to throw in the towel just yet.

The scrape of a boot had her turning to discover two of her pursuers rappelling down the side of the building behind her. Their ropes weren't twelve feet short, either. She caught movement in the corner of her eye and spun back around to find the ones in front had moved up while she was distracted. She couldn't win this. She was one, and they were many. Damn, maybe she *was* going to die tonight.

"Fuck," she swore, not caring who heard. Fucking *Nick Katsaros*. This was all his fault. Instead of running around Kansas, consorting with vampires, he should have been verifying the intel that sent her after the damn Talisman in the first place. *He'd* have caught the inconsistencies, the tells that would have warned that something wasn't quite right about this job. He had a real gift for it, a knowledge that exceeded her own, and she was a fucking expert. But it was too late. The only thing he could do for her now was to attend her damn funeral.

A sudden scream had her jerking back around, just in time to see one of her pursuers seemingly plucked off the wall and sent flying through the air to hit the opposite building with a sickening crunch.

What the hell?

A huge blond man stepped out of the alley between the two buildings and walked over to the injured man who lay on the ground groaning. Picking him up by his obviously broken arm, the blond giant held him for only a second before running him through with a big-ass sword, stabbing in below his arm to avoid the ballistic vest and right into his heart. Yep, that was another thing no magic user could survive, having his heart sliced in two. The second climber jumped to the ground and spun to fire his weapon at the newcomer, but the blond held the body-armor-wearing dead guy in front of him to absorb the gunfire as he advanced, then threw the body at the shooter, grabbed his weapon, and turned it on him, shooting him expertly three times. Once in the head, twice in the heart.

Casey stared. A triple tap. Who was this guy? But then she heard curses from the enemies still in front of her and decided it didn't matter. Whoever he was, he was on her side—at least for the time being—and she might survive this night, after all.

Bullets whizzed past her position as her enemies started firing at her erstwhile ally. Casey ducked back farther into the protection of the dumpster, taking advantage of the fact that they seemed to have forgotten about her. Slipping the backpack off her shoulder, she tucked it between the dumpster and the wall, then shuffled to the other end of the container, until her enemies were in sight. They weren't paying much attention to her anymore; they were totally focused on taking out the blond, stepping into the open to gain a better vantage, overwhelming him three to one. She waited until they were just past her position, then crept out of hiding behind them and picked them off one, two, three. Did she have a problem with shooting them in the back? Why no, she didn't.

As soon as they were down, she raced out of cover and over to where they lay on the ground, finishing each of them off with a bullet to the head. No telling who among them was a magic user.

She was breathing hard, standing over the last dead body, when a deep, rumbling growl reminded her of something she shouldn't have forgotten. The damn hellhounds were now unbound. One of these dead men had been their handler. Every instinct was screaming at her to back away, to run, but her brain was telling her that would be a mistake. She had to stand her ground, establish her dominance. Or at least try to. Logically, she knew that wouldn't last, but her only weapon was her Glock and there were those thick skulls to contend with.

One of the beasts took a threatening step closer. She jerked and instinctively started to step back.

"Stand your ground," a deep voice commanded.

She risked a glance over her shoulder to find her new ally striding up the alley toward her, bloody sword in one hand, a HK MP 5 submachine gun in the other.

"Eyes on the hound, woman, unless you want to die."

Casey's eyes narrowed in irritation. He might be her rescuer, but that didn't mean she had to put up with his macho bullshit. She'd kept herself alive this far . . . and okay, maybe there'd been a little help from him. She spun back around in time to see one of the hounds creeping close enough to reach her with a single leap. Damn. She raised her Glock. Maybe she couldn't kill it, but she could hurt it, slow it down. The other beast leapt suddenly, powerful hind legs propelling the creature ten feet to where she stood. She swung her Glock up and fired, watching the bullets hit its massive chest and knowing it wasn't going to be enough. She'd braced herself for impact, crouching down and protecting her face, ready to grab the beast and toss him through the air . . . when metal flashed in the dim light and a huge, fucking sword swung right over her head, slicing effortlessly through the hound's thick skin and taking off his head.

Casey screamed. Not in fear, but in disgust and anger as hot blood sprayed all over her, and the hound's head rolled to her feet. "Shit," she hissed, but kept her eye on the remaining beast. She wasn't going to make that mistake twice.

"Shall I kill that one for you also?" The same rumbling voice asked the question with a definite snarky edge.

"Would you?" she asked sweetly. "I'd be ever so grateful."

The blond snorted and lifted his blade, but the second hound growled loudly and backed away. He might be without a handler, but he wasn't without a brain, no matter how tiny. He'd seen what that blade had done to his partner.

"I can—" Casey lifted her Glock, intending to offer her assistance in dealing with the beast, something that involved shooting the creature as a distraction, if nothing else, but the arrogant ass cut her off.

"Your gun is useless," he said dismissively, then, using his left hand, he pulled a wicked knife from its sheath on his hip and threw it at the hell-hound, hitting the creature in the neck. Casey opened her mouth to warn him that that wouldn't be enough, but the man was already moving. He was on the hound almost before the blade struck, reaching out to grab the animal by the scruff as he shifted his grip on his sword, and efficiently removed its head.

Casey saw it coming this time and stepped away, smirking when she saw the creature's blood spurting all over the blond . . . when the thought suddenly struck her. Her pursuers were dead, the hounds were dead, and she was still alive. It was over, and she still had. . . . Shit! The Talisman. She rushed back to her hiding place behind the dumpster. No backpack. Heart sinking, she got down on hands and knees to peer underneath the filthy container, but it was gone. One of the bad guys must have snuck in and grabbed it, someone she hadn't even noticed was there. She climbed back to her feet, gasping as her wounded shoulder reminded her she'd been shot.

She felt awful. It wasn't the pain, or the exhaustion, or even the stinking hound's blood that coated her. She'd lost the fucking Talisman. She'd been searching for that damn thing for months, and she'd had it in her *hand*. She'd fought and clawed her way this far, and now it was gone again. She leaned bonelessly against the rough brick wall, eyes closed as she tried to find the strength to start all over.

"Your enemies are vanquished, woman," that deep voice growled. "The blood debt is paid."

Casey opened her eyes and found herself the target of an intense black stare. Her tired mind struggled to parse what he was saying. Blood debt? What was he talking about? And who was this guy anyway? She studied him closely for the first time. He was tall, a good five inches over her own nearly six feet, and he was big. Huge shoulders, beautifully defined arms, thick thighs, and that face. It was the face of a god from the old paintings, handsome but fierce, with a smoothly defined jaw and sensuous lips, those dark eyes seeming out of place with the blond hair that hung loose to his shoulders. Altogether, an extremely good-looking man, for all that he seemed to take the idea of cosplay to a whole new level.

He jammed the knife back into its sheath, then raised his sword and shook the blood away with a practiced flick of his wrist. Casey frowned. Apart from the ease with which he handled the heavy weapon, there simply weren't many people around anymore who understood blades well enough to know, much less execute, that maneuver. She studied his clothing, or rather his absence of clothing. He had no shirt on at all, and while the view was nice, when combined with leather pants and soft-soled boots, it didn't exactly scream modern soldier. She blinked, taking in the whole picture once more. And suddenly, it hit her. He glowed. Not like a light bulb, nothing an ordinary person would see, but to her eyes, and more importantly, to that part of her brain that registered magical force, he definitely glowed.

Put it all together . . . the magic, the clothes, the big-ass sword. She looked at her hand, turning it over as she stared at it, seeing her own blood soaked into the lines of her palm where it had dripped from her shoulder wound. A blood debt, he'd said. Her gaze traveled up the side of the Kalman building, but she couldn't see the front, couldn't see the Kalman Guardian, the statue which had stood watch for so many years . . . and who looked just like her new ally.

"Who are you?" she whispered, staring at him in disbelief. She'd worked for Nick for three years now, and there was only one order he gave to all of his hunters, sort of the prime directive of working for Nick Katsaros. And that was to be always on the lookout for certain statues. His "stone warriors," he called them. Was it possible that the Kalman Guardian was one of those statues? She hadn't felt even a twinge of magic from the thing. Was that how it had managed to sit under their noses this entire time, and they'd never known it? If so, then the big, blond lug was coming with her whether he wanted to or not. She needed to call Nick, but first she needed to convince the giant warrior to go along with her.

Currently, the giant warrior in question was giving her an irritated look, obviously waiting for her to absolve him of this supposed blood debt. But he drew himself up and answered her question anyway. "Damian Stephanos, in the service of my lord Nicodemus. And your name?"

Shit. She was nearly hyperventilating. She couldn't believe it. Nick, Nicodemus . . . they were practically the same thing. Had Nicodemus been one of Nick's ancestors? Was that why he was so interested in the statues? That had to be it. Nick must have had some many times great-grandfather who'd created a few ensorcelled statues, and he wanted them back. And, oh my God, now she *really* needed to call him!

She glanced up and realized that the big guy had told her his name, and she was supposed to reciprocate. She grimaced. She had to tell him something, but names had power. Few people realized it anymore, but your name could be used against you by someone with the right kind of magical talent, and enough ill intent. And this guy definitely had some magic going for him. Though it was odd, more like what she'd feel from an artifact rather than a person. But then, if her suspicions were right about him being . . . well, a *statue* up until a few minutes ago, he probably wasn't from this era, so who knew what sort of magic he possessed? It could well be something she'd never encountered before.

"Where'd you come from?" she asked him instead of answering his demand for her name.

His scowl deepened. "A place you've never heard of," he snapped. "Your name, woman?"

Woman again? He was *not* winning any points with that one. "Casey," she said shortly. It was a nickname, something that couldn't be used against her.

"Casey," he repeated, as if he was tasting something sour. Then he shrugged his massive shoulders and repeated his earlier mantra, "I saved your life. The blood debt is paid."

She considered the situation. He *had* saved her life, though she'd ended up losing the Talisman. And she couldn't be sure yet that he actually *was* one of Nick's statues. On the other hand, he definitely was a big fighting machine, and she could use that. He was a genius with a blade and seemed just as comfortable with that HK he was slinging around like an oversized pistol.

More to the point in this case, however, was that, unlike most people, she actually knew what a blood debt was, and so she knew they were real. As a so-called "sensitive," she was one of those rare humans who could detect the presence of magic in both people and things. Granted, her skill when it came to people wasn't that strong, and if the person's magical talent was weak, she might not detect it at all. But there was no one she knew who exceeded her ability when it came to artifacts and devices, except maybe Nick, who was also the only person who had a more exhaustive knowledge on the subject than she did. He had some minor magical talent of his own, too. She could sense it, but had never seen him use it. And now she had a new theory—that magical talent ran in his family from way back, a talent that he'd inherited, though his was vastly diminished.

She didn't have any ancient magical ancestors that she knew of. But her inborn sensitivity to magic had led her from the FBI academy at Quantico, where Nick had found and recruited her, all the way to this stinking alley in an undistinguished city in the Midwest, where a massive warrior was talking to her about blood debts.

In her book, hunting down magical artifacts meant she had to understand them. When the others in her FBI class had been studying federal law and penal codes, she'd been immersed in ancient texts and crumbling codices. So she knew that blood debts were one of the strongest bindings in the world of magic. Blood was life. But how had this dangerous man ended up blood-bound to her?

"Explain something to me," she said slowly. "This blood debt between us . . . when were we bound?"

The stranger, Damian, compressed his lips impatiently, but he had no choice really. If he wanted her to release him, he'd have to give her what she wanted. "You spilled your blood on me," he growled, every bit as savage-sounding as the hounds he'd just killed. "You gripped my arm and asked for my help."

"I gripped . . ." Casey stared, her gaze running up and down his heroic form. Her crazy theory didn't seem so crazy anymore, but still, she really needed to see for herself. She raced down the back of the building, up through the narrow alley, and finally around to the street where she could stare up at the top of the Kalman. The Guardian was gone. She swallowed hard. It was possible. She'd read about things like this, but even in a world where blood curses were real, she'd considered the idea of a cursed statue to be more fantasy than reality—the result of some ancient paralyzing disease that primitive humans back in the day had resorted to calling a magical curse in order to explain the phenomenon to themselves. But now . . . she turned to stare at Damian, who'd followed her around the side of the building and stood watching her with such impatience that she expected him to start tapping his foot at any moment. What he *didn't* do was follow her gaze to the roof and the empty space where the statue had been. Was it because he already knew what she'd find, or rather *not* find, there?

"The guardian?" she asked softly, as if by not saying it out loud, the illusion would shatter and it wouldn't be real.

Finally, he looked up at the top of the building, his expression a mixture of wistfulness and horror. "For a hundred years, I stood silent watch on this city, witnessing all manner of change. More than fifty of those years were on the top of that building. Before that . . ." He paused long enough that Casey thought he wasn't going to continue, but then his dark gaze swung to her, his eyes piercing her with their intensity. "Your plea for assistance, sealed with the offering of your blood, broke a curse that had trapped me for millennia. But now, I have saved your life, and the debt is paid."

Casey studied him thoughtfully. Swords were always useful when dealing with magic. Too many spells had the side effect of rendering mechanical weapons ineffective. Blades, on the other hand, worked pretty much all the time. She carried a knife as part of her regular equipment, but a *sword* wielded by someone who knew how to use it? Now *that* would come in handy.

On the other hand, it was never a good idea to mess with curses. They had a tendency to backfire on anyone who tried to cheat the terms or manipulate the result. She tried to remember exactly what she'd said up on the roof. She'd piled out of the elevator, blood dripping down her arm, so there was no mystery about the *blood* part of the debt. But what had she said to him? Maybe she should ask him. But then, he might only tell her whatever would get her to agree that this so-called debt had been paid.

"Let's say I buy into the idea of a blood debt," she said, pretending far more skepticism than she was feeling. "Does that work both ways? Do I have some debt to you, too?"

He narrowed his gaze on her. She might have laid her doubt on a little too thick.

"What did I say that started all of this?" she asked instead. Artifice had never been her strong suit. "I mean, don't get me wrong, I'm happy as hell to have freed you from what sounds like a nightmare existence, but how did I do it? Did I say the magic word, squeeze some mark on your arm . . . what?"

His expression pinched unhappily, and Casey thought, *Ah ha!*

"You asked for my help," he said sourly. "And the blood on your hand sealed the bond, breaking the curse."

"So it was the blood that did it? No one else in all these years has bled on you?"

"It was both," he admitted. "The combination of the blood and your plea for assistance."

"Huh. So I asked for your help."

He rolled his eyes, clearly seeing where she was going with this. But the very idea of an ancient warrior rolling his eyes startled her into laughing. And that, in turn, seemed to startle *him*. He got this surprised look on his face, and then he smiled. It wasn't a big smile, not a grin, but a wistful one that softened his entire demeanor and made him look more like a man and less like a warrior.

"I haven't heard that sound with my own ears in—" He paused, as if unsure how many years it had been. "—a very long time," he said finally, appearing sad for a brief moment, before his jaw clenched and he was a warrior again.

"I'm sorry," she said.

He raised his eyebrows in question.

"For whatever happened to you back then," she explained. Then she shrugged and added, "and for what I'm about to do now."

"The blood debt is paid," he repeated darkly. "We part company now, and I will be about my own business."

"What business is that?" she asked, more out of curiosity than anything else. She couldn't let him leave, even if she had to shoot him to stop him, because she had a strong feeling that Nick definitely would want to meet him. But what business could a thousands-year-old warrior possibly have in 21st century America?

"It has nothing to do with you," he said coolly, "but you did free me so I will tell you this much. I must find my brother warriors."

She frowned. "I don't mean to be insensitive, but they would have died a long time ago, wouldn't they? Unless . . . were they trapped in stone, too?" Was *that* what Nick's four statues were about? Were all of them ancient warriors who'd been cursed?

"That is not your concern."

Casey was getting a little pissed about being constantly brushed off like an irritating bug. So she took more pleasure than she should have from what she said next.

"Well, look, I hate to rain on your parade"—okay, that was a lie—"but I still need your help. They got the Talisman, and I need to get it back before people start dying."

DAMIAN SCOWLED at the woman while trying to decide if he was honor-bound to continue helping her or not. Typical woman. They used words as weapons to compensate for their other weaknesses, constantly twisting their meaning, pretending to say one thing while intending another. Unfortunately, this particular woman probably had the right of it this time. There was no question about what she'd said when she'd broken the curse. She'd asked for his help. A broad and nonspecific bond that he'd never have agreed to normally.

On the other hand, he didn't want to risk being trapped in that damn stone prison again. Helping her would mean delaying the search for his fellow warriors and for their leader, Nicodemus. Sotiris would never have succeeded in cursing Nico the way he had the rest of them. Damian believed this with all his heart. Nico was too powerful, Sotiris's equal even on a bad day. And if the day was good, Nico far surpassed him. Which was why Sotiris had resorted to cursing Damian and his fellow warriors instead, hoping to weaken Nico enough to defeat him.

But unless Sotiris had succeeded in killing him on that long-ago battlefield, Nico would still be alive even all these centuries later, because sorcerers were virtually immortal. Maybe he should find Nico first. It was possible that *he'd* already located the others, that Damian was the last of the four to be freed. That would be a joyous reunion.

First, however, he had to deal with this woman, and that meant helping her retrieve this *talisman* she was so concerned about. But a few days' delay was better than the alternative. And maybe while they recovered the artifact, he could do some searching of his own. She was a creature of this age, which meant she'd have modern devices at her disposal and the knowledge to use them.

He'd told her the truth about his imprisonment: he'd watched the world change and expand from within his confinement. But seeing something happen wasn't enough to *know* it. He knew things called computers existed, and he knew in principle what they were capable of. But he had no idea how to use one. He knew about cars, but not how to drive. About electric lights, but not how they were powered. On the other hand, give him a weapon, any weapon, and he would master it in an instant. It was in his DNA. He wasn't *a* warrior, he was *the* warrior, the archetype, and this Casey woman could certainly use his help. Look at the state she'd been in before he'd saved her life. So, he would help her and he would learn. And when they were finished, he would find Nico, and together they would free any of their fellow warriors who remained trapped.

"I will help you," he told the woman. "But I will need information. You will brief me, and I will set our strategy."

He didn't exactly get the reaction he'd expected.

She gave a very unwomanly snort and said, "Yeah, right. I don't think so, buddy. You've been stuck on a roof for a few decades, so I think I'll take this one. You can be the muscle."

The muscle? "Your ignorance is understandable," he said with forced patience. "You know nothing of me or my time. I am a veritable god of war. My knowledge of such things is unsurpassed."

"You *were* all of those things. Right now, you're becoming a pain in my ass, and I'm beginning to think you're more trouble than you're worth. I like the sword. But I can live without it. So there you go. You're free. Goodbye."

She turned her back on him and started off up the street, cursing under her breath, holding her bloody arm, and limping on one foot.

Damian frowned. She had powerful enemies. It wasn't just anyone who could call up hellhounds and force them to do a human's bidding. And she was a fool to go against them alone when he was willing to assist. But if the foolish woman wanted to fight her battles alone, he was more than willing to have his obligation discharged. She had to say the right words, however, or he could find himself trapped again.

He caught up with her in a few long strides. "You must say the words."

She gave him an irritated glance and kept walking. "I told you. You're free. Fly away, little birdie."

Damian drew himself up to his full height, galled by her dismissive attitude. She should be on her knees begging for his help. He smiled slightly, thinking of other things she could do for him while on her knees. For all her arrogance, she was a desirable female. Tall and lithe, with black hair and deep brown eyes. Too headstrong for his taste, however, and apparently a warrior. He'd never believed women belonged on the battlefield, never thought they had the courage for it, though there had certainly been some who disagreed with him. But in his opinion, women had been good for two things—sex and babies, preferably sons who would someday grow to be great warriors like their father. His mind shied away from those memories almost as soon as he thought them.

But just as he knew that there had been technological advances in this modern age, so, too, did he know of the social changes. Women now seemed to stand equal with men in almost every arena, but he still preferred *his* women to be more biddable. Not that he'd had a woman in a very long while. He'd been a silent witness to more sexual encounters than he could remember, but none had brought him any relief.

In the beginning, when he'd been buried in the dark, when he'd still believed his imprisonment would end quickly, he'd dreamt of what he would do when he was freed. But as the decades, the centuries, and finally the millennia unfolded, he'd resigned himself to his fate. Doing otherwise was more painful than simply accepting his lot. But he'd never forgotten the soft feel of a woman's body, the sweet fragrance of her perfume as she writhed beneath him.

With a shock, he found himself becoming erect. His first reaction was relief that he could still function, that his long imprisonment hadn't taken away his manhood. But hard on that thought was the knowledge that this was not the time or place. He'd find a willing woman soon enough—he'd never had any problem attracting female attention—but first, he had to deal with Casey and this damn curse.

"Let us be clear," he said, wondering in spite of himself where she was going with such determination on her face. "You agree that the blood debt is paid."

"Yeah, yeah. Look, you seem like a nice guy and all that . . . Not. But I've got bigger problems. I can't let Sotiris get his hands—"

Damian reached out to touch the woman's shoulder, halting her resolute stride. "Did you say Sotiris?" he demanded in disbelief. "He still lives?"

THE FEW DOUBTS that Casey had clung to about Damian's identity vanished in a heartbeat. He didn't ask who Sotiris was, he asked if he *still* lived. This was one of Nick's stone warriors. More than once, she'd seen him eyeing the small set of statues that held the place of honor in his vault back home. It was where he kept everything of value, all of those dangerous artifacts she and the other hunters searched out for him. He'd invited her in on occasion, when she was delivering a particularly crucial device or charm, one that he didn't want to touch himself for reasons that he'd never explained, and she'd never questioned. But she'd noticed those statues and the sadness in his eyes whenever he looked at them. She didn't know exactly what they meant to him or even who they were, but she'd never asked, and never discussed it with any of the others, either.

That didn't mean she'd missed the obvious, however. The connection between the statues in his vault and his prime directive about actual magical statues was too obvious to ignore. Especially now, when she was pretty damn sure that one of those statues was standing before her in the flesh. As tempted as she'd been to walk away before, there was no question of what she had to do now. She looked up at the big warrior. "You know Sotiris?" she asked, already knowing what his answer would be.

"He's the one who cursed me and the others," he said, seeming more hurt and confused than angry. "And you're telling me he still lives in this time?"

"Maybe it's a different man," she said hopefully. "The name—"

"The name means nothing. The man you speak of is a powerful sorcerer?"

Casey nodded. "Not just powerful, but evil in the deepest sense of that word."

"It is he," Damian said, mostly to himself. "Are there others like him?" he asked her.

"I don't think so. No one on his level, anyway," she said, shaking her head. "Look, this is all beyond my pay grade. But my boss will know. He knows everything." She intentionally avoided mentioning Nick by name. He was obviously not the Nicodemus that Damian was looking for; that man had to be long dead. She didn't know exactly how long ago Damian had been cursed, but it was probably measured in millennia rather than centuries. Only a truly powerful sorcerer could still be alive after all this time, and as she'd told Damian, Sotiris was the only sorcerer around anymore with that kind of juice. Magic was her business; she'd know if there was anyone else. And if she didn't know, Nick would, and he'd have shared it with his team. Power like that was a threat they all needed to know about.

On the other hand, "Nick" was close enough for anyone with a brain to make the same familial connection that she had, and she'd seen nothing to indicate that Damian was a stupid man. But if he *was* one of the statues, then it was up to her Nick to decide what happened next. She'd call him first chance she got, but right now. . . . She abruptly realized that Damian was still holding on to her arm, gripping it like a lifeline, and it occurred to her how horribly disorienting all of this must be to him. Sure, he was a big guy who could hold his own in a fight. But this morning he'd been a fucking *statue!* And then, from one minute to the next, he'd been thrust back into a world he couldn't possibly understand, and now he'd discovered that his ancient enemy, the very sorcerer responsible for trapping him all those centuries ago, was still alive, still spreading evil.

"Look," she told him. "Why don't I stash you someplace safe, someplace with room service and satellite TV. You can rest up, *catch* up on the world, get something to eat . . ." Her voice trailed off. How long had it been since he'd eaten? He wouldn't even recognize most of the food on a menu today. She'd have to walk him through it, but she didn't have time to babysit. Every minute that passed was another mile that the Talisman traveled away from her. What the hell was she going to do?

Damian took the decision away from her. "I will not *rest up* while my enemy still lives," he said disdainfully. "I may not understand everything

18

about your world, but I can still fight and kill, and you need my skill far more than my knowledge of modern customs. You and I will travel together. We will find this *talisman* that you seek, and I will kill Sotiris once and for all. And then, I will find my brothers and together we will reunite with our leader."

"What was your leader's name again?" she asked, holding her breath against his answer.

He tilted his head, as if intrigued by her question. "Nicodemus Katsaros."

Casey closed her eyes. Christ. She couldn't let anything happen to him. Nick would kill her. Which meant she couldn't stash him away in a hotel, no matter how tempting it was. He'd never stay there, for one thing. But for another, she'd couldn't keep an eye on him if he wasn't with her.

"Okay," she agreed. "We'll work together. But we'll have to do something about your sword first. If a cop sees you with that . . . ." Her voice trailed off as he slung the sword over his head and down his back, as if expecting a scabbard to be there. She drew breath to call out before he sliced his back open, but then the blade just . . . disappeared. She stared. "How'd you do that?" she asked, walking around him and finding no trace of the substantial weapon. Curiosity overcame good sense, and she stretched out her hand toward what looked like smooth skin over a muscular back, coming up short when she ran into what sure as hell felt like a leather scabbard.

Damian eyed her over his shoulder, his amusement obvious. "It's magic, woman. You must be familiar with it. Nicodemus crafted this for me so that I would never have to leave the blade behind."

"He did a good job of it," she breathed, tracing the lines of the scabbard. So, this Nicodemus fellow was a sorcerer, too?"

"Far greater than Sotiris, which is why the bastard resorted to curses in hopes of weakening Nico enough to defeat him."

"Obviously it worked, because Sotiris is still around, but I've never heard of Nicodemus," she muttered, thinking out loud and never intending him to hear it. But the stricken look on his face told her that he had, and she hurried on, trying to soften the blow. "But that doesn't necessarily mean. . . . I work almost exclusively in the US, so if he's in another country. . . . I mean, it's not like Sotiris is the only sorcerer in the world; there are others for sure. And maybe your friend is using a different name now, right?" she said, though she didn't really believe it.

He studied her distrustfully—smart man—and she could tell he still had questions. But he also seemed to understand, with the instincts of the warrior he'd once been and clearly still was, that this wasn't the time or place. He nodded. "We will talk more before this is over, and you will tell me what you know."

Casey nodded. They were going to have a long talk soon. But not until she'd had a chance to talk to Nick. He was the one who'd earned her loyalty, not some sword-wielding warrior whom she'd just met. Nick had been good to her. He'd snatched her away from the FBI and given her a mission that was something only she could do. He valued not only her magic sensitivity, which was something she'd been born with, but her investigative and fighting skills as well. She was one of his top hunters, one of those he trusted with the most difficult assignments. And for that, for valuing her and giving her purpose, he had her loyalty and her affection. Besides, she'd be happy to turn the whole ancient statue thing over to him to deal with.

Chapter Two

CASEY DROVE BACK to the city, constantly checking her rearview mirror for suspicious vehicles, or familiar headlights, but found none. It was almost humiliating. Apparently, she was no threat to Sotiris at all now that they'd recovered the Talisman from her. She wasn't even worth a little demolition-derby action. Not that she particularly wanted to be run off the road, but it would have been nice to know someone wanted her dead.

She frowned. That was a damn twisted thought. She really needed some sleep. And something to eat.

The next order of business had to be food and rest. And she needed to deal with her shoulder, which was still slowly leaking blood. It should have stopped by now, which meant either the bullet had damaged something important, or it had been enchanted to amplify the destruction. Either way, she needed to take care of it. Now that the adrenaline had dissipated from the fight, the pain nearly whited out her thoughts every time she moved the arm, and the loss of blood was making her lightheaded. Add that to the fact of her exhaustion, and it was hard to think straight. Which wouldn't do. She'd need to be at the top of her game if she was going to figure out where Sotiris's people would take the Talisman next, and then get it back. Assuming Sotiris was behind this, that was. But the more she thought about it, the more convinced she was.

The logical next move would be for his people to get the Talisman to Sotiris himself, but she didn't think that was their plan. It was a dangerous artifact, probably not worth much when it had originally been crafted, but the perfect weapon in a digitized society. And Sotiris had become a broker of sorts in this century, a supplier of death and destruction rather than the destroyer himself. The buyer of record for the Talisman had clearly been a nobody, a front arranged by Sotiris to fool both customs and anyone who might look too closely. It had certainly fooled her. But he probably had a real buyer lined up, which meant his people, the ones who'd stolen it back from her tonight, would need someplace safe to store it. Someplace to keep it inert until the buyer paid for it and could accept delivery.

She glanced at Damian. He'd been quiet ever since he'd discovered that Sotiris was still alive, while Nicodemus was . . . well . . . *way* dead. He'd apparently lived long enough to produce descendants, and they, in turn, had produced more descendants, and on down the line, until *her* Nick Katsaros had inherited the family name and legend. But Damian's *Nicodemus* was dead, and they'd clearly been close. So, of course, he was quiet.

Despite all of that, however, she wasn't fooled by his silence. Nor by his newfound compliance. She had no doubt he'd recover quickly enough and be a big pain in her ass again. In the meantime, though, he needed a few things for his new life, like clothes. He couldn't walk around half-dressed and looking like an extra for some medieval adventure show. And he'd probably enjoy a shower. She didn't know exactly what kind of bathing facilities they'd had back in the prehistoric mists of time or whatever, but she was pretty sure it didn't involve indoor plumbing. Come to think of it . . .

"How'd you eat?" she asked without turning away from the traffic, which was getting heavier the closer she got to the newer part of the city. "I mean when you were, you know, a statue."

She felt his gaze on her a moment before he answered. "I had no need of food, or . . . other things."

The way he said "other things," she knew he wasn't talking about water. Sex probably. The way he looked, he'd probably mowed down the women of his time. Shit. A few thousand years without sex. Yikes. He'd be a fucking machine. Talk about stamina. All that built-up need. . . . Whoa. She definitely needed a bed if she was lusting after former statues. A bed for sleep, that was. Of course, Damian would be there, too. She couldn't leave him alone, and he'd probably sleep naked. . . .

Damn, Casey, think about something else!

"How come you speak English?" she demanded, almost desperately. Anything to get the image of a naked Damian out of her head.

"English?" he repeated.

"The language I'm using," she explained. "How come you know it?" Now that she thought about it, that should have been one of her first questions. He'd talked about being trapped for millennia, and the English language wasn't that old.

"Ah. Is that what you call this language? I've known many. I believe it's part of my curse. Sotiris wanted us—my fellow warriors and I—to suffer. It wouldn't do if we didn't understand what was happening around us, if we couldn't see the occasional danger and be helpless to stop it. I've understood every language spoken around me since I woke in my stone prison, from the scavengers who first unearthed me, to the sailors who brought me over the ocean, from the men and women who mingled in Lester Kalman's garden estate, to those who spent time on my rooftop." He paused thoughtfully, then turned and gave her that same wistful smile from earlier. "But your English is the first language I've *spoken* since the day I was cursed."

Casey tried again to steel herself against that sad smile and failed. All of this must be so disorienting. He needed her help.

"I'm taking you back to my hotel," she said, having just decided on that course for the two of them. There was a safe house nearby, but she'd been saving that for *after* she'd retrieved the Talisman, a place to lie low until the heat died down. In the meantime, she'd checked into a hotel, taking advantage of the gym and room service while she waited for the Talisman to turn up. All of her leads had told her it would end up in this city eventually, and it had. Until she'd lost it. She shook off the guilt that thought brought with it. She'd done her best under the circumstances.

But now she was reduced to waiting again. Listening, watching for some sign of where the Talisman would surface next. And that meant staying in this area, at least for a time. Damian might have been more secure at the safe house, rather than in a public place like a hotel. But she wasn't yet sure enough of him to reveal the house's location. It had taken Nick years to set up a reliable network of safe houses, places used not only by her, but by other hunters as well, and she couldn't jeopardize all of that on a whim. So, that meant going back to the hotel.

It was close to the airport and also had a couple of big-box stores nearby where she could pick up clothes for Damian without looking suspicious. She didn't have any familiarity with men's clothing sizes, but she'd have to figure out something for him, because she sure as hell couldn't take him with her to try stuff on. He'd stand out like a sore thumb, and they'd be found in no time. Sotiris's people hadn't bothered to tail her, but that didn't mean they wouldn't kill her if the opportunity presented itself. And what about Damian? If Sotiris had cursed him, wouldn't he want to get his hands on him again now that he was freed?

"Hotel?" Damian asked, jarring her from her thoughts.

"Like an inn, but much bigger," she said, trying to come up with some equivalent from his life.

He chuckled. "I know what a hotel is, woman. People came to my roof for privacy quite frequently, and I've heard enough conversations to know what goes on in a hotel room."

"What goes on . . . ," she repeated, then blushed. "Okay, it's not just for . . . um, romantic get-togethers, all right? It's for travelers, too."

His laugh was louder this time. "I'm aware of that." He eyed her curiously. "Have no fear, Casey. I have no sexual expectations of you."

She didn't know whether to be relieved or insulted. "Well," she muttered. "Anyway, we can clean up and get something to eat. I'll go out and buy some clothes for you. My boss will reimburse me."

"Your boss must be generous. Who is he?"

"Sorry, that's need-to-know information."

"I need to know."

"You *want* to know. There's a difference. And his name doesn't matter; what does is the fact that he knows more about magic and magical devices than anyone I've ever met. And I know he'll be interested in *you*."

"When do we meet him?"

"I'm not sure," she said evasively. She wasn't sure there would even *be* a meeting, much less when it would be. It hadn't escaped her attention that Damian would be the perfect Trojan horse, the perfect weapon against Nick and his allies. He claimed that her blood had freed him, but who really knew? Sotiris was the one who'd cursed Damian, so what was there to stop him from *un*cursing him, and sending him out to wreak destruction? Maybe even to assassinate Nick. Just because he was one of the statues come to life, that didn't mean he was necessarily a good guy. *That* decision was for Nick to make, not her. Hell, if Nick decided he was a threat, she couldn't even promise he'd live through the next forty-eight hours.

But he didn't need to know that just yet. "He doesn't live around here."

"Where does he live then?"

"Florida. We both do. The offices are there," she said absently, her attention on maneuvering into the right exit lane.

"Florida," he repeated, and she immediately regretted giving him that much information. She needed to be sharper in dealing with him. He was way too shrewd.

"Okay, this is the hotel," she said, hoping to distract him. They turned into the parking lot. "We'll go through the side entrance. You're not exactly average-looking, and I don't want to draw any attention, just in case someone's looking for us."

DAMIAN FOLLOWED the woman across the parking lot and into the hotel, watching with interest as she slid a small plastic card through a device next to the door, which then made a buzzing noise and popped open. The card looked like a credit card; he'd seen many of those during his imprisonment, and heard enough conversations to know their function. But this one seemed to substitute for the door key. Interesting.

The woman . . . *Casey,* he reminded himself, then frowned and said, "Casey. Is that a diminutive for Cassiopeia?"

She stopped and studied him, her dark eyes muddy with suspicion, as if deciding whether he could be trusted with her true name or not. It was plain that she had doubts about him. Her concerns were unfounded, but she didn't understand that yet. Still, she must have believed in at least some part of his good intentions, because her gaze cleared, and she said, "It's Cassandra, and that's bad enough."

He smiled at this indication of some small trust on her part. "Cassandra is lovely name," he commented as they bypassed the elevator in favor of the stairs. He'd never ridden in an elevator, though he'd heard the box function on his rooftop as people were disgorged behind him, and seen the boxes in action when people were delivered to the rooftop across the street. But he wasn't eager for the experience either. The boxes were small and confining, and an enemy could be lying in wait when the doors opened. You could be dead in seconds, and all because you were too foolish to simply climb the stairs instead.

Cassandra started up first, and he couldn't help appreciating the roundness of her ass, the strength in her long legs. She reminded him of the Amazon warriors of his time, and one in particular whom he chose not to think about unless absolutely necessary.

"This is it," she said, sliding the same card into a slot and opening the room door.

He would have entered first, on the possibility that their enemy lay in wait, but she didn't give him the chance. She pushed through the door without so much as drawing her weapon, which he thought was reckless.

"What if your enemy had been waiting for you?"

"They don't know about this place."

"Why would you assume that? You've obviously been staying here for more than a day," he commented, looking around the messy room.

"They didn't have a reason to track me before today, okay? I wasn't on their radar until I stole the Talisman."

He didn't know what radar was, but he got the gist of what she was saying. There was much he was going to have to learn.

She crossed the room and disarmed herself, dropping her gun and knife on a table already littered with weapons, wincing when she reached for the gun with her right hand before switching to her left. "I have to clean up this shoulder," she said, her voice strained.

"I can help you," he said quietly, laying his blade on one of the two beds. From what he could see, Casey favored guns, other than a small knife. He was grateful that his own blades had made the transition through time with him. His sword had been naked in his hand at the moment of his curse, so there was a logic to its survival. But he'd worried about his knife and, above all, the charmed scabbard that Nico had created for him. But both were with him, along with the blade that had been his and his alone. He laid the gun that he'd picked up from one of their dead pursuers next to his sword on the bed, and then turned to face Cassandra. "I have a great deal of experience with wounds like yours," he assured her.

Her eyes, when they met his, were filled with pain. "It's a bullet wound. I'm pretty sure they didn't have guns back when—"

"The weapon doesn't matter," he interrupted. "The wound needs to be cleaned, the bleeding stopped, and the arm immobilized. I can do that."

She was giving him a searching look, and there was something in her eyes that he'd never expected to see from someone as fierce as she was. Fear. "I think the bullet is still in there," she told him. "You'll have to dig it out."

He held her gaze without flinching and gave a single sharp nod. "I understand."

She swallowed hard. "All right. There's a first-aid kit in my duffel—that's the big bag over there. It has tweezers, but . . . you might have to use a knife."

"I don't know what tweezers are," he joked, trying to lighten her fear. "But I'm very good with blades, no matter the size."

She smiled. It was perhaps the first true smile he'd seen from her, and it made him feel strangely proud. "I need to shower first," she said. "Otherwise, I'll just get the bandage wet when you're finished. Here . . ." She picked up a small black device and aimed it at a glass screen on the wall. An image flared to life. "You can watch—"

"Television," he said delightedly. "I've heard so much about this. How do I select the channels?"

She gave him an amused look. "You know about channels?"

"I told you. I've heard conversations on just about everything over the years. Your television shows are a frequent topic of lunchtime conversations."

"I'm sure." She handed him the small black box, then leaned in close enough to point at the various brightly colored buttons. "This is a remote. It lets you control the television from wherever you are in the room, as long as you're line-of-sight to the screen. Line-of-sight means—"

"I can figure that one out for myself," he said dryly.

"Right. Okay, here's volume, that's sound, up and down. That one's for the channel. You don't have a whole lot of choice here, but it's a start. Once we get back to—" She stopped whatever she'd been about to say, but Damian didn't need to hear the rest to understand. She'd been about to say something that implied a future friendship between them.

"Anyway," she said instead. "There should be enough here to keep you amused while I shower."

"Excellent." He took the remote and began running through the channels, but as soon as she'd closed the door on the bathing room—no, they called it a bathroom now—and he heard the water start running—indoor plumbing, another modern improvement he was eager to try—he dropped the channel device and rummaged through her duffel instead. He pulled out the bandage kit, first. It was easily recognizable by the red cross on its case. He'd seen those on the ship during his journey here, and in the museum basement where he'd resided briefly after being purchased by Lester Kalman. Setting the case aside, in the event Cassandra inquired as to what he was doing, he continued his search through her bag, looking for anything that would tell him more about not only her, but her boss. He'd seen something in her reaction to him, especially when she'd realized he was the Kalman Guardian brought to life. There'd been a recognition of sorts in her eyes, and she'd been all too willing to accept his history. After all, how many people had spent the last few millennia as a statue? And yet, she hadn't blinked an eye.

"You won't find it."

He froze at the sound of her voice, then straightened and turned to face her, almost faltering when he saw she wore nothing but a towel, albeit one that covered her from chest to mid-thigh. She made a very tempting sight, bloody shoulder notwithstanding. "I was looking for this," he said finally, holding up the bandage kit.

"Uh huh. Let me save you some time. When I go on a job, I carry nothing that could lead back to my life or work. And that includes my boss's information."

Damian raised an eyebrow. "Is Cassandra your real name?"

"It is," she admitted grudgingly. "It's easier that way, but nothing else is real."

"May I examine your weapons at least?"

"Sure, why not. We'll both be better off if you know how to work them."

"Thank you."

"Whatever. I came out here for some clean underwear. Do you mind?"

"Of course not," he said lightly, then leaned over and dug out a pair of fresh panties and a bra from her duffel and handed them to her with a grin. He'd seen plenty of those in his years on the rooftop, as well. Being both torn off and put back on.

She closed her eyes briefly. "Thank you," she said calmly enough, though she couldn't hide the blush of embarrassment that brightened her cheeks before she turned and went back into the bathroom, closing the door behind her.

A moment later, he heard sounds that told him she was bathing. He shrugged and continued his search of her things. She said there was nothing for him to find, but he preferred to discover that for himself.

CASEY TURNED ON the shower, but let it run while she moved to the opposite end of the big bathroom. She wasn't sure why she'd trusted Damian with her real name. It had been gut instinct more than anything else, and she always listened to her gut. Her head wasn't quite as sure that he could be trusted, which was why she'd only given him her first name, thus limiting the risk. A truly dangerous spell would require either her middle or last name as well, in order to target the effects. Cassandra wasn't a common name, but it wasn't rare either. She'd also considered the fact that she needed him to remain with her, at least until she could reach Nick. A gesture of trust on her part might go a long way in that respect. After all, why would he trust her, when she didn't trust him?

But now, she had to track down Nick. He had a tendency to go off on his own business, whatever that was, and he sometimes dropped off the grid for days. With a guilty glance at the closed bathroom door, she pulled her cell phone from the pocket of her bloodied combat pants, where they lay on the counter, and hit Nick's speed dial. It went straight to voicemail. What the hell was he doing that he couldn't answer the damn phone? With an impatient breath, she hung up and immediately called again. Maybe if she just kept calling, he'd get the idea and answer the fucking phone. She tried that four times before finally leaving a whispered message, covering her mouth while straining to hear, over the shower, any sounds of Damian moving around out in the other room.

She made sure the ringer was off before tucking the phone back into her pocket, then opened the shower door and edged reluctantly toward the hot spray, knowing it was going to hurt. And she'd pretty much reached her limit on pain for the night.

"Just do it, Casey," she muttered to herself. She squinted her eyes shut and stepped under the water. She ground her teeth together to keep from doing anything more than hissing in pain, then reached for the soap.

She didn't linger, but it still felt like forever before she'd done enough to justify setting aside the soap and turning off the water to step out of the shower. Grabbing one of the hotel's big fluffy towels, she dried off carefully. There was one thing she never stinted on when she was working, and that was hotels. She liked her creature comforts—a nice shower, a big tub, good towels. There were times when she had no choice, but in a city like this, with a big airport, she could always find a top-notch hotel or two.

Unfortunately, the pain in her shoulder was making it really difficult to enjoy the fluffy towels. The painkiller she'd taken on the drive here had helped somewhat, but it was wearing off already, and the hot shower— while necessary from a hygienic point of view—hadn't helped the pain angle. It was as if the hot water had reawakened every nerve ending on the right side of her body. Not to mention what the water had done to encourage bleeding, which was currently ruining one of those nice hotel towels she was so fond of. She might have felt guilty about that, if she'd had two brain cells left to consider anything except the pain.

She forced herself to dry off completely, then pulled on the pair of boy-shorts underwear that Damian had so casually dug out of her duffel for her. She looked at the bra, but gave it up as a lost cause without even trying. It was a sports bra. There was just no way she was going to be able to get that on one-handed, even if she'd wanted to try.

Far too aware of the good-looking god of war in the next room, she did what any self-respecting woman would do. She ignored the pain and stepped over to the mirror to study the wreckage. She'd done a half-assed job of washing her long hair, pouring on some of the hotel's conditioner to help with the comb-out, though it wore her out just to think about that.

Normally, she'd have slapped a quick bandage on her arm, taken a couple of pills, slept for about ten hours, and figured out what to do when she woke up.

But she didn't have that luxury tonight. First of all, as she'd told Damian, she was worried that the bullet was still in her shoulder. Something certainly was. From what she could see, she guessed there'd likely be an exit hole in the mess of her shoulder, but there was still something firm in there, something that didn't belong. She couldn't risk going to a hospital, of course. Bullet wounds were automatically reported, and it wasn't only the good guys like her who could do a decent computer hack. If her enemies were still tracking her, that would be one of the easiest ways to do it. They had to know she'd been shot. She hoped that Damian really did know what he was doing. He'd probably never touched a gun before tonight, much less pulled a bullet out of someone.

And he was the other reason she couldn't blank out tonight. If she got a lead on the Talisman, they needed to be ready to go, and Damian needed clothes. He drew attention simply by existing—his height and his good looks, not to mention his overbearing personality, were hard to ignore. Leaving him half-naked on top of everything else was out of the question. She'd have to run over to the store down the road. But she couldn't do that until whatever was grinding in her shoulder was removed, and the wound bandaged well enough to stop bleeding. Not even in a big-box store would she be able to hide that she was dripping blood on the floors. She doubted the staff would appreciate having to clean up that mess.

Sighing, she ran a wide-toothed comb through her hair using her left hand, which was awkward as hell. This should be a lesson for her. She was too dependent on her right hand. She should have been working with both hands all along, strengthening her left against just this possibility.

With her hair done, or as done as it was going to get, she wrapped a towel around herself, securing it tightly, then grabbed her dirty clothes, including her pants with her cell phone in the pocket. If her new roommate had been one of the men she sometimes worked with, she'd have taken the situation in stride. Bodies were bodies. She'd patched them up, and they'd done the same for her more than once. But there was a distinctly sexual quality to Damian that changed the equation. Maybe it was just his combination of confidence and supreme arrogance—historically, she did tend to find such men attractive—but whatever it was, it made her reluctant to get naked around him.

She opened the bathroom door, then stood there like a terrified virgin, holding her clothes in one hand and clutching the towel over her breasts with the other, staring at Damian, who was kicked back on the bed, one arm behind his neck, looking like an invitation to sin.

"I need your help," she said, trying not to sound defensive.

His dark eyes took in her wet hair, lingered at her breasts beneath the towel she was gripping so tightly, and then traveled down over her bare legs and back up to meet her eyes at last. Casey simmered slowly. She was so tempted to tell him to go fuck himself. He could have the damn room. She'd get another, or maybe go to the safe house. She could do some research while her arm recovered, and then go after the Talisman once she found it. She'd done it on her own before; she could do it again.

If only she could be sure the arrogant bastard wasn't important to Nick.

"Can you do it?" she asked with forced patience.

He grinned, and she ground her teeth when she realized her mistake. Everything would have sexual overtones for this guy. She'd have to watch her words.

"Can you help me with my shoulder?" she asked, her voice flat, her meaning unequivocal.

He stood and, without a word, pulled a leather cord from his wrist and tied back his long hair. "We'll need light," he informed her. "The bathroom is the brightest, but the work will be painful, and the bed will be more comfortable for you."

Casey wanted to tell him that she could tough it out; that sitting on the closed toilet seat while he dug into her shoulder wouldn't be a problem. But that wasn't true, and it would be far less humiliating to admit it now, than to wake up from a dead faint on the bathroom floor.

"We can move the lamps around in here," she said instead. "The desk lamp over there is an LED. Um, that means it's very bright. If we move it to the bedside table, it should be enough. Just pull the cord there from the electrical outlet . . . the thing in the wall."

Damian started for the desk, speaking over his shoulder. "Don't worry. I've done this sort of thing by candlelight. This will be easy."

"For you," she muttered. She eyed the bed, then considered the towel and underwear which were all she had on. Her arm and shoulder, front and back, would have to remain bare, but she could at least put on some pants. Walking over to the other bed, she shoved her dirty clothes into the duffel, pulled out a pair of cotton sleep pants, then pawed through the rest, hoping against hope that a tube top would magically appear. That didn't happen, of course. She'd never owned a tube top in her life, and her duffel contained only an assortment of T-shirts, along with black combat pants, and one pair of jeans.

Her clothing was the story of her life. Her mom had taken off when Casey was barely walking, leaving her with her drill-sergeant father and two much-older brothers. Her father had treated all of them more like recruits than children, so she'd never had much of a chance to be a little girl. She'd been one of the boys her entire life. It was no surprise she'd ended up as one of Nick's hunters. Or thieves. It was all a matter of perspective.

Yanking the sleep pants up her legs, she secured the towel, then turned around to see that Damian had set up his operating theater. She was rather impressed. He'd organized the bandages from the first-aid kit and set them within reach, and he was just coming out of the bathroom where he'd clearly been washing the instruments he'd be using to dig into her shoulder.

Damn, she was *so* not looking forward to that.

She met his eyes across the room. She didn't know what hers showed, but his were patient and waiting. Everything about him told her this was her choice, her timetable, and he'd wait as long as it took.

She gave a resigned sigh. "Let's do this," she said, and had to swallow to avoid throwing up.

"Drink this," he said, holding out several mini-bar-sized bottles of vodka.

Casey laughed in surprise. "How'd you know about those?" She'd never considered the mini-bar, hadn't even remembered it was there. Stupid of her, really, because the alcohol was good for more than just anesthetizing her against the pain. It could also be used to sterilize the instruments.

"I explored while you were showering. I recognized the labels, although these bottles are ridiculously tiny."

"Not if you drink enough of them," she commented. "But you can also use that to clean the tweezers and stuff. I have some alcohol wipes, but probably not enough."

"I used soap and hot water. Your soap is milder than ours, but it should do."

"Oh. Well, yeah, that'll work," she muttered. "That antiseptic spray will work for bandaging, and there are gloves in the kit, too. You know, if you don't want blood all over your hands." She took the vodka from him and cracked open the first one, drinking it down like water while he went to the bathroom and grabbed more towels. Tears filled her eyes at the strong alcohol flavor, and she sat down on the bed. She wasn't much of a drinker normally, which worked in her favor. By the time she'd gulped the second tiny bottle, she was feeling buzzed. "Buzzed," she murmured and smiled.

Damian smiled back, his hand warm on her back as he urged her to turn. Wait. His hand was on bare skin, which meant. . . . She clutched the towel to her breasts, stifling a cry when the sudden movement jerked her bad shoulder.

"Stop that," he said impatiently. "I've seen breasts before, and I've no intention of spying on yours."

Casey frowned. What was wrong with her breasts? She realized the drunken thought for what it was, but couldn't quite shake the suspicion that he didn't find her breasts worth looking at. Fortunately, her head was turned away from him, and he couldn't see the expression on her face.

"I apologize in advance, Cassandra," he murmured, as she heard the snap of gloves being pulled on. The nitrile gloves from her first-aid kit, her brain supplied, eager for any thought which avoided contemplating what was about to happen.

There was the touch of cool metal and then a pain like nothing she'd ever felt before. She fisted her good hand against her mouth to keep from sobbing and waited to pass out. *Hoped* to pass out.

"Not a bullet," he said, mostly to himself, but she heard him.

"What was it?" she asked. There were tears in her voice, but she didn't care. He was lucky she hadn't drawn security with her screams.

"You were shot, but the bullet went all the way through. A sharp chip of stone was lodged in your muscle, right by the bone," he told her. "Were you standing next to a wall when you were shot?"

Casey tried to think through the pain, replaying the moment she'd been wounded. "Yeah," she said grimly. "I'd made it into the house and back out undetected, but someone shot from a balcony. The facing on the building was marble."

"That's it," he agreed, and she heard the click of a small stone hitting the table.

Part of her was registering the fact that this was good news, but it was hard for that to sink in—*sink in, ha ha*—when her arm was on fire from the antiseptic liquid he was currently pouring over and around the wound. She shoved her fist into her mouth again, tears flowing freely down her face.

"The front wound is minor," he said calmly and used tape to fix a small square of gauze over the bloody hole. Non-adhesive tape, she reminded herself. It was the only kind in her kit, because she was allergic to adhesive. He went to work on the exit wound on the back of her shoulder, smearing antibiotic ointment around it, then covering it with a thick pad of dry gauze and securing it with more tape. The care he took with all of this almost made her want to like him.

From the corner of her eye, she saw him pick up the Ace wrap. "I need to be able to move the arm," she told him.

He paused a moment, his fingers light on her shoulder, then said, "Understood." With a few deft movements, he managed to stabilize her shoulder while still leaving her enough mobility to function.

"There's a plastic bottle of antibiotics in there," she said, hearing the slur in her words. It wasn't all vodka at this point. She was exhausted. "The brown container with a white cap," she clarified for him, just in case. "I'll need two pills."

"Here," he said, then handed her a glass of water and the medication. She took the antibiotics as he collected the empty packaging from the gauze, crushing it all into a wad and tossing it in the trash.

"I have to go to the store," she said wearily. "You need clothes."

He grinned, switching from caring medic to cocky warrior in an instant. This was the Damian she'd come to expect over the course of their short acquaintance. "You don't like the look?" he asked.

She was just drunk enough to let him see the appreciation in her eyes as she did a slow scan of his naked chest and shoulders. "You don't exactly blend."

He laughed out loud at that. "I never have." He gathered the tweezers and other instruments in one big hand. "I'll clean these in the bathroom," he told her. "And then I'll make use of the shower. You should sleep. That's what I'll be doing soon, and I won't need any clothes for that. We can shop tomorrow."

"Not 'we,'" she insisted, pulling the covers back with her good arm, then sliding onto the bed. "Me," she mumbled, and closed her eyes as the meaning of his words sank in. No clothes for sleeping?

DAMIAN STOOD OVER Cassandra, admiring the expanse of unblemished skin on her naked back, the curve of one full breast just visible above the towel she'd clutched so desperately against her chest. His fingertips tingled, remembering the satin feel of that skin, but then his gaze caught on the stark white bandage and he flinched. The wound was vicious, for all that the bullet had missed the bone and savaged only soft tissue. The weapons of his time had been brutal and efficient, but humans had come a long way since then. Not only in destructive power, but in the ability to strike from a distance. On the battlefields he'd known, men had to put themselves at risk to succeed. Not so today. The gun that had torn through Cassandra's shoulder had been fired from far enough away that the shooter had missed his target. The shot had no doubt been intended to kill, not merely wound.

He reached down and pulled the blanket up, covering her completely. He'd lied when he said he had no desire to see her breasts. She was a beautiful woman, and he was a man who hadn't had the pleasure of a woman's body in a very long time. A man who'd had a different woman in his bed every night, sometimes more than one. But these were difficult times they found themselves in. More than simple strangers, he and Cassandra were from entirely different worlds in more ways than one. Besides, he was first and foremost a warrior, and sex had no place on the battlefield. It was what had condemned him in the first place, the root of the curse Sotiris had used to secure his prison.

Damian Stephanos, warrior and lover, who bedded the Amazon queen, but refused to take the battlefield by her side.

Those words had haunted him for centuries, repeating in his head over and over as he'd lain buried in a cave, waiting, hoping that someone would find him, longing for the sun on his face, the breeze against his skin. And he'd remembered the fury in Queen Hippolyta's eyes when he'd relegated her Amazons to the rear of the battle, safe behind the same walls that guarded the children, the ancients, and the rest of the women. She'd considered herself a great warrior, but all he'd seen were her delicate bones and the naked skin designed to entice a man, to distract him from the defense of his own life. He'd been convinced that women had no place on the battlefield.

And yet, as he gazed down at Cassandra, at her slender form outlined beneath the blanket, the elegant line of her features, smoothed now in sleep, he saw a warrior. For all her delicate appearance, she was as strong as any of his fighters had been back then, and with courage and determination that surpassed many of them. Times had changed. Logically, he knew that, but he hadn't lived those changes. She considered herself the leader of their duo. He understood why she would think so; this was her time, not his. But he was a god of war. He had only to touch a weapon and it became his. He was able to comprehend and adapt to events on a battlefield with a speed that she couldn't hope to match.

He sighed. As odd as it seemed, he was tired. After all those years in stone, one would think he'd be eager to stretch his legs, to run until his muscles gave out. But it seemed that instead of storing energy, his long imprisonment had weakened him. His body would recover soon enough, far faster than a regular human's. But he still needed rest, and found himself suddenly longing for the genuine simplicity of closing his eyes and sleeping.

Crossing to the bathroom, he tossed the scissors and other implements into the basin, then-bathed them in soapy water, while mentally tallying up the list of supplies they would need to replenish Cassandra's first-aid kit. Returning to the bedroom, he sat on the edge of the bed and untied and removed his boots. Then, suffering from none of Cassandra's modesty, he stood to unlace his leather pants. He was a little surprised that the leather had held up, that it didn't immediately shred in his hands as he pulled the pants down his legs and kicked them aside. Whatever else he and Cassandra might disagree on, they were in perfect accord with regard to this. He needed new clothing.

Standing perfectly naked, he stretched his arms to the ceiling. By all that was holy, it felt good to be alive again, to feel the taut pull of his muscles, the hot rush of his blood beneath the skin. He tipped his head from side to side, hearing the crack of bone as his spine adjusted to the full range of motion once more. And then his gaze fell on the shower behind its enclosure of clear glass. He knew what a shower was, had heard hundreds, maybe thousands, of people refer to it during his long sojourn in stone . . . and he'd covertly admired Cassandra's form behind the steam-blurred glass when he'd gone in to get towels while she showered earlier.

He strode into the bathroom now and opened the shower door, then reached in and turned the knobs. It took a few minutes, but he learned how to balance the hot and cold water quickly enough, then stepped underneath the pounding spray. He swallowed a groan of intense pleasure. Indoor plumbing might very well be the greatest invention of this time. It was sheer luxury to soap his body, to empty the small bottle of shampoo over his head and wash his hair. He stood under the flow of hot water until he thought he'd sleep where he stood, until his skin was wrinkled with exposure, then he turned off the water and grabbed one of the big towels sitting in a fluffy pile on the countertop. He toweled himself dry, marveling at the soft, absorbent fabric as he walked out into the bedroom, the air cool after the steam-filled bathroom.

Dropping the towel to the floor, abruptly exhausted, he eyed the sleeping choices available. There were two beds side-by-side, both the same size, although not big enough to suit his liking. One was covered with Cassandra's various pieces of gear—her duffel bag, computer case, and boxes of ammunition for the many weapons arrayed on the table against the far wall. She slept in the other. He knew where he would have preferred to sleep. He smiled, imagining her reaction upon waking to find him lying next to her . . . naked. His cock stirred at the thought, but he wasn't that big a fool. Or that rude. Women came to him willingly; he had no need to trick them.

He gripped the edges of the heavy covering on the second bed, gathered them together along with all of her gear, and deposited it on the floor. Then he slipped beneath the soft sheets, put his head on a pillow, and truly slept for the first time since he'd been cursed.

Chapter Three

Lawrence, Kansas

NICK STARED DOWN at the list of missed calls and saw Cassandra's name over and over. Four calls in the space of a couple of minutes, but only one voicemail, which had been left after the last call. What the hell? She'd been sent on what should have been a straightforward recovery. The target device was dangerous enough, but the creep who'd bought it was a nobody with no magical talent and no record of having purchased any other artifacts. Nick wasn't convinced that the guy even knew what he'd bought. He'd probably thought he was getting nothing more than a beautiful and unique piece of glass sculpture that matched his house decor.

The Talisman was indeed beautiful, and so unique that when one spoke of *the* Talisman, no one questioned which artifact you meant. But its uniqueness went well beyond the beauty of its form. Rich green in color, it had the appearance of a rare emerald of unusual size and shape. It was round and flat, like a stone, smooth, rather than faceted. But the absence of faceting did nothing to dull the brilliant light deep within. It was mounted, as if for a breastplate or necklace, surrounded by an elaborate bronze setting that twined up and around the gem like a cage. The bronze spoke to the antiquity of the piece; it was a metal that few would use in the modern age. Nick knew about the Talisman because he'd seen it in the home of its creator—a sorcerer of modest skill who he knew for a fact was long dead . . . because he'd been the one to kill him.

The man had made the fatal error of mistaking youth for weakness, and had tried to seize one of Nick's territories, a small but fertile strip of land with a single, well-constructed fortress where the farmers and their families had lived. The Talisman had disappeared in the subsequent fighting, and Nick had lost track of it because he'd been rather abruptly called back to his father's court. He'd been only fourteen years old at the time, and still very much under his father's rule, despite the burgeoning power of his sorcery. Two years later, he'd disavowed his father and established his own authority, but by then, the Talisman had become less than even a faint memory.

But now it had turned up again, unearthed by chance in the Caucasus Mountains. Nick doubted it was happenstance that had made that rediscovery possible. Certain magical devices were created to be easily found, and he suspected this one qualified. He still didn't know what the artifact's original purpose had been. Back then, he'd detected an odd energy about the piece, but it hadn't troubled him enough to pursue it any further. In today's world, however, with its dependence on electronics for almost everything, that same odd energy had the potential to do incredible harm. So much so that he'd considered sending another operative along with Casey to be certain of the recovery.

In the final analysis, however, he'd discarded that idea, believing it would only call more attention to the Talisman, perhaps the very attention he was trying to avoid. And, alone of his hunters, Casey had the best chance of figuring out how the thing worked. Her talent was one in ten thousand, maybe even rarer than that. He didn't have cause to admit it very often, but her skill exceeded even his when it came to seeing magical devices not so much for what they did as for *how* they did it. And, in the final analysis, understanding *that* was the key to destroying just about anything on this earth.

Frowning, he played her lone voicemail.

"Nick, we need to talk," she said. Her voice was so soft that she was practically whispering, and it sounded like she had a shower running in the background. That was the sort of thing a person did to conceal the fact that she was on the phone, so no one would overhear. What the hell? Who was she hiding from? "The Talisman," she said, then paused, as if listening to something. "I had it," she continued, speaking even more quietly. "They took it back, but I'm on it. I know where it's going, and I'll get it back if I have to kill every one of those bastards to do it."

His frown deepened. Some of his hunters were former military, accustomed to shooting their way out of a situation. But Casey wasn't one of them. Something must have happened to have her reacting this way. "That's not why we have to talk, but I don't want to say too much in a message like this. You never know who's listening, right? Nick . . . remember the prime directive? The statues? Well, I think I might have one. So, call me, okay? It's important."

Nick froze, staring down at his phone. Casey had located one of the statues? It was suddenly hard to breathe. *Calm down*, he warned himself. She could be mistaken. She'd used the word "might." He hit return on Casey's message and listened to her phone ring . . . and ring. No answer. His gut tightened in apprehension as he imagined all the reasons why that might happen. *Stop it. She could be in the fucking shower.* Right. The shower where she'd been hiding earlier. Or she could be sleeping. She was running the op alone, at least as far as he knew, and she could have turned off her phone to rest, if she was in a secure place . . . or to stop it from ringing if she wasn't. He checked his watch. Two a.m., and he and Casey were in the same time zone. He revised his earlier assessment. She was almost certainly asleep, which meant there was nothing he could do until she woke up and called him back.

Her phone rang a final time, and his call switched over to voicemail. "It's me, Casey," he said. "Call when you get this. I don't care what time it is."

SOMEWHERE IN *the Midwest*

Casey woke slowly, consciousness returning in tiny increments of increasing pain. First was the headache, which puzzled her at first, until she remembered the vodka. She groaned softly. There was a reason she rarely drank. But the discomfort quickly faded in importance compared to the rest of her body, which felt as if someone had been pounding on her with a mallet. Every bone in her body hurt, every muscle ached. She catalogued her symptoms as the previous day's events came rushing back. Infection was a real possibility from the shoulder wound. That could be why she felt so awful. She remembered taking antibiotics, but the oral meds might not have been enough.

She forced herself to sit up. It wasn't unusual to be stiff and sore after an escape like she'd been through. No matter the shape one was in—and she was in great shape—all that running and crawling and crouching took a toll, especially when the adrenaline got pumping. Sometimes, you didn't know how badly you'd been hurt until the adrenaline wore off. Of course, she'd never been *shot* before!

She swung her legs over the side of the bed, reflexively grabbing the towel that fell away from her naked breasts. And that made her remember Damian. Her head came up, her gaze quickly falling on the opposite bed where he slept, seemingly unaware of her movements. Not quite trusting his innocent pose, she kept the towel over her breasts as she stood and walked the short distance to the bathroom. The light was on, the door cracked open to admit just a sliver of illumination into the dark room. She didn't know why Damian had left it like that, but she appreciated it. Blackout curtains could leave hotel rooms so dark that you couldn't even walk to the bathroom without stubbing your toe.

Closing the bathroom door behind her, she let the towel drop and stepped over to the full-length mirror on the wall, leaning in to check out her shoulder and anything else she might have missed. Between the gunfight and the long drive, and then the stress of having her shoulder cleaned up and bandaged, she'd been pretty foggy last night. She breathed a sigh of relief when she found only the usual cuts and scrapes and, of course, the big honking bandage on her shoulder.

She moved her arm carefully, testing her range of motion and the limits of her pain. She had to admit, it felt a lot better than it had before Damian worked on it. Getting that piece of marble out had probably made a huge difference. She saw her first-aid kit sitting on the counter and took another two antibiotic pills, along with some acetaminophen for the pain. She had stronger pain meds in there, but she needed her head clear. Today was the beginning of a new campaign to recover the Talisman.

The wordless rumble of a deep voice reminded her of her roommate. Pulling on one of the hotel robes, she cracked the door open, and found Damian sitting on the side of the bed, looking confused.

He looked up and saw her. "Leave the door open please." His voice was rough with emotion, and she realized it wasn't confusion on his face, it was dread, and more than a little horror. She gave herself a mental slap upside the head. Of course! That was why he'd left the light on in the dark room. He'd been buried in a cave for centuries. The pitch-black hotel room had probably brought back those nightmare years.

"Sorry," she said and opened the door wider. The light fell on his sitting form, and she saw that he was completely, *perfectly*, naked. Fuck.

No! No fuck! Her first order of business had to be a trip to the store to get him some clothes. "Are you hungry?" she asked, mostly to get her mind off the fact that he was naked and *ripped*. Damn! But then she told herself to stop ogling and get back to business. Was he hungry? Of course he was hungry. Forget the millennia trapped in stone, he hadn't even eaten anything since he'd been freed yesterday. And that was her fault. They'd been so busy getting away, and then dealing with her wound that they hadn't ordered any food. And since she'd passed out, he probably hadn't known how to pick up the phone and call room service. He'd experienced a lot of life up there on the roof, but she doubted ordering room service was part of it. Or using a hotel phone, for that matter.

He nodded, his head still bowed as he sat on the side of the bed. "I am hungry," he said, without looking at her, as if he was embarrassed at being afraid of the dark. Though she doubted he would describe it quite that way.

She grabbed the other robe, then walked over, and reached for the bedside lamp. "Do you mind?" she asked.

He made a grunting noise that she took for assent, so she flicked the switch on the lamp. It didn't light the room completely, but it was better than just the bathroom light. She turned and offered him the robe. "It's not quite god-sized," she joked lamely. "But it will keep you decent when the room service waiter arrives."

He cracked a smile at last, a wicked grin that made his opinion on that very clear. He didn't care who saw him naked. If she'd had a body like his, she probably wouldn't have cared either. If she'd been a man, that was. Since she was a woman, having his body would be rather odd. *Focus, Casey.* Damn. Put a gorgeous, naked god in her vicinity, and she lost her mind.

She crossed to the desk and found the room-service menu. When she turned back, Damian was standing and had donned the robe. She bit her lip. Yeah, the robe was definitely not sized for a god, but at least it made him a little less distracting. She opened the folio to breakfast and handed it to him.

"Knock yourself out, big guy."

He gave the menu a puzzled look, and she realized he might not understand the colloquialism. "It means—"

"I know what it means," he assured her. "I'm simply amazed at the variety of foods available."

"There's coffee too, or tea. Or I'm sure I can get wine, if that's what you're accustomed to."

Damian sank back onto the bed and perused his breakfast options. Typical male—he paid no attention at all to the spread of his legs and the subsequent display of his . . . *junk* to anyone who happened to be sitting on the opposite bed. Which Casey was. And she couldn't stop herself from looking. It was an impressive display.

Damn it. She stood quickly and sat next to him instead. "Tell me what you want, and I'll call it in," she said, pretending she had only moved to bring the hotel phone closer. "Or if you have any questions."

"What will you be eating?" he asked, one thick finger running down the list.

"I'm not much of a breakfast person," she said. "Coffee, of course, and maybe some fruit and a bagel."

He looked up, and she realized, for the first time, that he'd showered at some point last night. His hair was clean and shiny and fell over his shoulders in golden waves that looked a hell of a lot better than hers did. He smelled good, too.

Shit. She was doing it again.

"You should eat something," he told her. "Preferably meat. Your body will need the energy."

"Energy for what?" she asked suspiciously.

His eyes crinkled first, followed by a slow grin that made her want to squirm, aware of her own nakedness beneath the robe. "Energy to heal," he clarified solemnly, but with hints of the grin still playing around his mouth.

Casey felt her blush and was glad for the dimly lit room. "You're right," she agreed quickly, wanting to change the flirtatious undercurrent of the conversation. "I'll get some eggs."

A soft snort told her what he thought of that, but he didn't comment until he looked up from the menu again, and said, "Steak is meat, isn't it?"

"Most of the time," she agreed. "Definitely in this case. It's beef."

"Okay, I'll have the steak and eggs. I want the meat bloody, whatever you call it here, and the eggs fried. Also, the fruit platter and the lox . . . that's salmon, right?" he asked, then continued when she nodded. "Good. And a pastry basket and coffee, too. I've never had coffee, but everyone in your time seems to crave it. And water."

She regarded him with raised eyebrows. "Is that it?"

He studied the menu again, missing her sarcasm completely. A small frown marred that perfect forehead, and he nodded. "For now."

Casey smiled at his bent head. "Okay. I'll call it in, and then I'll get dressed. As soon as we finish breakfast, I'll go out and get you some clothes. After that, we can figure out what to do next."

"Our next task is simple. We find those who stole this Talisman from you—"

"Well, I stole it from them first," she admitted.

He shrugged. "In my time, possession was the only thing that mattered. They have it and you want it, therefore, we will go get it."

"If only it was that simple," she said. "I have a good idea of where they'll go, but I'll need to do some checking first, call some people." His eyes were already glazing over with boredom. It didn't surprise her. He probably hadn't been the guy who ran reconnaissance for the armies. He'd been the guy who stood at the vanguard and inspired the others to throw their lives into the crucible of battle. "Don't worry about it," she said finally. "I'll handle that part."

"I'm relieved," he said dryly, then gave her an assessing look. "Will you need help getting dressed?"

It was her turn to snort derisively. "You wish. I'll be fine."

"Then I shall watch more of your television," he said, not at all put off by her rejection of his assistance. Apparently, she really *didn't* exist for him as a female, she thought, frowning as he settled back against the headboard, looking completely relaxed as he clicked the remote from channel to channel. He'd clearly forgotten about her altogether. Hanging around him was *such* an ego boost.

After breakfast, which Damian inhaled as if he hadn't eaten in hundreds of years—bad choice of analogy, since he actually *hadn't*—she began the onerous task of getting dressed. She'd lied to Damian about that. She really could have used his help. It was not only that her shoulder protested any movement on her part, but it was also thick with bandages. Both of those things greatly limited her wardrobe options. Every top she'd brought with her was a pullover. Normally, she would have borrowed a button-up shirt from Damian. Most of the guys she knew had at least a couple of those. In this case, however, he had even fewer clothes than she did.

And then there was the bra situation. Her breasts were too big, and she was too self-conscious about it, to go braless. She briefly considered asking Damian to wrap her chest in gauze from the first aid kit, but then couldn't believe she'd entertained that idea for even an instant. She tried to imagine which outcome would be worse. Having him wrap her up like a sausage without even noticing she had breasts? Or ogling her like a teenager who'd never seen naked breasts before? Based on his earlier comments, she was afraid it would be option number one, which wasn't exactly an ego booster.

Fortunately, she got to skip the whole comedy routine. She had one old bra that she kept in the bottom of her duffel just in case she ended up on a long flight or even a long train ride. It was stretched out enough to be comfortable to sleep in, but still retained sufficient structure to be marginally decent, and, best of all, it had a front closure. She pulled on a front-zip hoodie as a top—her bandaged arm was a tight fit, but it worked—and she went with leggings and her UGG boots in order to avoid the need to button or lace up anything. After all, she was going to big-box heaven, not Rodeo Drive. She'd likely be one of the best-dressed people there.

Stepping back, she eyed herself in the mirror. Okay, so it wasn't her best look. Her big sunglasses concealed most of her face, and since braiding her hair had been out of the question, it hung long and wavy over her shoulders, which was pretty good camouflage all by itself since she rarely wore it that way. Anonymity was doubly desirable today—first, so the bad guys wouldn't recognize her, and second, so nobody she knew would recognize her in this outfit. She might be a badass magic hunter, but she was also a girl.

Taking off the glasses for now, she walked back out into the main room. Her godlike roommate hadn't moved at all, as far as she could tell. He was still lying on the bed, still wearing the too-short robe, his gaze riveted to the TV. She glanced over to see what he was watching.

"Hey!" she protested. "Did you buy a movie?"

"Did I?" he asked, and she just *knew* he was only pretending not to understand. He might be irritating as hell, and a real blow to her femininity, but he was also damn smart. He'd had to be in order to have comprehended and retained as much information as he had from within his stone prison. How he'd remained sane was another matter, but it certainly spoke to an iron will and intellectual discipline, and probably a deep-seated drive for revenge on the sorcerer who'd put him there. And then there was his desire to be reunited with his fellow warriors, which was clearly what drove him.

She frowned as unexpected sympathy bloomed in her heart. She wanted him to succeed, wanted to see the four men reunited, to see the look on that fucker Sotiris's face when he realized his plan had failed, and that they were whole again.

"Watch whatever you want," she told him, waving a dismissive hand. Nick was paying the bill anyhow, and he had plenty of money. "Where're your clothes from yesterday?"

He hit the pause button—he'd sure learned the remote fast enough—and tilted his head to study her quizzically. "Do you think taking my clothes away will keep me in this room? I assure you, it will not."

Casey rolled her eyes. "I'm not taking your clothes," she said dryly. "I'm going to measure them, so I know what sizes to get you."

"Oh," he said cheerfully. "Good. I've been looking at your magazine—" He rolled over and grabbed her favorite entertainment magazine from the table. "—and this is what I want." He leaned forward and tossed the open magazine on the bed for her to see.

She already had a good idea of what was going to be available at the store, and what she planned to buy for him, but she picked up the magazine out of curiosity. It was a picture of a currently popular action hero, who happened to be an excellent match for Damian in terms of size and looks. In the magazine photo, the actor was wearing a tux. And while it looked great on him and would probably look even better on her roommate, she doubted the nearby stores would have them in stock.

"Nice," she commented. "I'll keep it in mind for our next shopping trip. But for now, something more suitable for chasing down bad guys might be in order." She flipped through the pages until she found the same actor wearing jeans and a T-shirt. "This is what I'll be buying you."

He gave her a skeptical look, but took the magazine back, and held it under the lamp's light. And that reminded Casey that the sun was up and they didn't need to dwell in the dark. She had no reason to think anyone was lurking in the parking lot with a spy scope, or that her enemies even knew where she was. Walking over to the window, she hit the button on the automatic control panel and opened first the drapes and then the shades underneath.

Sunlight flooded into the room. Damian stood and walked over to stand next to her. "Beautiful," he whispered. Casey figured he must mean the sun in the sky, because the view wasn't that great. He turned to look at her, his gaze lingering on the lump of bulky bandage straining the shoulder of her hoodie. "I will help you measure my clothing."

"Thanks," she said, somewhat surprised. She'd begun to think of him as some kind of entitled prince, one who was used to being surrounded by servants. But maybe that was her projecting a history on him, rather than seeing who he really was. "I don't have a measuring tape, but I have string. I figure I can cut off pieces to the right length and measure them against clothing in the store."

He nodded then walked over to the closet and retrieved his leather pants and boots from the shelf where he'd folded them neatly. Interesting. It made her wonder again about his upbringing. Maybe he wasn't used to servants, after all.

While he came back with his clothes, she dug into her duffel bag and produced a ball of plain, white string. That and duct tape were the two things she always brought with her. Well, that and her guns. And her knives.

She measured off the pants first—inseam and waist—and then the sole of his boots. The boots would be tricky. But once he had contemporary clothing, he could accompany her to the store and try on the different footwear options. A good-fitting pair of boots was vitally important in her line of work. After doing what she could with the boots, she paused. She knew what she had to do next, but found herself strangely reluctant.

"If you could sit down here," she said, indicating the chair by the window. "I need to measure your chest and arms."

He immediately sat down and stripped away the robe, letting it fall to his waist to reveal a staggeringly gorgeous body. His shoulders were broad and thickly padded with muscle, and his torso was a work of art. His abdomen was ripped and his belly was perfectly flat. She raised her eyes to his face and found he'd been watching her as she studied his body. He gave her a smug smile. Now *that* was the Damian she'd come to expect.

Pretending he hadn't just caught her admiring him, she went ahead with her measurements, as her cheeks heated with embarrassment. He had beautiful skin, smooth and golden. Was there anything about him that wasn't perfect?

"Is there anything else you'd like to see, Cassandra?" he asked, giving her a wink.

Oh, right. His ego. That definitely wasn't perfect. She snatched her hands away, her eyes narrowing with irritation. "Hold out your arm," she ordered.

He chuckled, but did as she asked. She took one final measurement and then stepped away, sucking in a relieved breath. Maybe he really had been a god in his day. He certainly unsettled her, and she was usually tougher than this. Of course, she also usually worked alone, which forced her to focus absolutely on the task. She scowled at the thought. Except in this case, the task had been revised to include Damian, because of Nick's prime directive. Thinking of Nick reminded her that she hadn't checked her messages yet, and she really needed to do that.

Adding the last of her measurements to the notes on her cell phone, she switched over to messages and saw that Nick had called very early this morning. She frowned until she remembered that his current job involved vampires.

Without thinking, she put the message on speaker while she gathered the rest of her things. "It's me, Casey," Nick's voice informed her. "Call when you get—"

Damian's reaction drowned out whatever Nick said next. He was on his feet, staring at her phone. "Who was that?" he demanded, lifting his eyes to regard her intently. "That voice. Who was it?"

At first, Casey thought that he was simply confused by a voice coming from the phone, but quickly realized that couldn't be it. He'd already told her about the many people he'd observed on the roof, all talking on their phones. And hard on that thought came the truth. He'd recognized Nick's voice. If she'd needed any further proof that Damian was one of Nick's missing statues, she'd just gotten it.

"That was my boss," she said quietly. "His name is Nick Katsaros."

"Nico," he whispered almost reverently. He stiffened to attention and said, "You will take me to him."

She considered her next words carefully. "I will," she agreed calmly. "But I'm not sure where he is right now. He's traveling. I need to talk to him first, and let him know what's going on. And then we'll figure out where we can meet."

"I will talk to him also."

She nodded. "If that's what he wants."

Damian eyed her silently for a long moment. "He *will* want to talk to me," he said with complete certainty. "He is still my leader, no matter the passage of time."

"Um, well. This probably isn't *your* Nicodemus. You understand that, right?" she asked cautiously. "I mean it's been what? A few thousand years? This Nick is probably just his many times great-grandson."

Damian just stared at her with a curious look in his eyes. Almost as if he pitied her. What the hell?

"You will take me to him," he repeated. "Trust me. When he learns of my awakening, he *will* want us to meet." It was as if he hadn't heard anything she'd said. She blinked in slow realization. Or as if he knew far more about Nick than she did. She considered that possibility for a moment, then set it aside. She'd worked with Nick for years, and had met with him on many occasions, both personal and professional. The kind of magic that Damian had attributed to *his* Nicodemus would make him a very powerful sorcerer. And, even though her ability to detect magic in a person was weaker than in inanimate objects, there was still no way Nick could have concealed that much power from her.

She frowned. Was there? In all of their meetings, in all of the briefings with the other hunters, Nick had never dropped so much as a hint that he was anything but an exceptionally talented human. Would he have kept something that important from them? *Could* he have?

Damn it. She needed to talk to Nick sooner, rather than later. And he needed to answer some questions. But right now, she needed to get to the store while she had the energy to do it. And besides, she wanted to talk to Nick without Damian listening.

"I'm going to the store," she told Damian, scooping up her cell phone, along with the rest of what she considered to be the necessities. She checked her Glock quickly, verifying the full magazine, then put that and her wallet into the small backpack she used as a purse when she was working. A knife and a spare mag followed, and she was ready. In the unlikely event she was stopped, she had a valid concealed carry permit for this state. Similar permits for almost every state in the union were in a special folder in a hidden compartment of her duffel. Nick had friends in high places, and he always made sure his hunters had what they needed to protect themselves.

Except maybe the truth about who and what he really was.

Damn it. She had to stop obsessing about something that might be nothing more than Damian's need to believe, and get back to more practical matters.

Zipping everything into her pack, she turned to Damian. "I won't be long, but I've written my number on the pad by the phone, in case you need to contact me. Pick up the receiver, hit either button, and dial the number." She demonstrated before continuing. "I'll be getting clothes for both of us, and food for snacks and stuff. We might be here a couple of days before I pick up the trail of the Talisman again."

"I should go with you. If your enemies are looking for you, you'll need protection."

She ground her teeth together to avoid saying what she was thinking, which was along the lines of inviting him to do the anatomically impossible. He came from a different time, she reminded herself.

"I'll be fine," she said striving for calm. "I can protect myself." She nearly snapped that last bit before reining in her temper. "And you have no clothes to wear. That's why I'm doing this."

He shrugged. "I'm fine with the few things I have."

Casey regarded his bare chest, still visible beneath the loosely tied robe, the breadth of shoulders that nothing could conceal, the gorgeous face and thick blond hair. Yes, he was definitely fine. But he still wasn't going to the store with her.

"Your clothes may be fine, but they're bloody and dirty and they make you too noticeable. We're trying to blend in, and, buddy, you don't blend."

He shrugged carelessly. "And Nico?"

"Like I said, he's traveling. He's also probably asleep right now, since his current job involves vampires." She paused to peer at him curiously. "Did you have vampires back then?"

He frowned, shaking his head. "I don't know what those are."

"Huh. Well, we'll talk later. Anyway, I'll leave Nick a message while I'm out, and he'll call when he wakes up." She didn't tell him that what she really wanted was to call Nick from the car so they could have a private conversation before she dropped Damian on him. "Don't leave the room, okay?"

He gave her a disgusted look, but nodded his agreement. "I won't leave the room," he droned, sounding like a sulky child.

She pursed her lips, but didn't say anything. She needed to get going. She had a lot of work to do.

"I'll be back," she intoned, then realized he probably wouldn't get the movie reference. So she settled for a quick wave as she walked out the door.

CASEY WASN'T NAÏVE enough to believe that Damian wouldn't at least watch from the window while she walked to the car. She supposed one could call it protectiveness, but she suspected it was more that he didn't quite trust her yet. And why should he? Their meeting hadn't been exactly normal. If she'd been trapped in stone for a few millennia, she'd probably be suspicious of anything having to do with magic, too.

So, she crossed to the car, got inside, and drove away as if she had nothing planned other than a shopping trip. But the minute she got to the store parking lot—she didn't want to conduct this phone call while shouting into a speakerphone—she called Nick back.

"Casey. Talk to me," he answered, sounding like she'd just woken him.

"Good morning to you too, Nick."

"Cassandra," he growled.

"Okay, so here's the deal. You always told us to be on the lookout for certain statues, but you never said exactly why. And you never even *hinted* that they could come to life."

"To life," Nick repeated, sounding like he'd just witnessed a miracle. "Who . . ." His breath hitched. Was he *crying?* "Who is it, Casey?"

"He says his name is Damian Stephanos."

"Damian," he breathed, and there was definite emotion in his voice now. She waited, giving him time.

"Nick, you okay?"

"Yes. Yeah. Is he there? Can I talk to him?"

"He's back at the hotel. I wanted to talk to you first, because there's more going on here than any of us suspected. That easy in-and-out theft you sent me on? Well, it wasn't. The buyer had way more power than he should have. He's either a sorcerer himself, or he's working for one, and I think it's the latter. I think Sotiris is behind this."

"Sotiris. You're sure?"

"I'm not sure of anything, except that I was up against a hell of a lot of power last night. I'm still going after the damn Talisman, but I'm suddenly running blind, trying to fill in the blanks. And Damian is one giant blank spot. Don't you think it's convenient that he just happens to show up now? After all this time? What if Sotiris freed him a long time ago, and now he's the bait to get you to show yourself?"

"Damian wouldn't do that."

She paused at the certainty in his voice. He talked about Damian like he knew him. Personally.

"You don't know what Damian would do," she said tiredly, depressed by the growing conviction that Damian, whom she'd just met, had told her the truth, while Nick, a man she'd known and trusted for years, had been lying to her and everyone else this whole time. "He claims the curse was just broken last night, but who really knows? I was there, and I wouldn't swear that's what happened."

"What did you do?" he demanded. "I mean, how was he freed?"

Casey blinked at the abrupt question. "Um, well. I did manage to grab the Talisman initially, but I didn't make a clean getaway. I was under heavy fire, with a pair of hellhounds on my heels—hellhounds, Nick!" she interjected, wanting him to understand just what she'd been up against. "Anyway, I set a false trail, then climbed to the top of a building in old downtown, hoping to escape over the roofs. There's a statue there, or at least there *was,* that looks over the street, so I braced my hand on it to lean over and check out the guys chasing me. And I said, I don't know, something like, "I wish you could help out, big guy."

"That was it?"

"I'd been shot, so there was blood. Damian says—"

"Wait, you were shot? Are you okay?"

Casey felt a rush of affection for her boss. He might be a lying bastard, but the one thing she could always say about Nick was that he took care of his people. He sometimes had to send them on dangerous missions, but he provided the best resources available, and when the shit hit the fan, he was always there.

"I won't be doing push-ups any time soon, but I'm fine."

"Did you see a doctor?"

"Yeah, right," she scoffed. "You know they report bullet wounds, and I didn't want to deal with that. It was a clean shot to the upper arm, through and through. As far as I can tell, no bones were hit, but I'll have it x-rayed back home. Damian helped me clean it out."

"Right. Damian. So your hand was bloody when you braced it on the statue."

She nodded automatically, even though he couldn't see it. "Yeah. And now, according to him, he owes me a blood debt, and until I agree it's been satisfied, he's honor-bound to help me."

"What did he tell you about . . . himself?"

Casey heard the hesitance in Nick's voice. He was asking about Damian, but he also wanted to know what the newly freed warrior had told her. "That he's a god of war," she said casually.

Nick surprised her by snorting a laugh. "That sounds like him. He's not actually a god; he was just treated like one. If you're still going after the Talisman—"

"I am."

"Then from what you're telling me, you'll need help. I'll be finished here tonight, so I'll fly over there. But in the meantime, you should use Damian. He has remarkable skills when it comes to fighting. He's a genius tactician, and there's no weapon he can't master."

"So he says. He said something else, too," she added, deciding in that minute to just lay it all out there. "He said that *you* led an army back in the day, that he and his fellow warriors were your brothers-in-arms. Math was never my strong suit, but I'm pretty sure that makes you a few thousand years old, boss."

"Damn." She heard Nick's soft curse.

"So, it's true," she said, stunned. "Damn it, Nick, who *are* you? And how come you haven't told us? I mean, if you were around back then . . ."

"I was there, and yeah, I've been letting you and the others think I'm just like you, maybe a little stronger. But there's a reason for that, or there was. I thought if I laid low, hid in plain sight, so to speak, Sotiris wouldn't know where I was, and I could find my men. But I've been thinking about that lately, and, damn it, Damian's return just proves it. It's time for me to stop hiding and start knocking down some walls."

"Why weren't you cursed into a statue, too?"

"Power," he said simply. "Sotiris could never defeat me, one on one. That's why he struck against Damian and the others. He knew what it would do to me to lose them."

Casey concentrated on breathing normally as she took all of that in. First was the shock of what Nick was. He'd always struck her as a charming man, a salesman, maybe a bit of a con artist. But a sorcerer? And not just any sorcerer, but one who could take on Sotiris? No wonder he'd kept that part of his life a secret. Most people would be scared to death of him if they knew. She frowned. Hell, *she* was a little afraid now.

"So Damian was a friend?" she asked finally, changing the subject like a pro.

"More like a brother than a friend."

"Families have been known to hate and kill each other, Nick. Maybe he blames you for everything he's suffered all these years."

"Casey," he said, chiding her a little bit. "I told you, he'd never do that. Did you call just to argue with me?"

"No," she responded quietly. "I called because if this was *my* long-lost brother, I'd want to know about it. The decision has to be yours, Nick. I'll do whatever you want."

"But you don't want me there," he said flatly, as if she could stop him if he put his mind to it.

"It's not that. I just don't want you to walk into a trap." She waited, and when Nick didn't say anything, she said, "Look, he says he wants revenge on Sotiris—"

"Hell, yeah, he does. Wouldn't you?"

"I don't need an excuse to go after Sotiris. That bastard is evil and needs to die. But I see your point. And you're the one who said that he was handy in a fight. So, let me use him, and I'll check him out for you. If he's telling the truth, he'll help me recover the Talisman. If he's playing a game, then he'll get in my way, and we'll know."

"I already know," Nick said softly. "Damian would never betray me. But it doesn't hurt to do it your way, especially since I can't get there until late tonight. I don't want you to get hurt any more than you already are, babe. I'll feel better knowing he's with you."

"I've warned you about the *babe* thing, Nick," she joked, desperate for a return to their familiar banter. All this other stuff, the revelations about

Nick, the reality of a statue come to life . . . she'd process it eventually. She just needed time. Like a few hours. Something more than the length of a phone call.

"You can file with HR when you get back," he teased back. "You're sure about this, Casey? You're okay with Damian?"

"I'm sure."

"All right," he said, willing, in true Nick fashion, to respect her judgment on the situation. "But if you need me before tonight, I can be there in an hour."

"Okay. What do you want me to tell Damian?"

"Tell him I'm on my way, and tell him—" He drew a soft breath. "Tell him I love him."

She felt tears building behind her eyes. She could only imagine what he must be feeling. "I'll take care of him," she said.

He laughed. "Don't tell him that. You'll hurt his pride. Remember, I can be there in an hour."

"Yeah, boss. Love you, too."

"Smart ass. Talk to you later."

DAMIAN WAITED impatiently for Cassandra to return, pacing from the window to the door and back again. He told himself it was because he was bored, that he'd spent thousands of years trapped in stone, and now here he was, trapped within the four walls of a hotel room. That was true as far as it went, but his concern went beyond that. They faced a formidable enemy. Sotiris was not only powerful, but ruthless and cunning, and never one to forgive an insult. Cassandra seemed to think the ancient sorcerer would have forgotten about her now that he had the Talisman within his grasp, or very nearly, since it was in the hands of his agent. But Damian knew better than that. The fact that she'd managed to steal it in the first place would be enough to rank her among Sotiris's enemies, and the sorcerer certainly hadn't survived this long by leaving his foes at his back. Whether or not she recovered the Talisman again, Sotiris would want her dead.

The sorcerer definitely hadn't been in that alley last night. Damian would have sensed his presence. And, according to Cassandra, he hadn't been in residence at the home from which she'd stolen the Talisman, either. Which meant the device was still in the hands of Sotiris's agent, and their best chance to recover it was now, before the agent delivered the artifact, and they had to go up against Sotiris himself in order to recover it.

Damian suppressed a shudder. The sorcerer had captured him once, and he'd been helpless to resist. When Sotiris realized that the curse had been broken, and Damian freed, would he try to curse him anew? Damian wasn't afraid to admit that the idea of going up against Sotiris terrified him, especially without Nico at his side.

The thought of Nico made him frown. Cassandra was keeping something from him, holding back. He *knew* that had been his brother's voice on the phone, just as he knew Nico would come the moment he learned of Damian's freedom. Unless Cassandra persuaded him otherwise. She didn't trust him yet. She had no trouble believing that he'd been cursed and imprisoned, but she didn't seem altogether convinced that it had been her actions that had freed him.

His frown deepened as a thought occurred to him. Did she think he was working with Sotiris? That he'd ally with the creature who'd condemned him and his brothers to millennia of torture? He'd have to be insane to consider such a thing. His eyes widened. Maybe that was it. Maybe she feared his long ordeal had twisted his mind. It had, but not in the ways she might think. Before the curse, he'd done two things well. The first was war. He'd been the greatest warrior ever to exist, and that was not a prideful boast. No one had ever bested him on the battlefield . . . or in the bedroom.

And that had been his other accomplishment. Sex. Women had flocked to his bed, and he'd done his best to fuck as many of them as possible, taking pride in leaving them well satisfied. Including that damn Amazon queen who, for all her reputed prowess on the battlefield, had been a lousy lay. That fact only added fuel to the fire of his resentment that she'd been the catalyst of his nightmare. Though, admittedly, she'd had nothing to do with the curse itself. He and his fellow warriors had been betrayed. He still didn't know by whom, but it had to have been someone close, someone with access to their innermost sanctum. But while he hadn't figured out who the traitor was, he trusted that Nico had, and that the man was already suffering an eternity of torment.

Damian pulled back the curtain on the window again and looked down at the parking lot, his thoughts whirling. Nico. How was it that he happened to be here in this exact time and place? He hadn't been cursed directly; Damian was sure of that much. Sotiris's curses would never have worked on Nico. He had too much magic of his own, which had been the major source of friction between the two sorcerers. Sotiris had always resented the fact that Nico surpassed him in both power and skill, and that he'd done so from such a young age. Nico had been barely a teenager the first time he'd defeated Sotiris in battle.

And here they all were again. What were the chances that Damian would finally be freed in the precise time when both Nico and Sotiris were active? Was it Fate's way of slapping Sotiris down for daring to meddle with the sands of time? Were the gods about to reunite Nico and his warriors for one final battle against their age-old enemy? A fierce desire for revenge, for justice, nearly swamped him as he stared out the window. But he wasn't seeing the metal cars in the dingy parking lot, or even the airplanes drifting over the airport. His mind's eye saw only that last battlefield, the great armies arranged on either side, the stench of fear mixing with the musk of courage. And before them all stood Nicodemus and his warriors, shoulder to shoulder, grinning in expectation of the battle to come, confident in their victory because as long as they stood together, no one could defeat them.

And then had come the shattering knowledge that they'd been betrayed, the horror on Nico's face as the spell hit, the bloody sweat rolling down his face as he'd fought with every ounce of magic he possessed to counter the spell to save them, his brothers.

"I will find you." Nico's voice drifted through his mind as it had every day since he'd been trapped. It was that vow that had kept him sane, the absolute certainty that Nico would never give up.

The thin sound of plastic against the door's electronic lock had him turning, mind alert, muscles tensed and ready. But the moment the door cracked open, he knew it was Cassandra. He knew her scent by now, a combination of her soap and shampoo. Clean and feminine. It made his cock twitch, reminding him once again that he hadn't had a woman in far too long.

She looked up in surprise as she came through the door. "You're up!"

"You thought I'd lie in bed the entire morning? Your television isn't that interesting."

"I'm sorry," she said, seeming sincerely contrite. "It took longer than I expected. I've never bought clothes for a man before, and I wasn't sure about the sizes." She dumped two large bags on one of the unmade beds. "I ended up buying too much, but anything that doesn't fit we can donate. I saw a thrift store right down the road that benefits a homeless shelter."

He had no idea what she was talking about, but he liked the sound of her voice, the crackle of energy as she moved around the room.

She swung her small backpack onto the bed, along with yet another bag, this one with boxes in it. "The boots were the hardest. I hope one of these fits."

Damian eyed her in amusement. "And Nico?" he asked. "What did he have to say?"

Her eyes widened in surprise and maybe a touch of fear, before she replaced both expressions with a blank face.

"You have nothing to fear from me, Cassandra," he said as gently as he could.

"What makes you think I talked to him?" she said defiantly.

He grinned. "It was a guess, but your reaction tells me I'm right. What did he say?"

She gave him a narrow look, probably more pissed with herself than him at this moment. It only made him grin harder.

"He was . . . happy. Nick's usually a pretty controlled guy, but this. . . . It was genuine emotion. He's on another job, but it's not that far from here. About an hour's—"

"He's coming here?" Damian's heart lifted at the thought of soon seeing Nico again, but Cassandra was shaking her head.

"I told him not to, but he didn't listen."

He stared at her in disbelief. "Of course, he didn't listen. But why would you do that?"

"Because I don't know you or what your intentions are. Who knows better than Sotiris what the terms of your curse were? Maybe you were put in my path just so I'd take you back to Nick and you could kill him."

Damian was furious, but underneath the fury was respect. She was trying to protect Nico. He understood that. And in any other situation, she might even have been right. But not this one. There was no way in hell he would ever betray his brother, no spell strong enough to twist him against something so intrinsic to who he was.

"He's fully capable of defending himself, you know," he said tightly, unable to resist arguing, though he knew her actions came from a lack of understanding. "He's quite powerful."

"But not against you," she snapped. "He loves you. He said to tell you that. If you could have heard—" She stopped whatever she'd been about to say, but the emotion in her voice told him everything.

"You love him," he said, wondering why it irritated him to know this.

She shook her head. "I'm *loyal* to him. He's my boss, but he's also a friend. He was the first person in my life to believe in me. He showed me I was unique rather than weird, that I could actually help people."

Damian understood loyalty. The Nico he'd known had been young and full to bursting with the tremendous power he'd been born with, arrogant and smug with all of the benefits that power brought him. But even so, he'd inspired devotion amongst those who followed him. This Nico, the one Cassandra knew, was different. Older, of course. Confident rather than arrogant. But still with that core of strength that inspired steadfast loyalty.

"So what are your plans for me?" he asked.

"I don't have any plans for you," she countered. "I'm not even sure what's happening here. But I think we can help each other while I figure it out, and Nick agrees with me. I need to get the Talisman back before Sotiris uses it to kill a lot of people. And you want revenge for what he did to you and your friends."

"We were more than friends," he said quietly. "We were brothers. We are *still* brothers. If I live, then they do too, somewhere in this world that your people have created. And I will find them."

She nodded. "I can help you with that. I don't have magic. Not like Nick does, but I've made it my life's work to understand it. And magic is . . . avaricious. Do you understand? It's greedy and selfish, and . . . jealous in an odd way. It feeds on itself and it's drawn to bursts of power. Your release from Sotiris's curse will burn brightly on the magical horizon. A warrior god cursed and trapped for millennia, suddenly freed—"

"I'm not actually a god," he reluctantly admitted. But her reaction was a brilliant smile, bigger than any he'd seen from her so far.

"I know. Nick told me. But you were worshipped as one, and that kind of devotion has an energy all its own. I think when you broke the curse—"

"When *you* broke it," he corrected her.

She shrugged. "The details don't matter. The curse was broken, and you were thrust into this time and place. If I'm right, that will set in motion a chain of events that not even Sotiris will be able to stop. One by one, your . . . brothers will break their curses until all of you are free. And then—"

"And then Nico and his warriors will stand together again with only one goal. The death of Sotiris," he snarled.

He half expected her to recoil, to insist on justice, rather than revenge. To argue, as he'd heard so many in this time argue, that a criminal must be given the opportunity to answer for his crimes. But she proved him wrong again.

"Death," she agreed, her big, brown eyes cold and determined. "As painful and as lasting as we can make it."

Damian grinned. "A meeting of the minds at last, Cassandra."

She blushed and looked away, as if embarrassed by her own viciousness.

"You should try on the clothes," she said, shoving one of the bags closer to him. "If you're going to help me hunt down the Talisman, you can't wear that." She pointed to the too-short robe he was wearing. The *only* thing he was wearing.

Laughing privately, he untied the robe and dropped it to the floor in a single movement, leaving him completely naked as he reached for the pile of clothes. She sucked in a breath and her blush deepened to a furious red. But he noted smugly that it was a long moment before she looked away.

"Fuck," she swore softly. "You really . . . I'll just, um, I'll work over here." She snatched up her computer and all but ran the short distance to the opposite side of the room where there was a desk and chair against the wall.

Chuckling to himself, Damian went through the clothing choices, scowling at the stiff shirts with all their buttons, settling instead on several short-sleeved cotton shirts with colorful designs on the front. He tossed aside the package of underwear she'd bought him. No one had worn underwear like this in his previous life, and he didn't see the need for it now. Again, he rejected the too-stiff light-brown pants with many pockets that she'd purchased, going instead with what he knew were called jeans. Soft, faded-looking blue fabric that fit well through his hips and thighs, but were looser through his calves.

"They're just loose enough for boots," she said, drawing his attention and making him wonder if she'd been watching him the whole time.

He grunted as he considered the boots she'd purchased, settling on a pair of black leather, with reinforced toes and a lace-up shaft. "Good design." He stood up to take a few steps back and forth. "These are excellent," he said in some surprise. "Very good quality."

She nodded. "I found an army surplus store. It's a place that sells military-style clothing. Those are combat boots."

He looked up and gave her a grateful nod. "Everything fits. You did well."

She rolled her eyes. "Gee, thanks."

He knew she was being sarcastic, but didn't understand why since he'd paid her a compliment. But he'd learn. Women had always loved him. She would be no different.

"What about weapons?" he asked, doing a series of squats to work in the new clothing. A choking noise drew his attention back to Cassandra who switched her eyes away quickly.

"I have plenty of weapons," she said, her voice muffled somewhat by the fact that she was studiously avoiding look at him.

His male ego preened a little. So she wasn't as immune as she pretended. "These?" he said, walking over to the considerable arsenal spread out on the floor where he'd moved it so he could sleep in the other bed . . . all alone.

She nodded, still staring at her computer. "Those and others. They're nearby. Once you're dressed, we can go pick them up."

"Am I not already dressed?" he asked, holding his arms out and turning for her perusal.

She was forced to look up then, and he could see the same appreciation in her eyes that he'd seen in the gazes of a thousand women. Her throat worked in a swallow. "It's cold out. I bought you a jacket."

He spun back to the bed, his gaze taking in the various packages and bags until his eye fell on a large plastic bag with a hook protruding from the top. He picked it up, glancing at her for confirmation. She nodded, and he ripped the covering off to reveal a jacket of the softest leather, brushed brown with a quilted lining and zipped front. He picked it up and was assailed by the scent of well-cured ox hide. Finally, something familiar and welcome in this hard and unyielding world in which he'd ended up. Resisting the urge to bury his face in it, he pulled it on instead, then walked over to the mirrored closet door. It felt good on his shoulders, the weight comforting and right. How had she known?

He turned and found her still watching him. "I figured leather," she said. "It's been around forever."

"Thank you," he said sincerely, then grinned. "Shall we go get the weapons now?"

CASEY AGREED wordlessly, snapping her laptop shut, and all but jumping to her feet. Anything to get out of that confining hotel room and the suddenly sexy warrior god who was sucking up all of the oxygen and apparently her good sense, as well. Damian the insufferable ass was a lot easier to deal with than this new grateful and understanding Damian, not to mention blisteringly sexy. She hadn't missed the fact that he'd discarded the package of boxer briefs she'd bought, tossing them aside with barely a glance. On the other hand, the jeans fit him like they'd been tailor-made, caressing his thighs and very nice butt, cupping his crotch like a lover. Damn. Where had *that* thought come from?

"Pack up," she said abruptly, before she came up with any more poetic descriptions for Damian and his damn cock. "Here," she said, yanking a new duffel out of one of the bags and shoving it in his direction. "Put all of your clothes in there, and I'll pack the gear."

"Perhaps I should deal with the weapons—"

She gave him a disbelieving look. "Why? Because you have a penis? I don't think you need one of those to do this."

Damian gave a long-suffering sigh and began packing his new clothes, discarding as much as he packed. "What do I do with those items I won't be wearing?" he asked, continuing his sorting.

"Put them in one of the plastic bags. We'll drop them off on our way," she said, watching him shove the entire package of underwear into the discard bag. Great. Now she'd never get the picture of a commando Damian out of her head. That would be terrific for her concentration. Maybe she needed to dump him somewhere after all.

She dropped her small cosmetics bag into a side pocket, then, with all of the gear and weapons inside the big canvas duffel, she pulled the heavy-duty zipper shut. She straightened and looked at him.

"You ready to go?"

"Will you at least let me carry the heavy bag? Your shoulder is still injured."

She gave him a crooked smile. "Knock yourself out."

He tilted his head and gave her a puzzled look.

"It's a colloquialism. It's like saying, 'Sure, go ahead.' As for the bag, there's no question you're stronger than I am, and I'm always ready to use the best tool for the job."

"Are you calling me a tool?"

Casey laughed. "You know that word?"

"I've heard it. Did I use it correctly?"

She nodded. "And, no. You're not a tool. I'm just saying you're the best man for the job, and we need to get going. I'm getting a bad feeling, and I've learned to pay attention when that happens."

Damian hefted the big, heavy bag like it weighed nothing and slung it over his shoulder. "Are you a seer, then?"

"No, nothing that grand. I just get these warning twitches, usually when something bad is about to happen."

He nodded and pulled the room door open for her. "We should definitely leave, then. I serve Nicodemus Katsaros. I believe in magic."

Casey pulled on her winter jacket, the one she only wore when she was traveling. The hoodie she'd worn hadn't been enough. It was nearly summer, but the days here in the Midwest were a lot cooler than where she lived in Florida, and the nights seemed positively cold. Also, it was loose enough that she was able to fit it over her bandages without adding to her pain.

"I didn't see you in the parking lot," he commented as they took the stairs down. She noticed that he hadn't said a word about using the stairs instead of the elevator. Not even the other night when they'd both been exhausted, and she'd been leaking blood. She used elevators when she had to, like during her escape at the Kalman, but she found the metal boxes too confining. She wasn't claustrophobic, not exactly. It was just that her father's idea of how to discipline his young daughter had mostly consisted of locking her in a closet, as if she was one of his recruits being trained to withstand interrogation. He'd wanted her to learn discipline, and she had. Along with feelings of emotional abandonment and a healthy dislike of confined spaces. The claustrophobia she could compensate for. The other . . . well, let's just say that trust wasn't something she gave easily.

Besides, Damian was in such great shape that taking the stairs probably didn't matter to him. Actually, the exercise was probably a nice change, what with him having been a statue and all.

"I parked out back," she told him as they clambered down the stairs, filling the hollow space with noise that echoed. She was fighting to control her breath, because he was breathing as easily as if they were on a walk in the sunshine. Good thing he hadn't been with her coming up earlier, when she'd returned from the store. She considered herself to be in excellent shape, but eight floors with a healing bullet wound was pushing it. She'd actually waited down the hall before entering the hotel room, because she'd been panting so hard he might have been worried about her. And the last thing she needed was him trying to be the big man taking care of the little lady.

It was bad enough that he was bigger and stronger and undoubtedly a far better fighter than she was, with or without weapons. But this was still her mission, not his. He was there to help her, not take over. Besides, he might be a natural warrior—okay, yes, he obviously *was* a natural warrior—but she had an advantage he couldn't match. And that was time. As in, this was *her* time, *her* world. She understood this time period on a gut level. She'd grown up here. He hadn't.

They exited the stairwell into the rear of the first floor lobby, then made a right turn for the door to the parking lot behind the building.

"This is a different vehicle," he noted as they crossed the blacktop toward her GMC Yukon. "The weapons are inside?"

"Yeah," she said, beeping the locks open. It was the second Yukon she'd owned—only one year old, and her baby. "Kind of a mobile backup unit," she said, giving it a loving pat.

"I'll drive," he said with his typical arrogance.

She gave him a shocked look over the hood. She found the very idea of him behind the wheel of anything to be vaguely alarming, much less her beloved Yukon with its powerful V8 engine. "Again, no penis required here," she said sarcastically. "But for the record, do you even know how to drive?"

"No. But everyone does it, so how difficult can it be?"

"Yeah. Maybe later," she lied. Once he was no longer her responsibility, he could smash his way through half of the country for all she cared. But for now, she intended to keep him, and herself, in one piece.

"This is a personal vehicle," he reasoned thoughtfully, as she drove slowly from the lot. He tilted his head curiously. "But your home is in Florida, you said. You drove all the way here?"

She *knew* she shouldn't have told him that. Damn. Why did he have to be so sharp? And when had he'd studied a map anyway? She hated talking about this. "I like to drive," she said simply.

"From Florida," he reiterated, clearly angling for an explanation that she didn't want to provide.

"I travel a lot," she said, still hoping to avoid going into detail. Only her therapist knew about the closet. Nick had caught on to her claustrophobia a long time ago, and she was sure he had his theories about what had caused it. But he'd never pushed. Unlike *some* people. "Sometimes I feel like I live in my car," she told Damian, making light of it.

He was still studying her. "But that's not why you drove here. I studied the map of this continent while you were shopping—"

Well, that answered *one* question, but. . . . "Where'd you get the map?" she demanded.

"From your duffel," he said, not at all apologetic for snooping through her things *again*. She made an exasperated noise, which he ignored. "I don't know your city in Florida, but it's at least a day and a night to drive here from there, while you could fly on one of your planes in a few hours."

"How do you know *that?*" she asked in amazement. He hadn't gotten that off of any map.

"Google," he said matter-of-factly. "You left your computer on the table. I'll have to acquire one of my own very soon. It's a critical piece of equipment in this time."

"My password . . . ." she said, wondering why she bothered.

"It's buffEE. I watched you press the keys," he told her blithely. "Your computer doesn't think this is a very good password code, by the way."

"I know that," she snapped. "And it's just 'password', okay? Not password code. Also, just because you happened to see . . ." She stopped what she'd been about to say. What was the point? He'd just do whatever he wanted anyway. Besides, he was right. He *would* need to catch up on technology, and her password *was* crap. She sighed.

"I don't like to fly," she admitted quietly. "I can, but I prefer to drive. When Nick called, I was only a couple of hours away, finishing up on another job. I was the closest member of his team, though that's only part of the reason he called me. My talent goes beyond the ability to sense magic. I'm sort of a magical mechanic. I can see the flow of magic in a thing, and I'm also better versed than most in magic theory. Those two things combined mean I'm better than anyone I know at figuring out how complicated magical artifacts work."

"Better than Nico?" he asked, his tone clearly indicating his doubt.

"Yes," she drawled, "better even than him. At least, that's what he always told me. He claims to see the big picture, while I see the pieces and how they fit together. Or, in this case, the magical energies and how they interact. A lot of devices, probably most of them, are pretty black and white. They have a purpose and it's easy to see how they fulfill that purpose. But then there are the ones like the Talisman. Neither one of us is exactly sure how it works. Unfortunately, I didn't have it long enough to do much more than identify it as the artifact I was after before I shoved it in my pack and ran. And you know how *that* turned out. So once I have it . . . that is, once I get it back, my priority will be determining how it works."

"So you can use it yourself?"

"So Nick can destroy it," she corrected softly. "It's far too dangerous to permit in this world."

He considered that. "So Nico is your leader, just as he was mine."

"I guess so."

"And you're worried that I mean him harm, that I'm in league with Sotiris. But that would never happen. I am sworn to Nicodemus."

"That was a few millennia ago," she reminded him, as she made yet another turn, driving aimlessly up and down streets, watching her rearview mirror for anyone following.

"My oath was to the death. As long as there is breath in my lungs, my oath stands." He studied the side mirror. "You believe we're being followed?"

Casey closed her eyes briefly, struck by his remarkable ability to adapt. They might not even have had mirrors back in his time, not as such anyway. And yet he took all of this in stride—cars, mirrors, computers. Hell, what about weapons? He'd wielded an MP-5 automatic weapon last night as if he'd been born to it. She sure hoped he was on the up and up, because he'd be one hell of an asset for the good guys.

"No," she said, answering his question. "It doesn't seem like anyone's paying attention to us, but I don't expect that to last. I'm worried that Sotiris will learn that your curse was lifted and come after you. Will he? Do you know?" She glanced over and caught the shrug of his massive shoulders.

"I know nothing about it, but you should ask Nico. Or I could do it for you, if you'd let me talk to him." He sighed mournfully, or at least what probably passed for mournful from a warrior god.

Casey laughed. "You don't do the long-suffering martyr thing very well."

He grinned back at her. "It's not in my nature. I'm more likely to hunt down and kill my enemies than suffer their persecution. You're fortunate that I like you."

"Uh huh," she muttered. Although privately, it gave her a little thrill that he *liked* her. A thrill that only served as a warning. *Do not get too friendly with the ancient warrior god!*

"For what it's worth, I believe you're correct," he said. "As the crafter of the curse, Sotiris should be aware that it's now been lifted, and he's cruel enough to want to trap me anew if given the chance. But just because he knows I'm free, that doesn't mean he knows where I am. I could be anywhere in the world."

"At least until he gets his agent's report on last night's firefight and the big blond guy with a huge-ass sword. I figure we have a little bit of a window, a day or two at the most, before he decides we're worth his attention. If for no other reason than because we'll lead him to Nick."

"Nico does not fear Sotiris."

"No, but he worries about you and the other warriors. Apparently, he's been keeping his head down while he looked for you and the others, which was why he didn't tell anyone about his magic. I'm not sure Sotiris even knew he was in this time and place. But something happened on his latest job to change that."

"The job he's doing with vampires."

"That's the one," she agreed, noting again that Damian seemed to retain every bit of information she provided. And a lot more that she didn't.

"You think Sotiris will follow us and lay a trap for Nico," Damian deduced.

She nodded. "That's why I asked Nick not to come until Sotiris had been drawn out into the open."

"By us retrieving this Talisman of yours," Damian said.

"Exactly."

"Very well. I will help you."

"Gee, thanks. Just one thing, big guy. This is my world, and I'm in charge."

"And I am a god of war. You may find my knowledge of such things exceeds your own."

"Don't hold your breath waiting for that one. I'm in charge. Agreed?" When he didn't say anything, she added, "If not, then I'll do what I originally planned. I'll check you into a hotel with great room service and satellite TV and come back for you when it's over."

"You assume I'd stay there. I was imprisoned for millennia, Cassandra. I have no intention of consenting to a new jail cell, no matter how comfortable."

"I know that," she said quietly. "And that's not what I meant. But you're a warrior—you should understand that someone needs to be in charge. If you can't follow my lead, then we'll just get in each other's way. And this is too important. People will die if I fuck this up. I need to get that Talisman back."

"Will you at least take my advice on occasion?"

"Of course. I'm not stupid."

He smiled slightly. "Very well. Where do we start?"

A part of her wanted to hear the specific words, that he'd agree to follow her lead, but she figured this was as much of a commitment as she was going to get from him. Finally convinced that no one was following them, she headed directly to the other side of town and the new financial district, where one of her favorite hotels had just opened. "First, we're checking into a new hotel, and then . . . how are you at research?"

Chapter Four

DAMIAN SET ASIDE his laptop computer. It was his because Casey had made one additional stop on the way to this new hotel. Standing in the huge store, it had hit him just how out of time and place he really was. He hadn't known what half of the things in the damn store were supposed to do. There was only so much one could learn while trapped in stone on a roof-top. Sure, people came up there for clandestine meetings, or just to escape the pressures of work, and yeah, they talked to each other, and on their cell phones, but that was about it. They generally didn't drag their computers or elaborate music systems along. Casey had been very willing to answer his questions and to explain everything they saw, and he'd taken it in as he always did, making it part of his knowledge. But there was so *much* to learn, and in the end, it had only made him feel stupid. And for the first time in his life, a little bit lost. This wasn't his era. It wasn't where he belonged.

Except that it was now. And he would have to learn to live in it.

He shoved the computer farther away and leaned back, bouncing his head a few times against the elaborate headboard. This hotel was much like the last. Long, quiet corridors of widely-spaced doors that led to elegant, well-appointed rooms. This new room had two beds, just like the last, but it was larger with a separate sitting area and work desk. Cassandra sat at that desk, being much more productive on her computer than he'd been on his. It should have bothered him. It didn't particularly. Firstly, he couldn't be expected to work as well as she did on the unfamiliar device, and secondly, even in his own time, he had never been a scholar. Scholars had their place, but it wasn't on the battlefield. And that was precisely where he belonged.

Which raised a very good question. Why was he once again stuck within four walls, doing nothing but watching Cassandra work? Sure, he had his own computer, but that didn't mean he was doing anything useful with it. He'd learned very quickly that there was a vast difference between finding a Google map and actually doing research. A vast and *tedious* difference.

"You do know that I was trapped in a stone prison for thousands of years?" he asked, without any preamble.

It took a moment, but eventually Cassandra looked up. She had to blink a few times before she seemed to bring him into focus. "Huh?"

Well, *that* was hardly worth waiting for. "I said I'm bored. I spent a few thousand years in a dark cave with nothing to see at all, and the last hundred just watching, without any ability to interact with what I was seeing. I want to get out of this room. You wouldn't even agree to go to the steak house for dinner."

She scowled impatiently. "Look, I'm sorry about the restaurant, okay? But I'm sure the pictures in the hotel's brochure make it seem much nicer than it really is, and you *did* have steak for dinner from room service."

"Cold and overcooked."

"I warned you not to get it."

"Because it was room service. If we'd gone downstairs, I'm sure it would have been fine."

She rolled her eyes in an exaggerated way. "I said I was sorry, okay? I had work to do. I still *do*. I need to figure out where they'll take the Talisman, all right?"

"Of course. What you're doing is necessary and important."

"Thank you," she said and started to turn back to her computer.

"But there's no point in me being stuck up here, too."

"I thought you wanted to learn your new computer," she said without even glancing at him.

"I've learned enough for one night." Enough to know he'd never learn it all, at least not without a lot of help. But he wasn't going to tell her *that*. He rolled up and off in the bed in a single smooth movement, then reached back for his leather jacket. "I'm going downstairs."

That got her attention. "I don't think that's a good idea," she said, a worried look in her dark eyes.

"Why?" he demanded.

She stared at him for a moment, and he knew it wasn't because she lacked reasons for why he should stay, but because she was trying to find one that wouldn't insult him. "The restaurant is closed," she said finally.

"But the bar isn't."

"The bar?" she repeated, and he'd have sworn he could hear her heart racing anxiously from across the room.

"The place downstairs with people and music," he said dryly. "We walked past it earlier. I believe they offer alcoholic beverages there."

"I know what a bar is," she said impatiently. "It's just . . . it's really not . . . I mean, it's going to be really crowded."

"Good. If I'm to acclimate to this new reality, I need social interaction. Don't you agree?"

"Um. Sure. I guess I can do this stuff later. Just give me a few minutes—"

"I don't require a keeper, Cassandra. You remain here and do your research." He slipped his jacket on and headed for the door.

Cassandra was halfway out of her chair, frozen there as if torn between wanting to follow him or remaining with her computer to finish her research.

"Stay," he told her. "I'll be fine." And then he pulled the heavy door open and stepped into the hallway, not believing in his escape until the door slammed shut behind him.

CASEY STARED AT THE closed door, thinking she could hear Damian's footsteps as they moved down the carpeted hallway, which, of course, she couldn't. She did hear what she thought might have been the muted ding of the elevator. But then, Damian would probably take the stairs just as they had coming up here. They were only on the fourth floor of this very elegant boutique hotel. The room was going to cost Nick a small fortune, but at least they'd only needed one.

Although now that she thought about it, she wasn't at all sure it was a good idea to send Damian out alone into the world of expense accounts and dark hotel bars. Actually, she wasn't worried about him so much as the rest of the population. He'd told her he wanted to live after all his years of imprisonment, but looking the way he did, she suspected that was code for wanting to get laid. And who could blame him? He was gorgeous, tall, built, and irritatingly charming. He'd be a big hit in the average hotel bar. And he'd been driving her nuts all evening, restless and complaining, pacing around as if he couldn't sit still. But then, she supposed he'd done plenty of sitting—or standing—still up until now. He deserved to get out a little, and with him gone, she could do her work much more efficiently. She was used to working alone, after all. Used to having the quiet necessary to her concentration. She'd be much better off without him looking over her shoulder and asking questions, right?

So why couldn't she focus now that he was gone?

"Stop it, Case," she muttered and swung back to her computer, determined to figure out who Sotiris's buyer had been, and where he might have gone to ground. Lips pursed, she stopped herself right there. She shouldn't be assuming Sotiris was the one involved. The only thing she knew for certain was that there'd been major sorcery at work. It was the hellhounds that gave it away. One didn't simply visit the local animal shelter and adopt a couple of adorable hellhound puppies. It took some serious mojo to drag them through the dimensions and then, even more importantly, to control them enough to make it worthwhile.

But that didn't mean the magic worker was Sotiris, or even a full-fledged sorcerer. There were plenty of people wandering the world who could do a major spell or two. She'd cleaned up plenty of messes left by people who had enough magic to be dangerous, but no idea of what to do with it. That could be what had happened here. Maybe the buyer had found himself a fledgling magic worker to do the job for him. Or maybe he was working for someone else entirely.

It would be a serious mistake to focus her search too tightly this early in her investigation, and a fatal one if it kept her from finding whoever had grabbed the Talisman before they could use it. That was her greatest fear, that their plan was already in motion, and she had only days to find it and then figure out a way to stop it before the electrical grid shut down and planes started falling from the sky. Maybe she was living up to her name on this one, foreseeing doom where there was none. But the briefing Nick had provided when he'd given her this mission had mentioned the device's weird energy signature, and specifically, his concern that if properly boosted, it could act like an EMP, an electromagnetic pulse that had the potential for use as a weapon of terror. It could send planes crashing to earth, killing hundreds, or even thousands, of people. Less dramatic, perhaps, but with the same disastrous potential, would be using it to shut down Wall Street or one of the other major exchanges. It was the perfect weapon for someone whose only goal was to create chaos and destroy lives.

So with all of that at stake, why was she sitting there brooding about Damian and wondering what he was doing downstairs? She told herself that it made sense. That, while Damian was apparently some kind of super soldier, he didn't know this era, and their enemy could easily surprise him. Had he even taken a weapon with him? A gun or knife? There was his tremendous physical power, of course, and his intellect.

She frowned. Both of those would make him *very* popular with the ladies downstairs. But what did she care? Okay, sure, he was all of those things. You know, gorgeous and built . . . and smart. And, well, yeah, when he crossed a room, he didn't walk so much as he prowled, with every muscle moving in perfect harmony with all of the others. She could only imagine the sorts of things a man with that kind of muscle control could do in bed. And stamina. Oh, yes, Damian and his god-like powers would have stamina to spare, not to mention all that built-up need, passion . . . hunger.

Her gaze lifted slowly from the computer screen, her eyes narrowing in consideration. She was feeling a little bit hungry herself. A little . . . needy. Sexually. She tended to avoid long-term commitments with men, but she was hardly celibate. She thought back to her last affair—if one could call a three-day weekend an affair. It sounded nicer than the alternative, though, so she went with it. She counted back the time in her head. More than a year ago. As a matter of fact, she'd picked him up in a hotel much like this one.

She should walk away from this. Turn Damian over to Nick and be done with it.

But then, the image flashed in her head of him sitting downstairs, maybe being targeted by someone much like herself for an *affair,* and her eyes narrowed. What the fuck? Why should she sit up there like some medieval nun searching through scrolls, while the gorgeous man who happened to be *her* roommate was downstairs being hustled by someone else? If anyone was going to get lucky with the very munchable Damian tonight, it was going to be her. After all, *she* was the one who'd rescued his perfectly toned ass from that curse.

Well, fuck.

Yes. Exactly.

DAMIAN SMILED AT the woman sitting next to him—her name was Sabrina—as she told him her life's story. Or at least the story of her last few days, which included her reasons for being in this hotel at this point in time, and how she'd be going back home tomorrow, while tonight she had a room all to herself.

It was a story he was quite familiar with by now. Sabrina—if that was her real name—wasn't the first woman tonight who'd tried to seduce him. Though their pursuit couldn't really be called seduction. It was far too blatant. All of the women had been very clear about their intentions and his role in their plans for the night's activities. They wanted a bed partner for the night. Afterward, he and his bedmate would part ways and never see each other again. It was what he'd done all of his life, back in his own time. He'd been known for it. And yet, despite Sabrina's undeniable charms, he wasn't interested. Just as he hadn't been interested in the three women who'd sat on the barstool before her. He'd found fault with all of them. Too skinny, too brash, too perfumed . . . none of which would have bothered him before he'd been cursed.

He nodded at whatever Sabrina was saying, not really listening, but aware of her growing impatience. Apparently, he wasn't responding the way he should, which would have meant following her into the elevator and fucking her brains out. *That* would be exciting, right?

But imagining sex in the elevator only made him think about Cassandra and her dislike for the mechanical lifts. That, plus her avoidance of air travel, led to only one conclusion—she had a fear of tight places. He could empathize with that. He wasn't too crazy about confined spaces himself these days.

From the corner of his eye, he saw Sabrina pick up her glass of what-ever pink alcohol she was drinking, and drain the contents. She was just leaning in to whisper a final proposition in his ear, when movement near the doorway caught his attention. He swung around. It was Cassandra, and he suddenly understood why none of the women who'd accosted him to-night had been good enough. None of them had possessed her confidence, the spark of intellect in her gaze as she scanned the crowded room, memorizing every face, cataloging every exit. She was tall and ath-letic-looking, her long, black hair flowing in shining waves over her shoul-ders and down her back. Dark jeans clung to her long legs, and a dark green button-up sweater hugged the full swell of her breasts.

Compared to the perfumed and coiffed Sabrina, Cassandra looked like someone who didn't want to be noticed, though he wasn't the only man in the room who was watching her. It made him wonder what she looked like when she *did* want to be noticed. Was there a man waiting for her back home in Florida? Did she dress up for him? Maybe bare some of that creamy skin he'd seen when he was bandaging her shoulder? He'd bet her breasts were every bit as smooth and unblemished as her back had been.

Her gaze caught his across the room and her eyes narrowed as if she'd read his thoughts. Damian had a moment to wonder if she'd been concealing a talent for telepathy, and then she was pushing her way through the crowd, making straight for him and the lovely Sabrina.

"Cassandra, darling," he greeted her. "You decided to join us. This is Sabrina."

She gave Sabrina a quick, assessing glance. "Hi," she said, then moved closer, slipped her good arm over his shoulder, and leaned forward to take a sip from his drink.

Damian had to work hard to stifle a gleeful chortle. She was claiming him, clearly marking her territory not only with the physical gesture, but by drinking from his glass. It was a profoundly intimate act. He didn't know why she was doing it, but he was vain enough to be delighted.

Sabrina, on the other hand, was not. She'd sucked in a surprised breath when Cassandra showed up, and was now giving him a narrow look that was both embarrassed and irritated. As if he'd owed her honesty when she'd been anything but.

"Well," she said with brittle cheer. "It looks like my friends aren't going to show. Thanks for the drink, Damian," she said—another lie, since he hadn't bought a drink for her. But this one was aimed at Cassandra, which annoyed him for some reason. And it more than annoyed him when she took it a step further, saying to Cassandra, "Lovely to meet you . . . Sandra was it?"

But Cassandra only smiled, and he could feel her body shaking with suppressed laughter. She waited until Sabrina was out of earshot, lost in the crowd, before putting her mouth close to his ear and whispering, "She's married."

Damian pulled back and winked at her. "I know."

Her mouth tightened in aggravation. "And you were hustling her anyway?"

He laughed. "Sabrina was the one doing the hustling, darling. She was quite clear about what she wanted from me. And what she didn't."

"Humph. Bitch." She wrinkled her nose as she slid onto the seat Sabrina had vacated and rested her elbows on the bar. It had the immediate effect of making her full breasts look even more tempting, and he forced himself to look away before she caught him staring. "What's that you're drinking anyway?" she asked. "It's awful."

"That is twelve-year-old Macallan Single Malt, and it is most assuredly not awful," he informed her.

Her nose wrinkled again. "Scotch. I've heard it's an acquired taste, one I've never appreciated. How do you know about it anyway? I'm pretty sure they didn't have scotch way back when."

"They did not, but many a visitor to my rooftop carried a bottle with him, or at least waxed poetic about the flavor. I decided to try it, and the very helpful bartender over there—his name is George—suggested this one. He assures me it's the best they have."

"The most expensive anyway," she said dryly. "Did you put it on the room?"

He frowned for a moment. *On the room?*

She saw his confusion. "Did you charge it to our hotel room bill?" she clarified.

"Ah, that. Yes. George was very helpful there, as well."

Cassandra shrugged. "It's on Nick's tab, so go for it. I doubt he'll mind."

Damian sighed at the reminder of his absent brother. All of the pleasure of the evening drained away. He reached for his drink, wanting to recapture the mood, the normalcy of being just another visitor having a drink in a bar, surrounded by happy people and good music. The music seemed to shift in response to his need, as a happy, upbeat tune came on. Out on the dance floor, couples formed up and began bouncing around to the music. Calling what they were doing dancing would have been too kind, but they seemed to be enjoying themselves. Or maybe it was anticipation for what the rest of the night would bring. He wondered briefly how many of them had known each other before tonight. Something speculative must have shown in his face, because Cassandra suddenly laughed and nudged her good shoulder against his.

"I'd say nine out of ten," she murmured. "At least."

He gave her a questioning glance, and she lifted her chin in the direction of the dance floor.

"How many of them are just hooking up for tonight. Ninety percent or better."

"Hooking up?" he asked. He had a pretty good idea of what she meant, but he wanted to see the rise of color on her cheeks when she explained it to him.

"Sex," she said bluntly enough, but not without a telltale blush. "Like your girl Sabrina wanted with you."

"She wasn't mine in any sense of the word," he said with a touch of aggravation. Cassandra gave him a curious look, but before she could push for more, he slipped a hand over her arm and stood, taking her with him. "I want to dance," he said and started for the dance floor.

She didn't fight him, probably because she didn't want to attract attention. But she did lean in to deliver a hissed objection. "I don't dance."

"You mean you can't?"

"Of course not. I *can* dance. I just don't."

The music shifted again, this time becoming soft and romantic. The illicit couples all around them clutched each other almost frantically beneath the lowered lights.

"Shit," she muttered. "Damian, this isn't a good idea."

"One dance," he insisted. "It will calm you. You need to relax." He pulled her carefully into his arms. She started to slip her arms around his neck, but winced at the pain it caused and settled for hugging his waist instead. It reminded him of her wound and made him feel guilty. He hadn't even asked how she was feeling.

"How's your arm?" he asked.

"Better," she said unconvincingly.

He didn't push. He understood. They had a mission, and everything else would have to wait. He caught the scent of her clean hair, felt the press of her soft breasts against his chest. Well, perhaps not everything.

He nuzzled her hair with his chin and tightened his hold just a little bit. She felt good in his arms. Natural. Tall enough that all of the important body parts lined up nicely, and would do so even better in bed.

She sighed and looked up at him. Her big, brown eyes were soft, her plump lips glistening from whatever she'd slicked them with. It made him think of another pair of lips, much farther down her body. Those would be slick and glistening, too. His cock stirred at the imagery, and he shifted that tiny fraction of an inch, so she wouldn't feel his arousal.

"We probably shouldn't do this," she murmured, so softly that he had to lower his head to hear her.

"Do what?" he asked, his mouth almost touching hers when she lifted her face to his.

"Sex," she whispered, and it was everything he could do not to sweep her up and carry her upstairs to their very elegant room and its big beds.

"Why not?" he asked instead, smoothing his lips over hers.

Her body yearned upward. "Mixing business and pleasure," she said, her eyes closing when he slipped his tongue between her teeth and explored gently.

"I've never heard of that," he murmured, sliding his fingers through her hair to cup the back of her head as he deepened the kiss. Her mouth opened beneath his, her tongue stroking, inviting. Her body was soft against him, her fingers flexing in the muscles of his back. This was a different side of Cassandra, the woman instead of the warrior.

The music changed, the romantic song fading into something faster. Cassandra grabbed his wrist.

"Let's get out of here," she said, and tugged him insistently toward the door.

Damian followed, bemused, wondering at her sudden urgency. He could have stopped her and asked. As strong as she was, he was still immeasurably stronger. But since she was presumably taking him back to their room, he was more than willing to be dragged along. He laughed when she pushed the button for the hated elevator and hauled him inside, when she backed him against the wall and kissed him, swallowing his laughter and then his groan when she pressed her palm against his stiff cock, stroking him through the heavy denim fabric.

"By the gods, Cassandra," he muttered, cupping her round ass and lifting until her legs wrapped around his waist and his cock was nestled between her thighs. Her arms came around his neck then, their height difference unimportant when he was holding her the way he was. She kissed him again, a violent, biting sort of kiss that spoke of hunger, pure and simple. Cassandra wanted to fuck. She wanted to fuck badly enough that she'd climbed into an elevator with him to get to the room faster.

The elevator slowed and stopped. The doors opened with a chiming sound. Cassandra looked around at the carpeted hallway, and then grinned at him. "Can you walk?"

He grinned back. "Am I not a god?" He tightened his grip and carried her down the hall to their room, turning just enough that she could slide the card into the reader. The door popped open, and he turned, slamming his back against the door instead of hers, mindful that her back was injured, even with her pussy so hot that he could feel it against his denim-clad cock.

"Clothes," she muttered, tearing at his shirt before he'd even gotten the door shut.

He let her pull his shirt over his head, then released his grip on her ass, sliding her slowly down the front of his body, rubbing every long, lean inch of her against his cock. Her fingers played over the muscles of his arms and chest, squeezing and stroking, while her tongue licked and teased.

"Fuck, woman," he growled. He grabbed the two sides of her sweater and ripped it open, scattering small buttons.

She gave a laughing sort of gasp as he slid the sweater over her shoulders and off.

"I liked that sweater," she said, slapping a hand against his chest, a slap that quickly turned into an admiring stroke. "Christ, you have a great chest." She looked up at him with big eyes. "Do you work out?"

He couldn't help himself. He wrapped an arm around her waist and palmed her ass, pulling her into another vicious kiss. Her short nails scraped over the skin of his back when he bit her full lower lip, then soothed the sting with a swipe of his tongue, before licking his way over her jaw and down the elegant line of her neck, sucking gently, while his fingers were busy opening the clasp on her bra. He stepped back then, wanting to see the moment her breasts were revealed to him. Her eyes met his, her tongue wetting her lips in a nervous gesture.

He smiled. "You're beautiful, Cassandra."

And she blushed. The wildcat who'd dragged him from the dance floor, who'd attacked him in the elevator, blushed at the simple compliment. Something twisted in his chest, an ache as if a dead and unused organ was waking to life. He'd felt something like this before, but it was long ago, and only for his brothers-in-arms. Never for a woman.

"Clothes," he said hoarsely, reaching out to cup her breasts as he repeated her earlier demand.

He strummed her pretty nipples with his thumbs, and she reached for his belt buckle with a groan. "You first, big guy." She slid the zipper down and slipped clever fingers inside to wrap around his cock with a hum of pleasure. "And I do mean *big*," she murmured appreciatively, squeezing until he had to pull away. It was either that or humiliate himself by coming in his pants before he'd even touched her.

"Have pity," he muttered. "It's been a while."

"Oh," she crooned, moving in until her breasts were pressed against him, her nipples swollen and hard, scraping the skin of his chest. "Poor baby."

He laughed, but his laughter had an edge of danger to it. "You'll pay for that." Ripping open his pants, he shoved them down his legs, then did the same with hers, shoving jeans and panties down together, baring the smooth cleft of her pussy. His eyes widened at the sight, and he licked his lips hungrily. He raised his eyes to meet hers, then slid a hand over her belly and between her legs, holding her gaze as his roughened palm scraped over her clit while his fingers teased her slick cunt, dipping into her tight opening just enough for her to want more before sliding out again. He gave her one finger, then two, as her hips flexed against his hand, demanding.

"What do you want?" he murmured against the hot skin of her jaw, as he nipped his way to her mouth, then kissed her until she couldn't breathe.

"Damian," she gasped, sucking in a breath, while her hips thrust against his hand and her fingernails dug into his arms. "Damn it, don't tease."

"Poor baby," he whispered and saw the flash of frustrated awareness in her brown eyes. He slid two fingers deep into her pussy, feeling the tight walls close around him. His shaft swelled to a painful stiffness as he imagined how tight she would be around his cock, how hot and slick. He pulled his fingers out and shoved them into her again, while his thumb pressed against her clit.

She cried out. "Okay," she moaned. "You win. Now fuck me."

Damian withdrew his fingers completely, and spun her around, lifting her up and dropping her onto the bed, then gripping her hips and lifting her ass into the air. He held her there, one hand on her hip, while he removed her pants and panties completely, sliding them around her ankles, and tossing them aside before turning back to spread her legs wide.

"Ass in the air, Cassandra," he ordered. She obeyed, bending her knees and arching her back, even as she buried her face in her arms with a moan. It made him smile, these hints of embarrassment from his lover. But all embarrassment seemed to flee when he moved up behind her and stroked his cock through the wetness between her thighs.

She sucked in a harsh breath and arched her back, spreading her legs wider in invitation. "Now, Damian," she begged.

But he was in heaven. Gripping his cock, he grazed it through her slick heat again, closing his eyes against the delicious sensation. She made a soft noise of protest, and his eyes flashed open, sensation overcome by sheer lust at the sight before him. Her round ass in the air, firm thighs spread to bare every inch of her pussy, wet and pink and glistening.

His hand tightened around his cock as he positioned himself behind her, and then his patience snapped. He thrust into her without warning, one hand gripping her hip to hold her in place, the other guiding his cock into the hot and tight lushness of her body. She gave a muffled scream as her sheath stretched to accommodate him, as he slammed in, balls-deep, and felt the firm tip of her cervix. Damian paused, bent over her back, breathing hard, his cock buried in the fierce embrace of her cunt as he fought for control. Centuries. He'd waited centuries for this.

Her inner walls shivered over his length, and she moaned softly, wiggling, wanting him to move. Damian cupped his hand over the cheek of her ass and squeezed, before sliding that same hand around and burying it in her pussy. Her clit pulsed against his thumb as he began stroking her, circling around and then scraping the pad of his thumb across the sensitive nub, over and over, until she was panting hungrily, every breath a soft, needy cry as she writhed against his hand.

"No, no, no," she groaned as his fingers teased over her clit once more, bringing her to the edge of climax before slipping away again.

Leaning over, he kissed the back of her neck gently, softly. And then, without warning, he pinched her clit. She screamed into an orgasm and he began fucking her hard, slamming his cock in and out as she thrashed in climax, her pussy clenching around him while his shaft scraped against the sensitized walls of her sheath, driving his length in and out until a second orgasm ripped through her body, her channel closing around him so tight and hot that he could barely move. He wasn't sure he wanted to. He'd dreamt of this for centuries, the fervent clasp of a woman's sex, the volcanic heat of her arousal, the pulsing need of her climax.

But his body had needs of its own that his mind couldn't fight, couldn't slow down. Driven by the need to fuck her, he pounded his cock into her until the slick friction of her passage threatened to burn him, until the boiling demand of his own release shot down his cock in a rush of liquid heat. He threw his head back and roared, his thrusts becoming almost frantic as the climax overtook his senses.

Time seemed to stop for a moment. His mind shut down as he became nothing but sensation. The soft skin of her hip beneath his fingers, the fevered wetness surrounding his cock, dripping down her thighs—her climax and his, her soft cries fading into panted breaths that matched the beat of her heart, as his own heartbeat slowed from a gallop to its usual pounding rhythm. He soothed his fingers over her hip, knowing he'd gripped her too hard, that there would be bruises.

It was almost painful when he finally pulled out his cock, her inner muscles grasping at him, as if still unwilling to let go. His shaft was still half-rigid, his balls still tight, when he slid an arm around her waist and eased her to the bed, then stretched out beside her. He went to throw a leg over hers, and laughed.

"What?" she asked, sounding pissed and worried in equal measure.

"My boots are still on," he told her, nuzzling into her neck in apology. "I can't get my pants off."

She started laughing, reaching back to stroke a hand over his cheek. "You should probably do something about that before . . ." She broke off whatever she'd been about to say.

"Before?" he prodded. "Before what?"

"Before the next time." She pushed her ass against his cock, which was already growing harder by the minute. "I don't think we're finished here, do you?"

He grinned, then leaned in to close his teeth over her jaw. "Naughty girl. I like that."

"Damian." She whispered the objection, and he could feel the heat of her blush.

"And yet so sweet," he murmured.

She slapped his hip. He laughed and sat up, reaching down to untie his boots and kick them off, shoving his jeans to the floor after them. When he lay back down, he rolled to his back, taking her with him, so that she was stretched out on top of him.

"How's your shoulder?" he asked, touching the injured arm lightly and then smoothing his hands down her back to rest on her tight ass.

"It's fine," she said, but then gave a soft grunt of discomfort. "But it's better if I sit up." She put action to words and rolled into a sitting position, straddling his thighs. "Oh, look what I found!" She wrapped her hand around his dick and squeezed.

Damian groaned. He'd already been half-hard. One climax didn't come close to relieving the sexual hunger of centuries. But with her strong fingers now pumping up and down, squeezing and releasing in a sensual massage, his cock was swelling larger with every stroke. He slid his hands over her knees and gripped her thighs, spreading her legs until her pussy was wide open and on display. She tried to close them, to snug her knees against his hips, but he only chuckled, spreading her thighs even wider.

"Uh, uh, sweet naughty girl. You play with my cock, I get to play with your pussy."

"Not if I—" She started to slide down even farther, lowering her head to take him in her mouth. But as much as Damian would have welcomed her lips wrapped around his cock, he wanted to fuck her even more.

"That's not what we're doing, sweetheart," he said, sinking his fingers into her hips and lifting her easily until he could feel her heat above him. "Put me inside that tight little pussy of yours."

A hint of stubbornness flashed briefly in her dark eyes, but then he lowered her enough to slide his cock through her wetness, scraping his full length against her clit. She threw her head back in a moan, but when he lifted her up again, she took his cock and positioned it at the entrance to her sex, and then immediately tried to sit, to take him fully into her body, protesting angrily when she discovered she couldn't move.

Damian grinned. "I didn't tell you to sit on me. If I had, you'd be sitting a lot farther up," he added, licking his lips lewdly.

She gasped at the crude comment, and lowered her head so he wouldn't see her blush.

He really did love the way she reacted to him. He rewarded her, and himself, by lowering her a couple of inches, letting his cock sink into her slick and welcoming heat. But only briefly.

Wiggling her hips against his grip, she scowled in protest. "Damian!" It was a demand, rather than a plea, so he flexed his muscles and thrust upward, letting her feel his thickness once more.

"Ask nicely, Cassandra."

She slapped at his arms, but he only smiled. "Your ass is going to feel every one of those slaps before the night is over," he warned her. "I do love a nicely pinked ass."

"You wouldn't dare," she sputtered, glaring at him.

"Wouldn't I? Do I strike you as a man who makes idle threats?"

She wiggled again, trying to break free, but he only tightened his hold. "Ask nicely," he repeated in a singsong voice.

She narrowed her gaze at him, but finally said, "Damian, you insufferable ass, would you mind terribly putting your oh-so-big cock into my delicious little pussy?"

He grinned, and, without warning, dropped her onto his cock as he flexed upward, burying himself balls-deep in her admittedly delicious pussy. He groaned as her heat surrounded him, her sheath pulsing as it struggled to accommodate his intrusion, her inner walls already shivering with an arousal that had her growing even more slick and creamy wet.

"Damian," she breathed, her chest heaving, nipples flushed and swollen. She wrapped her fingers around his wrists, her head thrown back and eyes closed as she struggled visibly to deal with the overload of sensation.

He lifted her slightly and fucked her, thrusting into her sweet body, filling her completely as she hung helplessly in his grip.

"Oh God, I can't do this again," she whispered as her stomach clenched tightly and her pussy trembled around him.

"Come for me, Cassandra," he crooned, and she moaned.

"Please," she said on a sob, and he didn't know if she was begging for the climax that was about to wash over her, or pleading for him to free her from its grip.

It didn't matter in the end, because he had no intention of letting her go. He wanted to see her writhing above him, wanted to feel her pussy clamp down around him until he could barely move to fuck her.

She came without warning, her eyes opening wide in surprise as the orgasm roared through her body, bowing her back as she struggled to escape it, her fingers gripping her hair as she cried out over and over, her screams following the waves of climax that rippled over his cock until he joined her, crashing over the edge into carnal ecstasy.

Damian lowered her slowly, his cock still twitching inside her shuddering pussy as she collapsed against his chest. Her hair was silky and fragrant against his neck and he dipped his chin enough to kiss her forehead.

"I can't move," she muttered. "I know I should, but I can't."

He stroked a hand down her back, lifting her slightly as his cock slid out of her. Her cunt was hot and creamy against his thigh as she settled to her good side, one leg slung over his hip, one arm draped across his chest.

"You don't need to move. Just sleep."

He closed his eyes, but he could feel her chest move as her breathing deepened and her racing heartbeat slowed. Reaching down, he pulled the blanket over both of them, and then he slept.

CASEY WOKE SLOWLY, her body protesting the need to open her eyes. She was warm and cozy. She smiled as the word occurred to her. Cozy was not exactly something anyone would associate with Damian. But that was okay. She didn't want anyone to know him the way she did. He made her feel sexy and safe, treasured and protected. She'd lived most of her life being the one in charge, the one making the decisions and taking the risks. It was lovely to let go of that for a few hours, to let him be in charge. And the exquisite sexual pleasure that he delivered didn't hurt either. She'd never come more than once in a single night. Hell, there were plenty of nights when she'd faked even that one orgasm, just to get some sleep. But not with Damian. Her pussy clenched in reaction, just remembering the things he done to her. It was more than just his physical prowess—it was the enjoyment he took in fucking, the satisfaction he got from feeling her climax all around his cock. A cock that was thick and long and . . . Jesus! She needed to stop thinking about that, or she was going to climax all over again, just lying there.

She worked to regulate her breathing, to keep it even and relaxed. She didn't want to wake him, not yet. She wanted just to lie there for a few private moments. The day would begin soon enough, and work would claim them all over again. But for now, for a little bit longer, they were only Cassandra and Damian, two people who'd met on a rooftop and fucked themselves into oblivion.

She tried, but reality kept rearing its ugly head. The problem was the Talisman. *Well, duh.* More specifically, it was the fact that she was stymied in her attempts to follow its trail. Sometimes when she slept, or when her mind was turned to something else, solutions to whatever problem she was working on would float to the surface. But while Damian had sure as hell distracted her from her current problem, she'd had no brain cells left to think about anything else. Not with his cock slamming in and out, and. . . . Fuck! She was doing it again!

She forced herself to concentrate on emptying her mind. Now there was a fine conundrum. The whole idea was *not* to concentrate on anything, to let her thoughts float freely. Over the years she'd been working for Nick, some of her best leads had developed from exactly that strategy. It was as if her conscious mind inhibited whatever the part of her was that could detect magic, and by turning it off, the magic had a chance to do its thing. Whatever its thing was.

She still didn't quite understand it, but then she'd never met anyone who did. Even Nick couldn't provide rational explanations for most of it, which made sense now that she knew what he really was. If he'd been born with the kind of power that Damian attributed to him, he'd never had to think about why magic worked. It was a part of his blood and bone, hardwired into his nervous system. It simply *was.* There was a certain arrogance in that, and it showed in Nick's personality even now. To be sure, time and experience had probably worn the sharpest edges off, but Nick was always the guy in charge. And as generous as he could be, he never let you forget it.

Speaking of which, she wondered how he'd gotten along in Kansas with the vampires. If it had been your ordinary run-of-the-mill vampire, she wouldn't have thought twice about it. But Nick's mystery mission had something to do with Raphael, who was the Vampire Lord of the West and rumored to be the most powerful vampire not only in North America, but in the world. Some people still believed the old myths about vampires being risen from the dead and so on. The only part those myths had right was the blood drinking, and maybe the aversion to sunlight. Though it was unclear to her whether a vampire would actually crisp up like an overcooked piece of bacon, or if it was simply a sensitivity born of the vampire symbiote found in their blood.

Now *there* was a piece of magic. No one knew where the symbiote came from or how it did what it did, but there was no question in her mind that it was magic. The few times she'd gotten close to a vampire, the magic had flowed over her skin like warm silk. She could only imagine what it was like to stand next to someone like Raphael.

But that wouldn't be the challenge for Nick. No, she wondered how he'd respond to *not* being the guy in charge for a change. Because no matter how much sorcerous power he possessed, where vampires were concerned, the power only flowed one way. And that was in the direction of their Sire. It might be quite entertaining to watch Nick and Raphael spar, but only from a distance. She wouldn't want to be caught too close if they blew up at each other.

She closed her eyes, but a meditative state didn't come and neither did any bright ideas about the Talisman. There was only one thing to do. She'd have to go back to that house, the one she'd stolen the thing from in the first place, and dig around. Maybe there'd be some leftover piece of evidence that would steer her in the right direction. Or there was always the possibility that she'd pick up a magic trail that she could follow, if not to the Talisman itself, then at least to someone who could lead her to the next step and the one after that. This was what her work usually entailed—a series of small steps that eventually led to the prize. That was how she'd located the Talisman in the first place, and why it was so infuriating that she'd lost it. Months of research had been wasted. Unless the location turned up something useful tomorrow.

"You're thinking too loudly, Cassandra. I can't sleep."

She jerked at the sound of Damian's voice, wondering how long he'd been awake. "I barely moved," she protested.

"But your breathing changed, and so did your heartbeat." He stroked a big hand over her hip in a blatantly possessive move. "What are you thinking about?"

"The Talisman," she admitted, with a shrug that rubbed against his chest. "They were never supposed to get it back, and now I don't have a clue about where they'll take it next."

"You'll figure something out."

Her heart warmed at his confidence, even as a small voice warned her to be careful. This was sex, not a relationship. Damian was a natural leader; he was hard-wired to make the people around him feel strong and capable.

"We need to go back to that house, the one I stole it from. Or rather, I need to go back there. You can—"

"Cassandra," he chided, shaking his head on the pillow. "Do you really think I'd let you go after that thing without me? Even if Nico hadn't decided I should go with you, I'd have gone."

"Why?" she asked, wanting to know, but hating herself for asking. It made her seem so fucking needy.

He patted her butt, and then sat up, taking her with him. "Think about it," he said, kissing her forehead. "And let me know when you figure out why I'm still with you. Come on, let's take advantage of that big shower." He stood up next to the bed, bracing her when she wobbled.

"I'm okay," she said quickly. "Who gets the first shower?"

At that, he laughed and, bending over slightly, he scooped her into his arms and started for the bathroom. "That's not the question you should be asking. Rather, who gets the first climax?"

Cassandra's whole body reacted to that question, heat racing through her veins. How was it possible that he could turn her on like that? After the night they'd had, she should be completely sated for weeks at least. And yet, she was swamped with desire, her breasts feeling heavy and swollen, her nipples hard peaks begging to be sucked and bitten. "Damian," she whispered, barely able to get his name out.

"I've got this, Cassandra," he murmured, striding toward the shower. "Trust me."

"TRUST ME, HE SAYS," Cassandra grumbled as she shoved clothes and gear into her duffel. She could still taste his cock in her mouth, still feel the hard thrust against the back of her throat. And that was before he'd yanked her up and pounded into her against the tiled wall as the steaming hot water rushed all around them. As if Damian needed any help in heating things up. The man was insatiable and sexy as hell. It was tempting to stay in the hotel a little longer, just one more night in this luxurious room with nothing but that big bed and lots of room service. In between fucking, that was. Something to keep up their strength.

And just the fact that she was considering the idea told her how much trouble she was in.

"This doesn't change anything," she said, intentionally not looking up at him where he stood in the bathroom doorway, one towel wrapped around his hips while he rubbed at his wet hair with another.

"What doesn't change anything?" he asked.

She could hear the grin in his voice, and knew if she looked up, his expression would be the definition of smug. "Sex," she snapped. "This is still my investigation, my hunt. I say what we do, and when."

"Of course," he agreed smoothly. "Unless we do battle and then, of course, I'm in charge."

She looked up, straightening with both hands on her hips and a defiant glare. "Why's that? Because a set of balls somehow imbues you with superior skills?"

"No," he said patiently enough, but she could see the anger tensing his shoulders. Those beautiful broad shoulders, smooth golden skin, thick muscles . . .

Damn it, Casey! Stop that! She forced herself to maintain eye contact, refusing to look away. She was stronger than that.

"If we go into a fight, you'll listen to me because I've *won* more battles than you've read about in all of your studies combined. Because I've faced my enemies close enough to see the terror in their eyes when my sword took their lives."

In three long strides, he was right in front of her, forcing her to meet his gaze. And he was more than angry, she saw. He was furious.

"Because I'm the best chance you have of getting out of this alive, and I want you alive, Cassandra."

She stared up at him, breathing hard, her heart pounding in her chest. He was a formidable sight when he was angry. Even knowing he'd never hurt her, she could easily understand the terror his enemies must have felt, confronting the cold determination in his dark eyes.

"You're right," she said finally. "I don't have a lot of experience fighting, and sure as hell not killing. But I'm not someone who needs protecting, either. You saw me the other night. If it comes down to it, I'll fight and I'll win."

He opened his mouth to protest, but she stopped him.

"Having said that," she continued. "I'll admit that when the shit hits the fan, you're probably better at thinking on your feet than I am."

He scowled at her. "You people have the strangest way of saying things. Lucky for you I'm brilliant as well as handsome. And you're correct. When things get shitty, I'll be the last one standing."

Cassandra choked on a laugh, not sure if he'd meant to amuse her or not. His quick grin told her it was intentional, but he was as accomplished at covering up his true feelings as she was.

"Are we good?" she asked.

"Oh, Cassandra darling, we're so far above good that we're walking on clouds."

And with that pronouncement, he strolled over to the closet, dropped both towels to the floor, and stood there, naked, staring at his wardrobe long enough that she *knew* he was only doing it to tease her. He didn't have that many fucking clothes to choose from! He finally yanked his jeans from the shelf and she nearly choked on her tongue when he bent over to pull them on. Bastard.

She turned away, determined to get back in control, forcing her thoughts to where they were going and what needed to be done.

"So we're going back to that house?" he asked, his voice muffled by the T-shirt he was pulling over his head, his jeans still unzipped and clinging loosely to his narrow hips.

She dropped the file she was holding, raising one hand to her forehead in a frustrated gesture. "I'm sure they've cleared out by now, but there might be something I can use." She let out a long breath, blowing aside a few pieces of hair that had escaped the loose braid which was the best she could manage with her injured arm. "After that, we're moving to a safe house nearby. I can control security better there, both physical and Internet. Plus it's a four-bedroom house, so there'll be more room."

He was suddenly there, his heat surrounding her, making her think of . . . *things*. He put a finger under her chin, forcing her to look up at him. "We don't need room, do we, Cassandra?"

A blush heated her cheeks when she answered him. "It has a pool. And a hot tub. You'll like it."

"Excellent." He met her gaze, holding it intentionally as he adjusted himself and zipped up his pants.

She rolled her eyes. He was such a *guy*. Nice to know the species hadn't changed much in thousands of years. "We'll need to stop at the store," she said, turning back to her packing. "We'll get food. And anything else you need."

"Shopping?" he asked enthusiastically. "Great! I'll make a list."

Cassandra *hated* shopping. Just her luck she'd get the one ancient warrior god who liked it.

"NO, YOU CAN *NOT* drive," she insisted an hour later as they loaded up the back of her Yukon. "I told you"—*a hundred times*—"that you need a license. But more to the point, you don't know *how* to do it."

"So teach me. I'm a fast learner."

"Not now, okay?" she said in frustration, struggling to shove her heavy duffel into the cargo compartment. "I know you're a god and all that, but in this universe, you're just another ridiculously handsome man who knows how to shoot a gun. And that won't help when you're taking your test, okay?"

"So you think I'm handsome." He lifted the duffel with irritating ease, sliding it into the space where she normally stowed it.

Naturally, he'd seize on that. It was true, but he hardly needed her to tell him. Especially not after she'd spent most of the night and a good part of the morning worshipping his body.

"And my knowledge of weapons is not limited to guns, obviously. The sword goes without saying, and knives are as natural to me as breathing. But battle-axes were always my personal favorite. I was never fond of the flail, though. All that flailing around."

Casey sighed while he chuckled at his own joke, lame as it was. Hell, most people probably didn't even know what a flail was anymore— basically a spiked ball on a chain used during ye olde Medieval times. They were depicted in movies occasionally, but usually far larger than they'd ever been in real life. She could understand why Damian hadn't liked it. As brutal a weapon as it had been, it was probably too lightweight for him to use effectively. The battle-axe, on the other hand . . . yeah, she could picture that quite easily. And a nice picture it was, too.

"*Down!*"

She reacted instantly to Damian's shouted warning, dropping to the ground and rolling into the cover of a nearby vehicle, pulling her weapon and scanning the parking lot all at once. Thank God she'd paid attention to the instinct that had her wearing the Glock on her belt this morning. Her brain belatedly identified the sound of a weapon firing, even as she catalogued the information. Two shots, long-distance rifle. She scanned the parking lot and spotted Damian on the ground a few feet away, facing her, crouched between two trucks. She raised a hand to indicate she was all right. More than a little relief showed in his dark eyes, before he nodded to say he was also okay.

Casey smiled tightly, then quietly said, "rifle," figuring he'd understand. He was already familiar with modern weapons, though he'd only used a relative few. He proved this again when he nodded his agreement and pointed at an office building across the parking lot. If the shot had come from there, the shooter had to be using a rifle.

She didn't question Damian's judgment regarding the sniper's site, just scooted up and maneuvered over to look. Pain shot through her wounded arm, a reminder that she'd already been shot once this week, which was more than enough. She peered around the back end of the sedan she'd been hiding behind. The office building was maybe eight stories high, with row after row of tinted windows reflecting the morning sunlight.

It was modern enough that she doubted those windows opened. Most of the newer buildings were climate-controlled, and builders didn't want any stray currents of air drifting in to mess up the thermostat. That meant the shooter had either been on the roof, or had broken out a window, but she wasn't sure it made a difference. What mattered at this point was whether their assailant had accepted his failure and made an escape, or if he was sitting up there somewhere waiting for them to stick their heads out.

With nothing else to do—since she wasn't going to offer herself as a test target—she searched the blank windows and finally found one on the seventh floor that was suspiciously dark compared to all of the others, which were still reflecting the sun with a blinding glare. She saw movement in the dark hole and dragged her backpack over from where it was still sitting on the ground. Rummaging around inside, she pulled out a pair of powerful binoculars and scanned the building. It took her a minute to locate the broken window through the binocular's lenses, but she studied it until her eyes watered and she was satisfied there was no longer anyone there.

"He's gone," she told Damian, not bothering to speak quietly. He didn't take her word for it, but held out a hand in a silent request for the binoculars. Or maybe it was a demand, but Casey was giving him the benefit of the doubt and calling it a request. She shrugged and tossed them over. It was no skin off her nose if he wanted to double-check. Double-checking kept people alive sometimes.

"You're right," Damian said and straightened out of hiding, going directly to the RV which was parked next to her Yukon. He reached out and rubbed his fingers over two entry holes. "You're right about this, too," he continued, shoving his fingers in deeply enough to extract first one slug and then another. "Rifle, .300 caliber rounds."

"How the hell do you know that?" she demanded, taking one of the slugs from him. It was definitely a .300 Winchester mag round, but. . . . "I mean, I get that you know weapons, but ammunition? They didn't have guns back in your day, and we haven't had time to get to a range yet. So where'd you come up with this knowledge?"

"The Internet. I've been studying. If I'm to live my life in this reality, I need to have information regarding warfare in this time."

"When did you do all of this?"

He shrugged. "When you were gone the first day, and that night, when I couldn't sleep. Over the last few centuries, I've spent too many nights silent and alone. Now that I have a choice, I feel as if I'm wasting my time sleeping, when I could be *doing*." He flashed her a quick grin. "When I'm not doing you, that is."

"Nice," she said, flipping him off. "Which one of us do you think they were trying to kill?"

"I'm an unknown in this world, while you managed to locate and steal a precious artifact from them. You represent the greater threat."

"But I've never had anyone come after me like this. I mean, sure, I've been in a few firefights, like what happened the other night. But I've never had anyone try to kill me after the fact. Especially since they got the damn thing back. Why come after me now?"

"You fear they have plans to use the Talisman, and so are still pursuing the device. Perhaps *they* fear your pursuit will disrupt whatever those plans are."

"They don't need to kill me for that. They could simply secure the artifact somewhere I can't get to it. Take it out of the country, maybe overseas. Besides, it's not like I have a reputation or anything. I'm not exactly Lara Croft."

He considered her words for a moment, then said, "I don't know who that is. But there are many ways you could destroy their schemes without ever recovering the Talisman itself."

Casey didn't waste time trying to bring him up to date on popular culture. Especially since she was convinced it wasn't her they'd been after in the first place. It didn't take a forensic genius to look at those bullet holes and know the sniper had been gunning for Damian. He was several inches taller than she was, and he'd been walking on the side the shooter had seemed to be aiming at. It was sheer luck that the guy wasn't a better marksman, but it made more sense to think he'd missed by a few inches, rather than a few feet.

"Here's an idea . . . maybe they were after you," she said, meeting his obsidian gaze. "Tell me something. Would Nick benefit somehow from getting all of you guys back? I mean, apart from the obvious, the bonds of friendship and so on. But is there more? Do the four of you constitute a power matrix of some kind?"

Damian's usually expressive face shut down at her question, his mouth tightening into a narrow line as if to keep any stray words from escaping. "That's a question of magic. You should ask Nico about it," he said finally and then turned back to study the bullet holes in the unlucky RV.

So that's the way it was, she thought to herself. She'd ask Nick all right, but only for the details, because Damian's reaction had already told her she was right. She knew it was possible. She'd read about such things, but never encountered one. Nick might have used his magic to create a matrix, an amplifier of sorts that would make him infinitely stronger. And if he was already strong to begin with? Well, shit.

The downside was that, just as it enhanced his power, it was also bound into the four warriors. And when Sotiris had ripped them away. . . . Was that the real reason Nick had been hiding who he was for all these years? She couldn't blame him for lying about it. It must feel as if pieces of his soul had been ripped away. Not to mention, the shocking loss of power for a man accustomed to being a virtual god.

"We must return to Nicodemus," Damian said suddenly. "When Sotiris discovers his sniper has failed, he may target Nico instead."

Casey frowned. "I don't think so. He could have gone after Nick any time in the last two decades, when he first started working with the FBI to recover stuff like the Talisman. Why change that strategy now?"

"For the same reason he came after you today. Because one of you has the potential to disrupt his plans. When are we meeting Nico?"

"I'm not sure. He's probably still in Kansas."

"Cassandra," Damian said, giving her an almost pitying look. "He's here already. Though perhaps he hasn't called you yet," he added.

"How do you know that?" she demanded, frustrated beyond tolerance at being caught in a lie.

He grinned. "I didn't until you just told me. We should go to him now. He'll need our help."

She stared at him, furious with him for tricking her, furious with herself for falling for it. "Later," she conceded grudgingly. "Besides, Nick has plenty of protections in place; he doesn't need our help. We can brief him tonight, after we get to the safe house. Our best bet is to focus on the Talisman. It's at the center of all of this."

She could see Damian's jaw working as he fought the urge to argue with her. There was no argument he could make that would change her ·mind, but she could understand his desire to see Nick sooner, rather than later. After all, it had been centuries, and their parting hadn't exactly been planned.

Still, the next few hours would be a lot more pleasant if she wasn't dragging a sulking Damian along behind her. She stepped closer and put a hand on his arm. "The best way to protect him, to protect ourselves, is to find out who's behind the attack."

He nodded stiffly. "The decision is yours."

It was probably the best she was going to get, so she simply squeezed his arm and moved on. "All right. First order of business is to find out as much as we can about the shooter."

"How? He's long gone."

"Yes, but nothing happens in a vacuum anymore. Especially not in the age of terrorism in which we live. Our shooter had to get in and out of that building, and there's bound to be security. I'm betting they have cameras on every door, every elevator. Maybe even the parking lot."

"And they'll share that with *you*?"

Okay, the way he'd said that was almost insulting. She bared her teeth at him in what passed for a smile. "Watch and learn, big guy. Come on. There's no point in standing around here with targets on our backs. And we definitely don't want to be here when the guy who owns this RV discovers the bullet holes in his vehicle."

DAMIAN FROWNED in confusion when Cassandra drove them not to the shooter's building, and not even to the safe house she'd spoken of, but to a modest inn called a motel. It was in reasonably good repair, albeit painted a garish turquoise with pink trim. But that aside, he didn't understand her purpose in coming here.

"What are we doing?" he asked, when she parked in front of the glass-fronted motel office.

"You'll see."

And that was all she said, which was infuriating as hell. He understood the need for a chain of command. He'd even gone along with her decision to wait until later before briefing Nico. It was true what she said about his brother being able to protect himself, but Damian's purpose in life had been to watch Nico's back, and in his heart, he knew there was no more important task. But then, there were things he hadn't confided to her about himself and Nico. He liked Cassandra and admired her courage, but some things were not his to share. Or, not *only* his.

"I'm going to get a room," she said brusquely, and was out of the vehicle and heading for the office almost before she'd said the last word.

Damian sighed deeply. He could have gone to the office with her. He probably would have, if she'd given him time. But he doubted there was any danger, and Cassandra was more than capable of taking care of herself. Of course, there was her shoulder to consider. She wasn't exactly at full strength. Cursing under his breath, he shoved open the door and went after her, covering the short distance in a few quick strides. She glanced back in surprise when he walked into the office, but then smiled. A genuine smile this time, rather than the grimace of earlier.

"Hey, babe," she said casually, as if they were a couple on holiday.

Feeling reckless, Damian concealed a smile of his own and slipped up behind her, circling her slender waist with one arm and fitting his body against hers. "They got a room?" he asked, taking on the vernacular of some of the characters he'd watched on TV while waiting for her.

She stiffened at first, but then relaxed like the good operative she was. She wouldn't want the innkeeper to suspect anything. "Yep," she said, placing her hand over his and squeezing.

"Can't wait, darling," he murmured, nuzzling her ear.

Her nails dug into the back of his hand, and he had to fight the urge to laugh. Until she rubbed her ass against his groin, and he had to fight another urge altogether.

Fortunately, the innkeeper returned at that moment, and held out a key.

"Room 108's already been cleaned, so you can have that one. Just the one night?"

"Yes, thank you."

The innkeeper nodded. "Here you go, then." He looked up and gave Damian a knowing wink. "There's take-out menus in the room, in case you need 'em," he said.

Damian grinned back at him. "Good to know."

The man chuckled and turned back to his desk, already dismissing them.

Cassandra turned to leave, dislodging his arm, but Damian placed a possessive hand at the small of her back, urging her out the door. She went along with it until they were back in the truck.

"Very funny," she muttered, starting the engine and backing away from the office. Their room was at the far end of the long, two-story building.

"The innkeeper seemed to enjoy it," he said, not bothering to conceal his amusement. "Why are we here?" he asked again.

She sighed, but seemed to have forgotten her earlier insistence on playing him along. "The building where the sniper hid will have security. We'll need their cooperation in order to find out anything, so I need to be someone else."

"You're donning a disguise?"

"Sort of," she said, parking in front of room 108. "Come on."

He followed her around to the back of the SUV. She opened the cargo door and leaned inside, but instead of grabbing the expected duffel bag, she went for a suitcase, which she immediately shoved in his direction, and a slim hanging bag, which she kept for herself. She reached to close the door, but Damian was already there.

"You need to be more mindful of your arm," he murmured.

"I'm fine."

"Yes, but you won't be if you're not mindful."

"Anyone ever tell you you're a smug asshole?" she asked, smiling up at him as if they were about to spend the day doing exactly what the innkeeper had assumed.

Maybe not the day, he thought to himself. But when he got her alone tonight . . .

"Many times," he said, answering her question. "But I'm still right about this. Your arm needs to heal."

"Just take the damn suitcase and shut up, okay?"

He laughed. "Yes, darling." He grabbed his own laptop case and slung it over his shoulder, then picked up the suitcase by the handle and followed her the short distance to their room.

Once inside, he looked around. There wasn't much to see. It was nothing like the hotels they'd been in the last two nights, but it was clean enough. Cassandra followed him, shutting the door as he placed the suitcase on the lone bed, and then took the garment bag from her and hung it on the bathroom door. He turned to face her. "Okay, we're here. Now tell me why. If we're to function as a team, I need to know what we're doing."

She opened her mouth as if to disagree, then snapped it shut and nodded grimly instead. "You're right. Okay, so I told you that Nick saved my sanity, that he was the first person who ever understood what was happening with me. I always thought I was wired wrong or something, like my body chemistry was different from everyone else. But then Nick came along and showed me a whole new world inside this one. A world that most people didn't know existed. Suddenly, I wasn't twisted, I was unique."

"Nico sees the best in people and draws it out. It's what makes him a good leader."

She nodded. "That's true, but his instinctive way with people also lets him use them for what he wants. And what he wants is all those magical artifacts that have been left lying around in caves and museum basements because no one knows what they are anymore. But he can't just wander around the world searching for them, buying or stealing whatever he finds. He's only one man, and the world is a big place. He has money and connections, which got him a meeting with the powers that be at the FBI, and he persuaded them that these devices were dangerous, that they could be used against the interests of the United States. And, for the most part, he's right.

"Of course, I know now that he was also looking for you guys, and some of the things we found ended up in his private collection instead of being destroyed. But that's not my point. My point is this." She popped open the suitcase, reached into a side compartment, then pulled out a small leather folio and handed it to him. It contained a card with Cassandra's photo on it, along with a golden badge that had writing and an official-looking image on it.

"That's my FBI identification," she explained when he didn't react.

He looked up from the badge. "I don't know what this means, Cassandra. What is the FBI?"

She stared at him for a moment, then made an exasperated noise. But she was obviously irritated at herself, not him. "Of course, you don't," she muttered. "Okay, I don't suppose they had anything like this where, I mean *when* you come from, but the FBI, the Federal Bureau of Investigation, is like a national police department. That's a bad description, because they're totally different, but it gets to the heart of what they do. They have federal powers, which means they can investigate crimes or whatever anywhere in the country, and they're taken very seriously, especially now with everyone worried about terrorism."

"And Nico works for them?" he asked, somewhat puzzled. The Nicodemus he'd known didn't work *for* anybody. Others worked for *him* and considered themselves privileged to do so.

"Hmmm, it's more like he works *with* them. Nick's kind of a free spirit. But his team of hunters, me and a few others—that's what he calls us—we're all duly sworn FBI agents. We went through the academy and everything."

Damian nodded. That sounded more like Nico. He'd always been one to use whatever officials he needed and to make them feel special in doing so.

"So, you'll speak to these building security managers, and they will give you what you want because you are FBI. I assume you won't tell them the real reason for your hunt."

"I'll tell them it's a matter of national security, that lives are at stake. Which is true enough."

He nodded. "But why are we in this room?"

"I need to look the part." She turned and unzipped the garment bag to reveal some rather dull women's clothing—a dark-colored jacket and matching pants. "This is what they expect to see."

"I understand. Shall I help you disrobe?" he asked, raising one eyebrow in a leer that was only half-teasing.

She snorted. "With your *help,* we'll never get out of here."

"I am irresistible," he agreed. "I shall try to contain myself so that you can prepare."

She tried for a glare, but ended up laughing. "You do that," she said.

With nothing else to do, Damian took his laptop from its case and stretched out on the bed to continue his research on this world's weapons. He already had a mental list of which ones he'd like to acquire for himself, but that didn't mean he couldn't add more. He smiled happily and started reading.

CASEY EYED DAMIAN suspiciously. He'd taken all of that a little too well. She'd expected him to argue against Nick's affiliation with "the man," but almost as soon as she had the thought, she knew it didn't make sense. He wasn't some kind of social rebel from the 90s. Probably where he came from, where *Nick* came from, they *were* the men. Or at least Nick was. It sounded as if he'd had a lot of power, so why would Damian be surprised that he was hooked into the power structure of this world, too? Her scowl deepened. But now he was trolling through those weapons websites of his with a much too happy smile on his face. Like a kid in a candy store, picking out sweets.

She shook her head. That was a problem for another day. Right now, she needed to don her own powers-that-be mask. Bending over her suitcase, she dug out the sensible blue pumps that went with the pantsuit, and the plain white bra that she would wear under a crisp white blouse. The outfit was almost a stereotype uniform. Most female agents in the field wouldn't be this buttoned up, but it helped her play the part, and, as she'd told Damian, it was what the building's security people would expect to see.

Sighing deeply—she really despised wearing this stuff—she took her things into the bathroom to change. Not because Damian hadn't already seen her naked. Hell, between last night, and then this morning in the shower, he'd licked almost every inch of her naked skin. Which was the problem. Not that anything about sex with Damian was a *problem*. The very opposite, in fact. But if she stripped naked in front of him in that tiny little motel room, she'd end up beneath him on the bed, and then they'd never get out of there this afternoon. Not exactly a hardship, she reminded herself as she eyed him speculatively. He did look awfully enticing lying there, almost chirping with glee as he learned all the elegant, new ways to kill people in this century.

He glanced up as she stood in the bathroom doorway studying him, and from the smug smile he gave her, she probably had a stupid dreamy look on her face.

Fuck.

She backed up and slammed the door, then turned her energy to looking like she belonged with the Effing BI.

DAMIAN HELD THE door open for Casey when she walked into the Lorenzo office building—Lorenzo being the architectural firm which had designed the building where the sniper had set up his nest, and which now occupied the top four floors. She'd wanted Damian to remain with the vehicle, but he'd refused, reminding her that their shooter had fired from the seventh floor, which was one of the floors occupied by the Lorenzo people. She'd granted the possibility that someone from that firm had helped the shooter get into place, and then get away. But when he'd taken it a step further, and suggested that some bad guys might be waiting to ambush her when she came to investigate, she'd insisted that such a scenario wasn't at all likely. He'd agreed, but then he'd snottily pointed out that one didn't stay alive planning only for likely threats.

And that was why he was with her, posing as her sniper specialist. They'd stopped long enough to buy him a plain, blue windbreaker of the sort FBI agents used, but it really wasn't necessary for him to pass as FBI. He could be local SWAT, or even a civilian specialist, the latter of which wasn't far from the truth. He was a civilian, and oddly enough, he *was* a specialist. So, as long as she played her role well enough, the part of an uptight, by-the-book FBI agent, no one would question his presence. It was all about the bluff. She hoped she was up to it.

There were two security guards in the lobby. One stood near a short hallway to the elevators, arms crossed, eyeing everyone who walked past, while the other sat behind a marble façade desk. His main job, it seemed, was to answer visitors' questions. Casey couldn't help but notice that there was no security checkpoint—no building ID, no metal detectors, none of the usual security precautions. It was disturbingly light security for this day and age, and it made her wonder if she'd been too optimistic when she'd assumed that the building would have security cameras.

The guard was on the phone when she walked up to the desk, so she opened her ID and held it where he couldn't miss seeing it. His eyes widened perceptibly, and he immediately hustled the caller off the phone. He reached for Casey's ID, but she pulled it out of his reach—close enough to read, but not touch.

"Agent Lewis, and Stephens," she said, intentionally mispronouncing Damian's name and introducing him in such a way that the guard would logically assume he was also an agent. She crossed her fingers, hoping he didn't ask to see Damian's ID. It's what he *should* have done, but if he did it, the game was over.

The guard studied her ID then looked over her shoulder to where Damian waited with impressive patience. She'd had real doubts about bringing him this far, afraid that he wouldn't pass inspection, and they'd be out of luck. But when she glanced back at him, he was standing there looking all formidable and vaguely pissed off, as if he was ready to send someone's head rolling if the guard didn't get his ass in gear and give them access to the entire building ten minutes ago.

"How can I help you, Agent Lewis?" the guard asked finally.

"Your building was the base of an active shooter earlier today, and—"

"Dear God." The guard came half out of this chair. "Was anyone—?"

"You had no reports of gunfire from any of the building's tenants?"

"Absolutely not, and I've been on shift all day except for my lunch break. But there couldn't have been anyone injured, the police would have been. . . . Oh."

She smiled to take the sting out of it. "You may not have been aware"—she had to peer at his name badge—"Mr. McBride, because while the shooter used your building, his target was across the parking lot just east of here."

McBride drew a relieved breath. "Well, that's good at least. I mean . . . no one was injured over there, were they?"

"No, but it was only good luck or bad shooting that kept it that way. In any event, your building *is* part of the crime scene, and we have two requirements. First, my colleague"—she gestured Damian's way—"needs access to your seventh floor, so that he can investigate the shooter's location."

The guard glanced over her shoulder at Damian again, and then back at her. "I'm sure that won't be a problem. The seventh floor is occupied by Lorenzo Associates. I'll need to advise them of the situation, and have one of their reps come down to—"

"Stephens will go on up," she interrupted, referring to Damian by his fake name. "They can meet him there."

"Well, I guess . . . ," he started to say, but Damian was already on his way to the elevator.

"Does this building have security cameras?" Casey asked, drawing the guard's attention back her way. "I'm especially interested in exterior coverage, but if you have any here . . ." She looked around the lobby and spotted at least one camera, making a point of noting its placement before turning back to the guard. "I can get a warrant, if necessary."

"That won't be necessary," a new voice announced, and Casey looked up to see someone who was clearly the man in charge bearing down on her from a door that had opened behind the desk. "David Espinoza," he said holding out a hand. "I'm Director of Security for the Lorenzo. How can I help you, Agent Lewis?"

That he knew her name told her two things. One, he'd been not just watching, but also listening the whole time. Which meant, two, there were definitely more cameras in the lobby than the obvious one near the elevator hallway.

Casey shook his hand. "Someone was taking potshots at the parking lot behind your building this afternoon. We have a fairly narrow time frame, and I'd like to take a look at any video footage you might have. I can't be sure of when he arrived, but he had to have exited the building shortly after the incident, at the most within the last two hours."

Her cell phone rang. She checked the caller ID and said, "Excuse me a moment," then stepped away. "What do you have?" she asked Damian when she answered the call. That was the other item they'd picked up when they'd stopped for the windbreaker. Damian had required no more than a ten-minute tutorial, and he was swiping right and thumb typing like a fifteen-year-old girl. It was downright frightening.

"The room he used is obvious," Damian told her. "Our friends here were dismayed to discover the broken window, but the office was vacant, and no one seems to have noticed any strangers. On the other hand, they're not exactly observant. They barely noticed me, and, let's face it, I'm remarkable."

Casey ignored that part and got to the point. "Did he leave anything?" She actually hoped the sniper had taken all of his gear with him. It was unlikely to yield anything useful if he'd left it, while, on the other hand, if he was carrying a gun case, it would make him easier to spot on the security tapes.

"Nothing worth noting," Damian said.

"Any food wrappers? Soda cans? Anything we might get a fingerprint from?" She heard Damian's hesitation and wondered if he knew about fingerprints. It was so easy to forget that he was still new to this reality. "Does it look like he touched anything?" she asked instead.

"He rearranged some furniture for his setup, and there's the broken window, of course."

Casey frowned. It was just possible that the shooter had left a print on the furniture or the broken glass, and she had a kit in her truck. But there was likely to be a huge number of prints in that office, and no way to get elimination prints from everyone who'd ever used or visited the room. Not to mention that doing so might expose her rather precarious authority in this situation.

"Okay," she told Damian. "Come back down for now. They've got security footage. We can try to spot him there."

"Yes, ma'am," he snapped out solemnly, and she had to fight the urge to roll her eyes. He was loving this role-play shit a little too much, though she should have expected it. Now that he was free, he was all about the adventure, the challenge. Well, that and connecting with Nick to find and free his brother warriors, which was the biggest challenge of all.

Casey disconnected and turned to David Espinoza, who'd been politely pretending not to listen to her call. "My colleague is on his way down. The more eyes, the better on the video footage."

"Excellent. We can go ahead and get you set up. McBride will show your fellow agent back to our security office when he gets here."

An hour later, Casey was rubbing her sore eyes as she watched people come and go through the lobby. They were running the footage at an accelerated speed, which made the time literally fly by, but it also required more intense concentration to—"What's that?" she asked abruptly, and froze the image of a man carrying a long zippered case.

Damian leaned over her shoulder, and she wanted to preen at the sheer heat and presence of the man. He had one hand braced on the back of her chair and the other on the desk in front of her, which effectively bracketed her in his arms. It wasn't a bad feeling at all. In fact, it was a little too good. She wanted to move, to break the moment, but that would have given too much away, so she only bent forward to study the image more closely.

"Could that be a gun case he's carrying?" she asked quietly, though they were the only two people in the room. Espinoza had gotten quickly bored and gone back to his office.

"It's the right size and shape," Damian agreed. "Can you make the image of the case bigger?"

Casey zoomed in and saw what he'd been looking at.

"Pelican," he said, reading the logo on the case. "Is that——?"

"A well-known long gun case," she told him. "I suppose it could be something else, but what are the odds?" She dicked with the image some more, then *tsk*ed in exasperation. "I can't get his face on this angle. Let me try . . ." She'd become quite familiar with the security setup by now and switched deftly to a different angle, speeding through the footage until she found the right time stamp. "There," she said, pointing.

"Do you recognize him?" he asked her.

She stared at the man's face, trying to see it in a different setting. She nodded. "He was there. At the house, when I recovered the Talisman."

"All right," he said, "We have his face. How does that help us?"

She smiled grimly. "Turns out the Lorenzo folks are quite the voyeurs. They have cameras everywhere. Let's see if I can follow our guy to the parking lot."

"Cool," he said, and it was everything she could do not to laugh at that word coming from his mouth.

She switched angles again, bringing up all six exterior cameras and advancing them to the relevant time frame. The gun case made it easy to spot their guy after that, and they followed him to his vehicle, which was the ubiquitous white cargo van. There was a reason bad guys chose those vans. There were so many of them on the road, they simply blended into the scenery. But this one had a license plate, and that she could use. She zoomed in on the plate, then brought up a searchable database on her cell phone and inputted the number.

"The car is registered to a George Smith," she read off for Damian's sake. "No stolen vehicle report. The name's obviously a fake, but there's an address about an hour from here. That's worth checking out. It's legally registered, which means this might actually be a valid address."

"Why would Sotiris do that? It's too easy to follow."

"It's not Sotiris himself. He hired an agent to purchase the Talisman for him, and we know that agent had a house nearby, because that's where I stole it from in the first place. So, maybe the sniper lives around here, too."

"Are we going there now, or waiting for tonight?"

Casey considered it. There was always a danger that the bad guys might move, just disappear into the darkness. On the other hand, she was reminded of the other night, and how the defenses on the house had been hardened so much more than she'd expected. With just the two of them, they'd have to know exactly what they were getting into. They'd expect her this time, which would make it even more dangerous, and considering the last attempt had left her running from hellhounds *and* getting shot. . . . Let's just say she wanted to be prepared.

"We'll head to the safe house first. I want to research the location, at least check out the neighborhood and surrounding streets. I might even be able to get an up-to-date satellite image of the property."

"Research," he said glumly. "I'd like to say it's a waste of time, but unfortunately I think you're right. We'll be outnumbered and outgunned. The only thing you'll have going for you this time is superior knowledge . . . and, of course, me." He grinned at her. "So how far to this safe house?"

"It's in the same direction as the target, which is convenient. Just a little farther from the city." She pointed at the map on the cell phone's screen. Damian leaned forward as if memorizing it, and then glanced at her and jerked his chin upward, before stepping back. Taking the chin jerk—such a guy thing—to mean he'd seen everything he needed to, she logged out of the database on her phone, and then closed all of the video files she'd had open on the Lorenzo system, and erased all trace of her activities there. She hadn't done anything that was strictly illegal, but Nick always stressed that they should keep their FBI affiliation on the down-low, and she decided that was especially important on a case like this, when she'd used her FBI ID to gain admission under somewhat false circumstances.

She handed Damian her keys. "You should go ahead to the truck. I'll deal with Espinoza and join you."

"Does this mean I'm driving?" he asked, a teasing glint in his eyes.

"No," she said firmly and would have grabbed the keys back, but Espinoza had stepped out of his office, and the spectacle of her trying to get the keys from Damian wouldn't have done much to reinforce her image as a no-nonsense FBI agent. She leaned closer to Damian and hissed, "If you damage my truck, I'll stab you in your sleep."

He just laughed.

"I'll wait for you outside," he said loudly enough for Espinoza to hear.

Casey gave him a final warning glare, which only made him grin harder. Great. With every day he spent in this reality, he was becoming more and more confident in his surroundings. What little control she'd had over him was slipping away by the hour.

"Did you find what you were looking for?" David Espinoza asked from behind her.

She turned to face him, aware of Damian opening the door to the lobby on his way out to the parking lot. It struck her suddenly that the only sound had been the door itself. For such a big man, he moved almost silently.

"Agent Lewis?" Espinoza prodded her.

"I'm sorry," she said immediately. "I'm already thinking of our next steps. We retrieved an excellent image of the shooter, enough to move our investigation forward in a very positive way. Thank you for your cooperation, and for not making me get a warrant." She gave him a we're-in-this-together smile.

He responded with a dazzling smile of his own, and she realized for the first time that David Espinoza was a very good-looking man. Funny how she hadn't noticed that when Damian was around.

"We're always happy to help law enforcement here at the Lorenzo," he was saying. And that made her wonder when the Lorenzo had dealt with the police before.

Fortunately, that wasn't her problem. She produced one of the business cards Nick had provided for her and held it out. The card was very official, but it would send the caller to the office of Nick's assistant, who had very specific instructions for how to deal with any queries that came in on that line. All of Nick's hunters carried cards with the identical number.

Casey offered her hand and they shook. "Thank you again," she said sincerely, and would have left it at that, but Espinoza held on a fraction longer than courtesy required.

"Will you be staying in town?" His brown eyes were warm and interested.

She blinked in surprise. What was the deal lately? She'd gone a year without so much as an idle flirtation and now suddenly, she had Damian in her bed, and Espinoza stroking his thumb over the back of her hand.

"We won't actually," she said, emphasizing the *we*. "We're leaving right away."

"That's unfortunate," he murmured. "But if your investigation brings you back, I'd love to show you the city."

"I'd enjoy that," she lied, figuring that was the easiest way to extricate herself from what had become a very awkward situation. "I'll call you."

"Excellent," he said, giving her another one of those dazzling smiles. She'd bet he slayed 'em left and right with that charm.

"Cassandra." She spun in surprise at the sound of her name from a visibly unhappy Damian.

"Stephens?" She gave him a worried look, thinking something must have pulled him back into the building.

"We need to get going. The others are waiting for us."

"Right," she said. Confused, but not wanting to give anything away, she turned back to Espinoza. "Thank you again, David."

"My pleasure," Espinoza said, then aimed an arrogant smile over her head at Damian. "Stephens," he said flatly.

Damian bared his teeth. "Espinoza," he said in the exact same tone of voice.

Casey glanced between the two men, wondering what the hell was going on, but she took advantage of the stare-down between them to make her own escape, circling around Damian and heading for the door. He caught up with her and reached over her head to push open the heavy glass panel. Exquisitely aware of the many security cameras watching their every move, she waited until they were back in her Yukon and on their way out of the parking lot—with her driving—before looking over at Damian and saying, "What was all that?"

"All what?" he asked, giving her a bland look.

"At the end, you and Espinoza."

"He's attracted to you."

"Uh huh, and—?"

"And he can't be trusted. He would use you to gain inside information on our investigation."

So it was "our" investigation now. Interesting. "I've been doing this a while, you know," she told him. "I don't exactly go around spilling my guts to every handsome man who shakes my hand."

"So you think he's handsome?"

Casey rolled her eyes. "You didn't think so?" she asked innocently.

Damian was not amused, which both amused *her* and, at the same time, made her wonder why he cared. Did he care? Of course he didn't care. She was simply the only person he knew in this time. Which was fine with her. She wasn't exactly looking for a long-term commitment either. He was a gorgeous man and terrific in bed. Oh, yeah, and a great fighter. Good enough reasons to keep him around. For now.

She turned back to the road. Rush hour was in full swing, and she needed to pay attention to traffic. She took the ramp up onto the expressway, then gave him a quick wink. "Buckle up, cowboy. I like to drive fast."

Chapter Five

THE SAFE HOUSE was big and comfortable, with the pool and hot tub that she'd promised Damian. It was good luck that there was a place so close to their target. Nick maintained several safe houses throughout the country, but it was impossible—or impossibly expensive—to have them in every city, even if only the major ones. This one, for example, served the entire Midwestern region, and it was one of the nicer places. It sat on an acre and a half of land, with mature trees all around, providing the privacy necessary to come and go without the neighbors seeing the occupants' every move. Or noticing that the people who came and went weren't always the same ones.

Casey parked and stepped out of the vehicle to admire the broad front porch. She loved porches like this. Because her father was in the armed forces, she and her brothers had grown up in military housing, which hadn't concerned itself with design or style. At least, not for the non-commissioned officers like her father. Some of the big generals and their families had pretty, palatial homes, but she'd barely been permitted to walk through the front door of those places.

She stood for a moment longer, until Damian shifted impatiently. "Is there a problem?" he asked, searching the house with a warrior's eye.

"No," she said. "I was just admiring the porch."

He looked at it and grunted wordlessly. She didn't know if that meant he agreed with her, or thought she was wasting time. Frankly, she didn't care.

She walked around to the back of the Yukon and opened the hatch. "Let's get this stuff inside and I can get to work."

Together, they gathered their personal duffels, laptops, and the several bags of groceries—Damian really did love to shop. He carried the bulk of it, and she tilted her head in consideration, watching him march up to the porch, laden with bags that he seemed to carry with no effort at all. *One of the advantages of having a god on your side,* she thought with a smile. At least until he turned and gave her an impatient look that asked, *What the hell are you doing down there?*

She quickly grabbed the one bag he'd left her, then closed the cargo hatch and hurried up the stairs. "Sorry," she muttered. "I had an idea." That was a lie, but he didn't need to know that.

They dropped their duffels near the stairs to the second floor bedrooms, and carried the groceries into the kitchen. "I'll make dinner tonight," she said, then added, "but don't get used to it."

He shrugged. "I'm fully capable of preparing my own meals. Food is necessary to a warrior."

"Good, you can cook tomorrow. There's a grill outside."

She looked up to find him watching her. His lips lifted in a tiny smile when he caught her eye, then he winked. "I'll carry the bags upstairs." The words were innocuous enough, but the way he said them. . . . They conjured images of sweaty bodies and tangled sheets, or maybe it was tangled bodies and sweaty sheets.

Either way, Casey suddenly found it difficult to breathe. She managed to nod in agreement, until he strode from the kitchen, and her lungs remembered how to function. She was getting in over her head when it came to him, and it couldn't lead to anything good. Why? Well, hell, because he was one of Nick's statues! An ancient warrior brought back to life with some sort of mysterious destiny. It was all tied up with Nick and his secrets, not to mention the other, equally mysterious, stone warriors, and she had a feeling she wasn't part of that destiny. Which meant anything between her and Damian would end when the job was finished. Even if they succeeded in recovering the Talisman, which they would, she'd probably never see him again. She'd continue her work for Nick, roaming around the country, and Damian would either remain in Florida with Nick, or maybe travel the world searching out the other statues. It was all very logical.

So why did the thought make her heart feel as if someone had grabbed it in a fist and squeezed?

She looked up as he dropped their gear with a thump on the floor upstairs. A moment later, there was the sound of running water, and he called down to her.

"I'm taking a shower!"

"Okay," she shouted back, then spent the next several minutes trying to get the image of a naked Damian out of her head—water running over his sleek skin, every muscle defined and toned, like a textbook of the human body on display just for her. She could go up there. Strip down and step into the shower with him. She remembered doing just that this morning. Sex in the shower. Damian pounding into her against the tile wall. "Damn it, Casey," she hissed. "Get a grip."

It was an effort, but she managed to turn her thoughts to something more practical. Like the dinner she'd promised to make. She'd already put away most of the groceries they'd bought, moving automatically while her thoughts had been focused on her urge to molest Damian in the shower. Going over to the fridge, she opened the door and surveyed the options. They were both hungry. Other than breakfast, they hadn't had much more

than snack food today, and she knew from living with her father and brothers that big men needed a lot more fuel than that.

"Steak it is," she decided and grabbed the package of three filets. She'd
be lucky to eat one, but she'd bet Damian would eat the other two, and
probably want more. So . . . side dishes. She turned on the oven, then
wrapped four potatoes in foil and popped them inside. Anything left over
could be used for breakfast tomorrow. Next, salad. They'd bought a bunch
of veggies, but she'd also picked up a prepared salad from the deli section,
which would save her some chopping. A quick check told her she'd somehow managed to buy all the fixings they'd need for the potatoes, so she
grabbed a dish, mixed up a quick marinade, and added the filets just as the
shower went off upstairs.

Good. She could shower while the potatoes baked, and then the two
of them would enjoy a nice, civilized meal together, after which she could
get started on her research. That's why they were there, after all. This wasn't
a private sexcapade getaway, she reminded herself. She marched up the
stairs, determined to remember that this mission was serious. Lives de-
pended on her.

There were four bedrooms on the second level. She found her things,
along with Damian's, in what would be the master suite, with a huge,
king-sized four-poster bed that looked like it belonged in a fairy tale, not the
gritty safe house of some clandestine government operation. She briefly,
very briefly, considered insisting on separate bedrooms, but immediately
realized how stupid that would be. They'd been sleeping in the same room
since she'd found him, having sex almost that long. Good sex. Fantastic
sex.

Damian walked in from the bathroom, naked, of course. It was his de-
fault condition. He had a towel in one hand, rubbing it over his wet hair,
and she couldn't help smiling. The towel was snowy white, his skin golden
brown, his body sculpted perfection. She met his eyes, and his smile was
just for her. Was that just part of his charm? To make everyone feel as if
they were special to him? She sighed. She wasn't usually this insecure. Hell,
she was *never* this insecure when she was doing her usual breaking and entering, stealing away treasures. Love had done this to her. Made her doubt
everything about herself, made her question every word, every—

Wait, what? Love? She wasn't in love. She *couldn't* be in fucking love!

"Cassandra?"

She shook herself slightly. Of course she wasn't in love. She'd simply
gotten carried away at the sight of all that golden flesh. And who wouldn't?
She forced a smile.

"Sorry, I was just thinking about . . . you know. Anyway, I thought I'd
wash up while the potatoes cook. How's the shower?"

He stepped right into her space and stroked his callused fingers over
her cheek. "Not as good as this morning's. I missed you."

She drew in his clean soap scent, could feel the heat of his skin, and, oh, my God, the press of his growing erection. "Damian," she whispered.

He leaned over and kissed her. Gentle, sensual, thorough. The kind of kiss she read about in romance novels. She sighed against his mouth. "We'll never get dinner," she warned him, smiling.

He grinned back at her. "Are you hungry?"

"Starving," she said, intentionally rubbing against his hard shaft.

He grunted. "Cassandra." Just her name, a warning. But then his stomach growled loudly, and they both laughed.

"There's always dessert," she said, crooking one eyebrow.

"And after-dinner drinks," he agreed, biting her lower lip before smoothing his tongue over the small hurt.

"It's a date. I'm going to shower now, and you're going to put on some clothes."

"Why?"

"The shower or—"

"The clothes. If I put them on now, you'll only tear them off when you attack me later."

"Yes," she agreed. "But that's half the fun."

He laughed and turned her toward the bathroom with a swat on her ass. "Don't take too long, woman. I'm hungry."

She rolled her eyes, but resisted the urge to punch him over the "woman" comment. They'd only end up in bed, and she really needed a shower. She also needed some distance from Damian. She couldn't seem to think straight when he was so close. It made her start wanting things she couldn't have.

Stopping at the walk-in closet, she stripped off everything, feeling more relaxed now that they were away from predator hotel bars and shooting gallery parking lots.

She walked into the master bath and stopped. It was like a mini-spa, with marble floors and a floating vanity. There was even a selection of bath products in a basket on the counter. What the hell was this? She'd used other safe houses, but they hadn't been this elegant. It made her wonder what Nick used the place for when it wasn't needed as a safe house. A venue for secret assignations, maybe? Did Nick have a lover no one knew about? Actually, if rumors were true, he had several. One in every city. Although that last part seemed a bit of an exaggeration.

She laughed softly, wondering why she was wasting time wondering about Nick's love life, when she should be focused on her own. That thought sent her over to glance in one of the mirrors, and her laughter died. Good God, she looked awful. It was a miracle that Damian wanted to have sex with her at all. There were dark circles under her eyes, her skin looked like it had never seen an ounce of moisturizer, and her hair . . . there were probably small animals nesting in there somewhere.

She shuddered at the thought, which jarred her injured shoulder beneath its voluminous bandage. It was the same bandage Damian had applied, and it was probably time for a change. She started tearing away the tape, wincing at the occasional tug on her skin, dreading what she was going to find. The bloody bandage went into the trash, and then she stood in front of the mirror with her eyes closed, steeling herself for what she was about to see.

She opened her eyes. Okay. It wasn't as bad as she'd thought. It wasn't pretty, but at least it wasn't green. A part of her had feared finding a big, swollen, infected mass of green goo underneath the bandage. But no, Damian had done a good job of cleaning it out, and although her arm and shoulder were purple with bruising, the wound itself looked good. It was definitely going to leave a scar, though. She might even need to see a plastic surgeon to make sure the scar tissue didn't limit her range of motion. But right now, tonight, she'd settle for cleaning it up and applying a new bandage.

"Cassandra." Damian knocked on the door and entered without waiting. She whirled, catching up a towel to cover herself, which was pretty ridiculous. Her face heated with embarrassment, but it was too late.

"I thought you might need help with your shoulder." His eyes were twinkling in amusement.

She swallowed. He was wearing a pair of unbuttoned jeans and nothing else. And she had only her towel. But then she caught her reflection and remembered. She looked awful. "I've got it," she told him.

He held her gaze a moment longer. "If you need anything," he said finally. "Call me."

She nodded. "I will."

He gave her a little smile, then backed out of the bathroom and closed the door.

Casey leaned weakly against the vanity, no longer sure she was up to this. She knew better than to get involved with a man like Damian. *But it's just sex,* her brain reminded her. She wasn't getting involved, they were just having sex. And that was something she hadn't had nearly enough of in the last few years. She straightened, then marched over and turned on the hot water in the shower, filling the enclosure with steam. Just sex. She could do this. She *would* do this.

DAMIAN COULD SMELL something baking when he got downstairs after talking to Cassandra, and he found meat sitting in a glass dish, soaking in a liquid that smelled of oil and herbs. He didn't have much to offer when it came to cooking in this modern era, but one thing remained constant through ages and worlds, and that was wine. It was one of the oldest alcoholic beverages in the history of man, and his samplings from room service over the past couple of days proved that the process had improved dramatically.

This house had been set up by Nico, and judging by its opulence, he knew that his friend stayed here himself on occasion. Which meant there had to be alcohol in the house somewhere. A quick perusal of the kitchen showed him a glass-fronted cabinet with several bottles of wine inside. Opening the door, he read the labels and made a selection. A wooden block of knives produced a blade suited to the task, and he soon had the cork out of the bottle. The room service waiter had used a clever device for the same purpose, but he saw no reason to change what didn't need changing.

A search of the cabinets turned up a variety of glasses. He chose two and set them on the counter, then filled one with the rich, red vintage he'd chosen. He smiled at the bouquet of fruit and oak that wafted into the air as he poured. A quick taste gave him all of those flavors, along with just a touch of black pepper. His smile widened. Winemaking had indeed come a long way while he'd been imprisoned.

Carrying his glass, he walked over and opened the sliding glass door to the backyard, where a turquoise pool wafted steam into the cool air. The temperature was just on the edge of being too cold, which was perfect for him. But then, any fresh air felt good on his skin these days. He didn't care if it was freezing cold, or steamy hot, or anything in between. He walked over and sat in one of the chairs, staring out into the moonlit night, seeing nothing but open space. . . .

He sucked in a breath against the emotion that threatened to overwhelm him. So much had happened since his release, so many new things to learn, people to remember . . . not to mention keeping himself and Cassandra alive. He felt as if this quiet moment sitting next to the pool was the first chance he'd had to truly appreciate his long-delayed freedom. There had been entire decades, centuries even, when he'd been trapped within that statue, that he'd despaired of ever seeing the curse lifted. Times when he'd thought he would go mad, and had tormented himself with thinking up ways to end his existence.

But Sotiris had planned well. He'd been no more capable of killing himself, than he'd been of freeing himself. Thank the gods that Cassandra had come along when she had. He was even grateful that she'd been shot, as selfish as that seemed. Because if she hadn't been, if blood hadn't been dripping over her hand, she could have gripped his stone arm all night long, and his curse still wouldn't have been lifted.

The glass door opened behind him. "Hey," Cassandra said. "You okay out here?"

He glanced up as she came around his chair. She was wearing skin-tight pants of some stretchy fabric that emphasized the elegant strength in her long legs, and over that, a long-sleeved sweater that kept slipping from her uninjured shoulder. And she wasn't wearing a bra. He'd seen plenty of bras during his tenure on the roof, and he knew they could be lovely adornments to a woman's breasts. But nothing was sexier than the sway of Cassandra's full, naked breasts beneath the silky sweater.

He watched silently as she took the chair across from him and leaned back to take a sip from the glass she carried. "Good choice on the wine."

He nodded. "This house fairly screams of my old friend Nico. He also had excellent taste."

She took another small sip. "I'm no connoisseur, but this is delicious."

He smiled at her enjoyment, then gave a somber nod in her direction. "Your arm?"

"Still sore, but it's better," she said cheerfully. "*Much* better than I expected. You did a good job of cleaning it out. I put a new bandage on. A lot smaller," she added with a chuckle.

He nodded, then turned his attention back to the seemingly endless emptiness around them. Cassandra didn't say anything for several minutes, then asked, "Does it bother you? The wide-open space, I mean?"

Damian looked at her in surprise. "On the contrary. It's a balm to my very soul," he said somberly. "Every single sensation—from the moisture in the air to the sounds all around me—is brighter, sharper, richer than anything I could have imagined, even in my darkest hours of entrapment. Sometimes I think I finally died within the tomb Sotiris crafted for me, and that this is Elysium."

She tilted her head curiously. "Elysium. The Roman version of heaven. But from what Nick's told me, and what you've said yourself, you guys predate Rome by a whole lot of years."

He shrugged. "Elysium, Valhalla, nirvana, heaven . . . it doesn't matter what you call it. They're all the same."

She studied him a moment longer. "But you know this isn't heaven, that you're alive, right? Because I'm definitely alive, and you're here with me."

He grinned and scooted forward, resting his elbows on his thighs, hands dangling between his legs, the wine held loosely in his fingers. "Are you sure of that, Cassandra?"

She laughed. He could have told her that her laugh was one of those sounds that was pure sweetness to his ears. "I'm sure," she told him. "And I'm hungry. How about you?"

"Ravenous," he growled and was rewarded with a hot blush that stole over her chest and neck to color her cheeks. He loved the way she blushed like a virgin, but fucked like a siren.

"Damn it. You do that to me every time. I'm going inside to the put the steaks on before this gets any worse." She stood and started to walk past him, but then stopped. "Would you rather eat out here?"

A rush of warmth filled his chest. She was so busy convincing herself she didn't care, that she forgot not to do it. She'd taken to heart his comments about being free to breathe the fresh air, but her concern wasn't necessary. He'd been teasing her, saying he didn't know if he really was alive and free. But he was certain of both. Just as he was certain no one would ever imprison him again. He'd happily die first. But because he knew it down to the depths of his soul, and because he was a man, not a needy child, he didn't require constant reinforcement of the truth. And besides, it was too cool out here for Cassandra.

"We should sit inside," he told her. "It's the civilized thing to do."

"Okay, let's be civilized." She winked. "Until after dinner anyway."

CASEY TOOK ANOTHER sip of her delicious wine. The food had been great so far, and she was really looking forward to dessert. So when the hell was Damian going to make his move? Or maybe he was waiting for her? This was stupid. They'd already fucked once. Well, actually more than once. So why the teenaged nerves now?

"Come here," Damian said, and lifted her hand from the table, urging her out of her chair and around the edge of the table onto his lap.

She frowned. Had she ever sat on a man's lap before? She didn't think so, not even her father's. *Especially* not her father's.

"Relax," Damian murmured, one hand massaging up and down her back, strong fingers shaping her spine. That's all he did for a long time. It was just the two of them in the candlelit room, the patio door open enough to admit the sounds of the night and the fresh air that Damian craved. The movement of his hand was almost hypnotic, his big body so warm. All of her muscles slowly relaxed, one at a time, and she found herself leaning into his heat. She wrapped her arms around his neck and nestled into his shoulder, rubbing her cheek against his jaw.

Damian made a sound low in his throat as his hand skimmed over her ribs and around to brush the underside of her breast. Casey arched her back in invitation, and he slipped his hand under her sweater to squeeze her breast gently, his thumb dragging over her nipple, rubbing back and forth until it was wildly aroused and exquisitely sensitive. The sensation was almost too much for her and she wanted to sob in relief when he freed her nipple with a gentle caress, only to switch to her other breast to give it the same achingly delicious treatment.

Every movement was so slow, so desperately erotic. She wanted it to go on forever, even as she thought she couldn't stand another moment. The tension was nearly overwhelming. How long had it been since a man had made love to her like this? Not the quick meet in a bar, have sex, and never see each other again kind of hook-up, but like this . . . slow and seductive.

Hell, she wasn't sure she'd *ever* experienced anything like this. Like Damian.

His lips touched her neck, warm and wet as he nibbled his way to her mouth, kissing just the corner, before gliding his tongue over the crease of her lips in both invitation and demand. Casey opened her mouth with a soft moan, meeting the spear of his tongue with the tentative touch of her own. His lips moved over hers with a luxurious slowness, as if he had all night to kiss her. She moaned again, almost embarrassed by her easy arousal, by the slick heat building between her thighs.

"Damian," she whispered, turning into his kiss, twining her tongue around his.

He gripped the bottom of her sweater, and she lifted her arms as he tugged it over her head. She had an instant of embarrassment over her own nakedness, but that was soon lost in the wash of sensation as Damian lowered his head to one breast and sucked her nipple into his warm mouth, his tongue lashing the swollen peak, his teeth coming together in soft bites that flirted with the edge of pain, turning it into the most erotic sensation. She could have sat there all night, letting him worship her breasts.

Thankfully Damian had other plans.

He stood, slipping one arm under her legs and taking her with him, carrying her as if she weighed nothing. She rested her head on his shoulder as he climbed the stairs, trying to remember if anything had ever felt this *right* before. This wasn't just sex anymore. She was fooling herself.

Damian must have felt her growing tension, or maybe he understood her better than she knew. Because he tightened his grip and tipped his head down to bite her cheek. "Relax, Cassandra. You'll love dessert."

She laughed and bit him back. "Will there be chocolate syrup?"

"Oh, baby," he murmured, kicking the bedroom door open. He strode over and dropped her onto the bed, following her down. "We don't need chocolate syrup. You're going to be sticky enough when I'm finished with you."

Casey shivered, not with the cold—who could be cold with Damian's heat surrounding her?—but with anticipation. She watched hungrily as he moved away enough to tear off his T-shirt and toss it aside, and then grabbed the waist of her yoga pants and tugged them down her legs, snagging the silk panties she'd donned just to tease him. They were stripped off along with her pants and thrown on the floor on top of his shirt.

Feeling suddenly vulnerable in her nakedness, she opened her mouth to say something, but was stopped when he knelt between her legs, pushing her knees wider as he massaged her calves. His eyes studied her, grazing over her flesh, his regard so intense that it was like a brand, searing his mark into her wherever his gaze landed.

He kissed her, beginning with her knees, the inside of her thighs and then stretching out on top of her to kiss her lips, his tongue tangling with hers, caressing her mouth until her heart was pounding so hard, he had to feel it thumping in rhythm against his chest.

His kisses moved downward to her neck, her breasts, her belly, while his hands stroked every inch of her. She gasped when his broad shoulders spread her thighs and she felt the warm brush of his breath against her heated flesh. She wanted his mouth on her sex. She flexed her hips, thrusting upward, but he placed one big hand on her belly and held her down while he continued tormenting her, licking her swollen outer lips, murmuring about her waxed-bare pussy.

"Smooth as silk, my Cassandra," he said, a moment before he slid one thick finger into her pussy, her sex so slick and wet with arousal that he'd barely begun before he added a second finger, pumping in and out, while she bucked against his hand, wanting more.

Then she felt the wet heat of his mouth surrounding her clit.

She nearly came off the bed, shocked at the intensity of sensation when he sucked her clit into his mouth, his tongue rasping over the sensitive nub, swelling it, making it throb in rhythm with his fingers as they pumped in and out of her soaking wet pussy. She twisted her fingers into his long hair, moaning softly, her knees hugging his shoulders. He was a solid presence between her legs, an immoveable force.

"Please, Damian," she whispered, her voice catching on a sob.

His tongue swirled around her clit, pressing hard. She cried out, her hips jerking, pushing her pussy against his demanding mouth. He chuckled, his breath an aching brush against her too sensitive flesh, and then, with no warning, he sucked the rigid nub into his mouth and bit down, his teeth scraping against the aching bundle of nerves.

She came like a rocket, crying out over and over, his hold on her the only thing keeping her from bucking off the bed, she was thrashing so hard. Waves of intense sensation unlike anything she'd ever felt before rippled through her body, pulsing in time with her pounding heart. She clutched her fingers in his hair, tugging hard enough to cause pain, desperate for something, anything, to break the cycle of consuming pleasure that had taken over every inch of her body.

He growled low in his throat, the sound vibrating over her throbbing clit, and she groaned his name, "Damian." It was half worship for the man who could bring her this much pleasure, and half a plea for it to stop before she lost herself completely.

"Open your eyes," he demanded, and she could feel the heat of his breath on her sex-slicked thighs.

She fought to obey, struggled to find the right nerves and muscles to lift her eyelids and gaze down at him. With a wicked smile, he slid his fingers out of her pussy, and slowly, deliberately licked her juices off of each thick digit. She blushed at the sight. She couldn't help it. This was more than sex. This was lust, dark and sinful, addictive, delicious. And she wanted more.

"Fuck me," she growled, fisting her fingers in his hair and yanking, wanting to know that he felt *something,* even if it was only pain.

Damian's smug smile disappeared in an instant, replaced by a desire so fierce that her heart stuttered. Without warning, he pushed upright, her straining thighs closing over her bare pussy, which was suddenly bereft of his warmth. But not for long. His eyes never leaving hers, he pushed his jeans down his legs to the floor, leaving him completely naked at last. His cock jutted out, thick and long and hard as he dropped one knee to the bed. She licked her lips, and he gave an evil laugh that held nothing good, but promised all sorts of delicious bad.

"Spread your legs, Cassandra," he ordered impatiently, and she did. Eagerly, hungrily. "Wider, darling," he chided. "I want to see you."

That touch of sin, the forbidden wantonness, made her blush, and she thought of resisting. But she couldn't. She wanted him to fuck her, wanted that beautiful cock, which jerked under the weight of her gaze. She lifted her eyes at this evidence of his arousal, seeing a hunger to match her own, proof that she wasn't the only one sinning tonight.

"Fuck me, Damian," she whispered again.

He knelt on the bed, his rough fingers gripping her ankles as he bent her legs, pushing her knees to her chest, stretching her out even wider. Cassandra was totally exposed for an instant, brazenly on display, but then he thrust his cock into her empty pussy, gliding on the slippery cream of her climax, the juices of her renewed arousal coating her thighs. His eyes were hot with desire, black pupils all but erasing the coffee-dark brown of his irises.

He groaned as he pushed in deep. "By the gods, you're tight. A hot, tight glove that grips my cock and won't let go."

He fucked her slowly at first, long smooth thrusts that went as deep as he could go, before pulling out nearly all the way, until just the tip of his cock was buried in her pussy, and then doing it again. Fucking her steadily, slowly, while his mouth was everywhere, kissing her mouth, her cheeks, her eyes. Sucking on her neck as she clung to him, her arms strong around his shoulders, her legs around his hips, ankles crossed to hold him deeper with every thrust.

"Damian, Damian," she whispered, feeling another climax surging, threatening to swamp her senses once again. Everything disappeared but him—the hot friction of his cock, the pulse of her clit, the sound of her own blood rushing in her veins, her heart pounding . . . or was that his? She couldn't tell anymore. They were moving as one, soaring higher and higher, his thrusts becoming more frantic, going faster, harder . . . until the orgasm crashed over her and she shattered into tiny pieces of pure sensation. Somewhere in the midst of the drowning ecstasy, she felt Damian slam himself into her one last time, felt him stiffen with a groan as his cock bucked deep inside her, filling her with a heat that matched the crush of his arms around her. Inside and out, there was only Damian.

They lay there for a long moment, stunned by the power of their coupling. Casey concentrated on breathing, taking in oxygen. It was the only thing she still remembered how to do when everything else was buried in a haze of delicious bliss.

"I love it when you come around my cock, all creamy and wet." Damian's rough voice penetrated her awareness, and she blushed at the crude words, even as satisfaction added to the heat flushing her skin.

"And I love it when you make me come," she murmured, finding the energy somehow to flex her hips against his.

He growled and slid his cock idly in and out, cruising on the combined wetness of their climaxes. Casey gasped as her body responded instantly, her clit sending a jolt of desire that made her nipples tighten again.

"What have you done to me?" she whispered, not sure she wanted him to hear.

He thrust his hips, pushing his cock into her pussy once again, setting off little shocks of pleasure. "I'm not the only one in this seduction, sweetheart. You've got me harder than a teenaged boy."

Casey hummed her satisfaction, stroking her hands over his body, shaping the sheer beauty of his thick muscles, the strong column of his neck. "I think we should—"

She never finished her thought as Damian stiffened and then, without warning, rolled off the bed and to his feet. Grabbing his jeans, he picked up her clothes and tossed them to her.

"Get dressed, Cassandra," he said, his manner deadly serious.

"What is it?" she asked, jumping to her feet, thinking two steps ahead—get to her gun, push on her shoes—as every sense she possessed strained for signs of trouble. But she heard nothing, felt nothing. "What is it, Damian?" she repeated.

He slipped on his jeans and pulled the shirt over his head before answering. "Nico is coming."

Chapter Six

MOVING WITH THE preternatural silence that was the side effect of his tremendous skill as a warrior, Damian slipped down the stairs. Behind him, Cassandra was pulling on her shoes, grabbing her guns, and hissing at him to wait. But there was no need for her weapons, no danger from the man walking up the driveway.

The waning moon was just visible through the surrounding trees when he opened the front door and stepped outside. The gravel was sharp against his bare feet, but he barely felt it. A man rounded the last curve of the drive, his figure wrapped in shadows despite the still-bright moonlight.

The shadows disintegrated like wisps of paper, and the man grinned. "Damian."

He felt his face stretching in an answering smile. "Nico."

The two men strode toward each other, coming together in a clash of strength as they embraced, arms tightening as if each feared the other would disappear if they let go. Thousands of years had passed while they'd waited for this moment, and they were taking no chances now that it was finally here. Tears filled his eyes and Damian let them fall unashamedly, tasting the salt of Nico's tears as they kissed cheeks, first one, then the other and then all over again. They were laughing like lunatics, Damian's cheeks hurting from a smile that wouldn't let go.

Nico pounded him on the back, and then pulled away, his expression crumpling. "I'm so sorry, Damian," he whispered finally. "So damn sorry."

Damian jolted as he realized Nico had spoken in the ancient language that was the first tongue to both of them, a language he hadn't heard in so long. His chest tightened. It wasn't the words. It was what they meant. Cassandra kept remarking on how rapidly he was adjusting to her time, but here, at last, was someone who had shared the only existence he'd known until just a few days ago, someone who'd *lived* it with him. He staggered at the sheer relief of no longer needing to fit only into *this* world.

Nico caught him, gripping him tightly, and hissing the foulest curses in their native tongue, berating himself, taking blame for everything that had happened. But Damian would have none of it.

"Stop," he grated, so overcome with emotion that he could barely get the word out. "I know what you did. That you never stopped searching."

"But it never would have—"

"We were betrayed."

Nico speared him with a hard stare. "It was Antioch," he said fiercely. "That bastard thought to sell us out."

Antioch. Damian repeated the name in his thoughts. He could hardly believe it. The man had been like family to Nico. His people had served Nico's family for generations. But that's what had made him the perfect weapon for Sotiris. He'd had access to the innermost sanctum of the warriors. He'd have known which of their many personal possessions were truly personal, not valuable in terms of money, but those that they valued above all others. The ones that could anchor the curse of Sotiris's devastating spell.

"Did he suffer?" Damian demanded, already knowing the answer. Cassandra thought her "Nick" was harmless, a bookkeeper who sent people out to hunt down treasures for him. She didn't know the real Nicodemus. He was as cold and efficient a killer as the world had ever seen.

Nico bared his teeth in a predator's grin. "Long and hard, brother. He begged for death, and still he suffered, until finally I grew tired of hearing him scream." He laughed. "And then I cut out his tongue, boiled him alive, and fed him to the pigs."

"Excellent," Damian growled and started grinning all over again. "It is *so* good to see you," he said fervently. "From the moment Cassandra freed me, my soul has been searching, seeking its missing piece."

Nico grabbed him and pounded his back again. "So I'm your missing piece, eh?"

Damian laughed, feeling truly free at last.

"How do you like my Casey?" Nico asked, and Damian scowled back at him.

"She's yours?"

"Relax, brother. She's under my protection, but only as one of my hunters." He gave Damian a knowing look. "But she's not a plaything. I don't want her hurt."

He was offended. "When have I ever hurt a woman?"

"Physically? Never. But you know as well as I that you have broken a few hearts."

"Ah. Well, that's hardly my fault. I made no promises."

"And Casey?"

CASEY STILLED JUST inside the house, hidden in the shadows of the open doorway. She couldn't move with Damian's unnatural level of silence, but she could be sneaky enough when she wanted to be, and the two men were too busy hugging out their bromance to pay attention to her. She'd hoped to get some clue as to their history together, but, instead, she'd been treated to a discussion of her delicate self. Apparently, she was a thing in need of protection.

"I made no promises," Damian had said. He wasn't talking about her, but he might as well have been. What did she care anyway? Hadn't she been thinking the same thing earlier? She had no intention of making any promises either, so why did it bother her that he'd said that?

"And Casey?" Nick asked. She froze, waiting to hear what Damian would say.

"Cassandra thinks I need protecting," he said with a dismissive snort. "Hell, she thinks *you* need protecting. And she prefers to work alone."

Nick shrugged. "She doesn't trust easily, but she's a good hunter with a unique skill, and she never gives up once she scents her prey." He shifted abruptly, meeting Damian's gaze head-on. "How much does she know?"

"Why don't you ask me that question?" Casey stepped out onto the low porch. Damian turned with a smile and stretched out his hand, inviting her to join them, but she held her ground. "What is it that I'm not supposed to know, Nick? Besides the truth about who and what you are?"

"You know better, Case. It's never that simple."

"So use small words. I'll figure it out."

Nick sighed impatiently. "Can we take this inside? Or are we going to stand out here all night?"

It was Casey's turn to shrug. She wasn't the one who'd shown up without warning and hugged out a reunion in the driveway.

Damian was eyeing her curiously. She figured he was wondering how much she'd heard and how he could explain it to her. At least, that's what she thought until he grinned suddenly and said, "Cassandra thinks there's a connection between us, between all four of us and you, that is. She thinks that without us, your power is diminished."

Nick gave her a startled glance, before covering quickly by saying, "Let's hope Sotiris thinks the same. I'm tired of hiding. It's time to find the others and take the battle to him. But this time, he dies. I swear it, Damian."

"He dies," Damian agreed. "I pledge my life to it."

"Not your life," Nick objected immediately, as if to take back any ill fortune that could result from Damian's pledge. "Not again, brother. No one dies this time but Sotiris."

But while they were busy pledging fealty to each other and death to Sotiris, Casey was stuck on that brief, unguarded moment when Nick had reacted to Damian's half-joking comment. She *had* shared with Damian her speculation that Nick's power might be enhanced by having his warriors close, and that, conversely, he was weakened by their absence. But that's all it had been, speculation. Now, seeing Nick and Damian together—the magical energy swirling around them—she thought it just might be true.

She also thought Nick owed her a few damn answers.

Damian was nodding grimly at something Nick was saying. "Where do I find the others? Do you know?" he asked.

"I'll tell you everything I've discovered, but first I think we need to talk to Casey before she shoots us both."

Damian strolled over and slung an arm around her shoulders. Casey stiffened slightly, not quite comfortable with the PDA in front of Nick, but also not sure how she felt about Damian and his "no promises." But if he felt her hesitation, he gave no indication, other than a slight squeeze of his arm. "Cassandra won't shoot me, brother. You, maybe. But not me."

Casey cast him a scowling glance. What the fuck did that mean? Did he think that because they'd had sex, she was now one of his groupies? Like those oh-so-many women he'd fucked and left behind back in the day? She shrugged his arm off her shoulders and stepped away. "I'm not shooting anyone," she said, trying to keep the snap out of her voice, not wanting them to know that anything she'd overheard had bothered her. "But you're right, Nick. We should take the conversation inside."

She led the way into the kitchen, choosing one of the three high barstools and sitting with the width of the marble-topped island between her and the two men. Damian ignored the stool and walked around to stand facing her, with one hip against the island. It put him close to her, almost an embrace with their bodies nearly touching. It was the kind of thing a lover would do, and it reminded Casey that just a few minutes earlier, Damian had brought her to a screaming orgasm. She shivered at the memory and looked up to find him watching her intently. He'd done it on purpose, she knew suddenly. He'd sensed her distance and reacted by forcing her to remember that they were, in fact, lovers. And maybe something more, she realized with a sinking heart. Damn it.

"Okay, Nick," she said, determinedly ignoring all the confusing emotional crap between her and Damian, and focusing on what she could understand. "What's going on? And the truth this time, please. Why didn't I ever see the real you before? For that matter, I never even had the urge to *look*. Why was that?"

He sighed. "Because I didn't want you to. It's a small look-away spell on me, not you. It just kept you from seeing too deeply."

Casey hated the idea that she'd been manipulated like that, but she wasn't going to beat herself up about it. Now that she could see him for what he was, Nick was damn powerful. The most powerful sorcerer she'd ever come across in person. She couldn't have stopped him from doing whatever he'd wanted. Hell, she couldn't even get upset with him. He'd only been protecting himself. She'd probably have done the same thing.

"All right," she said. "So that explains *you*. But what does Damian have to do with it? Someone tried to kill him this afternoon."

Nick shot Damian an alarmed look. "Why didn't you—"

"Because he's trying like crazy to pretend they were shooting at me, not him. But they weren't. So talk to me, Nick. What's really happening? And why would someone want Damian dead?"

He eyed her silently for a long moment. "Can I get some water first?" he asked.

Damian walked the two steps to the fridge, opened the door, grabbed a bottle of water, and tossed it at Nick, who snagged it from the air with a grin. By the time he'd opened the bottle and taken a sip, Damian was back, leaning against the island even closer than before. Near enough this time that they *were* touching.

Nick eyed the two of them silently, and then started talking. "My warriors, Damian and the others . . . I used magic to bring them to my side. From the corners of the earth, through the mists of space and time. I called and they came, one by one. But Damian—"

He broke off when Damian suddenly straightened away from the island, and headed for the sliding glass door that led out to the pool. He pulled the door open, and paused, giving Casey a nervous glance. "I know this part," he said, with a forced chuckle. "I'll be outside."

She frowned at the empty space where he'd been.

"He doesn't like this story," Nick said, drawing her attention.

"Why?"

"You'll understand." He took another sip of water, and then continued. "I called all of my warriors with magic, but Damian . . . he was my first. I was only a child, just beginning to learn how to live with the tremendous power burning inside me. I was small for my age, and sometimes, I felt like the magic was a flame that would consume me before I had a chance to grow. I felt out of control, helpless. And I was lonely. I had two brothers, both older. All of us were born of the same mother and father, which was uncommon in our society. My father had concubines, but if any of them bore a child to him, I never knew of it. Later, when I was old enough to understand such things, I suspected he'd paid some minor sorcerer for a charm that ensured his seed took root only in my mother. Bastard children could tear a territory apart and he wanted to avoid that. I sometimes wondered if he saw me the same way, as something that could destroy his legacy."

"But he must have valued your power, if nothing else," Casey commented. "You said sorcerers were rare even then."

Nick breathed a bitter laugh. "Rare and unpredictable. I could prove to be his greatest asset or his greatest enemy, and there was no guarantee either way. If I decided to support him, I had the power to ensure his continued domination of the territory. His worry, and that of my brothers, was that I would seize the territory for myself. And I could have. I had no particular loyalty to my father. I rarely saw him. But my brothers, I saw them far too much. They tormented me at every opportunity."

"But you had magic. Didn't they worry what you could do to them?" she asked.

"Not until later, once I'd grown into my power enough to control it, instead of letting it control me. Once I learned how to wield it as a weapon. But it was long before that when everything happened with Damian. I was young, no more than five years old. And small, as I said . . ."

SOMEWHERE IN THE mists of time . . .

Nicodemus shoved the big door closed, pushing against it with all his might, which wasn't much. He was small and weak, and his brothers were so much older, big and brawny like their father the king. He tried a small spell, something to hide the entrance, to send his brothers far down the hall, chasing shadows. He leaned against the rough wood, sucking in a breath when the movement put too much pressure on his injured arm. He thought it might be broken. His oldest brother certainly had intended to break it. But his magic was already healing the break, the heat almost too much as his body raced to heal itself.

He heard the thunder of his tormentors' booted feet as they stormed down the hallway, bypassing the door behind which he cowered like the weakling he was. He sank to the floor, his back against the door, his legs pulled up to his chest. Resting his head on his knees, he fought the tears that wanted to come. Everyone said he was special, unique. A gift to his father from the gods. But where were those gods when his brothers were slamming him against the stone fountain in the courtyard? Where was his oh-so-unique gift when they tried to drown him in that very same fountain? He hated what he was. Why couldn't he have been normal? A warrior like his father?

A scuffed footfall made him look up, listening intently. But whoever it was continued down the hallway. Nico stared around the room he'd taken refuge in. It was a women's parlor, one of many scattered throughout the palace. A place where his mother and her sisters, along with all of their ladies, would sit in the sun and sew, making the stunning tapestries that hung on the walls and kept out the bitter cold when winter set in. The ladies and their sewing moved from room to room, according to his mother's whim or the season. Some rooms got more sunlight than others. Nico looked around with a small smile on his face. There was one trick he could do already. It wasn't very useful against his brothers, but it always made his mother smile.

He called up a bit of the magic that was always within him, waiting like a great dragon to pounce the moment he lost control. Freeing just a tiny peek, like a wink from the dragon's eye, he filled the room with sunlight. As unnatural as it was, it sought out every shadow, every nook and cranny, and filled the room with light and warmth. His smile grew . . . and then, without warning, the door behind him trembled as his oldest brother, Straton, pounded on the wood. The sunlight scattered into shadows.

"I know you're in there, freak," Straton bellowed. Nico couldn't believe sometimes that their father found Straton to be a worthy successor. He was a boor, a bully who used his physical size to get what he wanted. He might make a worthy warrior, someone to throw into the midst of a battle, but he would never be a leader like their father.

On the other hand, Nico thought, as Straton's fist collided again with the heavy door, there was something to be said for brute strength. He held his breath, but his locking spell held, and the door remained shut. He listened to his brother muttering as he stomped away down the hall, and he sighed. He couldn't escape forever. Eventually, Straton would find him. Why couldn't he have just one good brother? Someone who'd stand with him, no matter what.

Everyone praised his magical talent, but no one took his side, not even his parents who simply forbade him to use that magic against his bully of a brother. He glared at the fractured sunlight that he'd been so proud of just moments before. Was this the only thing his magic was good for? He didn't want sunlight, he wanted a defender, a friend. . . . Thoughts stuttered, and his breath caught in his chest as shadows that shouldn't have been there coalesced into a form. He froze in both fear and wonder. Fear because he'd been warned about enemy sorcerers who wanted him dead, and wonder because that was how his sorcerer's mind worked. It was curious and analytical. And something was happening in that dark corner, something that called to the magic inside him.

He leaned forward intently, feeling the eager smile that crossed his face, all thoughts of danger gone. The shadows evaporated in a burst of sunlight so bright that Nico started to raise a hand to shield his eyes, but then the light faded as quickly as it had come. And in its place, there stood . . . a boy. Someone he'd never seen before, someone who'd inextricably entered the locked room, breaking Nico's protective spell. The boy stumbled a little, and Nico started forward reflexively to help him, but then the boy grinned. And Nico found himself grinning back.

"Who are you?" he asked, though he had a growing feeling that he knew the answer to that. The boy only tilted his head, as if confused. Nico tried again, "What's your name?"

The boy's eyes widened in understanding. "Damian," he said, but that seemed to be the extent of his words. And honestly, Nico wasn't totally surprised by that.

"Nico," he said, touching his own chest. "And we're going to be friends."

BACK AT THE SAFE house, in the American Midwest

Nick blinked out of his detour into the past and glanced nervously at Casey, wondering how long he'd been sitting there staring at nothing, and whether she'd noticed. He took a long draw off his water bottle to cover. "I hadn't meant to call Damian that day, but that's what I did. It was the first great magic I'd ever performed, and I'd done it completely by accident." He smiled in remembrance. "It was days before my parents realized that there was a strange child living in their home, and by then, it was too late. We were inseparable. My father permitted him to stay, because it was obvious that Damian was warrior-born, and that was the one thing my father respected without question. Damian was only a few years older than I was, and already he could wield a sword better than boys twice his age. My father decided I'd need a bodyguard going forward, and Damian was to be that man." He gazed out the window where Damian was sitting on a lounge chair just beyond the lights of the patio.

"And your brother Straton?" Casey asked, pulling his attention back to the present. "How did he feel about your new friend?"

Nick smiled, remembering. "Straton and Damian fought only once. My brother never bothered me after that." He sharpened his gaze on Casey. "So, you see, Damian is far more to me than just a warrior among warriors. He is my oldest and truest friend, my brother in every way that counts."

She nodded. "I see that, you know. When I look at the two of you. Your magic and his—"

"Damian doesn't have any magic."

Casey gave him a bemused look. "You really don't see it, do you? Maybe it's too much like your own. You look at him, and all you see is you."

"That's not true. Damian is—"

"I don't mean physically. Obviously, he's a separate person. But his magical energy derives from yours—"

Nick nodded.

"—just like certain aspects of your energy come from him."

He scowled at that. "I told you, Case. Damian doesn't have magic."

"No, but he has other qualities. When you created him that day, you didn't only wish for a friend. You wanted a different brother, one who'd defend you against all others, who'd stand by you no matter what. One who had all the traits that your warrior father would have wished for in a son. Your energies are linked, but it's not you feeding Damian. It's Damian feeding you. That's why you're stronger when he's around, more intent on confronting your enemies. You're like the cowardly lion, Nicky, and Damian's your courage."

"Let's not get carried away. I'm not skipping down that road. It's not like I've been hiding in my bedroom all these centuries."

"And yet . . . Damian's curse is lifted and suddenly you're taking the fight to Sotiris. Coincidence?"

"I'm a fucking sorcerer. I don't believe in coincidence. Not around me, anyway."

"Exactly. Damian makes you stronger, and I think you know it."

"Maybe I'm just more willing to take risks with someone I trust at my back. Maybe it's the synergy of men at war."

She shrugged. "Maybe," she said, in a tone that said she didn't believe it for one minute.

"Smartass. Sometimes I think I should have left you sitting in that FBI classroom."

She grinned. "You'd have missed me," she said, and then sobered almost immediately. "What about the other warriors? You said they were different from Damian?"

He nodded. "As I grew, so did my magic. And my list of enemies. I quickly understood that I'd need men I could trust to stand with me. So I called them the same way I had Damian, albeit with greater finesse and intent. From the four corners, I drew them. Damian, I considered to be from the East, as that was where my father's territory lay. And then there was Dragan Fiachna, a son of kings, from the West; Urban Halldor from the cold North; and Kato Amadi from the hot sands of the South. They were mine, body and soul, called by my magic, bound by my blood."

His smile faded. "But when it mattered, when it was *my* turn to protect *them*, I failed utterly."

CASEY RESTED HER hand on Nick's forearm where it lay on the table between them. It felt odd to be the one comforting him, instead of the other way around. "We'll get them back," she told him confidently. "You have Damian already, and you know how magic works. Damian is the beginning, the unraveling of Sotiris's spell. The others will follow."

"You may be right." He didn't say anything for a moment, and then asked, "Does he hate me?"

Casey frowned, but then her eyes widened in understanding. "Damian? Hell, no. That's all he's talked about . . . getting back to you and finding the others."

"Not the only thing," he said shrewdly. And just like that, they were back on their usual footing, with Nick seeing far more than she wanted him to. "What are you two up to?"

She couldn't stop the blush that heated her face. "He saved me the other night. I'd never have gotten out of there alive without him. There was a hell of a lot more resistance than I expected."

Nick grinned. "He *is* good in a fight, isn't he? A thing of beauty to watch."

Casey lowered her head to conceal her reaction. "Yeah, well, I was too busy staying alive to admire his dance moves."

He grinned again, and she had the feeling he was seeing right through her. His next words confirmed it. "Don't be too charmed by him. Damian is a love 'em and leave 'em kind of guy. So much that it formed the root of his curse. Why do you think it took your blood, a *woman's* blood, to free him? Sotiris assumed it would never happen. He intended that curse to last an eternity, and not only for Damian. The others were similarly crafted."

Casey nodded, desperate to change the subject. "So while the others were already alive when they came to you," she said, forcing their conversation back to a path she was comfortable with, "Damian was different. Did he even exist before you conjured him?"

"Casey, I don't—"

"I know it happened a long time ago, and it's difficult for you to remember, but . . . I mean this explains so much—"

"What does it explain, Cassandra?" Damian's flat voice broke into her spinning thoughts.

She twisted on her seat and saw him standing there, his expression bleak. Eyes that were usually so full of energy, so in love with life, were steeped in misery as he stared at her. She played back the last few words she'd said to Nick, and she nearly panicked.

"Damian," she said, wanting to make him understand. But he strode off without a word, disappearing into the dark beneath the trees beyond the pool.

"Damn it," she swore softly and started after him.

"Casey," Nick said, stopping her. She paused long enough to look at him over her shoulder. "You hit a nerve, babe. If you care about him . . . you'll have to work for this one, but he's worth it."

She wanted to stop the flow of words from Nick's mouth, to tell him that he had the wrong idea. Yes, she cared about Damian and didn't want him hurt, but it wasn't the way Nick seemed to think. She wasn't in love with him or anything, she just. . . . She just what? All she knew was that she didn't have time to consider it all now. She had to find Damian and make him understand.

Without another word to Nick, she spun around and headed past the glow of the underwater lights, and into the shadows.

"I'll just wait here," Nick called from behind her, but she ignored him.

DAMIAN KNEW Cassandra was following him. He'd known even before he left her sitting in the kitchen with Nico that she'd come after him. She was practical, logical, but she wasn't cruel. She'd be feeling remorse for her cold assessment of who he was, of *what* he was. Hell, sometimes he didn't know what he was either, but for Cassandra to wonder. . . . She mattered more somehow. What she thought of *him* mattered more.

He stood in the darkness and watched her come to him, stepping carefully over roots and around rocks. She didn't have his night sight, and she hadn't bothered with any sort of light for herself. He sighed and stepped into the open where she could see him.

"Damian." His name was a relieved breath between her lips. She stretched out a hand when she came close enough and he took it, bracing her until she was right in front of him. He would have let go of her once she had her feet safely under her, but her fingers tightened, refusing to release him.

"You need to listen to me," she said urgently. "It wasn't what you—"

"Wasn't what, Cassandra? You telling Nico that I wasn't real? That I'm a figment of his magical thoughts and could disappear on a whim?"

She stared at him. "Are you insane?" she demanded. "Of course, you're real. That's not what I was saying at all!"

"I heard you, Cassandra. You said Nico's tale explained everything, that it explained—"

"That it explained what I see when I look at you, at the *two* of you together. What my magical senses *feel,* you ass. It has nothing to do with you being real and everything to do with the magic inside you. The magic that turns you into that big warrior god you're so damn proud of."

He studied her in the dark. He could see her far better than she could see him. And she was telling the truth. There was no artifice in her manner, no lie in her earnest expression. "You heard what Nico said, about the women I bedded."

"You're not winning any points here, bud."

"That's not what I'm trying—" His lips tightened in exasperation. "All of those women, Cassandra, and not one of them ever produced a child that was mine."

"So? Nick said his father had a spell to prevent—"

"But *I* didn't," he corrected her. "In my day, a warrior was judged on the battlefield, to be sure. But also on the strength of his sons."

"And daughters," she added automatically.

"There were daughters, of course," he agreed almost dismissively. "But sons were far more important." He shrugged when she scowled at him. "It was a different era. Hell, it might even have been a different world than this one. But none of that matters, because I didn't produce a son *or* a daughter."

"And you think. . . you thought *then* that it was because you weren't real."

A frown line deepened above his nose, but he nodded. "And I wasn't the only one who noticed. No one dared say anything to my face—not even Straton, Nico's bully of a brother—but it was whispered about behind my back."

"What about the women who lined up to fuck you?" she asked, reaching down to stroke his cock through the denim. "Did they complain that you weren't real? That this"—she pressed hard against his straining erection—"wasn't real?"

"No," he admitted.

"Consider this, then," she said patiently. "Did Nick have any children?"

He frowned, as if he'd never considered that before. "No. But no one expected—"

"No," she interrupted. "Probably because, like his father, he cast a spell to prevent such a thing from happening. And since the two of you are linked—"

"You think his spell affected me."

She lifted one shoulder in a shrug. "It makes sense."

He was quiet for a long moment, and then he asked, "What do you see when you look at me?"

"Magic-wise, you mean," she said with a small smile. "This isn't just you fishing for compliments, right?"

He gave in to his instincts and tugged her closer. He knew she didn't need protecting, but he couldn't help wanting to do it. There were beasts in the woods around here. Animals that would be drawn to the presence of two humans where they shouldn't be. Besides, he simply felt better when she was close.

"Magic-wise," he agreed. "What do you see?"

"The first time I saw you in that alley behind the Kalman, I sensed magic inside you. I'm not strong when it comes to personal magic—I'm better with things than with people—but with you. . . . I knew you weren't a sorcerer. It wasn't like that. But you resonated almost the same way. At first, I thought you were just a lesser magic-user—"

He snorted his opinion of that.

"I know," she said, patting his chest soothingly. "You couldn't possibly be a lesser anything." She rolled her eyes, which made him grin. "But don't worry, I dismissed that theory almost right away. It just didn't *feel* right. But then you told me about the statue, and the curse, and so I figured it was just a leftover residue from that, and it would fade. But it didn't do that either."

Damian frowned. "What am I, then?"

"Besides a person, you mean," she admonished, and didn't continue until he'd nodded his agreement. "I didn't fully understand until tonight, when I saw you standing there with Nick. For the first time since I've known him, he wasn't bothering to cover up what he is. He blazes so brightly, Damian. I wish you could see—"

"But I do. I mean, I probably don't see what you do, but Nico shines like the sun itself."

"Exactly. But that's my point. So do you. When the two of you were together earlier, you looked like two pieces of the same sun, each separate and strong, and yet far more powerful together. When it comes to you guys, the whole is way more than the sum of its parts. But here's the thing—*he* benefits more than you do. He's like this parasite, feeding—"

"My brother is not a fucking parasite, Cassandra."

"No, no, of course not. Bad choice of words on my part. But it's not quite symbiotic either, because once you're together, the energy only flows one way. From you, to him."

Damian considered that. "All right, I get your point. He's stronger with me back in the world, which explains why Sotiris wants me dead. He'd rather curse me back into the literal Stone Age, but if he can't do that, he'll settle for killing me outright."

She nodded. "I think our little vacation's over. We need to get back into the hunt." She started to turn, to head for the house, but Damian pulled her against his chest, sliding his hand around to rest on her hip, his fingers splayed just above the curve of her ass.

"One more thing, Cassandra," he murmured. She looked up at him with a question in her eyes, and he kissed her, soft and slow, nibbling on her plump lower lip, sliding his tongue between her teeth when she gasped with surprise, sucking her tongue into his mouth until her gasp became a moan. Her arms were around his waist, her body flush against his, her nipples taut peaks through the soft fabric of his T-shirt, and his cock grew heavy where it was trapped behind the zipper of his jeans.

"What was that for?" she asked, her voice raspy with desire as she rubbed herself against the thick bulge of his erection, making it even thicker, while her fingers dug into his back.

"A promise for later," he said, and then admitted the truth. "And a reminder of what's real."

"Damian," she whispered unhappily, but he stopped her with another kiss.

"I know, sweetheart. Let's get back to Nico."

She nodded, but stretched up on her toes for one final kiss before they threaded their way back through the trees to the bright beacon of the pool, and the house where Nick waited for them.

"I'LL SEND YOU whatever information I have," Nico told Damian as they walked back to his car. You won't catch Sotiris, not this time. And I'm not sure I want you to, anyway. He's far too dangerous. But make no mistake, these are his agents at work, and the Talisman must be recovered. Its potential for death and destruction in this era is devastating."

"Do you think he wants the device for himself?"

Nico shook his head. "Sotiris doesn't collect things, not the way I do. If he wants the Talisman, he has a purpose for it. But it could just be money that he's after. Whatever he's planning might simply be a demonstration of the device's destructive power, either for potential buyers, or to further a blackmail scheme of some kind. One thing is certain—Sotiris won't care how many people he kills to accomplish his goals." He shook his head. "I've asked my assistant, Lili, to send Casey the latest satellite images of the house where your sniper went to ground. That should help. And you'll keep me informed on the rest."

"Of course."

"And you'll take care of Casey?"

"I'll try, but I think she sees it the other way around," he said disgustedly. "She's taking care of *me*."

"She likes to be in control, and I told you, she doesn't trust easily. If you knew her father and husband, you'd understand."

"She has a husband?"

"Ex-husband."

Damian frowned. "Ex?"

"Former, no longer married, they're divorced."

"Ah, divorce. I understand."

"He's a real bastard, but that's not my story to tell." Then Nico grinned. "It is so good to have you back, brother. When this is over, you'll come stay with me in Florida, and we'll use it as a base while we locate the others."

"I look forward to it. But now I have to get back to the house, lest Cassandra think I've wandered off and been kidnapped."

The two men embraced again, and then Nico dropped down into the seat of a sleek, red machine of a car. He pushed the ignition and the car's powerful engine purred to life. Maybe Nico would let him drive it once they reached Florida. The gods knew Cassandra was never going to let him drive anything, he thought sourly.

The house was quiet when he closed and locked the door, then armed the security system. He'd had Nico give him the codes and demonstrate the device. With Sotiris doubly on their trail now—not only to stop them from stealing the Talisman, but to weaken Nico by killing Damian—he wanted to utilize every advantage this new age had to offer.

Cassandra was already asleep when he stripped off his jeans and T-shirt, the white bandage on her arm a gleaming reminder to him of how vulnerable she was. She didn't have his ability to heal quickly, and despite the power of her determination or her magical gift, her body was as fragile as any other human's. It terrified him to think about sending her into battle against an enemy as dangerous and utterly ruthless as Sotiris. But it wasn't up to him to send her or not. That decision lay firmly with Cassandra herself. All he could do was protect her as best he could. Including from herself.

She murmured wordlessly when he slid into bed behind her, wrapping her in his arms and pulling her into the shelter of his body. She stroked her hands over his forearms and smiled in her sleep, before the gentle rhythm of her breathing returned.

He lay awake, surrounded by the sweet fragrance of her hair. The much fainter scent of their lovemaking from earlier lingered in the room, and that made him smile. For the first time since he'd been freed from his stone prison, he thought he could sleep restfully. Seeing Nico, feeling the embrace of his brother again . . . it brought everything into stark relief at last. This world hadn't seemed quite real to him before tonight. But now it did. Now he stood where he belonged, with his leader and brother, Nicodemus. And with Cassandra, whether she liked it or not.

Chapter Seven

CASEY WAS ALONE when she woke the next morning. She sat up, wondering where Damian had gotten to, when splashing sounds from the pool drew her to the balcony window. He was swimming laps, powering back and forth with graceful strokes that barely rippled the water. But as she watched, she found herself frowning. Not at the picture he made—that was pretty enough—but at the realization that her first thought upon waking had been not of her mission to recover a dangerous artifact, but of Damian. She'd missed him. She couldn't remember the last time that had happened.

Actually, no, she *could* remember. It had been the first morning she'd woken up and realized that her dick of a husband wasn't where he should have been. The first time she'd been forced to acknowledge that coming home to their bed, to *her,* wasn't his top priority anymore . . . if it ever had been. It still made her flush with humiliation to remember how many times she'd let that happen before she'd finally walked out the door.

Ever since then, she'd carefully avoided emotional attachment, never giving anyone the power to tear her apart the way her ex had. Until Damian. He'd somehow slipped through her defenses and become important enough for her to *miss* him. She hadn't planned this, and she didn't want it.

She turned away from the window and stepped into the shower, her thoughts tumbling over one another as she stood beneath the pounding heat. There was no question that she would go after the Talisman. She'd known that from the moment she'd discovered it missing. But she'd lost track of that goal, gone off course somehow. Or not *somehow.* There was no question as to how she'd gotten off course. It was Damian. Getting involved with his situation, letting herself be seduced by him . . . it had made it easy to forget her purpose. Just like this house, with its elegant furnishings and expensive wines, had made her forget what she was—a hunter. She turned off the water, and stepped out of the shower. Even the oversized fluffy towel, on a rack that was as warm as the floor, was a distraction. It made her forget why she was here. Why *Damian* was here.

And it sure as hell wasn't so that the two of them could play beautiful house together. She'd let him get too close, become too important. Or maybe he'd just snuck in under the radar before she'd realized he was there. But whatever it was, it had to stop.

Evil existed, and it had a plan for the Talisman. *That* was why she was here. Her responsibility, her *purpose*, was to disrupt that plan by stealing the Talisman back and shutting it down.

Damian had pulled on some sweats, and was sitting at his laptop working away when she got downstairs. He was worse than she was now, the computer permanently attached to his fingertips. She walked over and stroked her fingers over the back of his neck, before realizing what she'd done. Yanking her hand back, she had to fight the urge to lean down and kiss him, which told her just how deeply he'd managed to infiltrate her heart, and how stupid she'd been to let him.

"I saw you swimming," she commented, putting physical distance between them, keeping her voice casual. She helped herself to the coffee he'd started. "Did you always do that for exercise? You know, before?"

He smiled without looking up from his computer screen. "*Before,* we didn't need to exercise. Life did it for us. But, no, I'd never actually swum before this morning."

She paused mid-sip and looked over at him. "But I saw you. You were doing laps."

"It's an intuitive response to water. The body doesn't want to drown, so I learned."

She gave the back of his head a narrow-eyed stare, trying to figure out if he was pulling her leg. But, no, she decided. He really *had* taught himself to swim in one morning. Or maybe with him, it was more that he'd simply let his body do what it did naturally. "Please tell me you'll at least need to work at maintaining that body now that the daily hardships of life won't be doing it for you anymore."

He looked up with a grin. "You like the body?"

Shit. Why had she said that? She blew out an intentionally dismissive breath. "Yeah, right. Like you need any more ego-stroking. Listen, this morning, Nick's assistant emailed some satellite images of the house where Sotiris's agents have gone to ground. They're less than twenty-four hours old, which means they're accurate. By tonight, I'll have blueprints or some other floor plan of the house itself."

He grunted. So charming. What the hell was he doing on that computer anyway? If he'd discovered fantasy football or some other shit, she was going to crack that damn thing over his head.

"Look," she said matter-of-factly. "I know what Nick said about us working together, but I've been thinking, and getting the Talisman back is my responsibility, not yours. So, if you'd rather start looking for your warrior brothers, I'd understand. I've been working alone for years, so I'm used to it."

"Maybe that's your problem," he said absently. "You've spent so much time alone, you've forgotten how to do anything else. You need to learn the value of depending on others." Then he spun his laptop around to show her what he'd found.

Casey stared. "Is that—?"

"Yes."

She pulled the computer closer and manipulated the image, verifying that it was what he claimed. He'd done her research for her. She'd figured on several hours today digging out information on the house where Sotiris's agents had taken refuge, maybe unearthing the original construction blueprints if the local county office had a record of the architect, or better yet, if they scanned the docs for their own files. Public databases were the easiest to sneak into, since they were designed to allow ready access.

But Damian had taken a much simpler route. Her preliminary search had already told her that ownership of the property had been transferred roughly six months ago in a private sale. But the house had apparently been listed and sold two years before that by a local Realtor, who still had the information available on his website. There were pictures of the interior and exterior, as well as a basic schematic of the layout.

"This is great, but how the hell did—"

"You admire the body, but you underestimate the intellect, Cassandra. I believe I'm insulted," he added, with a satisfied smile that told her he wasn't insulted at all. Damian didn't need her approval. He knew exactly what his worth was, in *every* arena.

"It's not a matter of underestimating your intellect," she protested. "Anyone in your position would take a while to catch up to this world. Why should I expect you to be any different?"

"Because I *am* different. You heard Nico. I was created to be the perfect warrior, which doesn't mean following someone else's orders. It means leading. And *that* means that strategy, tactics, and weapons are all second nature to me. And in this reality, it includes your Internet. And swimming. Therefore, darling, I learn."

"Lucky you," she muttered, stifling the irritating little thrill she got whenever he called her *darling*. "But, what about Nick?" she asked, mostly just curious. "You didn't lead when he was around. You followed. You still do."

He shook his head as if pitying her for not understanding. "Nicodemus was our leader, but we four fought *with* him, not behind him. No blade could touch him as long as we stood by his side. Why do you think Sotiris wanted us gone? Because there was no other way to kill Nico."

"But he didn't. Kill Nick, I mean. You four were gone, but Nick still survived."

"Nico's was always the superior mind, his power unmatched. It drove Sotiris mad with envy."

"Well, he sure as shit is crazy mad now. Which is why I have to get the Talisman back." She leaned over just enough to reach the computer keyboard, careful not to brush against him. "Thanks for doing all of this. If it's okay with you, I'll just email them to myself—"

"I already did that," he said, sounding almost bored.

"Okay, well thanks," she said awkwardly, standing back up.

He gave her a curious look, but then said, "I'm assuming the present owners will have upgraded whatever electronic security was built into the house, but I've identified all of the structural defenses. There are almost certainly arcane defenses as well, and since I'm assuming you'll want to come along, your talent will be useful to reveal, and hopefully disarm, those. I still want you out of the action, however, so once we're in, you'll remain in the rear."

Casey didn't answer. She *couldn't* answer. She was too busy staring at him. "Excuse me?" she said finally.

He sighed. "Don't be difficult, Cassandra. I'm far better equipped to conduct an assault of this nature. I've fought any number of magically skilled enemies on my own. I understand your desire to be involved, and I *can* use your help with the arcane defenses, but you must accept that I'm in charge and commit to maintaining your assigned position. If I can't trust you to fulfill your part of the plan—"

Casey finally opened her mouth to tell him where he could shove his *plan*, but he talked right over whatever she would have said.

"—and if you cannot trust *me* sufficiently to do what needs to be done, then we should not attempt this together. I will recover the Talisman alone, and bring it back here. You can then deal with—"

"What makes you think you're the only one who can get it back?" she finally interjected, pissed as hell that he'd all but hijacked her mission. "This isn't my first rodeo, you know. I'm perfectly capable of—"

"And you might succeed . . . *this* time—"

She sucked in a breath. Oh, he did *not* just throw that in her face. It wasn't her fault she'd lost the damn Talisman the first time she'd grabbed it. The intelligence had been woefully inadequate. She'd been facing hellhounds, for God's sake.

"—but it's just not in my nature to permit you to endanger yourself when I can accomplish the task alone."

"Not in your nature?" she growled. "Fuck your nature. This is *my* assignment, not yours. If *I* decide to let *you* help *me*—"

"Cassandra, be reasonable."

"Is that warrior code for 'stop being such a *woman*?' Because that's bullshit. Let's not forget who got whom off that damn rooftop, bucko." She regretted the words as soon as she said them, even though they had the desired effect. She'd wanted him angry, wanted a reason to let her own anger rise to the surface, to push him away, to get him out of her heart where he didn't belong. *Couldn't* belong.

And it worked. Damian showed real temper for the first time since she'd met him, tightly leashed, but obvious in the clench of his jaw, in the way he so carefully set the computer down and walked over to stand in front of her. "I have been pledged to the fight against Sotiris since I was a beardless boy, *millennia* before you were even born. I am a warrior, honed and shaped over decades of battle, and far more capable than you of accomplishing this task." He leaned closer, staring directly into her eyes. "And as for who did what on that rooftop, I saved your life that night, Cassandra. Let's not forget that either."

"This is *my* mission," she argued, her teeth clenched.

"Oh, no, darling," he said sweetly. "This is *my* mission, given to me by Nicodemus himself, the only man, only *person,* whose wishes matter. I could leave here right now, and have the damn Talisman back by noon, without any of your interference," he said, finishing with a snarl.

She blinked, reeling inwardly at the slap of his words, reminding herself that this was what she'd wanted. She stared up at him, and felt her own temper rising to meet his. She didn't usually permit herself to get angry. She preferred to remain in control of her emotions, just like the good little soldier she'd been raised to be. The fact that she now found herself getting more furious than she could ever remember being only confirmed in her thoughts what she already knew. She never should have fucked him. All those orgasms had freed up destructive emotions that she normally kept tightly leashed. Not to mention that having sex had blurred the lines of exactly who was in charge between them. She couldn't quite convince herself that it had all been a mistake, but it sure felt like one now.

His gaze was cool as he returned her stare, but there was something more than anger in his expression. She'd hurt him with her sharp words about the curse being broken. She'd taken what was undeniably the most horrific thing that had ever happened to him, and thrown it in his face. And knowing that, she realized it hurt *her* to know that she'd caused him pain. God, she was an asshole.

"I'm sorry," she said with real contrition. "What I said about the curse . . . that was cruel. You deserve better."

He nodded, but his gaze remained flat. He was giving her nothing back, no emotion of any kind. Panic froze suddenly in her chest. She could lose him over this. He really would walk out the door, and she'd never see him again. Oh, sure, maybe their paths would cross at Nick's house on one of the rare occasions they were both there. But that would be it. And wasn't that precisely what she'd wanted when she'd woken up this morning? When she'd been convinced that whatever this was between them had gone too far? She'd been certain that she needed to get out now, with no messy emotions, no aching heart, no roiling gut at the very thought of losing him. So why was she now suffering exactly that?

Her eyes were burning, but she refused to cry. Not just because it would prove his point, but because she wouldn't use tears as a weapon. She hated women who did that.

"Damian," she said, raising a hand to place it on his chest, but then closing it into a fist against her own chest instead. She didn't know what to say, how to make this better without making it so much worse. So she just swallowed and said, "Do you really think that the two of us working together has the greatest chance of success?"

He nodded curtly. "Yes."

It took willpower on her part, but she put away the guilt and the hurt, and all of those other unwanted emotions tumbling inside her, making her want to throw up. She boarded them up behind a lifetime of discipline. "Okay, we'll do it your way. But I'm not a novice at this, you know. I have skills. If you can't accept that, then—"

"I never doubted your abilities. The question is . . . can we trust each other?"

She stared at him for what seemed like a long time. Did she trust him? Trust didn't come easily to her, not even in a situation like this. He was right about her. She didn't trust other people to come through, to be there for her. It was why she preferred to work alone. Hell, to *live* alone. But he'd gone and shattered that, whether he knew it or not.

Today's mission demanded more from her than old insecurities. They were about to break into a house full of bad guys who'd have magical protection, to steal an artifact that those same bad guys would kill to protect, and then break back out with the artifact and with everyone—at least the good guys—unharmed.

And then there was Damian. He'd had every opportunity to walk away before this. Hell, she was surprised he hadn't taken off already. But he was still here. Not because of the adventure, or because it made him look good. And certainly not because of any affection for *her,* not after this morning. He was staying out of duty. Because he'd sworn an oath to Nick, and neither time nor distance could make him walk away from that.

"I trust you," she said finally.

He nodded. "Then, when we go in there tonight, you will do as I say. I won't order you around for no reason, but if I tell you to do something, you must do it, Cassandra. Both our lives will depend on it."

"Okay," she said slowly. "Is there something you're not telling me? Are you like prescient or something?"

"No," he said soberly. "Only experienced. We should study these plans together, but first I need to go out briefly. You said there was a military store nearby, where you acquired these boots."

"Army surplus, right. It's back near the airport, but we have time. What do you need?"

"Communication devices. You and I are likely to be separated tonight."

"Oh!" she said brightly. "I have those in my truck. Bluetooth. The latest, greatest model. They were on sale online at—Uh, yeah, never mind. Anyway, I have them. Anything else?"

"Ammunition."

"Also in my truck, though I'm not sure how much I have for the MP 5. We should check that."

He nodded again. "We can do that now. I'll just—"

"Wait. I need breakfast. It's the most important meal of the day."

He frowned at her, clearly not catching the contemporary reference, and not caring enough to ask. She already missed the old Damian. The one who'd joked and teased. The one she'd driven away.

"Never mind," she said. "It's unimportant. But I do need to eat. Aren't you hungry?"

His eyes flashed up to meet hers, and for a single second, she thought she saw passion in their depths, a little bit of the warmth that had been there before she'd been such an idiot. But then it was gone, and the new, cool Damian was back. "I am hungry," he agreed. "Shall I—"

"No, no," she said immediately. "I've got this. But maybe you can print out those floor plans and photos for us to work with later, while I cook. There's an office upstairs with a printer. Breakfast should be ready in half an hour."

He gave a brisk nod and closed the laptop as he stood. Casey couldn't help watching as he rose to his full height. He was such a beautiful man. She flashed back to the previous night when he'd been stretched out above her, all that heat surrounding her, his hips spreading her thighs, pounding . . . She swallowed a sob of grief and turned away, walking over to the refrigerator and pulling the door open, letting the cool air soothe her overheated skin.

She was counting eggs, listening to his departing footsteps, when a sudden thought intruded.

"Hey!" she called, just before he left the kitchen. "What about you?"

"Me?" he asked, confused.

"Well, me, actually. Do you trust *me* now?"

He regarded her in silence for long enough that she worried what he was going to say, but then he gave her a solemn nod. "I never stopped, Cassandra." And he left the room.

She stared after him. "Damn Casey," she muttered. "You really fucked that one up." And then she turned to do the one thing she still knew she was good at . . . scrambling some eggs.

NOT KNOWING WHAT level of sorcery they might encounter, they erred on the side of caution and left her Yukon a mile away. There hadn't been much in the way of physical security visible on the satellite images Nick had sent them, which was both good news and bad. The good part was obvious—no razor-wire-topped walls to scale, no guards to avoid. But their very absence was bad. It meant Sotiris's people were depending on arcane defenses, and those were much trickier. Casey's talent should detect the wards before they were triggered, but knowing they were there and defeating them were two different things. It would take time for her to analyze their structure and shut them down. Assuming she could. She wasn't a sorcerer. Whatever security they couldn't defeat, they would avoid. Her talent would definitely enable them to do that much.

Their assault plan involved the two of them splitting up, which would leave Damian vulnerable to whatever magical defenses he encountered. Casey seemed way more worried about that possibility than he did, and she didn't know how much was alpha male bravado and how much simple experience in dealing with sorcerers. She might have asked him, but while they'd agreed to work together, they were still tiptoeing around each other. Or rather, she was tiptoeing around *him*. He didn't seem to give a damn one way or the other. Her feelings might have been hurt if she hadn't been the one responsible for his change in attitude.

They paused when the house came in sight, both drawing up at the same time without the need to say anything. Casey scanned the property in the physical realm first, noting the few dim lights burning on the first floor, and the complete absence of exterior lights. That might have seemed like a good thing, but there was a huge expanse of lawn with a gravel driveway cutting through it. Walking up the driveway was out of the question when every step would announce their presence. But it was a dark night, with the moon a bare sliver of light behind unexpectedly heavy clouds. Damian wouldn't have a problem, but she'd have to be careful crossing the lawn or end up with a twisted ankle. How ignominious would that be? All of her bragging about skills, only to be taken down by a gopher hole in the grass.

She glanced up at the clouds and hoped they didn't mean rain, or worse. This time of year, the weather could go either way. Maybe she should have included a weather map among all of the research they'd done on this damn house.

"Comm check," she murmured and tapped the nearly invisible bud in her right ear.

"Check," Damian responded quietly, and she heard the corresponding electronic click from his device. But her thoughts were already several steps ahead in their plan, as she stared intently at the house.

"Cassandra," he said, as if pulling her back to the here and now. "Are you ready?"

His shoulder was warm where it touched hers. They were crouching side by side beneath the trees across from the house. That brush of heat *bothered* her, and she wanted to move away. She couldn't afford any distractions tonight, especially not ones that made her want things she couldn't have.

"Ready," she said, shoving everything else aside and keeping her eye on their target. "We'll rendezvous in the library."

When he didn't respond, she turned and caught the clench of his jaw before he said, "Be safe." Then, without a glance, he was gone, moving so swiftly that if she hadn't been looking for him, she'd have dismissed his passage as nothing more than the moonlight playing with shadows.

She tried to catch sight of him anyway, staring until her eyes burned before giving up. That was a handy talent to have. She wondered if it was some spell, or if he was just that much superior physically. She sighed. Whatever it was, she didn't have it.

They'd agreed that Damian would enter through the kitchen in the back of the house, while she'd aim for the sun porch that stuck out from the front on the left. She was hoping for a door, but she could break a window just as easily. Damian might not appreciate it, but she really did have skills other than her ability to sense magic. Most of her recoveries involved quiet thievery, not running gun battles. What had happened the other night was unique, to say the least. More often, she slipped in and out with no one the wiser. Damian might be able to move like a shadow, but she was a damn fine cat burglar.

She waited until the clouds shifted enough to cast a bit of moonlight on the front lawn, and then she took off, running low to the ground, her steps landing lightly until she was certain of her footing and then moving to the next. In only a few minutes, she was crouched next to the sun porch.

Dead shrubs surrounded by the detritus of a long winter huddled next to the solid half of the wall, while the windowed uppers were mostly bare, with one or two covered by crooked blinds. Overall, the sun porch had a vacant feeling, as if it hadn't been used in years rather than months. Creeping over to the door, she was surprised to find nothing but a rather flimsy lock. It was suspicious enough that she took a few minutes to scan for magical defenses and found none. The lock barely challenged her lock-picking skills, but once she was in, the reason for the crappy security became apparent. The only thing getting through that door got her was access to the porch itself. The lock on the door from the sun porch into the house proper was first class.

She knelt before that door, too, a little rush from the challenge making her hands tingle. Shaking her hands out, she went to work and wanted to crow with pride when the complex deadbolt gave way to her skills in just a few minutes. She found herself wishing Damian had been there in that moment, so he could appreciate her talent. She shut that thought down cold. She didn't need pats on the back from him or anyone else. She knew her own worth, and that was all that mattered.

Taking another minute to scan for magical influence, she opened the door slowly, expecting lights and shouting at any moment. But once she stepped fully into the house, the reason for the lack of a security response became obvious. The Talisman wasn't here.

"Damn it," she whispered. She needed to let Damian know she was in, but should she tell him about the missing Talisman? This was the problem with working with a partner. They probably should have agreed on stuff like this ahead of time. How much talking was usual for an operation like this one? She decided to wait until he confirmed his own entry, just in case. She didn't want to overload him with information at the wrong time.

She touched her ear bud. "I'm in," she said simply, and then proceeded the way she would have if she'd been alone. The Talisman was gone, but that didn't mean there wasn't anything worthwhile to be found here. If the house was a regular hideout for Sotiris or his people, there could be other artifacts concealed within, or valuable information left behind. This was still their best lead on the Talisman, and she worked in the same way she'd always conducted her hunts. Step by step. Anything she found here would tell her where they'd gone, and the information would be more than what she had now.

She came to her feet slowly, aware of every small movement around her, every shift of her clothing and backpack. Despite the absence of the Talisman, her magical senses were blaring a nearly constant warning, making her want to jump out of her skin. On top of that, she felt a persistent feeling of unease that spoke to the level of malevolence left over from whatever magic had been used here. This house fairly reeked of it. No question now. She needed to warn Damian.

A quick scan told her she was in a sitting room of some sort. It had one door to the sun porch, which she'd come through, and another door on the opposite wall, leading into the rest of the house. Antique-looking chairs and a sofa were gathered around a cold fireplace, and the coffee table in front of them was adorned with curlicues and elaborate carvings. Very expensive, she was sure, but not to her taste. Rather than huddle in the doorway, she slid farther into the room, sticking to the edges where the shadows were deepest. She hadn't heard even a whisper to indicate there was anyone in the house except her and Damian, but the stink of evil was too strong to be nothing more than an echo of old magic. There was an active malevolence in this house, but whether it was from a person or an artifact, she didn't know.

She paused before entering the main part of the house and listened with all her senses. When nothing came back at her, she put her hand on the wooden panel first, and then the knob. Still nothing. With a light twist, the knob turned and the door opened. She paused again and heard nothing, not even Damian, which didn't surprise her all that much. He moved like a ghost.

Reaching up, she clicked her ear bud and waited for a response. When none came, she clicked again. She didn't use these things often. Maybe they sometimes malfunctioned. She tried a third time, and when there was still no response, her perception of danger soared. There was no way Damian wouldn't have responded if he could have, even if it was nothing but a return click.

Stepping back into the sitting room, she leaned against the wall and closed her eyes, letting her magical senses tell her where to go. It was a big house, but mostly empty. If they'd really wanted to confuse her, they should have filled it with people. Human life force was so loud and distracting, it took effort to weed it out. But this house was a tomb. Big and echoing and deserted, except for that cold touch of very bad magic. It was everywhere, but spread thin. She'd never encountered an arcane security field that covered an entire house the way an electronic system would, but knew instinctively that this was what she was feeling. There was no other explanation, because the magic was too thin to be doing anything active.

Still, that wasn't what she was looking for. Pulling in her senses, she filtered out the weaker signatures and looked for hot spots. She and Damian had decided to meet at the library, only because it was central to the house. For all they knew, the room wasn't even used for books anymore; it was just a name on a floor plan. But in this eerily empty house, she was abruptly struck with the urge to find him as soon as possible. Picturing the floor plan in her head, she looked around, trying to figure out where the library was located relative to her current position. Damian might not be there yet, but like her, he'd be headed in that direction.

She started walking, moving quickly and quietly from room to room, all vacant, until suddenly, with no warning, magic flared so cold and bright in her mind's eye that she was temporarily blinded and had to cling to the heavy armoire that she'd practically run into. Fingers pressed against the hard wood, she kept her eyes closed, trying to minimize the sensory input while she reasoned out what must have happened. The library, or a room very close to it, had some heavy-duty shielding. Enough to block her senses, which was saying something, because she was *strong*. The existence of shielding wasn't the alarming part, though. No, it was the sheer, overwhelming force of magic that had suddenly blared from within the room, as if a door had opened. It wasn't the Talisman. She knew that for a fact. But it was something big.

She blinked in sudden awareness, as her human brain caught up with her arcane abilities. The Talisman wasn't in there ... but Damian was. Alarm brought a spike of fear, and she forced herself to keep going, despite all of the warnings flashing in her mind and her instincts screaming at her to run the other direction. She moved at a deliberate pace, continuously scanning for traps while keeping her mind's eye on that bright spot of magic growing closer with every step. The possibility hadn't escaped her notice that this could very well be a trap itself. Someone had opened that door on purpose. The shields on the room were such that if they'd left the door closed, she'd have continued to detect the general malevolence of the house, but never would have known about the hidden trove of magic. So why open the door unless they wanted to draw her in?

She drew her weapon as she got closer. Magic was her game, but very few magic users were powerful enough to defend themselves against projectile weapons, and even the few who could might be caught off guard. . . . But she knew that wasn't the case here. Whoever had opened that door was expecting her. The question was why.

Casey peered around a corner and stared down a long hallway. It was dark except for an open door near the middle, where a warm light spilled out and broke the darkness. It was so faint that it made her think of those nightlights parents bought to soothe young children. She'd never had one. The need for such comfort was considered a weakness and wasn't tolerated among her father's offspring. She thrust aside that useless memory and focused on the problem at hand.

That slight incandescent glow was meaningless. It told her the room beyond was mostly dark, but that was equally meaningless. Because what her physical eye was seeing was belied by her mind's eye. That dark room was seething with magic. And "seething" was the right word, because it wasn't only plentiful, it was the source of the malevolence she'd been feeling since entering the house. She didn't think it was just one artifact, but a collection of many in one place. This was most definitely an important stronghold for Sotiris and his agents.

Too bad for them that it would be hers by the end of the night, or at least Nick's.

She continued her cautious progress down the hall, keeping to the wall, weapon trained in front of her. As she drew closer, she was increasingly able to separate out individual signatures from the giant blob of magic that had been her sense of the room up until that point. None of the signatures meant anything to her except. . . . She frowned, then stared at the open door in alarm. Son of a bitch.

Two men sidestepped into the hallway, barely visible in the dim light of the doorway. One of them she didn't know at all, probably the lone agent left behind to guard the house. The other . . . Damian gazed at her calmly, appearing perfectly relaxed despite the 9mm automatic currently digging into his carotid.

"Damian," she said, meeting his eyes, letting none of her fear show. "What the hell, dude?"

A slight smile curved his lips. "I was distracted by all the pretty baubles."

She arched a brow. "Bad form for a god."

His captor scoffed loudly. "He's no god. Just a hyped-up playboy who's pretty useless without his boyfriend."

She studied the other man. He was big. Not as tall as Damian, but broad and tall enough that he could comfortably hold the gun against his prisoner's neck, while still remaining mostly hidden behind his bulk. Despite the man's size, though, it was the *gun* that gave him the advantage. Even if she succeeded in killing him with a single shot, if he somehow managed to pull the trigger first, or if his finger contracted at all and the gun fired, Damian's carotid would be shredded. He'd bleed out in minutes with no way of stopping it. Not even a god could survive that, and he wasn't really even one of those.

"You'd have killed him already if that's what you wanted," she said to the man. "So what *do* you want?"

"To live, of course," the man said mockingly. "Well, and for you to die."

Casey just stared at him, waiting.

"Fine. I was supposed to be gone by now, but I got delayed and then *you* showed up. So now, you're going to drop your weapon, and let me lock you inside that room. And then I'm going to walk out of the building. I don't care what you do after that. You'll try to escape. You might even succeed. I doubt it, but, hey, stranger things have happened, right? I will warn you that Lord Sotiris set the defenses himself, and somehow, I don't think you have anywhere near enough power to break them. Face it, bitch, you're nothing but a glorified Geiger counter."

That was essentially true, so the comparison didn't bother her. Especially not coming from this guy. Besides, while he was no doubt right about Sotiris setting the wards, he didn't seem to know that Nick was around. And while *she* couldn't break the wards, Nick almost certainly could. And when he couldn't reach them, he'd know where to look.

Of course, she had no intention of letting that happen. First, because she'd stab herself in the eye before she agreed to be locked in that room. She didn't know what was in there, but she wanted no part of it. But more importantly, what *wasn't* in there was the Talisman. It was gone, and this asshole was her best, and maybe her only, source of information about where it had been taken and what they planned to do with it.

She considered her options. Appearances aside, she was a fully trained FBI agent, and one of the first lessons she'd learned was never to surrender her weapon. There was nothing about this situation that made her think she or Damian would be well-served if she broke that rule. On the other hand, she couldn't just kill the guy. For all the reasons she'd already considered, she wanted him alive to question.

But on the third hand, nothing and no one mattered when counted against Damian's life. Not even the Talisman. If the asshole and his information had to die to save Damian, then so be it. She'd figure out some other way to track the Talisman. She'd done it before.

"Cassandra," Damian said, drawing her attention, her eyes locking with his. "Shoot him. It doesn't matter where."

"Shut the fuck up," his captor hissed, digging the barrel of the weapon so hard into his neck that it drew blood.

Casey's hands tightened on her weapon, which was still held low in front of her in a two-handed ready stance.

The man seemed to sense the shift in her posture. "I'll kill him," he warned her. "Don't think I won't."

But her attention was all on Damian. "Are you any good with that thing?" he asked.

She scowled at the unexpected question, but jerked her head in a nod. "The best."

"How's your shoulder?"

"Good. Not a problem." Why the fuck was he asking about that *now*?

"Just making conversation," he said as if reading her thoughts. "Do you trust me?"

"Yes. But, Damian, I'd rather keep him alive."

"Hey!" Sotiris's lackey shouted. "I said—"

But Casey was already firing. She shot out his left knee, which was the clearest shot she had from his concealment behind Damian. His howl of pain became a tortured gurgle when Damian moved like lightning, spinning away and turning on his captor, drawing his sword in a single graceful movement that ended with his blade against the man's throat, slicing through just the first layer of skin with incredible precision. A thin line of blood appeared as the scent of urine filled the air.

Casey stared. Her heart was fluttering in her chest, her fingers still locked around the Glock as she lowered it. Some of what she was feeling was adrenaline overload, but some of it, she admitted to herself, was stark terror. And a whole different part of her brain was marveling at the sheer skill Damian's maneuver had taken, not to mention the extraordinary edge on the blade itself.

She jumped when Damian flipped the sword again, this time to bring the pommel down hard on top of the man's head. He fell bonelessly to the floor, and she looked down, inching back quickly from the flow of urine.

Damian stepped between her and the unconscious man, his big hand reaching for her shoulder, but not quite touching her. "Are you okay?"

She managed to nod her head.

"Come on, then. He was right about one thing. We can close the door to this room, and no one will get inside, not until Nico arrives anyway. But before we do that, I'd like to take a look around. There are more than just artifacts in there, there are files and—"

"What if I'd missed?" she asked faintly.

He frowned. "What?"

"What if I'd missed? If I'd shot you instead, or worse, if I missed him and—"

"I had confidence in you."

"Why?" she asked almost plaintively.

He gave her a crooked smile. "You don't brag, Cassandra. If anything, you're too modest. So, if you said you were the best with that gun, then I knew it was true."

She waited until her heart rhythm had slowed, and then, striving for the same casual tone that he was using, she said, "I didn't know you had your sword with you."

"It's always with me. It's who I am. A warrior in the service of Nicodemus."

"I'll remember that next time."

He chuckled lightly. "Let's try not to do this again."

"Deal." She glanced down at their prisoner in distaste. "We need to put him somewhere. We'll check out the room first, so it can be closed up, but then, I think it's worth questioning him. He seemed like a talker to me."

"A talker maybe," Damian agreed with a shrug. "But I'd wager he's low-level. Why else would they leave him behind to clean up?"

"I think you're right. But sometimes guys like him know more than anyone gives them credit for. They're so low-level that they're invisible, and they hear stuff."

"It's worth a try." He walked a few feet down the hall to a closed door, and turned the knob to open it. "We can stash him in—Whoa! You smell that?"

Did she smell it? She was gagging with it. "Jesus," she said, swallowing hard. "What is that? Damian, don't—" But he was already gone, letting the door close behind him. It made the smell tolerable, although nothing was going to get rid of it now that it had been admitted into the hallway. And she couldn't see Damian anymore. There was no way in hell she was going to leave him alone to deal with whatever was making that smell. Or whatever had caused it. Because she knew what it was. There was a body in there, which meant someone had been killed, and the killer could still be in the house.

Cassandra was already moving as all those thoughts filtered through her head, so she was only a few steps behind Damian. She caught the door before it could close, and pushed through into the next room. It took some effort. The door was heavy and insulated, which explained why they hadn't smelled the body before this. When she looked around, she realized they were in a kitchen, which accounted for the tightly sealed door. People who could afford a home like this could also afford to be sure cooking smells didn't permeate the entire house. Damian looked over his shoulder when she walked in.

"You don't have to see this."

She wanted to protest his chauvinism, but she didn't, because she understood where it came from. And because she'd insulted him more than enough for one day. He was trying to protect her, which was generous, but unnecessary.

"I've seen a dead body before. I've actually caused a few."

He snorted softly. She didn't know what that meant. "Who do you think this is?" he asked, toeing the body lightly.

She stared down at the dead man. He'd been gutted, and left to die, which explained the horrific odor. That and the blood pooling all around him. It was a horrible death to contemplate, but she forced herself to think logically, scientifically. "I'm not pathologist, but I'd say this guy hasn't been dead more than an hour or two. Which means monkey boy out there probably knows who he is."

"Monkey boy?" Damian repeated.

"A primitive human being. It's an insult. From a favorite movie of mine."

"When this is over, maybe we can watch it."

She glanced up at him in surprise. "Maybe," she agreed softly.

"Do we need to get rid of the body?"

Casey pursed her lips, thinking. "Eventually, I suppose. What a pain in the ass. But leave him for now, and let's get the prisoner in here. Maybe spending some time with this lovely aroma will loosen his tongue."

"You're a cruel woman, Cassandra," Damian said.

She was surprised when he said that, because it mirrored what she'd been thinking about herself earlier. But he made it sound like a compliment.

"It's practical," she responded quietly. "Not all of us have a magic sword." The heat suddenly came on overhead, and a fresh whiff of decay struck her full in the face. Fighting down a new wave of nausea, she said, "Fuck, that stinks. Let's do what we have to do, and get out of here."

While Damian dragged their bound and unconscious prisoner from the hallway into the kitchen, Casey crossed to the wide-open door of the treasure room and stared, hating the idea of going inside. "Can you sense it, Damian?" she asked, when she heard him return.

He came up behind her, close enough that she could feel the comforting weight of his presence along her back. "I can't," he admitted. "That's not where my talents lie."

"I can," she whispered. "It's so damn cold. You said there's information in there. Files. How many?"

"There's a small desk with a few folders piled on top, but there's also a computer. Not a laptop like mine, but a bigger one with a separate screen. It was still on when I first entered the room, as if someone had recently left. Maybe our prisoner."

She nodded. "We should grab everything in there first, including the computer. We can take it all with us eventually, but for now, let's at least get it out of that room, just in case. There's always a chance the door is on a timer of some sort, and we don't want to risk it closing before we're finished. Besides," she said shuddering, "I don't want to spend any more time in there than I have to."

"I can do it. The room doesn't bother me."

"No, that's okay. We'll do it together; it'll go faster. I'm also going to do a quick inventory and snap a few pictures. Nick will want to know what we see. After that, we can close it up and question our new friend."

His hand rested briefly on her hip before he gave it a reassuring squeeze. "Whenever you're ready."

Her voice deserted her. His touch comforted her and made her sad at the same time. Their intimate familiarity was gone, and it was her fault.

"Let's go," she managed to say, finally. "We need to finish up and get on the road. Weather dot com said there's a freeze coming tonight."

TWO HOURS LATER, Damian was ready to call it quits in what he thought of as the treasure room. It was perhaps a misnomer to call it that— "treasure"—as if the things stored there were something to be cherished. To the average person, most of the artifacts would have minimal value. A few were embellished with jewels, and gold was commonly used. But the real treasure was the magic that had gone into the making of the devices, and what was still stored within them, ready to be used.

As Damian had told Cassandra, his talents didn't include sensing such magic, but one of the artifacts in that room had called to him so strongly that Sotiris's man had managed to sneak up on him and put a gun to his neck. The item would mean nothing to Cassandra, perhaps not even register to her considerably more acute magical senses. But to Damian . . . and to Nico . . . it was a treasure indeed, and so intensely personal that he hadn't even mentioned it to Cassandra. He'd simply concealed it within the spell of his scabbard, and planned to see it safely delivered or die trying.

From the other side of the room came a small noise of distress, and he spun around to find Cassandra lowering herself slowly onto a wooden chair, her face buried in her hands. With every passing moment they'd spent in this cursed room, she'd gotten steadily paler and more distressed. He was still angry at her, still struggling to understand why she'd been so determined to push him away this morning. Hell, he'd been *legendary* for his refusal to commit to one woman, and even *he* was willing to pursue what they had together. What was she so afraid of?

Despite all of that, however, his feelings hadn't changed. He was ready to pick her up bodily and haul her out of this place that was making her so sick. Hell, he wanted her out of the house entirely.

He walked over and crouched at her side, taking her hands in his. They were so cold. "We're done here," he said, and she nodded wearily. "Come on." He helped her up and ushered her out into the relative sanctuary of the hallway. "Here." He dragged a chair from a nearby room. "Sit down, and I'll do the rest." That she didn't protest told him how much being in there had worn on her. She'd only been in the hallway a few minutes, and already her color was returning.

"How do we lock it?" he asked as he carried the computer tower out into the hallway, and set it on a nearby table. At his question, she started to stand, but he waved her down. "Just tell me, Cassandra. I'm sure even I can manage to close a door."

"Don't close it yet," she said, surprising him.

"It's making you sick," he said flatly.

"I'm okay out here. Besides, I have a plan for our prisoner. He knows more than he's telling."

Damian regarded her quizzically. He forgot sometimes that she was more than just an expert in all things magical. She was a fighter, a warrior even. And always thinking two steps ahead to get the job done.

"You want to shove him in there and leave him to die?" he guessed. "I'm good with that."

When she met his curious gaze, there was a gleam in her eye that was positively predatory. "Maybe we'll leave him there afterward," she agreed. "But first we need answers—" She held up a hand when he opened his mouth to protest that she was too exhausted. "I'm okay, Damian. And he's our best lead. Will you get him out here in the hall for me? Please?"

Damian shrugged. He knew better than to think he could talk her out of it, whatever the plan was. He suspected he had far more experience than she did when it came to extracting information from unwilling sources, but he'd go along with her for now.

Their prisoner swung his head around as soon as Damian opened the kitchen door, his eyes wide above a vomit-soaked gag. Oh, yeah. He should have thought about that. They were probably lucky the man hadn't choked on his own vomit and died. Not that his death would be a great loss to the world, but then Cassandra wouldn't have been able to ask her questions.

He walked over and ripped the man's gag off, then picked him up by his bound hands and started dragging him toward the door, while the man screamed profanities.

"Shut the fuck up, monkey boy. Or I'll gag you again, and this time I'll leave you here for the maggots."

That shut him up, except for an occasional pathetic whimper. Monkey boy, indeed.

Damian drew a carefully concealed breath of the slightly fresher air as soon as they were back in the hallway. Cassandra was on her feet, her attention shifting from the device she held in her hand to their prisoner, and then back again. She was stroking the artifact in a focused, almost sensuous, way that made him frown. Was it magical? And had she gone back into the treasure room for it? Why would she do that, when it had obviously made her sick? He glanced down at the prisoner and saw him staring, his gaze fixed on the movement of Cassandra's hands over the device, in a way that Damian found deeply troubling. He took a step forward, prepared to knock the damn thing out of her hands, when she looked up and gave him a quick wink.

He breathed a long sigh of relief. Shit. He'd been more than half-convinced that she'd been overtaken by some evil piece of magic from the collection. A soft whimper from their prisoner had him looking down at the man. Apparently, their prisoner had also been taken in by whatever game Cassandra was playing.

"What's your name?" she asked suddenly.

The prisoner jumped at the sound of her voice, and struggled to inch closer to Damian, until Cassandra slanted an impatient glance his way, and he shouted in his eagerness to comply. "Graham Lockhart."

"Tell me . . . *Graham,*" she crooned. "Who's the dead guy?"

Damian could tell the man didn't want to answer, but he was too afraid of Cassandra and whatever she had in her hand to resist. "Eli," he mumbled.

"And who was Eli?" she coaxed in an almost singsong voice.

"An asshole," Graham hissed, then jerked a fearful look at her. "My brother," he amended.

"You killed your own brother?" Damian demanded in disbelief. It was one thing to hate your brother. Gods knew Nico hated his, and for good reason. But it was another matter entirely to murder your own blood.

"Why not?" Graham snarled. "He treated me like shit all our lives, told me I was stupid, just because he had magic and I didn't. All of them were like that, thinking they were so much better than the rest of us."

"My, my," Cassandra interrupted, laughing breathily. "So much hatred. Tell me what happened."

Damian shivered. He knew she was playing a part, but in that moment, she sounded almost greedy for the details, as if the kind of hatred that could drive a man to kill his own brother was the most delectable treat she could imagine.

"They left us behind," the man explained sullenly. "Eli was the trusted one. He was supposed to secure the house and then catch up to the others. They took the Talisman, but all the rest of this junk"—he jerked his head in the direction of the open door—"they didn't have room for it, or maybe they just didn't feel like dragging it along with them. I didn't ask, and nobody would have explained it to me if I had. I was the lowest of the low. No magic, no skills. Just a strong back and a pathetic willingness to do whatever they asked."

"You *do* seem pathetic," she agreed silkily.

Graham flushed and for a moment, his hatred showed through. But then he lowered his gaze and continued. "I wanted inside that room. It was a waste to leave all of those valuable things behind. That's what I told Eli. What would it hurt if I lifted a few of them? I've earned that and more over the years, but no one was ever going to pay up. Besides, they didn't remember even half of what they'd shoved in there. They'd never miss a pretty piece or two, right? But Eli wanted no part of it. He came right out and said that my empty human soul would suck the magic right out of whatever I touched. Arrogant bastard," he snarled.

"So you killed him."

"I killed him," Graham agreed. "Best night of my life. I was getting ready to grab a few things and run, until you two came along and fucked it up."

Cassandra smiled sweetly. "That was a wonderful story, Graham. And now you're going to tell me everything you know about where your friends have gone."

He grunted. "They're not my *friends*. And they don't tell me anything."

"Graham, Graham," she chided. "A sneaky fellow like you must have listened to things he wasn't supposed to. And you're going to tell me all about it."

"Why would I do that? You're just going to kill me anyway."

"True," she agreed cheerfully, but then her voice darkened and she turned a threatening gaze on him. "But you see, Graham, there's death, and then there's *death*. Do you know what this device does?" She offered the pretty artifact she'd been rolling back and forth in her hands.

He stared at the bauble sitting in the center of her palm, and so did Damian. It was globe-shaped, made of gold with black marks of inscription covering its surface, in a language Damian didn't recognize. Graham shook his head wordlessly.

"When a person is killed by violence, his spirit often lingers near his body, too confused to move on. This device"—she hefted it slightly—"captures stray spirits. It doesn't even have to be activated. It's always searching, always hungry."

The prisoner stared at it in growing horror. "Are you saying you've got Eli in there?"

Cassandra gave him a lazy look. "I do, and you know what else?"

He shook his head silently.

"I'm going to put you in there with him. I won't even kill you first. I'm still vexed with you for trying to hurt my Damian," she added almost sulkily. "So I'm going to steal your soul and trap you inside. You and Eli, together for eternity. Except . . . you'll still be alive. Won't that be fun?"

Graham was shaking his head, his whole body trembling in terror. "Please," he whispered. "Please don't. I'll tell you anything, everything. Whatever I know."

She smiled delightedly. "Will you? That'd be *great!*"

Fuck. She sounded like some crazy axe murderess or something, and Damian wondered what it meant that she could switch personalities so easily. Maybe there were depths to Cassandra that he'd yet to discover. He eyed her appreciatively, remembering, in great detail, all of her depths he'd already explored. Somehow she intrigued him even more now that he knew this side of her.

"They're going north to Chicago," Graham said, the words gushing forth in his eagerness. "I don't know the target. I swear!" he added, all but screaming when Cassandra gave him a skeptical look. "But I know it's big.

142

They talked about planes falling from the sky."

She froze for a moment at that piece of news, and Damian knew it was important. How could it not be? Planes falling from the sky? What the hell did that damn Talisman do, anyway?

"When did they leave?" he asked the man, since Cassandra seemed to be too deep in thought to follow up.

"I told you. Less than an hour before you got here. You just missed them."

"And when's the attack?"

"Tomorrow, in the afternoon, when they said all the TV news would be watching."

Damian called up the map he'd memorized in his head, but nothing stood out for him. He didn't know this area, or even this world, well enough to spot its weaknesses. That wasn't true of Cassandra, though. She was staring at the man with an awareness that very nearly broke through the creepy character she'd donned. But she recovered quickly enough.

"Thank you, Graham," she said silkily, then lifted her gaze to Damian. "Damian, darling?"

Darling? He repeated silently to himself, and then, out loud, said cautiously. "Cassandra?"

"Would you dispose of this trash for me?"

"Certainly," he said and reached over his shoulder, drawing his sword in a single, practiced move.

"Wait!" Graham shouted. "You promised—"

"I promised nothing," she snapped, all traces of the hypnotic sorceress gone. "You killed your own brother, and you did it out of jealousy. That's not even original, and it's not why you're going to die. You're dying because I won't gamble thousands of lives on your cowardice, on the chance that the moment we leave, you'll call your cronies and warn them we're coming."

"What about Eli?" he whispered, staring at the globe in her hand. "Don't, *please*."

"Oh, this?" she asked, tossing it up in the air and catching it. "This is nothing. The ancient equivalent of a pet rock. It looks mysterious as shit, and if you touch it, you'll get a little zap, like an electrostatic shock. But that's it."

He sobbed out a breath. "But you said—"

"Well, obviously, I lied, Graham. I think your brother must have been right about you being stupid."

His head shot up, pure hatred in his eyes. "Bitch."

"Probably," she said, with a sadness that was far too genuine. And that was enough for Damian. Grabbing the man by his hair, he dragged him into the kitchen.

"Please, don't," Graham begged.

"May your gods be merciful," Damian muttered.

"I won't tell anyone. You can—"

He sliced the man's throat with a single, clean, and merciful stroke, shoving the body aside before the blood could spray all over him. He gave his blade a cleansing flick, and slipped it back into the scabbard, then took a quick look around the kitchen with its two dead bodies and cooling pools of blood. He could almost pity whoever ended up finding this disaster.

Cassandra was waiting for him in the hallway, looking as exhausted as he'd ever seen her.

"I'm sorry," she said immediately.

He gave her a puzzled look.

"I should have killed him myself. It wasn't fair to ask—"

"Cassandra," he said, interrupting her. "I thought we were partners?"

She frowned. "We are, but what—"

"That means we each do those things we do well. His death meant nothing to me. Can you say the same?"

She stared at him a long moment, then shook her head. "I've killed. You know I have."

He nodded and waited.

"Thank you," she said simply.

Unable to stop himself, he walked over and stroked her pale cheek. Her eyes closed as she leaned in to the touch, and a single tear escaped. Damian cupped her chin and lowered his head to capture the salty drop with a touch of his tongue, his mouth lingering over her soft skin, skimming down along her jaw to brush his lips over hers in a quick kiss. But when her lips opened beneath his, he couldn't resist. He deepened the kiss, sliding his tongue between her teeth, exploring her warm mouth, feeling a surge of satisfaction at her soft moan, at the responding stroke of her tongue against his. But it wasn't the time or place. And this was Cassandra. Too much had happened between them for any of this to be easy.

He ended the kiss gently, reluctantly, going back for more before finally breaking away with a final touch of lips that was like the quick kiss he'd intended all along. She licked her lips, as if savoring his taste, and he nearly groaned.

"Cassandra," he murmured, his voice deep with a lust he tried to conceal.

She opened her eyes and looked at him. And there it was. All of the heat and desire he was feeling mirrored back at him. She blushed and looked away. "We should get out of here. We'll aim for Chicago, and hope I figure out something more specific before we get there."

The corner of his mouth lifted in a grin. "Can I drive?"

Her answering smile was weak, but it was there. "I'm driving."

DAMIAN SAT IN the passenger seat of Cassandra's SUV, the seat pushed all the way back to accommodate his long legs. It was a big vehicle, but tonight it felt too small, a sensation that had nothing to do with his size or hers. It was emotion that was filling every inch of space, unspoken feelings, frustrated desire. He wasn't a particularly intuitive man, but he'd seen the hunger in her eyes after he'd kissed her. Hell, he'd seen that same hunger before, when he was buried inside her, with her pussy creaming all over him. But that was just sex, chemistry. And he'd never doubted the chemistry between him and Cassandra. If that's all there had been, it wouldn't have mattered what insults they threw at each other in the heat of an argument. If anything, anger would have made the sex burn even hotter.

But there was more between them than that. He'd seen proof of that tonight, too. There'd been torment in her eyes when he'd told her to shoot Graham while the man still had him at gunpoint, when she'd believed he was about to die no matter what she did.

He could have warned her that the idiot would never succeed in getting the fatal shot off. But then, maybe *he* was the idiot for getting caught at all. He was only grateful there'd been no witnesses, or he'd never have lived it down. Cassandra knew, of course, but he trusted her to keep his secret. And wasn't that what it came down to? Trust?

Which reminded him . . . he'd have to tell her about the item he'd taken from the treasure room, because he'd be meeting Nico to turn it over to him, and Cassandra wouldn't forgive him if he snuck away to meet Nico on his own. There was already so much between them, keeping them apart. A secret like that might sound the death knell to any future for the two of them. Assuming they had one left at all.

He sighed and stretched out as best he could.

"Would you rather sit in the back? I don't mind," Cassandra said, concern for him evident in her voice, though why, he didn't know. If anyone had been traumatized by the night's events, it was her, not him.

"I'd rather stay up here." *With you,* he added mentally, then leaned forward to stare through the windshield. It had rained earlier, but the sky had cleared, leaving a pitch-black night. "How can you drive in this? I can't see a thing, and my eyesight is extraordinary."

That made her smile. "Of course it is," she murmured. "I'm used to driving at night," she told him, then glanced at the exterior temperature read-out with a frown. "This could be bad, though. Can you bring up the weather report on the radio?" She rattled off three numbers. He fiddled with the controls until he found the right button, then adjusted it until the numbers on the display matched the ones she'd given him. The sound was scratchy, the signal distorted, but he caught a few words. Multi-car pileup, black ice, and several closed roads. Next to him, Cassandra cursed.

"That affects us?" he asked.

She nodded, reaching out to touch the vehicle's central display, zooming in on the map there. "There's a massive accident up ahead." She pointed at a big yellow symbol. "See that? That's the accident, and look at all that red between us and it."

He studied the map. It had just as much detail as the one he'd pulled up on his laptop, which he found amazing. "That's us?" he asked, pointing at another marker.

She nodded again, then swore as their SUV was suddenly floating, as if on water. But it was far too cold for water out there, which meant . . .

"Ice," she said tightly. "Black ice, we call it. It's from all the rain we had earlier, combined with these freezing temperatures. It's not common this time of year around here, but it happens." She shook her head in disgust. "I don't think we're going to get very far tonight. But the good news is, neither will our enemies. That accident was more than an hour ago, which means they're probably just as stuck as we are. If we're really lucky, they died in the crash. But at least we know they're not getting through." She tapped more buttons on the display. "It won't help if we get killed in a crash, or freeze to death on the side of the road, because we insisted on following the Talisman, so we'll have to . . ." The picture on the display changed to reveal a list of hotels. "Damn," she breathed.

"Is there a problem?"

"Not a decent hotel among them," she muttered.

Despite the storm that had turned the road to ice and was now keeping them from their prey, he wanted to laugh. Cassandra valued her comforts. She wasn't worried about the ice endangering their lives at this very moment. She only cared about the quality of their lodgings for the night.

"We'll just have to suffer," he murmured, trying to keep his amusement from showing.

She gave him a sharp glance. "Okay, look, I need to pay attention to this road, so you'll have to start calling. It's a touchscreen, and that's a list of hotels at the next couple of off-ramps, starting maybe half a mile from here. We won't be the only ones looking, so you might have to go down the list, but the more stars the better. Find us a room."

Damian didn't quite understand the process, but once he touched the first hotel on the list, he realized the in-dash system was linked to her cell phone and could make calls for him. He grinned. The strategist in him simply loved the technology of this era.

It was more than two off-ramps before they found a hotel with a room. Cassandra insisted the price was outrageous, given the accommodations, but the authorities had closed the road up ahead, which made it likely that this was their last chance to avoid sleeping in their vehicle. He had no doubt there were times when Cassandra had slept in the back of the SUV, but he'd seen enough of it to know that the two of them wouldn't fit, no matter how familiar they were willing to get.

He had very fond memories of getting completely familiar with every part of her long, lean body, and, if he was honest, admitted he was looking forward to doing it again. He was willing to move beyond the insults they'd flung at each other earlier, and suspected that Cassandra's defensiveness had more to do with her own insecurities than any real anger at him. It was almost as if she'd been looking for a reason for them to argue, because she didn't trust what they had between them.

When he considered what Nico had told him about her history, or rather what he *hadn't* told him, certain things became clear. Some man in her past—most likely the ex-husband—had fucked with her head, making her feel less than desirable, of little value as a woman. And that was absurd on the face of it. She was beautiful and intelligent and possessed a courage that put her life in danger almost every day in order to protect a population that didn't even know it needed protecting.

He'd like to get his hands on whoever it was that had destroyed her sense of worth. Even more, he'd like to get his hands on every inch of Cassandra to prove once and for all that she was as desirable a woman as he'd ever met. And not only his hands either, he thought, stealing a private look at her in the dark vehicle. His cock twitched at the thought of all the things he'd like to do to her.

But while Cassandra definitely still wanted him, she seemed to accept the end of the relationship as inevitable. She acted almost as if it was better to get it out of the way, to avoid prolonging the pain. He didn't accept that. Which meant he was going to have to seduce her . . . again. And all while chasing bad guys over half the country on ice-covered roads.

Cassandra angled toward their turnoff, swearing when they slid uncontrollably down the long ramp, and managing to slow them down just before they hit the busy road below. They hit the curb hard enough that their vehicle jerked with the force of it, and she muttered a string of curses. But Damian turned away with a smile. It seemed he was going to have time for that seduction after all.

CASSANDRA COULD barely hold her head up by the time they found the hotel, got checked in, and finally made it to their room. Their only room. Sure, they'd shared way more than a room for the last two nights, but everything was changed now, even if she didn't want it to be. Or wait, she *did* want it to be, didn't she?

She didn't know anymore. When they'd first argued, when she'd said those horrible things to Damian, and he'd finally gotten angry, she'd been relieved. It was better for them to end now, better for both of them, before things got any more complicated and people got hurt. People like her. She couldn't afford to let another man into her heart, couldn't risk that horrible vulnerability.

And, as for Damian, he and Nick had both made it clear that he was a player. Nick had even warned her away from him. Damian hadn't settled down with one woman in his previous life, so why would he do anything else now? Especially now, when he'd been trapped in that stone for so long. He'd want his freedom, all of it. Including the freedom to fuck as many women as he wanted. And God knew the women would line up for the privilege. Why settle for her when he could have all of that?

But now he'd confused her all over again by being so sweet this afternoon, by kissing her like he still wanted her. What was she supposed to do with that?

Unfortunately, they had no choice tonight. There was only one room, and practically speaking, it was more secure for them to stick together anyway. Sotiris or his flunkies—it was still very unclear to her whether the sorcerer himself was involved in whatever plan was afoot—knew she and Damian were coming after the Talisman, and he might consider it to be well worth the effort to stop them before they disrupted his plans.

"What do you think their target is?" Damian asked, as they rode the elevator up. Their room was on the tenth floor, and she was just too exhausted to worry about climbing stairs tonight. "Graham said 'north' but he specifically mentioned Chicago."

"I don't trust that," she said tiredly, wishing this was all over with already. Had she ever been this exhausted on a hunt before? Had the stakes ever been this high? She sighed. "I mean, I think they really did go north, but Chicago could mean anything. It's a huge city, with a huge suburban population. Not to mention that there are several major airports on the northern corridor. We need to narrow it down."

"How do we do that?"

The elevator door opened. She grabbed the strap of her duffel, intending to hitch it up to her shoulder, but a jolt of pain had her crying out in surprise before she'd gotten it even halfway. Damian took it from her, and she let him. She was so tired, so overall aching, that she'd nearly forgotten her injured shoulder.

"You need to go easy on that arm," he scolded her. "You don't have to do everything alone, you know."

Her lips tightened in an almost automatic response, because for the last five years, she'd done exactly that. She'd worked all alone and loved it. There'd been no one to argue over her choices on the big things, or quibble over details on the little ones. She'd been a one-woman army, and she'd liked it that way. But then Damian had shoved his gorgeous self into her life and made her feel lonely for the first time since she'd joined the FBI and been recruited by Nick.

No risk, no pain. That had been her heart's motto, and it had worked for her. She'd been happy. But Damian made her yearn for more. Made her want things she'd thought were safely locked away forever.

With a resigned sigh, she watched, as he hefted the bag as if it weighed nothing. "Show off," she muttered and picked up her much lighter backpack. Then she headed left down the hall to their room, where she fumbled the key card into the lock. Damian pushed open the door from behind her, placing a big hand on the panel above her head and giving a shove.

The room smelled like every mid-range hotel room she'd ever stayed in, and there had been more than a few of those, despite her preference for five stars. Outside of the big cities, five-star accommodations were hard to come by. Her steps dragged as she moved down the short entry hall. She passed a standard bathroom setup on her left, but came to a stunned halt when she hit the main room.

Sharing a room with Damian? She'd make it work. But sharing a *bed*? And not *just* a bed, but a bed that was like something out of every teenaged girl's fantasy. It was huge. A four-poster with a mile-high mattress and a mountain of lacy pillows. She glanced around in confusion. Was this the hotel's version of a honeymoon suite? Well, shit. That certainly explained the hotel clerk's smirking grin when he'd checked them in downstairs. The damn bed took up most of the room and, as big as it was, it seemed ten times bigger in her mind's eye. She swallowed a groan. She could survive letting him carry her duffel, could even survive his luscious and confusing kisses. But this? She walked past the bed and stared at the narrow strip of carpet in front of the wall heater.

Damian chuckled right behind her, so close that she could feel the warm rush of his breath. "Don't worry, sweetheart. I'll be good."

She shivered. That's what she was worried about. He *was* good. Very, very good.

"Come on," he said, dropping the duffel onto the long dresser and turning her around with both hands on her shoulders. "You're exhausted. You take the first shower—"

"I need to call Lilia, figure out where they're going."

"Lilia?"

"Nick's personal assistant. I have an idea—"

"You can call her after you shower," he insisted, walking her to the bathroom and turning her through the doorway, swatting her butt to get her moving when she just stood there.

She scowled at him over her shoulder, but the swat had the desired effect. Closing the door, she turned on the hot water, then stripped off every piece of clothing before realizing she hadn't brought anything in with her to change into. She briefly contemplated putting her clothes back on and venturing out to grab some fresh ones, but that seemed like way too much work. So instead she pulled back the shower curtain—she *hated* shower curtains—checked it for mold, and then, finding it clean, ducked under the water and pulled the curtain shut.

The water pressure was exactly what she'd expected—which was crappy—but it was hot and clean, which was everything she wasn't. She stood under the weak spray for a long time, letting the heat seep into her bones. Eventually, she opened the small bottle of shampoo and sniffed, then poured it over her head, and washed her hair. She rinsed, added the complimentary conditioner, and let it sit while she tried to avoid thinking about everything that had happened in the past few hours. It didn't work. She felt . . . contaminated. Even though Damian had killed Graham in the other room where she wouldn't have to see it, in her mind's eye, she was splattered with the man's blood, sticky with bits of pink flesh.

Using the provided bar of soap, she washed every inch of her body, then went back and did it all over again. Even the bottoms of her feet got scrubbed, and between her toes. She was overreacting; she knew it. She frequently dealt with bad people, and some of them were bad enough that they'd tried to kill her, so she'd killed them first. But tonight, she was overwrought, at her literal wit's end. Between the freezing cold stench of that awful room, and then the dead body in the kitchen, and the persona she'd been forced to adopt in order to get the information she needed from Graham . . . she had nothing left to give.

She just stood under the hot water, and kept scrubbing the filth from her body. She probably would have rubbed off some of her skin if Damian hadn't opened the bathroom door to admit a sobering draft of cool air.

"I'm leaving some clothes on the sink for you," he called over the shower.

It took her a moment to leave her world of scrubbing frenzy behind, but she managed to yell back her thanks with enough enthusiasm to convince him she wasn't drowning. He closed the door, and she peeked around the shower curtain to see what he'd left her. A clean T-shirt and some underwear. She sighed. Once again, Damian had dug through her duffel and selected a pair of panties for her. Silky pink panties that she was supposed to wear to bed. The bed she'd be sharing with *him*. Sweatpants would have been the better choice, although she didn't think even that would be enough armor to help her resist him. Hell, she didn't even know if he'd try anything. Or if she wanted him to. She thought for a moment. No, she definitely wanted him to. And what did that say about her? That she was too weak to resist a relationship that couldn't possibly go anywhere. As soon as he started meeting other women, she'd become just one more among many.

She finished her shower quickly after that, reminding herself that Damian might like to clean up, too. After all, he'd been the one dealing with dead bodies, not her. She rinsed her hair, then wrapped one towel around her head and another around her body and pulled the curtain back to discover that he hadn't only provided clothes, he'd left her small cosmetic tote sitting on the sink. How could you resist a guy who understood the need for a comb and moisturizer?

On the other hand, there were the pretty pink panties. He'd probably had a great time picking out those.

When she was dressed and more or less ready, she opened the bathroom door, shivering slightly in the cooler air. It wasn't actually cold; it just felt that way compared to the steamy bathroom. And her bare legs didn't help any. Tugging down the T-shirt as much as she could, she ventured past the mirrored closet wall and around into the main room. Damian was there, looking pretty much the way he always did. He'd kicked off his boots and was sitting up on the bed, back against the headboard, pillows piled behind him, and long legs stretched out in front of him, with his computer open on his lap.

He looked up and smiled. "You look better."

She could have made some snarky comment about his implicit suggestion that she looked bad *before*, but she didn't have it in her. "I feel better," she said instead. "The bathroom's all yours."

He nodded and went back to his typing. "In a minute," he said without looking up.

Casey scowled. So much for worrying about them sharing a bed. There she was in her pink panties and bare legs, and he was ignoring her. Apparently, she was perfectly safe. She knew she should be relieved, but all she was feeling in that moment was disappointment.

"They have a coffee shop downstairs," he said absently. "And they'll do room service for a fee. The menu's there on the desk."

She did a quick scan of the desk and spotted the single piece of pink paper that served as a room service menu. It was fairly simple stuff, but it included cheeseburgers, which was good enough for her.

"Should I go ahead and order?" she asked, still perusing the menu. "Cheeseburgers and fries? How many will you—" She squeaked as two big hands slid beneath her T-shirt and settled against the bare skin of her belly.

"You smell great," he murmured, his lips nuzzling her ear through her wet hair. "Your hair, too."

Casey froze, her heart racing with something close to fear, even as a warmth filled her belly beneath the too-familiar heat of his hands. "Thanks," she whispered and then wanted to groan. *Thanks? What the hell?* She shivered and her head fell back on his shoulder when his lips closed over her neck, his tongue a wet, warm sweep of sensation before he sucked gently and moved on until he reached the corner of her mouth.

"I like the panties," he whispered.

Her heart felt like it was climbing up her throat. "You picked them out," she managed to say, rather proud of herself for sounding cool and calm.

"I know," he growled then slipped his fingers under the top edge of the silken material and teased downward, flirting with the edge of her pussy.

She sucked in a breath. Was he going to make love to her? Was this just a quick fuck to release adrenaline after a fight? Or was it something more? She wasn't sure she wanted to know.

His teeth closed over her earlobe. "Delicious," he murmured, and then abruptly straightened, his hands lingering only slightly as he took away their warmth and tugged her T-shirt back into place. "I'm going to shower. You should order some food. Two burgers for me, two fries, and a chocolate shake."

Casey blinked at the sudden change in mood, but managed to take it in stride just as she did everything else, hiding her feelings behind a rigid self-control. "I'll call it in," she said, all cool and collected. *Move along, nothing to see here.*

She heard the shower go on and fought against the picture that wanted to form in her head of Damian stripping off his clothes, and stepping naked under the hot water.

"Cassandra?" he said from way too close.

She spun around to see him leaning around the corner, his broad shoulders and muscular chest enticingly exposed. That mental image of a naked Damian took on a new dimension.

"Cassandra?" he repeated, and she blinked, forcing her gaze to his face, which was more than enough to contribute to her daydreams.

"Damian?"

"No onions on the burgers, yeah?" He gave her a playful wink, and ducked out of sight. A heartbeat later, she heard the slide of the shower curtain followed by splashing water.

"Damn," she whispered. She would have liked to believe nothing was going to happen between them tonight. But that would have been a lie.

Nonetheless, she did what she could to armor herself against seduction. She pulled on her rattiest, most comfortable sweatpants, and a slouchy sweater whose neck was so stretched out that it kept falling off her shoulder. After adding a pair of heavy socks to keep her feet warm, she was wearing the uniform of a woman who planned to stay home alone and watch old movies. This was definitely not what one wore when a warrior god was whistling in the shower only a few feet away. And, yes, he really was whistling.

Casting a scowl in his general direction, Casey put their room service order in, and then opened her laptop. She wanted to organize all of her facts before she called Lilia. She pulled up a map of the area, but didn't really need it. She had travelled this part of the country enough times to know the major cities and highways. But looking at the map helped her think. When she'd considered all of the options and everything they knew, she picked up her phone.

Lilia was Nick's personal assistant. At least, that was her official title. But she did a hell of a lot more than you'd normally find on a PA job description. As far as Casey could tell, the woman lived on Nick's rather expensive Florida estate, and, yet, there wasn't a hint of romance between them. Not that Casey had ever seen, anyway. Nick was a bit of a dog when it came to women, with a girl in every port. Lilia . . . well, she didn't seem to have a life outside of her job. So despite the late hour, nearly ten o'clock in Florida, Casey knew the woman would still be at the office. Or if not in the actual office, then at least reachable . . . because she always was.

"Casey, my love," Lilia answered, her words redolent of the deep South. Casey didn't know if that's where she came from, or if she just liked the way it sounded. "I hear you've recovered a long-sought-after treasure."

Casey considered how to respond. Lilia knew that Casey was chasing the Talisman—she always knew the details of the hunts Nick sent them on—but she apparently didn't know that it had been recovered, and then lost again.

"Not yet I haven't," she admitted. "I had it in my hands, but it slipped away."

"Oh, my," Lilia breathed, doing an excellent impression of a Southern belle from all the bad movies. "Was it . . . big?"

She frowned. "I guess. I mean you could probably wear it around your neck, but—"

"Whatever are you talking about?" Lilia asked, dropping the breathless accent.

"The Talisman," Casey said, puzzled. "What are you—" On the other side of the wall, the shower turned off. Damian. Lilia was asking about Damian. "Lilia Wilson, get your mind out of the gutter!"

She laughed. "Oh, come on, Case, like you haven't been lusting after the man. Nick says he's gorgeous, and *he* knows his stuff when it comes to looks, male or female. "

"Staring at yourself in the mirror doesn't make you an expert on good looks," Casey observed tartly.

Lilia just laughed. "So you're saying this Damian person *isn't* gorgeous?"

"Of course, he is but—" She paused long enough to listen carefully, wanting to be sure Damian wasn't eavesdropping on her conversation. He was sneaky like that. "We're working together, Lili. We're partners. And he's still adjusting to this new reality. It wouldn't be right to take advantage—" She stopped, pretty sure Lilia wasn't listening anymore, considering her hoots of amusement.

"Oh, God," the other woman finally said, sniffing away her tears of laughter. "Thanks, I needed a good howl. So, you're fucking him, right?"

"Lili!" she said in exasperation, then sighed. "It's complicated, okay?"

"Only you would find that complicated," Lilia said with a sigh. "But tell me, in a perfect world, would you like to fuck him?"

"Nick's right," she whispered. "He's gorgeous, okay?"

"And you're whispering," Lilia said, whispering herself. "Are you sharing a room? Ooooh, my. You'll have to tell me all about it."

Casey started to agree, then realized she didn't want to discuss the intimate details of Damian with anyone else. The memories of her time with him would be for her alone. But her silence spoke too loudly.

"Oh, Casey," Lilia breathed. "You like him. Be careful, hon."

"I know. I'm an idiot."

"No, you're not. And not every man is a jerk like your idiot ex."

"I know." She sucked in a long breath. "But I didn't call you to discuss my love life. I need a favor."

"What can I do for you?" she asked, taking Casey's cue and shifting to all business.

"I'm speculating here, but . . . I think they're going to hit Chicago's O'Hare Airport. You have that list of properties that we know belong to Sotiris, right?"

"Right. And you want me to see if any of them have suddenly gone active, anything that would suggest the bad guys are holing up there, waiting to strike. What timeframe?"

"Within the last week. The first whispers about the Talisman didn't start until ten days ago, so they couldn't have been planning it for much longer than that."

"Unless they've known all along where the Talisman was, and just didn't go after it until they were ready to use it."

"Maybe. They clearly had safeguards set up in case anyone else tried to grab it. Like me. But if O'Hare's their target, I still think they'll have waited until the last minute to set up shop nearby. They know we're after the device, and that we'll try to stop whatever they're planning. And they have to at least suspect that we can track their movements. So why advertise their presence?"

Lilia made a wordless sound of agreement. "I'll dig into it and let you know what I find. Shall I get some of the other hunters moving in your direction? Terrell is already on his way back here; I could reroute him to you. And Carmen's cooling her heels in New York, waiting on customs. She'd jump at the chance to get in on some real action."

Casey thought about her fellow hunters and what they could bring to the game, but decided against it for now. "No," she said. "I think this one's going to require more stealth than firepower. Besides, if it comes to actual fighting, Damian's all the army I need."

"Is he?" Lilia purred.

"Yeah, yeah. You'll meet him soon enough. Look, the weather is keeping us here tonight, but we'll be on the road tomorrow. I'll call Nick, but he never answers his phone. So if you talk to him first, let him know what's up."

"I will, but I don't think he'll need it. He's following you pretty closely on this one. Damian's important to him."

"I know," she said quietly, thinking to herself that Damian was important to more than just Nick. "See what you can find out about the safe houses, okay? And get back to me either way."

"I'll do that, darling. You take care."

The dead air told Casey that her friend had disconnected, so she did the same, noting that her cell phone battery was down to less than fifty percent. She was bent over, digging out her charger when someone knocked on the door. Figuring it was room service, she started for the door, but Damian got there first. Dressed in nothing but a pair of the black boxer briefs she'd bought for him—she guessed he'd kept at least one pair—he stepped out of the dressing area near the bathroom and pulled the door open without even checking the peephole.

"Damian," she cautioned, but it was too late. Frankly though, her warning wasn't necessary, since the unmistakable scent of hamburger and fries hit her the minute the door opened.

"Well, hi there." The voice was young and female, and plainly interested in a hell of a lot more than a good tip. Casey peered around Damian to find a young woman who looked no more than sixteen years old. But that didn't stop her from gawking at a half-naked Damian. Casey stepped between him and the perky teenager. "I've got this," she said, shooing him away from the door.

The young woman—really little more than a girl—shifted her reluctant attention to Casey. "Oh, hi," she said, eyeing Casey's shapeless outfit with an expression just short of a snicker. "You ordered food?" She gestured to the tray of covered dishes on a cart next to her.

"I'll take that," Damian said, pushing past Casey and lifting the heavy tray like it weighed nothing. And coincidentally flexing a few muscles, much to the delight of the delivery girl, whose eyes followed his every move.

Casey half-closed the door and stepped primly into the opening to block the girl's view of Damian carrying the tray into the room. "You need me to sign something?"

"Yeah," the teen said. "Or he could."

Casey narrowed her eyes at the girl, and grabbed the check, signing it quickly and adding a generous tip, just to prove she wasn't threatened by a ponytailed teenager. "Thanks," she said, before all but slamming the door in her face. Because, really, the girl had just been rude the way she'd been eyeing Damian. He wasn't some piece of meat. She turned around to find him grinning at her.

"Aren't you cold?" she asked, and busied herself with finding her charger and plugging in her phone. But when she turned back, he was still smiling. "What?" she demanded.

His grin widened. "You're jealous."

"Hardly. Are you going to eat like that?"

"I'm comfortable," he said, thankfully letting the jealousy issue drop.

"Does it bother you if I wear this?"

"Not at all," she lied, and started unloading their food onto the small table.

Without warning, his arms came around her, his heat plastered against her back. How did he keep doing that? Moving so quickly and so silently?

"Are *you* cold, Cassandra?" He slipped a hand under her sweatshirt and flattened his palm against her bare skin. She was suddenly sweating.

"I was," she whispered. "Do you want—?" She sucked in a breath as his hand glided downward, past the loose waistband of her ratty sweats, his fingers barely skimming beneath the elastic band of the pink panties he'd picked out.

"Do I want?" he murmured. "Yes."

Casey leaned against his powerful body, sucked into his heat, moving without conscious thought to get closer. She'd missed him, missed this. They'd been together for only two days, and apart for nearly that long, but he'd gotten beneath her skin somehow. She'd never cared much about any of the guys she'd dated, or, even less, hooked up with. They were convenient, nothing more. But not Damian. He was definitely more.

"Damian," she whispered, reaching up to stroke the back of his neck, twisting her fingers in his long hair.

His arms surrounded her, his hands coming up to squeeze her breasts gently, weighing them in his big hands, the callused palms of a swordsman rough against her soft skin, rolling over her nipples until they were tight peaks of hunger, begging for attention. She arched her back, wanting more. Needing more. She felt sexual and feminine, powerful and needy at the same time. Damian flattened his hand against her belly, controlling her, holding her in place as he ground his cock against her ass. His long, hard, very aroused cock. She moaned at this evidence of his desire, proof that his hunger, his *need* matched her own.

Her sweats slipped off her hips, the worn elastic no match for the friction of Damian's hard body rubbing against her. Straining against him, she turned her head, wanting his mouth. He kissed her briefly, a ravenous, biting kiss, his tongue stabbing in her mouth, in and out, teeth closing over her lip in a not-so-gentle bite. Strong fingers fisted in her hair, tugging her head back, as he trailed his tongue along the line of her jaw, closing his mouth over the vulnerable pulse point of her neck, sucking hard. She cried out, feeling every tug of his lips against her throat as if he was kissing her breasts, her belly, her clit. Her pussy clenched in sudden need and she sobbed his name. "Damian."

"Let go, baby," he murmured. "You can let go. I've got you." Holding her tightly against his body, he turned to the tall, old-fashioned bed and bent her over until she was braced on the soft mattress, her ass high and crushed against his cock. He swore quietly and slipped a finger under the sodden silk of her panties, stroking her once before sliding his finger into her pussy. "Cassandra," he murmured almost reverently. "You're so wet. So fucking wet for me."

She could only moan softly, her face buried in her arms as he fucked her with his rough finger, adding a second that stretched her tender tissues. She'd never liked this position with anyone else. She'd felt trapped, humiliated. But the only thing she felt right now was hotter, wetter, more excited than she'd ever been. Wanting more, she braced herself on one arm and reached for her panties with the other, tearing the delicate silk as she struggled to yank them over her hips.

But Damian was having none of it. He grabbed her hand and pressed it back to the bed over her head, holding it there as he growled, "Uh-uh, sweetheart. That pussy is mine."

Casey growled in turn, wiggling her ass. "Then fuck me, damn it."

Damian only laughed, the sound coming out in a hissed curse as he slowly, so fucking slowly, dragged her panties down her thighs and left them there, trapping her legs together. She felt the touch of soft cotton on her bare ass, the scrape of his hand as he pushed his briefs aside. The hot, silken rod of his cock brushed against her ass, and then he took hold of himself, dragging the tip of his penis through the creamy wetness of her pussy before pushing through her swollen folds, and entering her. There was no hesitation, no slow build-up, no gentleness. His hips flexed and he filled her in a single, forceful thrust, her inner tissues stretching around him, even as they welcomed the intrusion, caressing his hard length. He pulled back once, never leaving her body, and then he stilled, letting her adjust to his size. He made every inch of her feel wanted, claimed, cherished.

"Okay?" he murmured, then slipped a hand around her hips and between her thighs, teasing her clit, circling but never touching, building the hunger, the raw need until she thought she'd scream. Wanting more, wanting him to know she could *take* more, she lifted her hips higher, spreading her thighs as much as she could in lewd invitation. "Damn it, Cassandra," he hissed and began fucking her, one thumb on her clit, the other hand gripping her hip, holding her in place as he pounded into her, making her body jolt with every thrust.

She moaned, her face buried in her arms, desperate for release, craving more—more of his touch, more of his cock driving into her liquid heat. He always made her feel like a raw virgin, as if she'd never fucked before, never felt the incredible sensation humming along her nerves, her pussy clenching around him over and over again. She writhed on the edge of climax, refusing to tip over, to surrender to the sensual feast of having his body against hers, inside hers.

Without warning, he pulled her upright, her back to his chest, as he surrounded her with his arms, caressing her, sparking so many sensations, emotions. The orgasm slammed into her without warning, taking her from a sweet swell of overwhelming pleasure to a crashing wave of passion that threatened to tear her apart. She thrashed in his arms, her nails digging in, blood trailing over his skin as he hissed his pleasure, fucking her through her climax, his grip almost punishing as he held her in place, his cock pounding into her from behind. And then it was Damian who was coming, a hot rush of liquid heat pouring into her body, his hips pumping, until finally with a soft grunt, he slowly stilled and wrapped his arms around her as they both collapsed onto the bed.

Casey closed her eyes, waiting for the inevitable rejection, for him to realize what he'd done and walk away, leaving her cold, wet and alone. But it never happened. Tears leaked from beneath her eyelids as Damian curled his body around her, kissing her neck, tasting the sweat on her skin as he bit her jaw gently.

"Cassandra?" he said quietly, noticing her tears. She flushed with embarrassment.

"I didn't think . . ." She sucked in a breath for courage. "I thought you'd never want me after . . . after what I said."

"You were angry. We both were. Things were said—"

"It's not easy for me," she said in a rush, before she could change her mind. "None of this."

"I'll tell you a secret, sweetheart. It's not easy for anyone."

She nodded, embarrassed, but relieved at the same time. He wasn't making a big deal out of it, wasn't demanding she bare her soul to reveal the soft underbelly of who she was. She placed her arms over his where they circled her waist, frowning when her hands encountered the raw furrowed flesh she'd left there, the sticky blood.

"Oh my God," she gasped, horrified at what she'd done. "Your poor arms!"

But he only chuckled, sounding more arrogant than wounded. "I'll heal," he assured her. "I like that I can drive you to such violence."

That only reminded her of her cruel outburst, spoken from the depths of a rare anger. "I'm not usually a violent person," she protested weakly.

"Exactly," he said, and there was no doubting the smugness in that single word.

The attitude was so very *Damian.* It made her smile at last, and she sighed her own satisfaction, lying there in the circle of his arms, listening to the silence outside their hotel room, the occasional slam of a door down the hall. And then her stomach rumbled loudly.

"We need to feed you," he murmured in his deep, sexy voice, his hand slipping down between her thighs, rubbing her clit idly, skimming through the cream of her orgasm. He chuckled arrogantly when her pussy clenched and she jerked against him.

Casey reached up and yanked his hair. "No teasing."

His only answer was a thrust of his hips against her ass, his thick cock sliding easily through the swollen folds of her soaking wet pussy and deep into her body. "Does that feel like I'm teasing, Cassandra?" he asked. And her entire body tightened.

She moaned, pushing her ass against him in demand, protesting when he pulled out, crying out her relief when he rolled her to her back and spread her legs, slipping between her thighs and plunging his cock deep into her.

"I want to see your face," he murmured, kissing her eyes, her cheeks, the corners of her mouth. "I want to watch you come."

She wrapped both arms around him, burying her face in the crook of his neck. "Damian," she whispered, overcome by the emotion of the moment.

"Wrap those beautiful legs around me," he growled, as he fucked her slow and easy, gliding on the juices of her climax, her breasts crushed against his chest.

Casey squeezed him between her thighs, relishing the scrape of her nipples through the rough hair on his chest, the tender skin of her thighs as his hips flexed, driving himself in and out of her pussy. She held him close, loving the weight of him crushing her into the mattress, the hard press of his muscles as he grew closer to climaxing, every thrust gaining urgency. It made her feel feminine and powerful to know this beautiful man could be so turned on by her, so driven to come not once, but twice.

Her own arousal snuck up on her, her pussy tingling, nerves alive and singing with desire. Her inner muscles contracted suddenly, squeezing his cock, and her gasp of surprise became a tortured groan when Damian grabbed her ass in both hands and lifted her higher, changing the angle of his penetration so he could go deeper, harder, his balls slapping her ass with every thrust.

Casey struggled to breathe as her climax built, her heart galloping in her chest, crushing her lungs as the orgasm crashed over her. She came hard, crying out as her sex clenched tightly, moaning when his cock bucked inside her and he crashed over the edge with her, his orgasm filling her with heat as they clung together, until finally they collapsed, shivering in the cool air. Damian reached down and pulled the sheet up over their sweat-soaked bodies.

They lay there a long time, exhausted, hearts pounding in rhythm, until Casey finally sighed. "The burgers are probably cold," she said woefully, hungrier than ever. Sex with Damian burned a lot of calories. "Do you think they'd bring us new ones?"

Damian was stroking his hand up and down her back. It was big and warm and soothing, and if she hadn't been so hungry, she'd have fallen asleep.

"I'm sure Bonnie won't mind," he murmured.

"Bonnie?" she repeated sharply.

He chuckled. "I knew you were jealous," he said, his delight obvious.

She slapped his hard-as-a-rock belly. "Maybe this time they'll send a *guy* to flirt with *me*."

"Not if he values his life," he snarled, just as both of their stomachs rumbled in unison.

"I'll call in the order," she said briskly, bending over to kiss him as she climbed from the bed.

"And I'll answer the door when it comes," he said, caressing her breast as he slid from the big bed after her.

"Okay, but put some clothes on this time," she said playfully. But then her phone chimed an incoming text, the screen giving her Lilia's name. It was a stark reminder of the reason they were here in this weird hotel room with its big, romantic bed, and Casey sighed. "Lilia Wilson," she told him. "Nick's assistant."

"What does she say?" he asked, the mood completely gone.

"Damn," she breathed as she skimmed the message. "She has a location, and it's every bit as bad as I thought."

Chapter Eight

"WHAT DOES SHE say?" Damian repeated. He wanted details.

"One of Sotiris's properties just went live, and it's close to Chicago O'Hare."

"Cassandra," he said patiently. "Explain." None of what she'd just said meant anything to him.

She glanced up, and he saw understanding register in her eyes. "You've never flown," she said softly.

He shrugged, embarrassed for some reason, even though it was hardly his fault. "When Kalman brought me to this country, it was by ship."

She walked over and put her arms around his waist, lifting her face for a kiss. "That must have been awful."

"It was better than the cave," he murmured, stroking her soft cheek with his knuckles. "And the rooftop, being out in the world . . . it gave me hope."

"Damian," she whispered, pain in every syllable as she hugged him tightly. "We're going to hunt down that fucker Sotiris and make him pay."

"We'll hunt him down, but the last part we leave to Nico," he said seriously. "Promise me, Cassandra. Sotiris's powers are beyond either one of us."

"I know that," she said, patting his chest. "I'll settle for stealing the Talisman back. Which takes us back to Lilia's message and Sotiris's network of safe houses." Turning away, she flipped open her laptop and pulled up a map, not unlike the one in her SUV. Except this map was of the entire North American continent and had several bright, blue dots scattered throughout. "Nick's not the only one who has a network of safe houses," she said, working the keyboard. "We've been tracking Sotiris's property acquisitions for years, identifying purchases made by any of the shell corporations that we know are associated with him. A shell corporation—"

"I know that part," he interrupted. "Kalman was a financial firm, after all. I heard lots of private negotiations on the rooftop, and not all of them were legal."

"Really?" she said, arching a brow. "We should compare notes when this is all over with."

"Sounds boring. The notes part," he assured her, tugging her hair. "Not the company."

"I knew what you meant. Anyway, we've been tracking Sotiris's properties, and every time we locate one that looks promising, we install some discreet little spies on the local utilities. Electric and phone especially, because they're easiest to track and everyone uses them. Cell phones are everywhere, but a lot of security systems utilize landlines, and Sotiris is old enough that he still distrusts cell phone communications. It's true they can be intercepted, but he'd be better off buying a box of burner phones."

"If you say so," he said absently, making mental notes to himself. He hated not understanding what was going on, but hated even more the necessity of constantly asking questions. So he simply stored questions away and looked them all up later on his laptop. The only reason he'd asked for an explanation earlier was because it was crucial to continuing their investigation.

"Anyway, the point is that we have a lot of Sotiris's safe houses identified. We can't monitor all of them all the time, but in a case like this," she tapped her keyboard and zoomed in on a regional map which he recognized as the general area they were currently traveling through, "Lilia can activate our spybots and see if any of the houses are drawing power. And this one is." She zoomed even closer, then pointed to the image of a small airplane. "And *that* is O'Hare International Airport, one of the largest and busiest airports in the world."

"You think Sotiris is targeting this airport? Why? What exactly was the Talisman created to do?"

"According to Nick, not much, at least, not when it was created. But now . . . maybe it was just dumb luck, or maybe its creator had tremendous foresight—not that it did him much good, since he's well and truly dead. That's also according to Nick. But anyway, what was once a pretty but useless bauble is now one of the most destructive artifacts in the world. Everything in today's world is run with electronics, and I mean everything. From a child's toy to the most powerful weapons in the world, and everything in between, including airplanes. It's not a matter of software encryption; it doesn't involve hacking into anyone's computer system. It's simple physics. There's a thing called an electromagnetic pulse, or EMP. Send out a big enough one and it knocks out every electronic signal within range. There are weapons that are designed to do just that. And the Talisman, in turns out, has the potential to be the most powerful weapon of all. Sotiris could kill thousands of people in just minutes, if he's figured out how to use it. And we have to assume he has, because, otherwise, why would he bother to steal it? There are air traffic control systems that guide planes through the air and keep them from crashing into each other. They could all be knocked out by this device, leaving planes stranded in midflight. But it wouldn't even matter, because the planes themselves would fall from the sky when their on-board systems suffered a massive failure."

Damian had been listening closely, following her explanation. "Sotiris is certainly cruel enough to kill thousands simply because he can," he agreed. "But it's far more likely that he will want to gain from it somehow."

She nodded. "We think it might be intended as a demonstration of the Talisman's power. He either plans to blackmail governments, or sell the weapon to the highest bidder. If we fail to stop this demonstration, the government could well step in and purchase the device outright, even knowing they were succumbing to blackmail. Fortunately, there aren't that many parties—whether government or private—who could afford the price tag Sotiris would set on it, so we'd be all but sure of getting it. Unfortunately, this second line of defense won't work until Sotiris offers the device to the highest bidder, with thousands of deaths serving to motivate buyers."

"Better to stop him now," Damian said absently, studying her map. "You're convinced this O'Hare Airport is his target."

"Yes." She glanced up at him. "But you're not," she said curiously. "Why is that?"

"You're assuming Sotiris doesn't know that you can track his movements by virtue of these safe houses? Why?"

"We've identified locations in the past this way, even derailed some of his plans because of it, and he's never caught on."

Damian shrugged slightly. "How significant were these plans? Maybe they were sacrificial goats, gifts to the gods, so to speak."

"Are we the gods in that analogy?" she asked, amused. "You're the only god around here, big guy. And we've had no evidence that any of his operatives know we could track them."

"Maybe the low-level operatives were unaware of your scrutiny. But that doesn't mean Sotiris is equally unaware. He would be just as willing to sacrifice his own agents as someone else's."

"So you don't think we should check out the house Lilia found then?"

"I didn't say that. With so much at stake, we have to assume the worst. But your friend Lilia should keep looking."

She turned and studied him thoughtfully, hands on her hips. "You might be right. I'll tell her. But that house," she pointed at the laptop, where the indicated house was now marked by a blinking cursor, "needs to be checked. Are you going with me?"

He glanced at her impatiently. "There's no need to be pissy about it, Cassandra. Of course, I'll go with you. I didn't dismiss your house-tracking scheme, I only suggested an alternative way of looking at it."

"I'm not pissy," she insisted, sounding extremely pissy.

He raised a silent eyebrow.

She regarded him with narrowed eyes. "Fine. But I hope you're wrong, because if not, then the whole world might be up shit creek."

He rolled his eyes. "Whatever that means."

CASSANDRA STARED straight ahead as she drove through the dark night, grateful that the weather, at least, was on her side. The unusual cold had moved on and so had the rain, leaving the road in front of her only slightly wet, and, at this late hour, only lightly travelled. According to the nav system, the house in question was still a hundred miles southeast. Figuring a predawn excursion would be ideal, they'd set out in the middle of the night, hoping to avoid even the slight chance that someone who knew them would see them leave the hotel. She was driving well over the speed limit, which meant she was also checking her mirrors constantly, keeping a close eye out for any state or local police who might object to her lead foot, or, for that matter, anyone who might try to follow them. It didn't exactly make for a peaceful driving experience. At least, not for her. Damian, on the other hand, was as relaxed as a person could get. He was sound asleep, probably digesting the three fast-food burgers he'd wolfed down in lieu of a room service breakfast. Not that he'd complained. In fact, she was pretty sure he was becoming a fan of drive-through.

She cast him a sour glance, even while admitting—to herself anyway—that the problem with her mood was more hers than his. The idea that Damian had planted, that Sotiris could have been tricking them with the safe houses all this time, and that they'd been so arrogant as to fall for it, really pissed her off. It made sense that it would take someone like Damian—someone not invested in the system, not familiar with their methods—to see the flaw in their program. But if it turned out he was right, they'd have to reevaluate so many of their assumptions about the enemy, and even worse . . . Damian would probably never let her forget it.

She sniffed irritably and turned back to the road. They'd know before the day was over, and she was confident he'd be proved wrong. There was no shame in it for him. No matter how quickly he'd caught up, he was still new to modern technology. So much of it must seem unlikely to him. No wonder he doubted the accuracy of their conclusions.

Damian finally stirred when she left the interstate, her slowing speed and the sway of the vehicle on the curving off-ramp enough of a change to wake him. He straightened in his seat and looked around. "Are we nearly there?"

"Ten minutes."

"You must be tired. You should have woken me. I could have driven partway."

"You don't have a driver's license," she droned, for what seemed like the hundredth time.

"It's not that difficult," he said with a dismissive shrug. "I've been watching others do it on your television."

"Watching isn't driving."

"It is when you're me."

"You did *not* just say that."

Damian

"Oh, yes, I *did.*"

The sound of Damian channeling a teenaged girl from the 'hood made her laugh out loud. And when he grinned, she knew he'd done it intentionally. "Where'd you hear *that?*" she asked him. "That doesn't sound like any rooftop negotiation."

"No, that's your daytime television. You left me in the room alone for hours, remember?"

"Geez, you make it sound like I abandoned you, like a puppy. Or worse, chained you to the bed."

"Would you like to?"

"Like to what?"

"Chain me to the bed."

Her eyebrows shot up in surprise. He couldn't be into that, could he? He was the very definition of an alpha male. He'd be more likely to be the one chaining someone down, not vice versa. "Are you, um, into that?" she asked.

He laughed. "You should hear yourself. No, Cassandra, I'm not *into* that. I didn't say I'd *let* you chain me down. I just wanted to know if you'd enjoy it for a brief time before I broke the chains, and made you pay for trying. I'd definitely enjoy *that.*"

"I bet you would. Okay," she said, studying the street signs. "This is it." She pulled over a full block away from the house and turned off the engine. "It's the one on the left with the dark sedan in the driveway. No exterior lights, but it looks like there may be one lamp shining through the door glass."

Damian leaned forward, his sharp gaze scanning not just the target house, but the street all around them. "It's a quiet neighborhood, no cars or people on the streets at this hour. How do you want to handle it?"

She did her own survey, seeing things he probably didn't because she knew what to look for. This was a working-class, family neighborhood. The cars on the street and in the driveways were mini-vans and mid-sized sedans, with the occasional pickup truck. Front lawns were postage stamp sized, with slightly larger spaces in the back, all of them unfenced, probably at the insistence of the Homeowners Association. There were basketball hoops above garage doors and backyard swing sets on more houses than not, and while a few had porch lights burning, far more were dark, conserving energy and saving on the electric bill.

In short, it was the perfect place to locate a safe house. There were enough "For Sale" signs that no one would notice a new face on the street, and Sotiris's agents would be far too discreet to call attention to themselves.

"We'll go in together. It looks quiet enough. I don't expect any real resistance. If there's a lookout, we'll take him out. The rest we'll rouse from their sleep."

"How many do you anticipate?"

"I don't know. There was a small army at the house when I stole the Talisman in the first place. But I don't think they could hide that much movement in a neighborhood like this. I think it'll be fewer than five."

"All right. We'll enter through the back."

She shrugged. It didn't matter to her. Not wanting to miss any sudden departures or other activity, she maintained her watch on the house, but tossed him her phone. He caught it, of course. There was no such thing as taking Damian by surprise. "Call Lilia—she's on my call list—and tell her where we are and what we're about to do. Just in case."

He turned on her phone and smiled way too happily as he started scrolling through every screen.

"Hey! No snooping."

"I wasn't snooping, I was learning."

"Learning what?"

"About you."

Well, shit. That was sort of sweet, wasn't it? On the other hand, this was Damian, so maybe not. "Instead of being so nosy, you should just call Lilia."

"Yes, ma'am."

She scowled at him, but he pretended not to see as he finally, *finally*, did as she asked and hit Lilia's call-back.

"Lilia," Damian crooned in his sexiest voice. "This is Damian."

Casey couldn't hear Lilia's response, but she could imagine it.

"I'm very pleased to meet you, too, at least over the phone. Cassandra speaks very highly of you."

"Just get on with it," she muttered. The bastard turned to give her a wide grin.

"I'm sorry, Lilia, I missed that. Cassandra was asking me a question." He listened for a minute and then laughed, which made Casey very suspicious.

"What'd she say?" she demanded, but he ignored her and kept talking to Lilia.

"We'll definitely be visiting Florida when this is over, and I'd love to get together with you."

"What?" What the hell? Was Lilia asking him out on a *date*? "Give me the phone," she snapped.

He shifted the phone to his right hand and leaned away from her. As if she could have taken it from him anyway. He outweighed her by a good hundred pounds of muscle.

"I'm afraid we'll have to cut this short, Lilia. Cassandra wants to talk to you." He smiled at whatever Lili said next. "I'd enjoy that. Good-bye for now."

Casey snatched the phone that he held out. "Watch the house," she ordered him, then turned her attention to Lilia. "Did you have a nice chat?"

she asked snarkily. "Don't worry, it's just the end of the world we're trying to prevent here."

"Oooh, is that jealousy I hear rearing its ugly head?" Lilia teased.

Casey made a scoffing noise. "Can we get back to saving lives now?"

"I'm sorry, you're right," Lilia said, sounding so abruptly subdued that Casey felt guilty.

"Look, Lili, I'm—" she start to say, then paused, scowling, when Lili started laughing. "Shit. I almost fell for that."

"You like him," Lilia said in a singsong tone.

Casey closed her eyes briefly. "Can we just stick to business for now?" she asked quietly.

"What do you need?" her friend asked. She must have heard something in Casey's voice. Maybe some of the desperate confusion Casey was feeling, wondering where the hell the relationship was going, if it was a relationship at all, and what the fuck she was doing to herself.

"This is just a heads-up," she told Lilia. "Damian and I are sitting a block away from the Sotiris safe house that went live in the last forty-eight hours. It's thirty minutes from O'Hare. We're going in there, but if this is the place they're using for a staging area, we could encounter resistance. It might be a while before we can get back to you."

"Maybe you should just sit on the place until I can arrange some backup."

"No can do. The timeline's too short. But, don't worry, and don't tell Damian I said this"—he gave her a sardonic look from his seat right next to her—"but he really is a god when it comes to fighting. It's like having my own personal spec ops team."

"Well," Lili drawled. "Aren't you the lucky one? Any other tidbits you'd like to share?"

"No," Casey said shortly. "We'll check in as soon as we can."

"I'll keep the lines open. Good luck, Casey. Be careful, and give Damian my—" Casey hung up before she could finish the sentence.

"Lilia says 'good luck.'"

"What else did she say?" he asked, giving her a wink.

"She offered to send backup."

He looked briefly offended, before understanding struck. "And you told her you didn't need it. What's spec ops?"

"Special operations. They're the most elite of our soldiers."

"Hmm. Your description of my skills sounds about right, then."

"Oh my God, could you be any more arrogant?"

"It's only the truth, Cassandra. You said so yourself."

"Right. We should probably get out of this car before you suck up *all* of the oxygen. Are you ready?"

"I'm always ready," he said.

She would have scoffed at the arrogance in that statement, but in his case, it was probably true.

DAMIAN STUDIED THE neighborhood as he and Cassandra strolled down the darkened street toward the safe house. They didn't hold hands—it would take too long to draw a weapon if necessary, and seconds could matter—but their body language was comfortable and affectionate, just another couple out for a stroll. All they needed was a dog to complete the picture. He'd never had a dog, there'd been no time or place for one in the life he and Nico had led, but he thought he might like one when this was over and he was settled in Florida. He frowned at the thought. There was no doubt in his mind that his home, his place, was at Nico's side. But now there was Cassandra.

And he needed to focus his attention on their mission tonight, instead of worrying about the future.

"Are you getting anything?" he asked, leaning in and whispering in her ear. Her shiver made him smile, but he let it go. She needed her mind on what they were doing, too.

She frowned in concentration, then shook her head. "We might be too far away for me to detect anything, especially if they're shielding it somehow." But she didn't sound very convinced.

Her report didn't surprise Damian. He didn't think they were going to find the Talisman here. Granted, he hadn't fought against Sotiris in a very long time, but before his imprisonment, he'd battled the sorcerer and his ilk on an almost daily basis. The wars between Nico and the few other sorcerers who were on his level in terms of magical ability had been constant. Damian didn't know modern technology as well as he'd like, but he sure as hell knew Sotiris. The man was evil, but he was also brilliant. He wouldn't be caught by something as obvious as turning on the lights in a safe house.

They walked right past the safe house and up the driveway of its neighbor, then strolled down the yard between the two houses, as if they belonged there. Damian's senses were on full alert. He picked up the soft movement of people in the neighbor's house—footsteps, the sound of running water—but there was no sound at all coming from the safe house. Nothing. The drapes were all drawn, the shades dropped. There were two separate light sources, one from the back of the house—probably the kitchen, based on the floor plans from the sales brochure for this development—and another in an upstairs bedroom. But no people. That damn house was empty. He knew it.

They entered the backyard through the unlocked gate, and crossed the small patio, where Cassandra eased up to the sliding glass door on the back of the house. Pulling a small flashlight, she examined the edges of the door all around, then focused on the handle and lock itself. From the look on her face, she didn't like what she was seeing. He crouched down next to her.

"I'm not finding any sensors. No security system." She paused, her lips tight with irritation or thought, he didn't know which. "Let me check something," she said, then stood without warning and walked quickly and silently over to the nearest window. The flashlight came out again, and she did much the same inspection, before coming back to kneel next to him. "Nothing on the windows either," she told him.

Damian waited.

"It could be they're only using magical intrusion measures," she said half-heartedly.

He nodded. It *could* mean that. "Are you sensing the Talisman?" He remembered her certainty at the previous house. How she'd known the moment she stepped inside that the Talisman wasn't there. But maybe she needed to get within the outer walls before she could be sure.

"Nothing from here," she admitted. "How about you?"

He tilted his head curiously. "I told you. I have no ability to sense—"

"Not magic," she whispered impatiently. "Breathing, grunting, anything to indicate there are people inside. I know you hear stuff regular people can't."

Damian tried to decide whether he should be insulted or flattered by the "regular people" reference. He wasn't sure he wanted to be considered regular, but on the other hand . . .

"Nothing," he told her.

"You think it's empty."

He shrugged and nodded.

"Shit," she hissed, then she turned without warning and punched a gloved fist at the closed glass door. It didn't budge, didn't break. Surely she hadn't expected that it would? "You're stronger than I am," she said moving out of the way. "Break the damn glass."

He gave her a puzzled look, but scooted over to examine the door handle himself. He glanced briefly at Cassandra, then gripped the handle and yanked it, breaking the lock and sliding the glass door back several inches.

"Show-off," she muttered, then leaned in through the open door and sniffed the interior.

Damian didn't know what the hell she was doing, but he knew she wasn't being very cautious about it. Reaching out, he gripped her upper arms and moved her aside, then pulled the door all the way open. "You're going to get yourself killed," he said at her look of outrage. He slipped through the flimsy drapes and into the house.

He stood for a long moment, ignoring Cassandra fuming at his back, focusing instead on the rest of the house. No, he couldn't sense magic, but most people weren't magical. They were just ordinary humans, who made ordinary human noises. And he'd been right. There was nobody here. He walked over to the light switch and flipped it on, flooding the big room with light.

"It's empty," he said, and strode from the kitchen into the main living room of the house, turning on lights as he went. He took the stairs three at a time and quickly searched the upstairs bedrooms and bathrooms, even the walk-in closets. When he went back down the stairs and into the kitchen, he found Cassandra on her phone, having an intense, whispered conversation with Lilia. She shot him an irritated glance, as if it was *his* fault he'd been right, and they'd been wrong. He wondered how many investigations had just been turned on their heads.

"Fuck," Cassandra swore viciously. "No, not you, Lili. That was a generalized fuck. Look, we're going to clear out of here while we still can. For all I know, they've booby-trapped these houses just to make this situation worse. Ping me when you get something more." She hung up and dropped the phone into her pocket. "You heard," she said, avoiding his gaze. "We should clear out—"

"Cassandra," he said, forcing her to look at him. "This isn't your fault."

"No?" she demanded. "Do you know how many of these damn houses I've scoped out before this? And not once did it occur to me that we were being played."

"Some of them must have turned up something, or you would have figured it out before now."

"Sure, yeah. And it's not just me. I'm only part of the team. We caught a few of Sotiris's agents—obviously the ones he considered to be disposable, as we now know. And we picked up an artifact or two. But never anything significant, nothing that comes close to the Talisman."

"I doubt there are many devices that do. From what you've told me, the Talisman is not your typical target either."

"You're right. And I'm not usually sent on the more dangerous missions. My skills don't run in that direction."

"But you do possess a rather extraordinary ability. One that was absolutely necessary to neutralizing the Talisman."

She gave him a grateful smile, then shrugged. "Lucky me."

"No. Lucky *me*," he said, hooking an arm around her neck and pulling her close. "We'll get this, Cassandra. We'll find him."

She leaned into him for half a second before straightening. "Okay. I don't think they bothered to booby trap this place, but I'd rather not amuse them by lingering, either. Let's get the hell out of here."

The walk back to the car was less of a stroll and more of a determined march. They were both tired, both disgusted at the waste of effort. And although Damian's theory on the safe houses had essentially been proven, he felt bad for Cassandra and the rest of her team. He was also surprised, frankly, that Nico hadn't known better. It made him wonder just how much his brother was involved in the activities of his hunters. Maybe he'd ask when he saw him next. Which would be soon. The item that he'd recovered from the treasure room was a heavy weight to bear. Not a physical weight, of course. Nothing that simple. But the knowledge of what was hidden in his scabbard weighed on his soul. He wanted to turn it over to Nico. His brother was the only one who might be able to make use of it.

"You drive," Cassandra said, tossing her keys his way and shocking the hell out him. He caught the keys and unlocked the doors with the remote, but then stared at her over the top of the SUV, eyebrows raised in question.

"I need to call Lili," she told him. "And I need to be able to focus on the conversation."

He shrugged. "Okay." He settled behind the wheel and dutifully fastened his seatbelt. "Where are we going?"

"Hotel. I don't know about you, but I'm tired and hungry, and it just so happens, there are something like a million hotels around here. Give me a minute and I'll tell you which one we're going to."

The night was cold, so he went ahead and started the engine, letting it idle while Cassandra worked the screen on her cell phone. A few minutes' worth of muttering later, she entered an address on the navigation screen. "One of my favorite places," she said. "At least something can be salvaged from this clusterfuck."

Damian had no response to that, so he wisely kept quiet and pulled the vehicle away from the curb, following the directions to the first turn. Cassandra, meanwhile, called Lilia and recounted the night's events.

"I think the model is still a good one," she told Lilia finally. "*Some* of those properties ended with successful raids, and I'm not buying the idea that they were all sacrificed to protect the larger goal. We just have to dig. He must have safe houses, but he's hidden them deeper than we thought."

She listened for a few minutes, and Damian could hear the soft burr of Lilia's voice, before Cassandra said, "That sounds great. We're going to find a hotel and sleep for a few hours, but I'll have my cell phone if anything comes up." She made a gasping noise in response to something Lilia said, but finished with, "Okay, I'll tell him. Thanks."

"Lilia says hi."

"Did she say she misses me?"

"She's never even met you."

"But we've spoken on the phone. I think we made a real connection."

Cassandra laughed. "Dream on. Don't listen to the nav. Turn here instead," she said, pointing.

Damian followed her directions and found himself in the drive-through of a restaurant whose name even he recognized. Cassandra ordered, shouting across him at the machine, much to his amusement. A few minutes after that, they had a bag of food, which they proceeded to scarf down while sitting right there in the parking lot.

"Damn, we must have been hungry. There's not even a French fry left in here." She balled up the empty bag, then opened her door, and walked over to dump it in the trash can.

"You are a good citizen," he commented, when she got back into the truck.

"Fuck that. I just like to keep my truck clean."

Damian smiled. "How far to the hotel from here?"

"Minutes. Pull out that way, and turn right."

It was farther than he expected, but before long, he was parking behind a multi-story hotel. A few minutes after that, they were climbing the stairs to their fourth-floor room. Once inside, Damian dumped the heavy duffel, then shrugged out of the scabbard, setting it carefully aside. Once he removed it from his back, it became visible, and so did everything it contained. But Cassandra was too busy with her own things to worry about his, or anything else.

Damian felt a twinge of guilt at keeping the item from her. There was no reason for it, other than the very bitter and personal relevance of this particular artifact, and Nico's general preference for secrecy. But, by now, Cassandra was too deeply involved in the battle against Sotiris to keep secrets from her. Damian's loyalty to Nico went too deep to move ahead without his agreement, but his feelings for Cassandra were strong, too. And growing stronger by the day. Maybe it was time to persuade Nico that it was time to share.

As he considered the state of his relationships with Nico and with Cassandra, Damian stripped off the rest of his clothes and headed for the shower. Cassandra was already there, enticingly naked as she leaned into the shower to start the hot water. She'd said this hotel was one of her favorites, which meant the bathroom was all marble and glass, with a walk-in shower that could accommodate four people.

Damian wrapped an arm around her belly and lifted her enough to carry her into the shower, while she laughed in surprise. He still loved the sound of her laugh. It was the strongest memory he had of returning to true life after years trapped in that damn statue. The sound of her laughter.

"Damian." She slapped his hands away playfully when he set her on the shower floor. The hot water was pouring down on them from above through a device called a rainfall showerhead. It was one of the best inventions of this time. The water was a steady, soft flow, like a natural waterfall in the mountains, but without the freezing temperature or the uneven stones underfoot.

Cassandra was currently hogging most of that lovely hot water, but the steam in the enclosure was enough to keep him comfortably warm. Especially with her luscious body to heat his blood. He watched as she poured half the bottle of shampoo on her long, wet hair, and then he took over, massaging the shampoo into a soapy lather with few firm strokes.

"Mmmmm," she groaned and leaned back into his chest, dropping her hands down to grip his thighs.

Damian's cock responded to the sensuality of that groan as much as the touch of her hands. He knew she didn't see herself as such, but Cassandra was a deeply sensuous woman. Her fingers were digging into his thighs, kneading the muscles, moving higher with every stroke. He took a step back, pulling her with him, which put her even more fully under the water flow. While the soapy shampoo slid down her shoulders and over her silky wet skin, he reached around and cupped her breasts, weighing their soft fullness in the palms of his hands before squeezing gently, twisting her rosy nipples between finger and thumb.

She moaned again, hungrier this time, as she rubbed her ass against his erection. Damian growled. He had plans for that ass, but first he was going to make her feel every ounce of her own sensuality. Reaching around her, he grabbed the bar of soap and used it to caress her arms and thighs, her back, her belly, flirting with the soft folds between her legs until he could feel the heat of her pussy against his fingers, but never delving into that hot, wet temptation. Cassandra dragged her strong fingers over his arms, dug her nails into his ass, and rubbed herself wantonly against his cock. But he resisted, washing her slowly, seductively, until she hissed in frustration.

"Damian," she demanded.

"What do you need, sweetheart?" he murmured, then dipped his hand between her thighs to stroke her sex. She was creamy and wet, and so sensitive to his touch. Her pussy shivered at the contact, her clit swollen, hard enough that he could feel it pulsing beneath the pressure of his thumb. Cassandra moaned, lifting her arms to curl around his neck, thrusting her breasts outward so he could see their lushness, could see water dripping from the peaks of her nipples. He covered his fingers in the cream of her pussy, teasing her clit until she was gasping for breath, her hips flexing in a plea for more. With a final caress, a last teasing pinch of her swollen clit, he flattened his hand against her belly, then slid his grip from her hip to her ass, his fingers digging in while he kissed her neck, tasting the salt on her skin as she writhed in the circle of his arms.

"Damian, please," she whispered.

"What do you want?" he asked again, then slipped his hand between the firm cheeks of her ass, his finger dipping into the tight hole of her anus at the same moment his other hand slid into the liquid heat of her pussy. Cassandra froze with a tiny gasp of shock.

"Damian . . ."

He stilled. "Do you want me to stop?" he whispered into the soft shell of her ear. For a long moment, he thought she'd say, "yes."

But then she shook her head in a jerky motion and murmured a soft, "No."

Damian outlined her ear with his tongue, biting the lobe gently as his fingers began fucking her pussy once again. One finger, then two, he filled her over and over until she was dripping wet, her juices coating his hand as she panted softly, making greedy little noises that made him want to bend her over and fuck her hard. But his Cassandra wasn't ready for that. He forced himself to go slowly, stroking her pussy to just short of climax, then circling her clit with his thumb, teasing, barely grazing. Over and over, until without warning, he took the firm little nub between his thumb and forefinger and squeezed, while he bit down hard on her neck. Cassandra cried out in surprise, and then pleasure, as the orgasm left her shaking, gasping for breath, his arms the only thing keeping her standing. And then he started over.

"Again, Cassandra," he ordered, slamming his fingers into her, feeling her sheath clench as she moaned helplessly.

"More," she whispered, begging for release of a different kind.

He waited until her body was pulsing around his fingers, the muscles of her belly contracting with the force of her orgasm, until his cock was slick with her juices, and then he slid slowly into her ass. She cried out, coming harder than ever, her pussy clamping down around his fingers, her cream gushing out to ease his passage as he pushed even deeper into her tight little hole. Hunger finally overtook his patience, and he shoved her against the wall with a dominating snarl, gripping her hip with a hand that was slick with her juices, digging in his fingers as he pumped her sweet ass. She was so tight, a velvet glove of heat around his cock, so fucking raw and erotic that he could barely hold back his own climax as he pushed her for another, pressing his rough thumb against her throbbing clit.

"Do it, Cassandra," he growled. "Come for me."

He groaned when he felt her stiffen, felt the orgasm hit her as she cried out in shock. He tightened his hold as she began to thrash in his arms, protecting her even as his own orgasm roared over him and he filled her ass with the hot rush of his release.

Damian clung to Cassandra as she trembled, the tiny aftershocks of her multiple climaxes jolting through her body, and rippling over his cock. With a flex of his hips, he eased out of her ass. She gave a sensuous little moan, and he cursed as his cock hardened all over again. Circling her with his arms, he kissed her temple. "You're beautiful when you come," he whispered as he reached for the soap.

He washed her ass first, caressing her cheeks, sliding his soapy fingers in and out of her tight little hole, and then moving to her pussy, where he was careful to avoid her tender clit as he washed her folds.

She shivered at his touch. "I can't," she moaned. "Damian, I'll fall apart."

"Ssh, baby, it's okay. I won't let you."

Holding her with one arm, he turned off the shower and grabbed one of the hotel's big, fluffy towels. Wrapping her tightly, he carried her over to the big bed and pulled back the covers. Then he laid her on the soft sheets, curled his body around hers, and pulled the covers over them both.

"Sleep," he murmured, and they both crashed.

Chapter Nine

DAMIAN WOKE TO the soft light of his laptop computer coming to life where it sat on the table against the wall. He'd left the computer open intentionally, expecting to hear from Nico, and not wanting to wake Cassandra with an audible signal. Or, at least, that's what he'd told himself. The real reason was that Nico would want to meet him privately when he discovered what he'd found. Damian was increasingly uncomfortable with the subterfuge and intended to tell Nico tonight that he was bringing Cassandra into their circle. But until then, he had to honor Nico's wish.

The room was dark, but he didn't need to see Cassandra to know she still slept deeply. Her slow, regular breathing, and the boneless way she lay sprawled over the bed told him enough. He slipped easily from beneath the sheets, not making a sound, barely shifting his weight on the mattress. The ability to move in near silence was an important skill for a warrior. And also for a man who rarely slept in the same woman's bed twice, but that was a very long time ago.

He went first to the computer and read Nico's message. His friend was already waiting downstairs, so Damian dressed quietly, then picked up his scabbard and slipped it over his back in a move so ingrained into his existence that it was second-nature, and made not a sound. The heavy door was more of a challenge, but he managed, moving slowly and deliberately until he was in the corridor outside their room. And then he went swiftly to the stairwell and took the stairs three at a time.

Once outside, he followed the tug on his soul, circling the hotel to find Nico standing next to that same bright red monster of a car on the far side of the parking lot. Despite the misgivings he had about keeping this meeting secret from Cassandra, he was still filled with joy at seeing his brother again. He strode across the lot, meeting Nico halfway. They embraced, holding each other tightly for a long moment, before letting go.

"I still can't believe you're real," Nico said, gripping his arms, seeming reluctant to release him.

"Real enough, brother," he said grinning back, and as he did, he wondered . . . how could he ever make Cassandra understand what Nico meant to him? What they meant to each other? She knew of his creation, how Nico had willed him into existence. But their connection was more than that. It was forged by decades spent side by side, fighting first Nico's brothers, and then his enemies as his power grew. Was she enough of a warrior to appreciate that? To understand that a piece of his heart would always belong to Nico?

"Everything okay?" Nico asked, seeing more than Damian wanted to reveal. But then, he'd always been able to do that.

"I don't like leaving Cassandra alone."

Nico tipped his head curiously. "You like her."

Damian shrugged. "It's not fair to keep this from her." He gestured between the two of them. "She won't understand why we deceived her, and she may not forgive. You're the one who warned me about her distrust of the men in her life."

"She might not forgive *me*, but she'll forgive *you*, my brother. You're hard to hold a grudge against."

Damian wasn't sure he agreed with that. "I'm telling her when I go back upstairs."

Nico laughed. "You *really* like her. Has a woman captured your legendary cold heart at last?"

Damian grinned abruptly. "My heart might have been cold, but my bed never was."

His brother gripped his shoulder hard. "Your heart was never cold, Damian. You just never found anyone worth giving it to."

Damian didn't want to discuss his feelings for Cassandra. He wasn't even sure what they were yet. So, he changed the subject. "I found something for you. It's the only reason I didn't bring Cassandra with me tonight. We were at one of Sotiris's safe houses, looking for the Talisman. Cassandra knew the moment she stepped inside that the Talisman wasn't there, but we found a vault-like room that served as a treasury of sorts. She was certain the room contained items important to Sotiris, but only of secondary value. I agreed for the most part, but then I found something he'd never have left behind on purpose. I suspect it was shoved aside by accident when the more valuable items were being loaded for transport elsewhere."

"Are you going to tell me what it is?" Nico asked dryly. "Something useful, I hope, because—" He sucked in a breath when he saw what Damian held in his hand. "Fuck me," he swore reverently. His hands shook when he reached for it, his knuckles whitening when he gripped the sides of the small chest, until Damian feared the ancient wood would crack.

"They're all there," Damian said quietly.

Nico opened the chest and touched the items contained inside, brushing his fingers over each in turn. There were four of them, one for each of the warriors Nico had lost to Sotiris's curse—the personal treasures that had been stolen by the traitor and sold to Sotiris. Items that were precious to the four warriors, but meaningless to anyone else. They'd been used as anchors, locking the curse irrevocably to each of the four men. Nico looked up, and there were tears in his eyes. "Do you know what this means?" he whispered.

Damian nodded. "Our brothers will soon be freed, and we'll be whole once again."

Nico barked out a short laugh. "Sotiris must be furious."

"If he knows. He might not yet."

"All the better. I'd love to be a fly on the wall when he learns of it, though. We might hear his scream all the way here." He leaned down and placed the small chest, now closed and latched, on the seat of his car, stroking the wood like a lover.

"Sotiris may be closer than you surmise," Damian commented. "Cassandra is convinced he means to target your O'Hare Airport with the Talisman."

Nico's attention sharpened. "Do you know where the artifact is now?"

"We surveyed a house your Lilia thought would be his staging area, but . . ." He was on the verge of telling Nico the tracking program was flawed, that Sotiris had laid a false trail for them to follow. But while his loyalty to his brother and fellow warrior was ancient and unbreakable, he'd discovered a growing loyalty to Cassandra as well. So he said nothing. It wasn't his place to discuss the methods she used on her assignments for Nico. He shrugged instead. "There was no one there. Lilia is going deeper, as Cassandra would say, and we hope to have more information soon."

Nico was giving him a bemused look, as if he knew better than Damian himself what the source of his reluctance was. "Go back to your warm woman, brother. But keep me informed. And tell Casey I'm staying in the area, just in case. I don't want the two of you going up against Sotiris without me."

They embraced again, holding tight for a long moment before pounding each other on the back and stepping away. "Tell Cassandra I said to be gentle with you."

"I don't think she cares what you say, brother," Damian said, laughing. "Besides, I like it rough."

"Don't let her go up against him alone," Nico said, his tone deadly serious. "Our Casey's got an ego. It gets her in trouble sometimes."

AN OBNOXIOUS trilling noise woke Casey from the best sleep she'd had in weeks. Her eyes opened on a nearly dark room, and she groaned. Yet another hotel room. Maybe it was time to go home for a while, maybe she should talk to Nick. . . . Shit!

She went from disoriented and half asleep to completely focused and wide awake in an instant. "Damian," she said, slapping the mattress as she reached for the phone on her bedside. She grabbed the phone, turning to frown at the vacant spot beside her as she hit the answer button. "Lili, what's up?" she asked as she turned on the light and stared around the empty room.

Yes, empty. Where the fuck was Damian?

"Another house just went live, Case," Lilia was saying. "But this one's buried deep, multiple layers of ownership. Even if Damian's right about the rest being a false trail, I don't think Sotiris can suspect we'd know about this house."

"Is it local?" Casey asked, climbing from the bed and walking around to the table where Damian had left his sword and jacket the previous night. Both were now gone.

"Even better," Lilia said eagerly. "Or, you know, worse, depending on your perspective. This house is *right* under the O'Hare flight path."

"Shit, okay." Casey turned on more lights. She didn't know why. It wasn't as if Damian could be hiding under a piece of furniture. "Text me the address, and I'll check it out. What time is it?" she asked, turning to stare at the red numbers on the bedside clock. Three in the morning. Where the fuck was Damian?

She caught sight of his laptop open on the table. Had he used it before he left? Hell, she was probably making something out of nothing. Maybe he'd needed some fresh air. The fact that he'd taken his sword meant nothing; he took that thing with him everywhere. Still . . . she hit the power key on Damian's laptop, bringing it to life. For all his criticism of her password earlier, he hadn't gotten around to adding one of his own. Which meant that the last page he'd been on came up when the screen lit. It was the messaging program, which she thought was odd. She leaned forward to read the last entry, ignoring a twinge of guilt. She really shouldn't be reading the man's messages without permission. But then, he should pass-word-protect his computer if he wanted privacy, she thought, and recognized it for what it was . . . a rationalization that let her read the damn note.

"Are you all right?" Lilia asked over the phone. "You sound distracted."

"Fine. Just tired, but I'll be okay after a cup of coffee." Her phone pinged with an incoming text from Lilia, which gave her the address of the latest house. "I got your text," she said. "I'll check it out and get back to you."

"Okay, but you be especially careful on this one, Case. If this is the real deal. . . . Maybe I should conference Nick in on this one."

Casey stared at the message history on Damian's computer. "Not yet," she said, struggling to keep the bitterness from her voice. "I'll call him if it pans out. No sense wasting his time."

"You sure you're okay? You really do sound funny."

"I'm fine, Lili. I'll call as soon as I know something, okay? Talk to you later."

She hung up before her friend could probe any further. Lilia was all too good at worming information out of people, and Casey had never been a good liar. Two more minutes and she might have been sobbing her heart out. What was it with her and men anyway? Why did she always fall for the good-looking jerks? Or maybe *she* was the jerk. No, just the idiot. While she worked with Lilia, stressing over Sotiris's next step, and terrified they wouldn't discover it in time, Nick and Damian were out somewhere indulging in a secret bromance. What a good chuckle they must have gotten out of her insistence that she needed to protect Nick from Damian. And her idea that he might be a spy, a mole sent in by Sotiris? How the two of them must have laughed at that one. Well, fuck Damian, and fuck Nick, too.

It took all of her discipline not to throw the damn computer at the wall. Hell, she wanted to gather all of Damian's things into his duffel and chuck it out the window. But, no, she had an even better idea. Storming over to the closet, she began pulling on her clothes. She wanted to be gone before he got back, wherever the hell he was. Nick's message hadn't given a place, just that he was "here." It could be miles away, or right downstairs in the lobby. Either way, she wouldn't be around when Damian returned. Let him be the one to wonder where *she'd* gone, for a change. She was done with waking up to find men gone. No more. Never again.

DAMIAN SLID THE card key into the reader, wincing as the lock gave a beep that he hoped was too faint for Cassandra to hear. Although, if she woke, it would be all the better. Because it was time to tell her about his and Nick's little subterfuge. If he came clean, if he explained their reasons, she might understand. And it had become very important that she not only understand, but that she forgive him.

But the moment the door opened, he knew he was too late. The same situational awareness that made him such an excellent warrior told him the room was empty even before he turned on the lights and saw that she was gone. And not just gone, but cleared out.

"Damn it," he swore, then dug the cell phone Cassandra had bought for him out of his pocket and scrolled through the contacts. It didn't take long because there were only three—Cassandra, Nico, and Lilia. He tried Cassandra first, but wasn't surprised when it rolled right to voicemail. He didn't bother leaving a message, because what could he say? What he needed to tell her was far too complicated for a phone message, especially since she'd probably delete it without listening.

He considered calling Nico next, but Nico wouldn't know where Cassandra had gone, and that was all that mattered right now. So, he called Lilia.

"Damian?" She sounded puzzled. Probably because, while his name would have come up as the caller, he'd never actually spoken to her on his own phone. She might not even have known he had one.

"Where is she, Lilia?" he asked, skipping the niceties.

"Where is . . . you mean Casey? I thought you were with her?"

"I was, but I went out to meet Nico, and now she's gone."

"Oh no! Damian, you have to go after her. I gave her a new location for the Talisman, and if you're not with her, that means she's decided to go alone."

"Damn it, Cassandra," he muttered to himself, then said, "Lilia, do you know where Nico is?"

"Of course, it's my job to—"

"I need you to get his ass back here right now."

"I can't—"

"Then tell him I said so. This is our fucking fault, and I don't have a damn car."

"Damian." Nico's voice was suddenly in his ear, courtesy of some of Lilia's computer wizardry, no doubt. "I'm on my way. Five minutes in front of the hotel."

There was a moment of dead air, and then Lilia's soft voice breathed, "You've got to catch up to her, Damian. I think this house is the real deal."

"Does Nico have the address?"

"Yes."

"Send it to my phone as well. I'm taking no more chances." He disconnected, then shoved the phone into his pocket and started for the door. Some instinct had him turning back to the table where his laptop, with its damning message, still stood open. And next to it, a Heckler & Koch MP5. The first gun he'd fired, the first gun he'd ever held in this reality or any other. And Cassandra had left it for him. It gave him hope, which was all he had to go on.

Well, that, and the fact that he was the greatest warrior alive today.

CASSANDRA FOUND it difficult to pay attention to what the nav was telling her, and had to backtrack more than once to make the right turn. She was so furious. With herself, with Damian, and even with Nick. All the years of loyal service she'd given that bastard and he'd pulled this crap on her. Damian, she could almost excuse. She knew about *esprit de corps*, and all the rest of it. She'd grown up hearing about the brotherhood of war, and about how a woman could never really understand such manly things. It was obvious that Nick and Damian had something similar going between them. She'd dismissed it as a bromance, but she'd known it was something much bigger. Nick held a special place in Damian's heart and history, and it went well beyond simple loyalty. If Nick had asked his warrior not to tell her about something, Damian's first instinct would be to obey. But that didn't let him off the hook entirely. Maybe his gut reaction was obedience, but at some point his brain, and, God damn it, his heart, should have kicked in with a more reasoned response.

She'd begun to believe that they had something together, that she *meant* something to him. Would she never learn?

Men like that—alpha males like her father or her ex, and now Damian, too—no one was more important to them than their own selfish needs. And the moment someone else's desires conflicted with their self-centered little worlds, they walked away without looking back.

Her needs meant nothing. It had been that way with her father, from the moment she'd informed him she would not be following the family tradition and enlisting in the military, but was instead joining the FBI. He'd looked at her as if she'd grown a second head, and then his eyes had gone cold and he'd walked out the door. That was the last time she'd heard from him.

And then there was her ex. Talk about a textbook daddy fixation. He'd been so much like her father, it was a wonder the two of them could exist in the same universe. And just like her father, he'd walked out of her life without a backward look the first time she'd disappointed him.

And now there was Damian. He was a warrior like her dad, and too handsome for his own good, just like her dad. She frowned. The analogy faltered there. She was the one walking away. But then, he'd lied to her, hadn't he? Made her feel like an idiot. What choice had he left her? Was she supposed to wait in that hotel like a good little girl, until the big man came back and deigned to offer an explanation? She was sure he had a million reasons for what he'd done. They always did. They could disappoint you over and over again, never show up when they said they would, miss your recitals, your graduations, year after year. And that was okay. But if she slipped up one time . . . bam! Good-bye, nice knowing you.

Her phone rang. She glanced at the dash screen, expecting it to be Damian again. But it was Nick. She ignored him, too, touching the decline button. Two minutes later, another call came through, this one from Lilia. No surprise there. Nick would have recruited her to talk some sense into Casey.

"Lilia," she answered.

"Casey, don't do this. Don't go in there alone."

"I don't know why not. I've been working alone for years. Hell, Nick's the one who originally gave me this assignment with no backup. So why the sudden hysteria?"

"Because there's more to it than Nick knew when he gave you that assignment. Come on, Case, you know that. You're the one those hell-hounds were chasing."

"I'm not stupid," she snapped, then immediately felt bad for doing it. None of this was Lilia's fault. "Look, Lili, I'm not going to storm the ramparts alone. I'm just going to check the place out discreetly. If it's nothing, like that last one, then we've wasted no one's time but mine."

"And if it's something? If the Talisman's in there?"

"Then I'll sit on the house to make sure the Talisman doesn't go anywhere, and I'll call in reinforcements."

"Reinforcements are already on the way. Nick and Damian, both. So why not wait—"

"Not *those* reinforcements. People I can trust. Terrell's waiting to hear from me, and—"

"Casey, I love you, but you're being an idiot. You can be pissed at the guy if you want, but Damian brings way more muscle to the game than Terrell ever could, and you know it. Not to mention Nick. And believe me, if—"

"Spare me the singing of Nick's praises. And I know better than you what Damian can do, but I don't *trust* either one of them."

Lilia sighed loudly. "Casey. Baby. Wait for—"

"Too late. I'm here. And I'm going to scope the place out. If you don't hear from me in an hour—"

"An hour?" Lilia scoffed. "Those two will be on you way before that."

"You think so?" Casey asked, watching as the garage door rolled up on the suspicious house, and a black Escalade with tinted windows backed down the drive and headed her way. She disconnected the call, turned off her engine and ducked down behind the wheel. She wouldn't be able to see them, but then, with those dark windows, she wouldn't have been able to see anyone in the vehicle anyway. More importantly, though, she couldn't risk them seeing *her*. The Escalade rolled past without stopping or even slowing down. Her Yukon fit right into the middle-class neighborhood, and it wasn't distinctive enough to call any attention to itself.

The Escalade, on the other hand, looked like it belonged in the motorcade of a president or a rock star. But that wasn't what made her slide carefully upright and snap a picture of the license plate before they turned the corner. No, what drew her attention, and what convinced her that this finally was the right place . . . was the fact that the Talisman was in the damn Escalade.

She reached down and pushed the starter button, wincing as the SUV's powerful engine came to life. But the Escalade was already gone, and no one at the house seemed to be paying any attention to the street. She executed a quick U-turn and went after the Escalade, inching forward at the intersection to be sure they were really gone, before she turned to follow. And then she called Lilia.

"Casey!" she answered. "Are you—?"

"I'm still fine, and I have a plate number for you." She started to read it off, but changed her mind. "I'll just text you the picture."

"Whose car is it?" Lili asked.

"I don't know, but it doesn't matter. What does matter is that the Talisman is on board. And I'm following it right now."

"Let me get the guys—"

"I'll lose it if I wait. You've got the plate, and I'll check in when I can." Then she hung up again. She hated doing that to Lilia, knowing she'd worry. But she couldn't deal with the other woman's mother-henning right now. She had the best of intentions, but Casey was an experienced operative. She sure as hell knew how to tail a suspect without getting caught.

The Escalade was easy to follow. Partly because of the thin early morning traffic, but also because it didn't belong. High-end SUV's were something drug dealers drove in this neighborhood, not hardworking folk. She hung back as far as she could, not wanting them to notice her. Her truck might fit in, but she still had to assume the driver was a professional. If he noticed the *same* truck in his rearview mirror, mile after mile, he might get suspicious. And she didn't want these people suspicious. She wanted them comfortable and secure, confident enough to take the Talisman wherever they needed it to be in order to complete their attack, so that she and her team would have a chance of snatching it before people started dying.

DAMIAN STRODE OUT of the hotel, blade on his back and MP5 in his hand. His sword was invisible in its enchanted scabbard, but the gun wasn't, and he was grateful when Nico pulled up before anyone had a chance to act on their alarm. Nico leaned over and opened the door before the car had even stopped, and Damian slid inside, dragging the door shut as they raced away with a crackling roar of the powerful engine.

"What the hell happened?" Nico asked, glancing at the in-dash display before making a tire-squealing turn onto the main road.

"As best I can tell, Cassandra woke and found me gone, and then somehow discovered that I'd slipped away to meet you without telling her. She cleared out of the room completely, and she won't answer my calls."

"What the hell is she thinking, taking this on alone?"

"She's thinking she can't trust us."

"It was only one fucking meeting."

"She doesn't know that."

"She'll understand once we find her, and you have a chance to explain. The good news is that she shouldn't be too far ahead of us. The bad news . . . Lilia's pretty convinced this latest address is the real deal."

"I should have told her I was meeting you. I shouldn't have just left," Damian muttered.

"You had your reasons, brother. We both did."

"They'll mean nothing if Cassandra gets hurt . . . or worse."

"That's not going to happen. We won't let it."

Damian gave him a bleak look. "We know better, Nico. Things happen, whether we want them to or not."

"Not this time," Nico said viciously. "I swear it, Damian. Not this time."

CASEY WATCHED THE Escalade turn into the driveway of a house that had seen better days. At least on the outside. The lawn was mostly dirt and old car parts, and the short driveway was cracked and overgrown with weeds. But the garage door slid up smoothly and quietly, closing behind the big SUV almost before the bumper cleared the space. She drove on by, just in case there was anyone watching, then circled the block and parked on a side street. She had no view of the house from there, but she wasn't planning any long-term surveillance. She wouldn't be practicing her cat burglar skills either. She'd already gone head-to-head with these people too many times in the last few days and, despite Damian's help, she hadn't made much progress. The thought of Damian was like a weight on her heart, and she pushed him out of her thoughts. It was an effort, but she wasn't going to think about him tonight. Eventually, she'd have to brief both him and Nick on what she found, but for now, she set everything aside except what she needed to accomplish the present task, which was gathering information.

Sotiris's people knew she was on to them by now, and they'd be waiting for her, expecting her to make a play for the Talisman before they could use it. They'd have a much heavier and much more alert guard on the device, wherever it was, which ruled out her sneaking in a window and snatching the thing as she had before. There was also the very strong possibility that Sotiris himself was in that house, maybe even in the Escalade she'd been following, and she wasn't ego-driven enough to take him on by herself. But she gave herself credit. If she hadn't acted as quickly as she had when Lilia called her, she would have missed the Escalade's departure from the other house. Instead of locating the Talisman and following it to the present hiding spot, she'd be sitting on her hands, watching another empty house.

By now, Lilia would have alerted Nick, and probably Damian, too. There was a tracker in her cell phone—standard equipment for all of Nick's hunters—which meant reinforcements were on the way. But that didn't mean she had to do nothing but wait. If she was careful, she could save everyone some time by gathering the information they'd need to breach the house's security.

She turned off her engine, then lowered her window and listened. It was something people rarely did anymore. The world had become such a noisy place that people were more interested in tuning it out than listening in. But you could tell a lot by listening. Especially in an old and established neighborhood like this. These few blocks probably saw a disproportionate amount of crime, which would seem to make it a perfect place for the bad guys to set up shop. But no matter how bad they were, they wouldn't fit in, and the local people would notice. As she sat there, she noted the same discrepancy with the sounds of the neighborhood as she had with the garage door. Just as the garage door had been too solid, its functioning too slick for the disreputable house, so the neighborhood was too quiet, even for this late at night. Hell, *especially* for this late at night. This was when criminals did some of their best work. So where were they?

Her guess was that the local bad guys had been warned off by the new crooks on the block. Either they'd been told to lay low—and had suffered a demonstration of the consequences—or Sotiris had placed a suppressing spell on the few square blocks surrounding the house. As soon as the thought occurred to her, she opened her senses, casting a wide net . . . and found it within seconds. It was stupid of Sotiris to use something so blunt, so obvious to someone with her particular sensitivity and training. He'd been too sure of himself, too certain he'd misdirected her investigation, and too determined to avoid a police presence, what with him plotting to shut down the Chicago air corridor and kill thousands of people from the rundown two-bedroom building down the block.

She ran her window back up, then opened the door and walked around to the back of the SUV to change clothes. Her jeans would work well enough, but she donned a black, oversized and fleece-lined hoodie. The nighttime air was cold, but that's not why she did it. Mostly she wanted to conceal her silhouette with the bulky clothes, and hide her face with the hood. It also happened to fit into the clothing style of the one or two people still on the street, though for all she knew, they could be working for Sotiris. The man hadn't survived this long by playing loose with his security.

Slamming the cargo hatch, she locked the doors, dropped the remote into an inside pocket of her jacket, and started off down the street, walking fast, as if she had someplace to go and wanted to get there. She headed away from the house first, turning for the alley that ran behind the yards. There were no streetlights back there, and very few houses offered anything more. One or two had weak lights over their back doors, but those did little more than add movement to the shadows. Casey stuck to the far side of the alley, ignoring the occasional barking dog and hoping the noise wouldn't draw any attention.

She slowed her pace, listening to every little sound, hyper-alert to her surroundings. The houses were small, she'd guess no more than two bedrooms. On the other hand, they all had ground-level windows, so she assumed there were basements. Basements were handy places to hide things, especially if you needed to shield the magical energy of something like the Talisman. It didn't work on her, because her talent was . . . what? Magical, she guessed. After all these years, it still struck her as odd that Sergeant Major Theodore "Ted" Lewis could have produced a child with such a fluffy gift.

She approached the target house. It was unremarkable to the naked eye, but she could feel the Talisman inside, like a beast testing the boundaries of its cage, waiting to get out. Pausing in the deep shadows cast by their back neighbor's tree, she crouched down and studied the house through the tall, chain-link fence that closed in the backyard. After a few minutes, she was forced to admit there was nothing to see. A little bit of light leaked around the drawn shades, and the infrequent passing shadow confirmed someone was inside. But there was nothing to distinguish this house from all the others, nothing except the shrieking of her magical senses, that was.

She had to believe they had some enhanced security on the place, but from where she stood, there was nothing obvious. Either the surveillance devices were all motion-sensitive and thus not detectable until it was too late, or Sotiris had set up magical wards that were too close-in for her to detect, until after she'd tripped one of them. She had no intention of testing her theory, however. By now, Nick was almost certainly on his way with Damian, and it was *his* job to handle Sotiris, not hers.

Rising from the crouch, she continued down the alley, intending to circle the block and do a walk-by of the front of the house from the other direction. A big, black dog with a mouthful of vicious-looking teeth came at her out of nowhere, straining against the chain holding it in place, and she jumped so violently that she nearly tripped. What was really creepy was that the dog didn't bark. Even its growl was more of a high whine, and she realized someone had severed the animal's vocal chords. Now *that* was someone she wouldn't mind meeting in a dark alley with Damian and his sword at her side.

She frowned. Why the hell had she put Damian in her little vengeance fantasy? She didn't need *either* of his swords. She shoved him out of her thoughts and reimagined herself in the dark alley with a big gun instead. Her frown only deepened. As vengeance fantasies went, it was much more satisfying when Damian had lopped off the man's head.

Speaking of heads . . . she needed to get hers back in the game. She walked on toward the opposite end of the alley, still alert, but fighting the urge to relax. That was the last thing she could afford to do. If there were any danger of detection, it would be on the other half of her little mission, when she planned to stroll right past the front of the house.

She reached the end of the alley and paused. Some instinct was warning her that there was danger here. She stretched her senses out as far as they could go, but felt nothing. Nothing magical, that was. She didn't have Damian's warrior instincts, which were pretty damn close to magic, too. And why was she thinking about him again? Determined to finish this recon and get back to her Yukon before he and Nick arrived, she marched to the end of the alley and turned . . . right into the arms of a big, burly guy who had one huge arm wrapped around her upper body, her arms pinned, and her mouth covered before she could so much as squeak a protest. He grinned down at her.

"You've caused a lot of trouble, bitch. It's time you made up for it."

The arm around her body jerked and suddenly his hand was on her breast, squeezing hard. She swallowed a gasp, more in anger than fear, and kicked back at him, thrashing as hard as she could.

"What the hell, Linwood?" another voice demanded. "The boss said to bring her around, not feel her up in the fucking alley."

"Fuck you," Linwood snarled. "It's not going to hurt the bitch, and the boss is too far into his big show-and-tell to notice a pipsqueak like me. Or her, for that matter."

"You maybe. But he asked for her specifically. Hand her over."

Well, *that* wasn't good, Casey thought to herself, then stumbled and nearly fell when the big thug abruptly shoved her in the direction of the other guy.

"You're back on patrol, Linwood. Try not to fuck it up," Thug Number Two snapped, then grabbed her arm and dragged her back down the alley. "Scream or make any noise at all, and I'll knock you out," he threatened.

"Thanks for the rescue," she said sarcastically.

"Shut the fuck up. You won't be so smart once the boss gets hold of you."

Casey had a feeling he was right about that. The "boss" had to be Sotiris, right? She'd been going head-to-head with his surrogates for almost as long as she'd been doing this job, but she'd never met the big man himself. And she couldn't say she was looking forward to it now. It seemed she'd walked right into a trap. He must have been aware of her following them the whole time. The big question was, why bother to capture her? Why not just kill her and be done with it?

Her captor dragged her through the dark backyard and up a few steps to the rear of the house. The door buzzed open almost the moment they hit the steps. It confirmed her assessment of the surveillance situation earlier. Not that it did her much good at this point.

They kept going through a small kitchen, into a hallway. They passed a dingy living room, and an even dingier bathroom, and then her captor was manhandling her down the stairs and into the basement. Nothing good ever happened in a basement.

"Cassandra Lewis," a smooth voice crooned. "We meet at last."

She spun around to find a man who could only be Sotiris standing there in the flesh. He wore a three-piece suit, of all things, and appeared older than she'd expected, given his ancient rivalry with Nick. Nick was late twenties, maybe thirty years old in appearance. But Sotiris looked to be in his late forties, a handsome man, with dark hair and elegant features.

She met his sneering gaze. "Uh huh," she said cautiously. "You could have called any time if you'd really wanted to meet me. We could have had a nice cup of coffee instead of freezing in this dumpy basement. Why'd you pick this house anyway? It's not exactly loaded with creature comforts," she added, casting a disapproving glance around the basement, her eye falling on a haphazard stack of empty wooden boxes, which, according to the stenciled labels, had once contained ammo and weapons. "Do we eat on the MP5 crate?" she asked.

Sotiris moved faster than she could follow, his right hand snapping out like a snake's strike, slapping her face. Hell, calling that a slap was too kind. It felt more like a truck hitting her as it knocked her to the floor.

"You will learn to respect your betters," he lectured, his voice completely devoid of emotion. No anger, no frustration. "Tie her up," he ordered someone behind her.

Suddenly, her arms were grabbed painfully tight, bound behind her back at the elbow and wrist, before she was spun around and shoved into a rickety chair in the middle of the basement. Her ears were still ringing, but while her captors tied her to the chair, she took the opportunity to check out the rest of the basement, looking for weaknesses, potential weapons, possible exits. And found not much.

She'd secretly hoped that someone had overlooked a stash of weapons in one of those boxes, but that seemed a vain hope. There was a plain concrete floor with two boarded-up windows high up on the wall, well out of her reach even if she wasn't bound to a chair. On the wall opposite the empty ammo boxes was an equally disorganized stack of old furniture and cardboard boxes. Everything there looked like it had simply been tossed into a big pile without any regard for the contents.

Granted, the furniture all looked as rickety as the chair she was tied to, but the boxes were taped shut and labeled, as if they had once mattered to someone. Maybe the previous owner of the house? She frowned, wondering if they'd left voluntarily—she chanced another glance around the cluttered basement—or if they'd left at all. That thought made her shudder, a reaction that Sotiris evidently took for stark terror. She wasn't terrified. Not yet. Scared out of her mind, for sure. But not terrified.

"Are you frightened, Ms. Lewis?" Sotiris simpered. But his next words were as hard and cold as ice. "You should be. Your life is now very much in my hands, and believe me, I've no care whatsoever for your continued well-being."

Casey forced herself to pay attention, to study him as she would any other problem. How did a human being turn into such a monster? Had he been born that way? Were sorcerers born to be good or evil? Nick probably knew, but they'd never discussed it, because until a few days ago, she hadn't known he was a sorcerer. She sighed. "What do you want?" she asked Sotiris, growing tired of the game.

"I want what's in that pretty little head of yours."

She gave him a puzzled look. "You mean the magic-sensing thing? Why would you—?"

"Don't be ridiculous. I'm a god in this reality. I don't need your puny talent."

"Then what?" she asked, truly confused.

"Information, you idiot. I want to know about your new friend."

She frowned again. "I don't know—"

The blow was a solid fist this time, from one of Sotiris's thugs. It connected with the side of her head, knocking her to the floor, chair and all. Her head hit the concrete floor, and she lay there a moment, nerves singing with too much pain to move, her thoughts too blurred to react in any way.

"Get her up."

She was jerked upright, the ropes ripping into her skin, her head still ringing from the double impact.

"Tell me about the warrior."

Casey blinked at Sotiris in confusion, and it wasn't an act. She was having trouble focusing her thoughts. "Warrior," she repeated, her tongue feeling clumsy and thick as she tried to make sense of the word.

She saw the blow coming this time and tried to duck away from it. The thug's fist missed her head, but she screamed when it hit her still-healing shoulder. "Stop it," she hissed desperately, tears streaming down her face. "What do you want?"

"Who's the warrior? What's his name?"

She had enough brain power left to be puzzled at the track of Sotiris's questions. He wanted Damian's name? Why would he. . . . *No*, he wanted to know which one of Nick's warriors had been freed from his curse. Why did it matter so much to him?

"He didn't tell me his name," she said quickly, to avoid getting hit again. "He doesn't speak any English, and whatever language he does speak, I've never heard before."

"You've spent several days with him. You must have learned something."

She shrugged, swallowing a pained cry for her poor shoulder. "He's pretty jumpy," she rasped. "Everything scares him, or at least, it freaks him out. Cars, phones, television, you name it," she continued, warming to her deception. "He's like a caveman or something."

"And the weapon?"

"You mean his sword?" she asked, playing dumb. She started to shrug again, but caught herself. "It's a big-ass sword," she said dully. "That's all I know. I don't do edged weapons."

Sotiris's hand snapped out, striking her across the face. It was better than being punched and shoved to the floor again, but as she tasted blood in her mouth and tongued a loose tooth, she thought that wasn't saying much.

"Where did he come from?"

"I don't know. I was too busy fighting for my life against a bunch of assholes to notice," she said bitterly. Then she couldn't help adding, "Oh, wait, the assholes are friends of yours, aren't they?"

"You're too smart by half, Ms. Lewis."

Not smart enough, obviously. Or she wouldn't be tied to a chair, playing punching bag to *this* asshole.

"It's really too bad you got suckered in by Katsaros and his noble intentions. Tell me, have you fucked him yet? That's usually his way."

Casey fought to control her reaction to the crude turn in the conversation. He'd probably done it on purpose, just to rattle her.

"I'll take that as a '*no*'," Sotiris continued with barely a breath in between. "That's all right, I don't need to know about Nicky boy, I know everything there is. After all, we practically grew up together."

Well, shit, then why wasn't he asking Nick these questions? "Look," she said, trying to sound reasonable. "I get it. You and Nick have a history. Or maybe you just don't like the competition. But whatever it is, I don't have your answers."

"I don't give a fuck about Katsaros. I want to know which one of his over-muscled followers turned up in that alley and why."

"And I'm telling you I don't know. He came out of nowhere and started waving a damn sword around. I thought he was nuts, but then he started killing your guys, so I didn't care. And afterward, Nick called and said he couldn't get away, so I've been stuck babysitting the guy."

"Really?" Sotiris said cynically. He gestured to the side, and one of his flunkies turned over what looked like . . . shit! They had her purse, which meant they had access to her damn cell phone. The flunky handed it to Sotiris. "Let's see whom we have here. He scanned her call log. "Well, there's Nick, of course. And that silly assistant of his. Too chipper by half, that one." He scrolled farther down the list. "A few unknown callers, probably junk but worth checking out." He frowned. "And that's it?" he asked in disbelief. "Goodness, you don't have much of a life do you? What does the warrior look like?" he snapped abruptly, clearly hoping to throw her off with the sudden change of subject.

She gave a genuine sigh. Her head was killing her, her jaw was throbbing in time with her racing heart, and it felt like her arm had been ripped from her shoulder *again*. And this guy wanted to go all fanboy on Damian for some reason.

"He's big, blond, and good with a sword. That's all I know."

"What does Katsaros call him?"

"I don't know. I've never seen them together. They've been having these private little meetings without telling me."

"You're annoyingly useless. Other than as an amusement for my men, of course. Lucky for you, they won't have as much time to play as they'd like." He looked over her head to the guy who'd punched and knocked her over her earlier. "Get rid of her, and make it messy. I want a pretty package waiting for Katsaros when he arrives."

He spun on his heel and headed up the stairs, calling orders as he went. She heard just a snippet of conversation from the top of the stairs, after he left the basement. It wasn't much. Just a few words, but with what she already knew, it was enough. He planned to auction off the Talisman to the highest bidder sometime very soon. And before *that*, he was going to do something spectacular enough to ensure the artifact fetched a high price.

They were officially out of time. They needed to stop him *now*. *She* needed to stop him. But how?

Her captor came around to stand in front of her, letting her see his face for the first time. To say he was pierced was an understatement. How the hell did this guy ever get through airport security? Both eyebrows, his nose, his lip, his ears . . . all had multiple piercings each. It made her wonder where else he was sporting metal, but as quickly as she had the thought, she shoved it away. She really didn't want to know.

He grinned, and she saw he'd filed his teeth to sharp points. And her fate was in this guy's hands. A guy who'd been ordered to "make it messy." Damn.

NICK DIDN'T BOTHER trying to be discreet as he roared down the Interstate. It was impossible with the Ferrari anyway. It was too noticeable, too much like an invitation to pull him over. Not for the first time, he wished he'd taken the time to switch out cars before leaving Kansas. But he'd been so excited when he'd heard Damian had been freed, that all he could think about was getting here. He could deal with the cops, if it came to that. Vampires weren't the only creatures who could magic their way out of a ticket. But he didn't want to waste the time it would take.

His phone rang and he glanced at the caller ID. Lilia. "Good morning, beautiful," he said. He always called her that, not because she was beautiful—or not *only* because she was beautiful because she sure as hell was—but because it made her cheeks pink up in a blush every time. He knew she was blushing now, even though he couldn't see her.

"Nick," she said in that breathy way she had when he'd caught her off-guard. She cleared her throat, then shifted into pure business mode. "Something weird is happening with the signal from Casey's phone," she said briskly.

"What?" Damian demanded from the passenger seat.

"Damian? It's good you're there. But you guys should have let me know you'd met up."

"Lilia," Nick chided. She had a tendency to get spun-up about details and forget the big picture. "What about the phone signal?"

"Right, sorry. Casey's phone stopped for a while, but it's moving again, and that doesn't make sense. I've tried calling her, but there's no answer, and that's not good, not normal. Casey *always* stays in touch. She's the only one of you guys who follows protocol on that. She might not be able to talk, but she'd at least answer the damn phone, even if it was only to let me hear what was happening on her end."

"Where is she now?"

"The *phone* was stationary for a long time, but it's now traveling down I-355."

Nick thought for a moment. "Okay, give me the address of her last stop, but keep tracking the phone."

"I'm sending the address to your nav system."

Nick glanced at the map and turned the wheel sharply, crossing three lanes of traffic to get to the off-ramp. It wasn't a great neighborhood, but he could see why Sotiris would have chosen it. An area like this, with its crime rate? No one would ask questions, because they wouldn't want to know. Knowledge wasn't always power in places like this. His engine screamed, waking neighbors and their dogs, as he braked to turn onto the street where Casey had stopped, or at least where her phone signal had paused before racing away.

"Shit, is that fire?" Damian was leaning forward to stare at a small house that did indeed seem to be on fire. "Is this the house? Is Cassandra in there?" he asked.

Nick shot a glance at his nav system. It was the right house. Fuck. Damian would be uncontrollable if something happened to Casey. "The signal's moving, Damian," he said, trying to sound reasonable. "She's not there anymore."

"Then who the fuck is that?"

Nick looked up to see two men race out of the burning residence, but instead of calling for help or acting like people who'd made a narrow escape, they were standing on the dead lawn and laughing their asses off.

"She's in there," Damian growled.

"You don't know—"

"I do, damn it. Stop the fucking car."

The two laughing idiots had turned to stare as the Ferrari drew closer, but when Nick roared to a tire-scorching stop in front of the burning house, they made a dash for their own car. Damian was on them in an instant, slamming one into the vehicle they'd been trying to reach, and grabbing the other by the neck, holding him several inches off the ground.

Nick crossed to the one lying on the ground next to the car and lined up the laser sight on his Glock 23 so that it painted a red dot on the asshole's forehead. The guy could see the light over the barrel, and knew what it meant.

"Where is she?" Nick demanded. "And where's the Talisman?"

The man grinned, displaying an impressive set of sharp teeth. Impressive in the sense that the guy was out of his fucking mind and yet still functioning.

"The Talisman's gone," he said, blood adding a gruesome touch to his grin. "And so's the bitch."

Damian spun at the man's words, his fingers still digging into the other asshole's throat, still choking the breath from him. With an almost absent gesture, Damian tightened his grip and twisted, breaking the man's neck. He tossed aside the limp body and, ignoring Nick's laser sight, grabbed the pierced idiot instead. But the guy only laughed.

"What're you going to do, big man? You can save the bitch or save the Talisman. But you can't do both. What's it going to be?"

A stricken look crossed Damian's face when he turned to stare at the burning house. Nick wanted to believe that Casey was still alive in there, but, even if she was, he couldn't set aside the thousands of people who might die if they didn't recover the Talisman. "You take the house," he said abruptly. "I'll go after the Talisman."

Damian nodded, then broke the pierced guy's neck as absently as he had the other's, before running into the burning building without even a heartbeat of hesitation. But that was Damian. He didn't know fear. He knew loyalty and love, and he'd give his life for the people he cared about. Which now included Casey.

Nick moved almost as fast as his brother, racing back to the still-running car to slide behind the wheel and tear away from the curb. He punched the number for Lilia.

"Did you find her?" she asked.

"Not yet," Nick said grimly. "Damian's on it. I need the phone signal."

"It should be on your nav system. I shared that with you earlier."

Nick glanced at the map displayed on the in-dash screen, and there it was. Casey's phone was still traveling due south on the I-355. Where the fuck was Sotiris going?

"Shit," Lili swore, all the more shocking because she did it so rarely. "The signal . . . it's gone."

"What do you mean 'gone'?" he demanded, knowing he sounded far harsher than he usually was with Lilia. He stared at the screen, which no longer showed any signal from the phone.

"I mean gone as in dead, kaput. No signal," she said, confirming what he was seeing.

"How the hell does that happen? Is the battery dead?"

"No," she said thoughtfully, and he could hear the soft tap of her computer keys. "They've either removed the battery, or crushed the whole thing so thoroughly that it's simply gone dead."

"Why would they do that?"

"Because they know we're tracking the phone, Nick," she said impatiently.

"Right. Okay, mark the spot it went dead. I'll get someone out there to search the ground, see if we can find it. In the meantime, I'm going back to Damian. If anything's happened to Casey, he'll—"

"If anything's happened to her, I will make it my personal ambition to destroy their virtual life," Lilia snarled. "I will wreak such havoc on their credit history, on any financial or social interaction they have, that they'll be reduced to living off the grid, in their car. If they're lucky."

Nick agreed with the sentiment. But he had ways of destroying an enemy that were far less virtual. And if they'd hurt Casey . . . well, she was *his,* and he would never again be forced to stand by while his people suffered. After a lifetime of rejecting everything his empire-building father stood for, he'd finally embraced what was very possibly the most important lesson his father had forced upon him: when attacked, you hit back ten times as hard and a thousand times more painfully. And Nick had had millennia to devise ways of inflicting pain.

IT WAS THE SMOKE that brought Casey back to consciousness. She coughed hard, choking, her eyes burning as she struggled to remember where she was. Something crashed near her head, sending embers flying, some of them landing on her bare skin, but when she tried to brush them away, she realized she was tied, hand and foot. The knowledge jolted her awake. She looked around, automatically taking stock of her situation. It wasn't good. She was in a basement with piles of junk all around, *flammable* junk, and dotted amongst the junk . . . dancing patches of smoky flame, growing bigger by the second.

Her mind froze for a moment, her thoughts nothing but white noise and fear. She was going to die. Tied to a chair, exhausted, too hurt to move, much less free herself, with the fire now burning hot enough that she could feel it on her bare skin. Her lungs were straining for air, short panting breaths that were making it difficult to think, and for some reason, her brain conjured up . . . Damian. Her own personal warrior god, who'd survived a thousand or more years trapped in a prison of stone, who'd held onto hope while buried for centuries in the utter darkness of a cave. If he could do that, then damn it, she could do this. She might die anyway, but at least she'd go down fighting.

She looked around with fresh determination, memory clearing her thoughts like a splash of ice-cold water. She remembered Sotiris's pierced and tattooed henchman bragging about his piercings, telling her about some of the ones she couldn't see, about how much it hurt when he was strung up by the steel loop in his dick, or the pins in his back, and how much he loved the pain.

"But you know what's even better?" he asked, flashing a short, very sharp-looking knife in front of her eyes. "Cutting someone else," he told her, the gleam of insanity so obvious in his eyes that she wondered how Sotiris had managed to contain him. He placed the flat of the blade just under her eye and scraped downward, not hurting her, not drawing blood. Not yet. But the point of the knife was so close to her eye that she could see it reflecting the orange and red. . . . Wait. Orange and red? She didn't dare turn her head, but she slid her gaze sideways and saw the first licks of flame among the boxes.

Her pierced friend followed her gaze, then straightened with a curse. "God damn it, you fucking pyro. I told you to wait."

A second man appeared on Casey's other side, a classic Zippo lighter in one hand, and a wild look in his eyes that made the pierced asshole seem sane. Where did Sotiris find these guys? He giggled. "It'll burn slow."

"No, it won't, you fucking moron. Damn it." He spun away, staring around him at the tinder-dry boxes, the old wooden furniture. "Shit. Let's get the fuck out of here."

"What about her?" the pyro thug asked, trailing the still-warm Zippo over her cheek.

"What about her, fuckwad? You wanna stay and fuck her while she burns, have at it. But I'm leaving."

Pyro's breathing increased, as if he was excited by the possibility. Casey swallowed hard. She didn't know what would be worse—dying in a fire, or having this creep rape her. Wait, yes, she did. The smoke would get her before the fire ever did, so she voted for fire over rape. Definitely.

"I'd love to stay," Pyro hissed in her ear, "but the master has such wonderful things planned. So much destruction." He licked her cheek, and then, laughing, flicked the Zippo open and tossed the open flame onto something she couldn't see, before shoving her chair over and slamming her head onto the hard floor one more time.

She'd lost consciousness then. She remembered that much. The blow to her head had been one too many. But, as grateful as she was to be alone and awake, her future looked pretty damn bleak. She couldn't make out much from her position on the floor, but she could see that the wooden stairs and bannister leading out of the basement were dotted with flame, almost like a deliberate pattern. Pyro's work, no doubt. But what worried her was the knowledge that he had to have used an accelerant for the pattern. And if there was more of that scattered around, the whole basement could explode into flames at any minute.

It would have been easy to simply lie there and go to sleep at that point. To accept the inevitable and let the smoke do the rest. But fuck that. She wasn't going to die for her enemies' convenience. She took stock of her situation.

She was still lying on her side and tied to a damn chair. Her lungs were burning, but at least the air was a little better down on the floor. She tested the ropes holding her and knew she'd never break them. Everything else in this basement was junk, but the ropes were new. On the other hand, the chair was part of the junk. It wobbled loosely when she moved and the seat under her ass, when she'd been upright, had been falling apart.

Twisting her head around, she focused on a stack of more solid-looking, wooden boxes and started scooting backward in that direction, thinking she could smash the chair—and herself, but, hey, no one said it was a perfect plan—against the boxes until something broke. Preferably the chair, not her bones. But once she started moving, she realized two things: one, it was damn difficult to move tied up the way she was, plus it hurt, and two, when she'd hit the floor that last time, the impact had actually cracked the wood under her left arm, weakening its connection to the chair. She pulled hard and it broke away completely.

Score! she thought to herself. Moving was easier now that she had greater flexibility in at least one arm, and she managed to drag herself over to the outer wall, with its row of three, high-up windows. Only one of those was uncovered, and that was only because someone had ripped away the tattered black cloth that had been nailed over it. She'd have to reach the window, break it, and then climb to the outside, and all with a chair tied to her ass.

"Damn it," she muttered, trying not to think about the fact that the smoke was getting thicker, the fire hotter. She searched the junk closest to the window, looking for something she could use, something within reach, and found an old length of galvanized pipe. Wielding it awkwardly with her left hand, she smashed the wood holding her right arm until she had both arms free. She still couldn't reach her legs, since they were tied to the back legs of the chair, which meant she could only stand in a hunched-over position as she began crawling over the junk below the window, dragging herself upward, inching closer to the uncovered window.

Behind her, the fire was spreading, with a thick smoke now blanketing the ceiling, making it harder to breathe the higher she climbed. She heard a distant siren that might be the fire department coming, but she wouldn't last that long.

Gripping the pipe in one hand, she crawled ever higher, surprised to discover a workbench of some kind just below the window. When she managed to clamber up onto it, it gave her a solid surface from which to swing the pipe. The glass shattered with a satisfying crack, but behind her, the fire made a whooshing sound as the cold air rushed in from outside to feed the flames. She didn't turn to look, didn't need to see. She could feel the heat growing against her back as she broke out the remaining glass in the window frame and saw her next problem. She could wiggle her way out that window, but the damn chair wasn't going to fit. She screamed in frustration.

DAMIAN SMASHED through the locked front door of the house and found the back of the small structure almost fully engulfed. He turned for the hallway and the two bedrooms, tearing them apart as he searched for Cassandra, convinced she was alive and in this house somewhere. Nico had his expensive car and his technology, but Damian had his gut. And it was telling him she was here.

Feeling sick at all the possibilities of what could happen, he raced out of the last bedroom and into the hallway, terrified that they'd left her in the kitchen at the heart of the fire. But on the way, he caught sight of an ordinary wooden door. He touched it in passing and slammed to a halt. It was hot, so hot that it wouldn't last much longer. There had to be a basement behind it—the heat was too intense for anything smaller, and the layout of the house permitted nothing else. Once again, his gut spoke, telling him Cassandra was down there in the heart of that fire. He took a step back and kicked open the door, flying back on his ass when flames erupted from the opening.

"Cassandra!" he called, his voice drowned by the steady rumble of the flames. He turned and raced from the house. He was fearless, not stupid. He'd never make it down those stairs through the fire, but there had to be another way into the lower level. He tore around to the back of the house, sucking in great lungsful of air as he went. If it was this bad for him after just a few minutes in that house, he could only imagine what it must be like for Cassandra. Was she conscious, injured, or even bound? Was she watching the flames come closer, her lungs filling with smoke, killing her slowly with every breath?

He rounded the building to the sound of shattering glass, followed by a woman's angry scream.

"Cassandra!" he roared and drew his blade. "Stay back!"

"There's no fucking room!" she shouted, and despite the anger, despite the hoarse growl in her voice, it was the sweetest sound he'd ever heard.

He dropped to his knees and saw she was right. His blade was preternaturally sharp, but he could as easily cut her as the wall, which was his target. Thinking quickly—which was, after all, what he did best—he ripped off his leather jacket and wrapped it around the blade to shorten it to a workable length. The edge would cut through the leather and then his hand soon enough, but he wouldn't need much time, and he would heal.

Using the blade like a long knife, he sliced through the old stucco and wood wall, until the opening was big enough that he could reach through and drag her out, cursing when her body got hung up on even the larger opening.

"I'm tied to this damn chair," she croaked, choking out a sobbing laugh.

"Hold on to me," he ordered, sheathing his blade. Her arms came around his neck, and he reached behind her to break away the remnants of a wooden chair, until finally, he could pull her all the way through the window and into the fresh air. Picking her up in his arms, he carried her to the far back end of the big yard next to a tall chain-link fence. It might have been safer to head for the street, but they were away from the burning house here, and the smoke was blowing in the opposite direction. Besides, he didn't know the situation on the street yet, didn't know if Sotiris had more men about, or if the human authorities would accost him the moment he appeared with Cassandra in his arms.

She clung to him for only a moment when he stopped at the fence and put her on her feet, coughing so viciously that he worried she couldn't stop. But eventually, she managed several deep breaths, and her fingers loosened their grip on his arm. And then, avoiding his eyes, she stepped back and asked, "Do you have a knife?"

"Cassandra," he murmured, frustrated and angry at the events that were tearing them apart.

"I need a knife, Damian."

"I'll do it, damn it." Gritting his teeth, he pulled the blade from his belt and cut through the remaining bindings on her arms, then reached for her wrist, which was swollen and bloody, still wrapped in lengths of rope. "Let me—" he started to say, but she snatched her arm away.

"I'll do it," she insisted, her hand trembling as she reached for the knife.

"Stop it," he said impatiently. "You'll cut yourself and only make it worse. Let me help you, damn it."

She pursed her lips angrily, but nodded and held out both wrists. Damian took one of her hands and carefully slid the sharp blade beneath the ropes. She hissed in pain when the back of the blade touched her raw skin, but he held her steady and sliced through the rope with a single move. Taking her other wrist, he did the same, then put a hand on her hip. "Hold still."

She stiffened beneath his touch, but he did what needed to be done, quickly removing the remains of the chair and the ropes from her legs. "We need to treat those rope burns. They'll fester."

"I'm aware of that," she snapped. She drew a calming breath through her nose, but then destroyed the image with another bout of coughing. Panting, breathless, she said, "We should leave before the authorities get here—"

"I've taken care of that," Nico said, coming around the house and crossing the deep yard to join them. "Cassandra," he said gently. "Do you need—?"

She flashed Nico an angry glare. "You can both go. I don't need anything from—"

"Damian, would you excuse us for a moment?" Nick snapped.

Damian stared at his old friend, confused.

"Just for a moment," Nico said, meeting his eyes. "Please."

Damian didn't want to leave Cassandra, even if she was so angry that she wouldn't look at him. He needed to explain, to make her understand why he and Nico had needed to meet, and he couldn't do that if he wasn't with her. On the other hand, this was Nico. The one person he trusted more than any other on this earth. He nodded. "I'll wait around front."

Nico frowned. "There will be firemen and police arriving soon. We'll want to leave before they get here."

"Cassandra," Damian said. "Where's your vehicle?"

She looked him in the face at last, and gratitude flashed in her eyes, there and gone so quickly, he might have imagined it. "Around the corner," she told him. "They took my purse, but there's a spare remote in a magnetic case in the rear passenger wheel well. You know which one that is?"

He smiled slightly, wondering if she was being intentionally insulting or if she really thought he was too stupid to understand her directions.

"He knows," Nico interrupted before they could use up time that they obviously didn't have.

"I'll find it," Damian told her and hopped over the tall fence into the alley, noting, as he did, that the house didn't have long before it would collapse.

CASSANDRA WATCHED as Damian easily levered himself up and over the tall fence. He was the very picture of athletic grace in his tight jeans and T-shirt, which was all he had on, despite the cold air. His leather jacket had been ruined when he'd used it to pad his grip on the sword, but—She frowned when she noticed the blood on the fence.

"He's bleeding," she said. "The blade must have cut through the leather of his jacket and into his hand." She started to go after him, but Nick stopped her.

"Damian knows blades. He knew what would happen, but he did it anyway. He cares about you, Casey."

"Not enough," she muttered.

"Oh, fuck that," he snapped angrily. "Stop feeling sorry for yourself."

Her eyes went wide. Had she ever seen Nick actually get angry? Had she ever seen *any* genuine emotion from the man?

"He's the best man you'll ever meet," he continued heatedly, "and you're sulking because he hasn't shared his soul with you? How long have you known him? A week? What the hell do you expect?"

"Honesty!" she shouted, her eyes filling with tears despite herself. She hurt everywhere; it hurt to *breathe*, for fuck's sake. And her heart was a raw ache inside her chest. The very last thing she needed right now was a lecture on her love life, especially not from Nick, whose idea of a long-term commitment was a few days. "*He* lied to me, and *you* made me feel like a fool."

"Well, welcome to the real world. There are things about my life, about my life with *Damian*, that could get people killed, people we love. So we made a mistake. *I* made a mistake. Don't blame Damian for it. He wanted to tell you everything. He *would* have told you everything if you'd been there when he got back to the hotel. I'm *old*, Casey. I've had several lifetimes of keeping secrets just to stay alive—my secrets and other people's too. You say trust doesn't come easily to you? Well, multiply that by a thousand, and that's how I feel. You don't think that's fair? Well, shit, Case. Life isn't fucking fair. But if you're stupid enough to walk away from Damian, then maybe you don't deserve him."

And with that, he spun around and hopped the fence with the same ease and athleticism that Damian had shown. More proof that he was the warrior Damian claimed, more evidence of just how little she'd really known him. The wind shifted and she looked around, nearly choking on the smoke from the burning wreck of a house. Why the hell was she still standing there, and why had they left her all alone? Oh, right. Because she'd asked them to. Probably not a good plan on her part. But wait, Damian had asked about her Yukon—

"Cassandra." Damian's deep voice cut through her self-pity. He touched her arm and she swung around to face him. It really was eerie the way he could sneak up on her. Behind him, the gate was hanging open in the back fence. "Your truck's in the alley," he said. "Come on."

She looked down at his hand on her arm. At the blood coating his fingers. "You're still bleeding."

He snatched his hand back and wiped it on his jeans. "Sorry."

As if she cared that he was getting blood on her. "Damian—"

"We need to get out of here," he said gruffly. "Can you walk?"

She nodded, even though she wasn't sure. She took a single step, wincing at the stabbing pain in her hip. She must have bruised it somewhere. Maybe when the chair had crashed to the floor the second time. She took a second step, but her foot never hit the ground. Damian swept her into his arms and started for the gate.

"Sorry, sweetheart. But we have to hurry."

She wanted to protest, but she was so tired and sore, so cold. And he was more than warm. He was hot, like a furnace, his chest deep and comforting. She sighed, relaxing into his strength. Then she noticed he was holding his bloody hand away at a weird angle, so it wouldn't touch her. Fuck.

"Damian—"

"Almost there," he said, again interrupting her before she could finish.

Was he afraid of what she was going to say? Did he really think she'd argue with him when he'd just swooped in like some mythological hero to save her life and carry her to safety? She thought about it. Well, yeah, he probably did. She'd had her reasons for leaving. Good reasons. But Nick's words came back to her. *Life isn't fucking fair.* Sure, her life hadn't been perfect. But it sure as hell had been better than what Damian had been through.

She rested her head against his shoulder, saying with her body what he wouldn't let her say with words. *Thank you. I trust you.*

THEY WERE BACK at the hotel, the same one she'd left that morning, the one she'd been convinced she'd never be coming back to, especially with Damian's arms around her. But she was too worn out to be angry, and she saw the situation a little differently now. She had a good idea of what, or *whom,* he and Nick were protecting—the other warriors, the ones still trapped by Sotiris's curse. And she knew how important the missing fighters were to Damian. And then there was what Nick had said about Damian wanting to tell her everything. It didn't surprise her that Nick kept secrets; she'd always known and accepted that. And she realized with a start that it wasn't the secret that was bothering her, it was the sense that Damian was choosing Nick over her. That the two of them had a relationship that would always take precedence over whoever else was in his life.

Damian slid the key into the lock and pushed the heavy door open, practically carrying her into the room, with his arm around her waist from behind. He sat her on the bed and kneeled in front of her, staring into her face. "Can you take off your clothes? Do you need help?"

She wanted to weep. He was being so sweet and so careful with her. "I can do it," she told him and began unbuttoning her blouse, realizing when she was halfway done that there wasn't much left of it. Between the fire and her own struggles to free herself, the thing was ruined. She might as well have asked Damian to cut it away with his knife.

And where was Damian anyway? She lifted her head to see him through the open door of the bathroom. The shower was running, the room filling with steam. He was half-naked, wearing only his jeans as he leaned against the marble sink, both hands on the sink top, his arms stiff while his head hung between his slumped shoulders in a pose of utter defeat. It hurt her heart to see him like that. A proud warrior brought low. Was he longing for the world he'd been sucked away from? For the friends he'd lost, or the days when he and Nick had fought the good fight against Sotiris, with an army at their backs?

She pulled the remains of her blouse down her arms and tossed the ruined garment onto the floor. She managed to unhook the front clasp on her bra, but when she went to slide it down her arms, she couldn't suppress a soft cry of pain.

Damian spun instantly and was at her side a moment later.

"It's okay," she said, raising a hand to forestall him. "It just surprised me, that's all."

He went to his knees in front of her, stroking a hand over her head and through her hair. "Let me help you, Cassandra. I know you don't want me here, but—"

"You're wrong," she said softly. "I do want you here. There's no one else I can trust. No one else I'd want." She grasped his arm. "Will you shower with me? I don't know if I can do it alone."

His head came up, his eyes meeting hers in surprise. "Of course. I'm here for you."

She nodded, then dug her fingers in where she was touching his arm. "It'll be easier to get these jeans off if I stand."

He remained on his knees, bracing her effortlessly as she stood, then helped her unbutton her jeans and slide them down her legs, cursing when he saw the bruising on her hip, when the pain brought tears to her eyes.

"By the gods, Cassandra, what did he do to you?"

She shook her head. "Sotiris never touched me. He left that to his creepy sidekick. Luckily, he didn't have much time. He knocked me around, but some of this is from me trying to get out of that house."

He hooked his thumbs in her plain cotton panties and pulled those down, too, so that she stood naked in front of him.

"Hey," she said half-joking. "No fair. You're still wearing clothes."

"Not for long," he muttered, then swung her into his arms with the effortless strength that made her belly heat with lust despite her injuries.

He carried her into the bathroom and set her on her feet in front of the open shower door. Reaching inside, he checked the water temperature, grunting in satisfaction.

"Can you stand on your own?" he asked. "Just long enough for me to take these off?" He gestured at his jeans.

She looked at the shower, with its soft rainfall showerhead and enticing steam. "I can manage." He held her hand until she was under the water, welcoming the sting of her various cuts and scrapes, the warmth sinking into her bruises. A moment later, he was in there with her, his big hands so careful as he soaped away the dirt and grime, his fingers massaging her scalp as he shampooed the smoke and soot from her hair.

She leaned back against his chest. "You should do this for a living," she murmured, feeling so much better than she had any right to expect after such a harrowing day.

He lifted the handheld shower attachment and rinsed her hair thoroughly. "You're going to be sore in the morning."

"How is that different from how I feel now?" she asked, twisting to see his face.

That finally got a smile out of him. "I see your point." He reached around her and turned off the water, then wrapped her in one of the big towels and dried her carefully. "Come on, let's get you into bed."

"Are you planning to take advantage of me?" she asked, so tired that she felt almost drunk. Which was the only explanation she could come up with for saying such a stupid thing.

"No," he said calmly. "I don't do that."

"I didn't mean—"

"Shh. I know. Come on, sweetheart." He didn't swoop her up this time, but simply guided her out of the bathroom and over to the bed. He'd already pulled the covers back at some point; she didn't remember when. But it was sheer heaven to slide between the fresh, clean sheets and close her eyes. His muted footsteps walked away from her and her eyes snapped open.

"Where are you going?"

"To dry off. I don't want to get the bed wet."

"Oh." Her eyes drifted closed. "Okay."

A few minutes later, the bed dipped and his heat seared her back a moment before he wrapped her in his arms and pulled her into the protective curve of his body. She felt the tears start, and told herself it was exhaustion. But that was a lie. She loved him. She didn't know how or when it had happened, but it had. She loved him, and it was going to hurt like hell when he walked away.

CASEY WOKE THE next morning to Damian's arm heavy over her hip, his heat at her back. And that wasn't the only thing she could feel at her back. His erection was a hard length against her ass, and they were both naked. She lay perfectly still, grateful that he was still sound asleep, his breathing slow and steady, his chest moving in rhythm. She closed her eyes and sorted through it all—everything that had happened yesterday and last night, what Nick had told her, what Damian had done. And how good, how right, it felt to wake up in his arms. Maybe it made her weak to need him the way she did, but where was it written that she had to be alone to be strong? Even if it only lasted a little while.

She wiggled her ass just a little bit, flexing the glutes she worked so hard to keep firm and strong, and was rewarded with a hitch in his breathing, a slight tightening of his fingers on her hip. She reached back and stroked his bare thigh, pushing her ass back to rub against his cock.

"Cassandra," he said, sounding almost breathless. "Sweetheart, wake up."

She smiled. He thought she was assaulting him in her sleep, and he was too much a gentleman to take advantage. Maybe he was one of the good guys, after all.

"I *am* awake," she said, digging her nails into his ass and pulling him closer.

He slid his hand down to her belly, caressing gently. "Baby," he said quietly. "You're still injured. We shouldn't—"

She grabbed his hand and squeezed. "I thought I was going to die in that basement," she said fiercely. "I thought about . . ." She sucked in a breath. Telling him what, or who, had filled her thoughts would cut too close to the bone. So, she lifted his hand and sucked his finger into her mouth, twirling her tongue around it sensuously before biting down just short of drawing blood.

"Fuck," he swore breathlessly.

"That's the idea, big guy."

"Are you cert—"

"Damian. Shut up and fuck me."

He pressed his face into her neck with a rumbling growl, then closed his teeth over the joint between her neck and shoulder, biting down just hard enough to leave a mark, before laving the spot with his tongue. His big hand slid down to grip her thigh, his fingers closing around it as he shoved it forward, baring her pussy to his cock. He toyed with her first, sliding the thick shaft between the swollen folds of her sex, the tip of his erection barely dipping into her opening.

"You're already wet," he murmured, his breath shivering over the delicate skin of her neck. "Were you dreaming of me, Cassandra?"

She would have answered, but he gripped his cock in that moment and with a single flex of his hips thrust deep inside her, gliding easily on the plentiful cream of her arousal. She blushed, almost embarrassed at how wet she was, at how much it told him about her. How badly she wanted him, how easily he turned her into a needy, wanton *thing*. But all she could do was moan and hope he wouldn't stop.

"I love fucking you," he murmured, his voice a deep rumble that vibrated in the marrow of her bones, as his cock thrust slowly in and out. "I love your luscious breasts"—he cupped both of her breasts in one hand, squeezing first one, then the other, rubbing her nipples into tight buds— "your round ass. And, most of all, Cassandra"—his voice went even deeper as his fingers smoothed over her belly and down between her thighs—"I love your cunt, so tight and wet, the way it grips my cock when you come, squeezing so hard that I can barely move."

She almost came right then, her pussy trembling around his shaft, her clit swollen and begging for his touch as he teased her, his fingers gliding through her slick folds, circling the sensitive nub, barely grazing it before drifting away, until she wanted to scream.

"Damian," she whispered, half plea and half demand.

"Sssh," he soothed, nibbling the smooth skin of her shoulder, kissing the still-tender wound where she'd been shot. "What do you want, sweetheart? What do you need?"

"I need—" She groaned as the rough skin of his thumb stroked directly over her clit. "Oh, God," she breathed. "I need your cock—"

"You have my cock," he murmured, thrusting harder, once quickly in and out, before resuming his long, slow, tortuous, glide.

She hiccupped a breath as her womb contracted, a sharp stab of pleasure that pierced her breasts, her pussy, leaving every inch of her begging for his touch. "I need to come," she said, hearing the pleading in her voice. She wanted to take it back, to deny that hint of vulnerability, but even more than that, she wanted to climax. Her entire body was throbbing in time to her pulsing clit, every ounce of awareness focused on that little bundle of nerves as his thumb circled closer and closer.

"Is this what you want?" His whisper was harsh against her ear, a moment before his thumb scraped over her clit and stayed there, crushing it, as shockwaves of erotic pleasure overwhelmed everything but her need to *feel* . . . his cock hard and thick, stabbing between her thighs; her inner muscles contracting around him, scraping along his length to the point of pain; her nipples engorged with blood, aching as his fingers pinched and squeezed. She threw her head back against his shoulder, twisting her neck, wanting his kiss. His mouth slammed down on hers, teeth clashing, tearing her lips with the violence of their meeting as he ravaged her mouth the same way his cock was ravaging her sex. It seemed to go on forever, waves of pleasure swamping her with sensation, while Damian held her tight, his hips the only thing moving, pistoning against her ass until finally, his fingers dug into her belly and he held her still while his cock bucked deep inside her, filling her with heat.

DAMIAN'S HEART WAS thundering in his chest, his blood pounding so loud that every pulse hammered in his eardrums, making it difficult to hear Cassandra's soft cries, her straining breaths. And he wanted to hear her pleas for release, her shocked gasps of pain, her cries of delight. Her pussy was still pulsing around his cock, her inner muscles still gripping him tightly as if not ready to let him go. He waited, holding her until the climax finally released her, until her muscles grew lax, and her breathing evened out. And then he held her a moment longer, just because he could.

He didn't understand yet why she had such a hold on him. Why this one woman, among the hundreds he'd bedded? How his fellow warriors would laugh if they could see him. He, who'd had more women than all of them combined, who'd been famous as much for his feelings, or his lack thereof, as for his conquests. He'd thought at first it was some perversion of gratitude that he was feeling toward her, because she'd been the one to free him from his long imprisonment. But then he'd gotten to know her, her courage and her intellect, the fierce loyalty she felt for Nico and the other hunters, the vulnerability that she worked so hard to hide.

She'd been the first woman he'd ever told, the first *person* he'd ever told, the truth of his making at Nico's hands. That he was a creation of sun and shadow, not a real man at all. There had always been a part of him when he'd been young, the frightened child who hid deep in his soul, who'd feared what would happen if he displeased Nico. What if Nico grew strong enough that he didn't need a protector anymore? Or what if he simply grew tired of Damian? Could he be made to disappear as readily as he'd appeared?

As the years passed and their friendship grew, he no longer worried about Nico discarding him, but he still wondered about his own humanity, about the fact that he'd fathered no children, and about his own mortality. He began to wonder if he would die, if he could. What did death mean to someone like him? There were stories of rewards for warriors who died in battle, of peaceful gardens and beautiful women. If he died, would he go to such a place? Or would he simply return to the sun and shadows of his creation, to nothingness?

And then, somewhere in the millennia of his captivity, Damian had moved beyond even that. Death, no matter what face it wore, held no fear for him anymore. The definition of life, *his* life had become unimportant. Until he'd met Cassandra, and he'd had to face a terrifying truth. He loved her. What *she* thought mattered. He needed *her* to see him as a fully-fleshed man, not some phantasm of Nico's creation.

He swallowed a sigh. Oh, sure, she'd wanted to fuck him this morning. She'd come close to dying yesterday—a thought that still had the power to stop his heart—and he knew better than most how a brush with death could make you want to embrace the pulse-pounding eroticism of sex and know you were *alive*. But that didn't erase the fact that, just yesterday, she'd gathered her things and left their room without so much as a note of good-bye.

She slapped his thigh, startling him out of his thoughts. "You're thinking too hard. I can hear the gears turning."

"Am I?"

"Look," she said, rolling to face him. She winced in pain, and he automatically soothed his hands over her. "I'm okay," she said, patting his chest. "Just sore . . . really sore. But nothing a bottle or two of ibuprofen won't take care of."

He stroked a careful hand over her head and down along her spine, fingers sliding through the silk of her hair, as her breathing eased. "Better?"

She nodded. "But, Damian—"

He waited for her to tell him that none of what they'd done this morning mattered, that he was nothing but a convenient fuck, just as he'd been to all of the women he'd bedded before, as, frankly, they'd been to him. Cassandra was different, but was he the only one who felt it?

"—look, I'm sorry."

What?

"I shouldn't have run out of here yesterday the way I did."

"You had your reasons," he offered and wondered why the hell he was making this easy for her.

"I know, but I should have talked to you about it instead of running away. I'm sure Nick's told you by now about my ex, and probably my father, too. Nick's very big on examining everyone else's trauma, while ignoring his own fucked-up psyche. But anyway, I know you guys are close, so he's probably warned you about me."

"Not at all——"

"The thing is, he's not far off. I don't trust people, and especially not men. So when I found out you and Nick had snuck away, I felt . . . excluded. Like you didn't trust me or my skills enough to let me be part of the inner circle. You two were hugging it out in a parking lot somewhere, and I wasn't even invited."

"Well, we didn't exactly——"

"Come on, I've seen you together. Tell me there wasn't a hug or three."

"I don't know what——"

"Fine, fine, keep your bromance secrets to yourself. But we're getting off track."

"Really?" He had no idea what the track was.

She gave him a narrow look, the stern effect of which was spoiled by the fact that her naked breasts were pressed up against his chest, her hard nipples stabbing into his skin. He dipped his chin and kissed her, a long, slow, indulgence of a kiss that had both their hearts racing by the time he lifted his head and slowly licked the corners of her luscious mouth. It was on his tongue to tell her how he felt, but reason prevailed, and he settled for a quick nip of her lips.

"I'm sorry."

"I'M SORRY." HER whispered apology overlapped his own, and they both sucked in a breath, laughing.

"I'll tell you anything you want to know," he told her.

Cassandra held her breath, worried that the wrong question, the wrong *word* would startle Damian into retreating back into the persona he wore so easily, the happy-go-lucky, let's-go-kill-something warrior, or worse, the legendary man-whore. Either one made her feel all alone when she was with him, but sometimes, *sometimes,* the real Damian would shine through. Like he did now. As strong and courageous as always, but with a hint of vulnerability, a *need* to be seen for who he really was.

But as worried as she was, she knew it was now or never. She needed to know that she could trust him. Not only with her life, but with her heart. If she went any deeper without that connection between them, she could end up devastated. Hell, it might already be too late.

"Why did you and Nick have to meet last night? And why not tell me?"

He nodded, as if to say he'd expected the question. But, of course, he had. It was the elephant in the room, the one event that had set off everything else in the last twenty-four hours.

"You're not going to like this," he warned her. "But let me finish before you get angry." He hugged her close, as if to keep her from leaving.

"No promises on the getting angry part. I can't control that. But I won't go anywhere until you're finished."

He nodded again, and drew in a breath before saying, "I found something in Sotiris's treasure room, and I took it with me."

Casey stiffened, her eyes going wide. *Son of a bitch.* When had he done that? And how?

"You promised," he reminded her.

"I'm still here," she added sharply. She wanted to demand answers, but let him continue.

"It belonged to Nico. Well, more accurately, it belonged to *all* of us, to me and the other warriors. But Nico's the only one who can make use of it now."

She frowned, admitting to herself that she was curious enough to listen.

"It was a small box, small enough that I could conceal it in my scabbard with ease. The box itself was of little value, and probably did belong to Sotiris at one point. But what it contained. . . . I told you about the spell he worked, that he used personal items stolen from each of us as a focus."

She nodded.

"That's what was in the box, Cassandra. I saw it, and all I could think of was getting it back to Nico, to help in the search for my brothers."

Casey opened her mouth, then paused, meeting his gaze as if to ask for permission. He smiled, as if he'd known she couldn't hold out until the end. "Go ahead, ask."

The words rushed out before he'd finished speaking. "Why not just tell me?" she asked, honestly confused. "What did you think I'd do?"

He frowned, looking uncertain for the first time. "It's. . . . It goes back to the beginning with us, back all those millennia to when Nico and I were fighting for survival, for ourselves and so many others. Magic was our weapon. There was so much more of it in the world then. You can't imagine what it was like. It was the very air we breathed.

"When Sotiris cast his curse, he twisted our lives, our histories, perverting them in a way even we can't fully understand. And that distortion continues to spread as long as at least one of us is still caught in the curse. Every decision that we make, that *I* make, has the potential to impact my brothers, even so far as to result in their freedom or their permanent imprisonment. Until Nico and I find them, until every one of us stands free, we have to tread so very carefully." He shook his head. "I'm a warrior. Give me the most complex battlefield and I can move men and equipment to ensure victory. But this? Manipulating magic through the mists of time with the lives of my brothers at stake? I don't know what's right or wrong.

"So, when I found that box and what it contained, the very keys to Sotiris's spell. . . . My first instinct, my *only* instinct, was to get it to Nico, and to tell no one else about it. By the time he and I actually met, I knew I'd made a mistake, and, whether you believe me or not, I fully intended to tell you everything when I returned to the hotel room. But you were gone."

"It was only supposed to be reconnaissance," she muttered, still pissed that she'd been caught unaware by Sotiris's thugs. "What does Nick say about the box? Will it help him?"

He studied her a moment, as if her question hadn't been the reaction he'd expected. What had he thought she'd do? She'd already done the whole storming-away-angry bit, and almost died in the process. She wasn't going to get angry all over again. That was the whole point of this exercise. She'd ask her questions, and he'd answer honestly.

"He says so," Damian answered cautiously. "You'd have to ask him about it."

"He probably won't tell me. What was your thing?"

"My thing?"

"In the box. Which of your possessions did the traitor steal as a focus?"

He shrugged. "A child's ring. Nico gave it to me. It was the first gift I had ever received, the first thing I'd ever owned, other than the clothes I wore."

"Do you think Sotiris knows the truth about you and Nick, about your creation?"

He frowned. He obviously still hated talking about the circumstances of his "birth." "I suppose he must. Why?"

"I'm not a sorcerer or anything, but I'm surprised he'd need a focus, like a ring, to work his spell on you."

"You mean because I'm a creature of magic just like the hellhounds or one of those artifacts you hunt?" he asked sharply.

"Don't be ridiculous," she snapped back. "I only meant that your connection to Nick is so strong that he shouldn't have needed anything else. You are fully human, Damian. No matter where you came from. Hell, you don't know for sure what happened that day you appeared. *Nick* doesn't even know. You were both too young and stupid to understand. Maybe he called you from another time, a time that hadn't occurred yet, and so when you walked out of the shadows, your life that would have been was nullified. It couldn't exist anymore, not even in memory, because it had never had a chance to happen."

He stared at her thoughtfully. "You make my brain hurt."

She let out a startled laugh. "Then I'd say we're even, because I hurt pretty much everywhere else."

His face crumpled into a worried scowl. "I was too rough," he said, smoothing his hands all over her, as if checking for injuries, until she grabbed his wrists, stopping him.

"No," she said, forcing him to meet her gaze. "The only good thing about this morning was making love with you. I wouldn't trade it, or you, for the world." She sat up, then leaned over and kissed him, a hard, passionate kiss that lasted longer than she'd planned. When she finally broke away, it was with a curse for the situation they were in. "All right," she said, letting her fingers play in his thick hair. "I say we go find that damn Talisman, lock it away once and for all, and then take a long vacation on a beach in Florida."

"You think it will be that easy?"

"Easy?" she repeated. "No. Doable? Yes. And we're going to finish it."

He sat up with her, wrapping his arms around her and standing to put them both on their feet. "We should shower separately," he said solemnly. "You can't resist my body."

She clapped a hand on his thick shoulder. "Come on, big guy. I'll try to restrain myself."

SHE DIDN'T. RESTRAIN herself that is. Although the fault might lie with him, Damian conceded. He wasn't strong enough to resist Cassandra when she was standing next to him naked, soap suds streaming over her body, dripping off the tips of her breasts. He took her fast and hard, backing her against the tile wall and slamming his cock into her, while her heels dug into his ass and her cries were as thick as the steam in the small enclosure. They clung to each other for a long moment afterward, eyes closed, his forehead resting against the tile, hers against his shoulder. Eventually, he eased her down slowly, holding on until her legs were steady, then used his fingers to gently wash away the evidence of their mutual climaxes.

They dried off and dressed quickly after that, with Cassandra stealing glimpses of his body, her face creased by a private, smug smile that made his heart swell.

"All right," Cassandra said, pouring herself a final cup of coffee from their room-service breakfast. "Where do we go from here?"

Damian sipped his tea. He'd tried coffee, but it wasn't to his taste. "I hate to ask this of you, but did you learn anything of Sotiris's plans while you were held captive? It's my experience that prisoners frequently observe more than their captors' intend."

She nodded. "He wasn't stupid, he was careful. Even though he planned to kill me," she added dryly. "But at the very end, when they were leaving, I heard enough to know that whatever he's planning will happen soon, maybe even today or tomorrow. And it'll be big, something to impress the buyers. Something splashy with lots of casualties. You and I can keep looking for the Talisman, but if we're going up against Sotiris himself—and I'm sure we are, why else would he be in town?—we're going to need Nick. Where is he, by the way? Can you tell?"

"I could tell you if he was walking down the hallway, or even through the parking lot, but no, I can't detect him at a distance. He wouldn't like that at all. Nico's a very private man."

"Aren't we all? But that doesn't stop him from putting trackers on all of our phones."

"Tracker," he repeated, pointing at her to emphasize the word. "You need to call Lilia. She was tracking your phone."

"*My* phone?" she said, her forehead creasing in thought. "But I don't have—Wait. Sotiris had it in the basement when he was questioning me. Are you saying Lilia tracked it after that?"

He nodded.

"I need to call her. Do you have your phone?"

He handed it over, and she manipulated the device much faster than he could have.

"Lili," she said. "Damian and I—Yes, I'm fine. A little bruised, but Damian's taking good care of me." She looked up and winked at him. "As soon as this job's over. I promise." She nodded at whatever Lilia was saying. "Right, that's why I'm calling. I'm going to put you on speaker so he can hear." She touched the phone's screen and set the device on the table between them. "Okay, Lili, go ahead."

"Hi Damian," Lilia said cheerfully.

"Lilia," he crooned.

She giggled, which had Cassandra scowling at the device. It delighted him that she was jealous, though there was no reason for it. He loved women, loved making them feel good, as he did with Lilia. But his feelings for Cassandra went far beyond what he'd ever felt for any other female.

"Damian, you're such a—"

"All right," Cassandra said, cutting off Lilia's chatter. "We've got a job to do. I hear you were tracking my phone. Is it still live?"

"Spoilsport," Lilia muttered. "No, it went off-line while we were tracking it. My guess is that it's been destroyed."

"Was that somewhere near O'Hare Airport?"

"No," Lilia said, her voice reflecting her surprise. "Whoever had the phone—"

"Sotiris," Cassandra supplied. "At least it was probably him. He had it at the house, and I saw him drop it into his pocket."

"So, maybe he forgot about it, then. We'd initially thought he was setting a fake trail, but maybe not. If he didn't remember he had it, he might have dumped it when he realized it was in his pocket."

"And that means it could be a good track. But you said it wasn't close to O'Hare?"

"Nope. He went right past there, heading south on I-355. That's where he was when he shucked the phone. We have the location. Nick sent a team out there to try and recover it."

"Where *is* Nick, by the way?"

"I don't know exactly."

"Can't you track his phone, too?"

"I can, but he wouldn't be happy about it, and I like my job."

"Great. All right, can you give me the coordinates where my phone died?"

"I'm texting them now. Whose phone is this you're calling from?"

"Damian's. I bought it for him, which means it doesn't have any of Nick's little trackers."

Lilia sighed. "That little tracker saved your life more than once, missy. Including today."

"Yeah, yeah. Send me that GPS, and we'll pull up a map to see if we can figure out where he's heading. Talk to you later."

She hung up without waiting for a response, then handed Damian his phone, which almost immediately dinged with an incoming message from Lilia containing the last known location of Cassandra's cell phone.

"Hold on to those," she said and walked over to her duffel, which Damian had brought up last night. It was sitting on the floor next to the table, and she squatted down to dig into it, doing all sorts of interesting things to showcase her lovely ass. He tilted his head, appreciating the view, which was what Cassandra caught him doing when she glanced back at him.

"Stop ogling my ass," she demanded, but the wide smile that accompanied it took away whatever snap her words might have contained. She returned to digging in her bag and emerged with her laptop in its hard case. "I'm pissed about my phone," she said, half to herself, "but not nearly as much as I'd be if I lost this." She extracted the computer from its case and walked over to the table.

Damian joined her as she pulled up a map of the Chicago area. He'd made a point of studying that map earlier, as well as the immediately surrounding states, but he didn't know it anywhere near as well as he would have liked. Cassandra, on the other hand, seemed to know exactly what she was looking for as she maneuvered around the digital map, zooming in on one section after another.

"There's I-355," she said absently. "Read me those GPS numbers that Lilia sent."

He did, but it didn't seem to help her much. "Where the hell is he going?" she muttered, drawing a line with her finger on the screen from O'Hare Airport to the 355. "There's nothing there."

"Maybe his target isn't an airport," he suggested.

"Is that consistent with what you know about Sotiris, though?" she asked. "Wouldn't he want the biggest target he could find?" She zoomed the map in again. "Shit, what if he's decided this area's too hot with all of us hanging around? The 80's right there," she added, pointing at another big highway. "If he took that, he could be going anywhere."

Damian studied the map. There were any number of smaller airports, in addition to O'Hare, but she was right. Sotiris wouldn't bother with those.

"What other facilities is this map showing?" he asked, noting that there were several structures blocked out in color that weren't airports.

"I started out only looking at airports," she explained, "because they're the biggest, most obvious targets. But then it hit me. We've been assuming he'll use the destructive power of the Talisman itself—the electromagnetic pulse effect that can knock out modern electronics. But what if he's figured out a way to use it as a trigger for something else instead? Something like a bomb? So, I expanded the search to include government buildings and hospitals. Any of those could contain hundreds, if not thousands, of people."

He frowned, considering her words, rejecting them in the end, though he didn't say so. At this point in their investigation, it wasn't wise to close off any possible avenue. But he tended to agree with her initial assumption that Sotiris would want something big and showy. "What's that?" he asked, pointing at a large yellow shape on the map. It was near the highway where Sotiris had probably tossed Cassandra's phone, but far enough away that it wasn't obvious.

"I don't know," she said, then centered and zoomed in on it. "Shit."

"What?"

"That's the Air Traffic Control Center, the facility that guides all of the planes around both O'Hare and Midway airports. If he lets the Talisman's power loose there, the center will go down without warning. Every plane in the air will be on its own. We could easily have midair crashes, and that's just the ones that stay in the air. Depending on a plane's altitude at the time, the Talisman might have a high-enough reach to scramble their electronics, too. They could literally fall from the sky. Shit!" She spun to stare at Damian.

"What's the range of its power, do you know?" he asked.

She shook her head. "No idea. But Nick might. You should call him," she said with more than a hint of sarcasm. "He'll probably take *your* call."

He sighed. She'd clearly forgiven him for meeting Nico without telling her, but, oddly enough, she seemed angrier with Nico. She'd known him longer, of course, and Damian suspected Nico was the first man she'd ever really trusted, which would make his actions seem like more of a betrayal. But Nico was a good man. Hell, he was a great man. She didn't know the wars he'd fought to protect his people from the excesses of monsters like Sotiris, and, unfortunately, there was no time now to educate her. He found Nico's number on his call list and touched the screen. It rang several times before his brother's voice came on, suggesting he leave a message.

He didn't bother to identify himself. Nico would know his voice. "We have a likely target," he said, and read off the name and address of the facility. "Cassandra and I are going there now. We're planning to sweep the area, hoping she'll pick up on the device. We need you there." And that's all he said. Cassandra might doubt, but Damian knew that Nico would come when he got the message.

"He'll be there," he told her, ignoring the skeptical rolling of her eyes.

"If he's not too late," she said, then closed her computer and began packing up their few things. "Let's take it all. One way or the other, we won't be coming back this time."

Chapter Ten

THEY CRUISED THE area around the FAA Air Traffic Control facility first. Cassandra let Damian drive. She'd never really doubted his driving ability; it had just been one small way she could establish control over an investigation that had felt like it was running away from her. But there was no time for dominance games anymore. She figured they had only hours before Sotiris would stage his little "demonstration." He knew they were close on his trail, which meant he had a limited window. But he wouldn't want to miss this opportunity. Not if he'd gone to any trouble to set things up, and especially not if he had potential buyers expecting a demonstration in a set timeframe.

This also happened to be a particularly good day and time if one wanted to do maximum damage. It was nearing the end of the work day and, since it was Friday, the end of the work week as well. There were lots of flights, with businessmen rushing home in both directions, and weekend getaways getting started. The timing was right for an attack, but there was more to it than that.

Cassandra was reasoning all of this out on the fly, but just as *she* didn't know the range on the Talisman, she figured Sotiris might not know either. This was probably his first real-life test of the device. And not knowing exactly what it might do, he wouldn't have wanted to risk triggering it earlier and drawing unwanted attention, not just from Nick, but from the human authorities whose notice might scare away his buyers, at least in the short term. But if this *was* his first test, he wouldn't want to take a chance on the device failing, either. He'd want to be as close to his mark as possible, to both maximize the effect and minimize the risk. She only hoped she was right about his target. It was all based on guesswork, on clues that might very well have been planted to mislead them. She was going with instinct on this one.

When they approached the FAA facility, she saw that it wasn't exactly isolated. There was a big hospital complex nearby, and, damn, an elementary school, too. Though it didn't really matter what was nearby. If planes started falling from the sky, no one for miles around would be truly safe.

They cruised the immediate streets around the FAA campus first, but no more than two blocks in any direction. She just didn't think Sotiris would take a chance on anything farther than that. When she didn't feel so much as a twinge of the Talisman's presence, she directed Damian back to the FAA center itself, where they began a circuit of the entire facility. They drove deliberately, not moving too slowly, and not speeding either. They didn't want to look like they were casing the parking lots, even though that's exactly what they were doing. She assumed there would be closed circuit surveillance, although probably not actively eyeballed 24/7. As a precaution, however, they'd parked her Yukon at the airport and were driving a nondescript rental sedan. Nothing blended in better around here than that.

Damian was keeping a lookout for the black Escalade, even though neither of them thought Sotiris would be foolish enough to use the same vehicle. But it was the magic sensor in Cassandra's head that was their secret weapon. No matter how much Sotiris tried to shield the Talisman, if they got close enough, she'd sense it. And if he tried using another spell to camouflage it, she'd simply detect that one instead. There was no hiding from her.

As they cruised around the corner of the main building and into the largest parking lot, she spied a cargo truck with double doors in the back. It was sitting almost dead center in the lot, with several smaller vehicles parked right next to it, even though the rest of the area was only sparsely filled. She'd noticed that the other lots were mostly empty, too, which had troubled her, until she realized that the facility would house more than just the Air Traffic Control Center, and that the people in all of those other offices would be clearing out for the weekend already. And she sure as hell didn't mind the absence of an audience for what would probably be a very flashy confrontation.

"See that?" she murmured to Damian, nodding her head toward the white truck. "We need to get closer."

He slowed to a stop and then pulled out a map, as if checking directions. "If we get too close, if he recognizes you, he'll kill you point-blank this time," he told her.

"Yeah, but he thinks I'm already dead, so he won't be looking for me. Come on, Damian, this is what we're here for. Just do a quick drive-by to see if I sniff anything funny."

"I'd hardly call it funny," he said unhappily, but he did as she asked, starting down the row where the white truck was parked, on a pass that would take them to within just a few feet of it.

It started as a tingle of awareness, an itchy sort of pressure that made her rub her scalp almost absently. But by the time they were ten feet from the truck, and then right on top of it, the itch had become a painful, squeezing pressure inside her head, like the worst headache she'd ever had . . . times ten. She sucked in a shocked breath. This was the Talisman, but so much stronger. Sotiris was boosting the power somehow. "Keep going," she gasped at Damian's concerned look. "Just . . . go."

She had to give him credit. He didn't panic, didn't stomp on the gas pedal and announce their presence. He simply kept moving at the same deliberate pace, until they were out of the parking lot and moving away from the facility.

She leaned over, clutching her head, as Damian pulled into the hospital parking lot, and immediately jumped out of the car, coming around to her side and opening the door. Squatting in from of her, he rested one hand on her thigh, and covered her hand on her head with the other.

"Cassandra?" he asked. His hands were like two spots of intense heat, sinking into her body, chasing away the cold of the Talisman. Was the cold part of its nature? Had it been created with ill intent? Or did it only reflect the intent of the user? If Nick took it in hand, would it feel the same? "Cassandra?" Damian repeated, more urgently this time.

"I'm fine," she assured him, threading her fingers with his and placing them over her racing heart. "That's definitely them," she said, with a cynical laugh. "Damn it," she swore, still trying to catch her breath.

"Take your time, sweetheart." He reached into a bag on the floor of the backseat. "Here, drink this." He offered her a bottle of a sports drink that contained lots of sugar, along with all the necessary electrolytes.

She didn't usually drink the sugary stuff, but she made an exception this time, sucking it down as if it was the first food she'd had in days. She finished off the bottle and handed it to him, with a grimace of distaste. "I hate that stuff."

"Really?" Damian asked, seeming honestly surprised. "I think it's great. Good for a quick recharge."

She shook her head. He was so single-minded. Everything came down to the battlefield, good or bad. Maybe that's what made him such a great warrior. Well, that and magic. She couldn't forget the fucking magic.

"What do you think we should do?" she asked. If one was going to consort with a warrior god, one might as well make good use of him.

"I think we wait for Nico." He stood and walked back around the front of the car to the open driver's door.

"I don't know," she said when he'd slid behind the wheel again. "That thing's powering up for something big. It didn't affect me like this earlier, when I followed them to the house. We might not have *time* to wait." She glanced over at him. "We could probably take them. I mean, how many thugs could there be in that truck? And with you, it's like having twenty guys at my back."

"Don't forget Sotiris," he reminded her dryly, as he pulled their car around to a spot under some trees, where they could see the back of the truck, but hopefully wouldn't be noticed themselves.

She *tsk*ed irritably. "Nick hasn't answered any of our calls, not even yours. What if he's not coming?"

"He'll be here," he said implacably.

"Yeah, right. He doesn't even—" She broke off as the back doors of the truck abruptly swung open, and two guys hopped out. The angle wasn't right for her to get much more than a flash of the interior cargo space, but there were definitely people in there, and she thought one of them might have been wearing a suit, just like Sotiris. The two men walked around to the cab and jumped inside. She waited for them to do something, like start the engine, maybe drive away. But they just sat there.

"What are they waiting for?" she asked, thinking out loud.

The back door of the sedan suddenly opened behind her. "You're wondering what they're waiting for," Nick said, as he slid across the rear seat and closed the door behind him.

She stared at him, then shifted to glare at Damian. "You knew he was close."

He shrugged. "You wouldn't have believed me."

"Okay, children," Nick said. "Let's bicker later. What's the plan, Casey?"

"Shouldn't that be your job?"

"Hell, no. I'm just the big gun. Tell her, Damian."

Damian sighed. "There are five men in the back of the truck," he said, as if reciting by rote. "Plus two more outside. Sotiris is one of those inside, and there is one man seated who appears to be restrained. The three others inside, as well as the two now sitting in the cab of the truck, are all carrying MP5s with standard 30-round magazines. The two in the cab—let's call them guards—are definitely wearing ballistic vests; I would assume the three guards on the inside are similarly attired. Sotiris is, of course, unarmed, except for his considerable power."

"But he won't use that against you or Casey," Nick chimed in. "He'll want to conserve his power in case I show up."

Damian nodded as if he was processing this bit of information. He glanced at Casey. "The Talisman is definitely there?"

She nodded.

"Then it's hidden. I saw nothing that matches its description—"

"You can't possibly have seen all of that. I had the same view, for the same period of time, maybe at an even better angle, and—"

"But I did, Cassandra. You joke about it, but there is a good reason that some worshipped me as a god."

"You four were the finest warriors the world had ever seen," Nick interjected almost angrily. "*You* still are, Damian, for all that you've been sealed away from the world for centuries. Sotiris knows damned well that with you at my side, the balance is tipped in my favor."

Damian turned to grin at Nick. "You won't need my help, brother, but Cassandra will."

She pressed her lips together, then nodded, and said, "Okay. So how do we do this?"

"First, the Talisman should be your first and only focus. You're the only one who can do this, and we can't afford for you to be distracted by anything else. Nico will deal with Sotiris, and I'll take out the others and keep them off your back."

"Wait, how do I know Nick can handle—"

"Give me a break, Casey," Nick muttered, but it was Damian who made the convincing argument.

"Because he's done it in the past," he told her. "Because Sotiris has always feared him over any other enemy. Look how far he went to weaken him by taking us away from him."

She shrugged in reluctant agreement. "What about you? I know I've said you're like twenty fighters in one, but Sotiris's people will put up a vicious defense. He'll kill them if they don't."

Damian shrugged, unconcerned. "They'll die either way. If they don't fight, Sotiris will kill them. If they do . . . at least I'll offer them a clean death. I doubt Sotiris can say—"

"All right," Casey interrupted, feeling like a third wheel and not liking it. "When do we do this?"

"I'd rather wait for dusk, but we can't take that chance. He could trigger the device at any moment." He met her gaze directly. "You will be careful, Cassandra. Wait until I clear the way for you. No heroics."

"What? You're the only one allowed to be a hero?"

"I'm stronger, faster, and I can heal almost immediately from any attack. That doesn't make me a hero."

"Whatever," she muttered, but he was still looking at her expectantly. "Fine, I'll be careful, okay?"

He smiled. "Thank you." Then he twisted around to address Nick. "Control yourself until we get closer."

Casey turned to stare at Nick, then lifted a brow. "What does that mean?"

Nick offered only a wicked grin, but Damian answered her. "Nico likes to make an entrance. He burns brightly enough that Sotiris will sense him coming anyway, but there's no need to draw his attention any sooner than necessary."

"Do you feel him burning like that? Because I get nothing from him except a vague irritation." She scowled at Nick, who winked back at her.

"Nico is like the sun rising on a new day," Damian said, pretending not to get her sarcasm. Or maybe he really didn't.

"You two like each other way too much," she said sourly. It was stupid to be jealous of their relationship, but she couldn't help it. "Can we just do this?" she snapped.

Damian's answer was to open the car door and step outside. Nick was right on his heels, exiting on the same side of the car, while Casey moved more cautiously. Her side was visible from the truck, so she wanted to appear more casual as she climbed from the car and walked around to meet the two men. No big deal. Just a woman going to work. Nothing to see here. Move along.

"I'll take out the two in the cab first. That's your signal, Nico," Damian said, gazing across the parking lot.

It was on Casey's tongue to ask Damian, again, if he was sure he could do this, but they'd already pretty much covered that territory, and she didn't want him to go into a fight thinking she doubted him. Because she really didn't. But she couldn't just let him stroll into danger either.

"Damian," she began, not wanting to let him go, but she didn't know how to finish. He smiled at her. It wasn't his usual confident grin, but a sweet smile, as if he knew what she was fighting not to say.

"Come here," he said, tugging her close. "Give me a kiss for luck."

She went up on her toes and kissed him, her hand gripping the back of his neck, fingers twisted in his long hair, trying to keep him with her just a little bit longer. When they finally broke apart, his eyes gleamed with the kind of sexual hunger for her that she'd never thought to see in a man.

"Be safe," he growled, then kissed her hard and took off.

He moved in that perfect silence of his—even his heavy boots on the gritty asphalt were soundless—and almost faster than her eyes could follow. One moment he was kissing her, and the next, he'd drawn his sword and was across the parking lot, pulling the door open and yanking the first guard from the cab, tossing aside the man's dead body to reach across the seat, and grab the second, who barely had time to raise his weapon before Damian's blade was taking off his head.

Nick's low voice interrupted her fascination. "Wait for your cue," he told her, and an instant later he was moving nearly as fast as Damian had, but with different intent. No blade for Nick. He circled wide to come in on the far side of the truck just as the back doors swung open. Sotiris stood there, his expression more one of irritation than anything else. Until he saw the dead guard's body lying several feet away. His searching gaze fixed on her first, registering obvious surprise before he smirked and opened his mouth, probably intending to cast a killing spell. But then Nick stepped into the open and Sotiris's eyes widened in shock. He shouted a warning, and tried to close the heavy doors, but at that moment, Damian came up on the other side of the truck, and grabbed one of the doors, nearly ripping it off its hinges.

Sotiris regarded Damian's sudden appearance with obvious dismay, but he reacted quickly enough. Jumping from the back of the truck, he manhandled the doors into place and sealed them with a burst of power. Casey couldn't catch the words, but it wouldn't have mattered if she had. She couldn't work magic herself, and so couldn't have undone the spell. But she sure as hell felt it when the spell snapped into place, and all but welded the damn doors shut. Fuck. How would they get to the Talisman now?

NICK STOOD HIS ground as Sotiris stalked closer, letting his smug grin speak for him.

"I thought I was rid of you," Sotiris said, the obvious hatred he felt for Nick making his words a low, vicious rasp of sound. "Thought you'd finally given up."

Nick scoffed. "You thought I'd give up on the men who were closer to me than my blooded brothers? You're a fool, but then, you never did understand loyalty."

"So you got the warrior back," Sotiris said dismissively. "He was always your favorite, your pet. But he's only one, you bastard. You still think to find the others?" He laughed.

Nick smiled, knowing something that Sotiris clearly did not. "Have you checked your vaults lately, Sottie?" he asked, using Sotiris's hated childhood nickname. "Maybe you should. Because I *will* find my brothers, every one of them."

Sotiris scowled, both annoyed and puzzled by Nick's confidence. "You won't find anything if I kill you first."

Nick laughed out loud, as if Sotiris had said something truly funny. And he had. Because they both knew the other sorcerer couldn't kill him. He didn't have the power. That had been the reason why he'd always hated him, why his hatred was so vicious that it had survived for millennia.

A car suddenly came flying across the lot, without a driver behind the wheel, just a handy couple of tons of metal that Sotiris had used magic to throw Nick's way. He spun aside just in time, the gap narrow enough that he felt the wind of the car's passage. He let his spin carry him full circle, back to facing Sotiris. He cast a deadly ball of energy at the other sorcerer, loading it with all the weight and density of a heavy medicine ball, slamming Sotiris with physical force on top of magical energy.

Sotiris grunted, not expecting the physical element to the attack. His back bowed as he struggled to repel the double hit of energy, fighting to remain upright. It was only seconds before he managed to dispel the energy, but both men knew that seconds could mean the difference between life and death in a magical duel.

But even as the hatred Nick felt for Sotiris burned in his veins, even as his magic roared, demanding release against this most ancient of enemies, he knew he couldn't kill him. It was complicated, but the lives of his missing warriors were at stake. And that meant he couldn't finish this. Not quite yet.

The arrogance was gone from Sotiris's expression when he finally gathered himself enough to meet Nick's gaze. Nick had always been stronger, but he'd also been very young back then. Aggressive and undisciplined in his attacks. He was none of those things now, and his enemy recognized it. He let a slow smile spread across his face. But it didn't last. Sotiris's eyes widened in something close to fear, and Nick knew suddenly what his enemy would do next.

"Damn it," he swore. He couldn't kill the bastard, but he could imprison him. He manipulated his magic feverishly, trying to contain the other sorcerer, to build a net that he couldn't escape. But Sotiris had too much experience in running away, in deserting his own men to their fate. With an explosive build-up of energy and a pounding clap of displaced air, he was gone. Nick reached out with his power, tunneling through the ether, laying down a chasing trail of magic that he could follow. But just as he was about to send himself rocketing after Sotiris, a wave of energy burst loose out of nowhere, and Damian's roar had him racing back to the truck.

CASEY HAD STUDIED the closed truck doors in dismay, feeling the heat of Sotiris's sealing spell like a sunburn on her skin. But then Damian had yelled, "Down!" and she'd dropped to her knees and rolled into a protective ball as if she'd been doing it all her life. Damian's blade sliced up and, with a shower of golden sparks, slashed through the bulk of the solid metal doors, nullifying the sealing spell. They fell open with a sizzling clang of fizzled magic and overheated metal, followed by the rat-a-tat of a submachine gun on full auto.

Bullets zinged through the now-empty space where she and Damian had been standing a moment earlier. She glanced at him from where she crouched on one side of the truck, meeting his eyes across the hail of bullets. What did they do next?

"On my mark," he mouthed, and she nodded her understanding.

They took up positions on either side of the open back of the truck, where the doors hung from broken hinges and the metal was still distorted from the heat.

Damian stared at her meaningfully, then lifted a hand with three fingers showing. He counted down, dropping one finger after another, and then he was moving, swinging up and into the truck. Casey cursed, forced to follow more cautiously as gunfire erupted from deep inside the cargo space. Maybe god boy was immune to bullets, but she sure as hell wasn't.

A body came flying out a moment later, and she took advantage of it, swinging up into the truck, and hunkering down behind one of the wooden boxes that littered the inside. She wondered what was in them, and if she needed to be worried about it. But then a bullet slammed into the metal siding next to her head, and she decided she should probably worry less about unknown crates, and more about the assholes who were shooting at her. She gripped her weapon, and was waiting for a break in the fire to shoot back, when abruptly the shooting stopped. Just . . . stopped.

She peered over the crate and saw Damian standing at the back wall of the truck's big cargo area. He caught her eye and motioned her closer. The remaining guards, who'd presumably been firing at them earlier, now lay sprawled at Damian's feet, bloody but no longer bleeding, since they were both quite dead. Apparently, Damian's style of fighting didn't include taking prisoners.

Stepping over their bodies, she was glad for her boots, but still kind of grossed out. The truck box was a contained space and the smell was . . . fragrant. She moved up right next to Damian, and looked around, somewhat puzzled. The Talisman should have been right here. She could feel it reaching out to her senses with a cold, oily touch, but. . . She studied the piles of boxes that cluttered the cargo space behind her, but almost immediately swung back around to the wall between the cargo box and the truck cab. She frowned.

"You said there was a fifth man in here, and that he was restrained. So where is he?"

"Could Sotiris have—?"

"No," she interrupted absently. "He's still here, with the Talisman." She closed her eyes, shutting out everything except the pull of the magical device they were after. In less than a minute, her eyes flashed open. She stepped over to the cab wall and placed her hand against it.

"It's back here," she told Damian, absolutely certain she was right.

He cocked his head, staring curiously at the plywood barrier. "Be ready, Cassandra. There may be more guards than we saw earlier." His blade came out and sliced through the fake wall like it was paper, and they both stepped back as a fresh hail of gunfire greeted them. Or at least Casey stepped back, taking cover behind a big wooden crate. And then, using the advantage of Damian's fearless assault, she lined up her target over the top of the crate and fired three shots, hitting her man center mass all three times. He slumped to the ground just as a bloody Damian gripped a second man by the throat and choked off his air, waiting until his weapon fell from lifeless fingers, and then waiting longer to be absolutely certain.

Not all of the blood covering Damian was from the dead man, but she knew better than to make a fuss over his wounds, at least until they were out of the combat zone. She briefly touched his side, where blood had his T-shirt clinging to his ribs, and then looked up and waited for his studly nod that said he was fine. She permitted herself a tiny smile, but then caught sight of the man sitting in the corner and could only stare.

"Shit," she breathed. She inched closer, meeting his terrified gaze and trying to project a confidence she definitely wasn't feeling. "What's your name?" she asked, wanting him to calm down as much as possible, to think about something other than the nasty magical thing about to go off in his face. There wouldn't be an explosion, not precisely, but the energy release would be hellish nonetheless.

"Basil," the man whispered.

Casey studied the setup with horrified fascination. She'd never seen anything like this, never dealt with this kind of brutality. Sotiris had shackled the man to the truck floor, then tied him to a chair and handed him the

Talisman. Why? She studied him first, noting his sallow complexion, and the way his tendons and muscles were standing out, straining in stark relief. She'd bet Basil was a minor sorcerer, someone whom Sotiris had probably hired to work with the many devices he owned. Unfortunately for Basil, he'd actually been recruited for a suicide mission.

Willingly or otherwise—it was difficult for her to tell at this stage—he was feeding his energy, his very life force, into the Talisman. Casey forced herself to ignore the man's terror, and to study the energy flow of the device, instead. She needed to figure out what was happening and how to stop it. That was why she was here. To save thousands of lives, not Basil's.

But the poor bastard was the key. There had to be a reason why Sotiris had linked him to the device. And then she saw it. The Talisman contained a tremendous amount of energy within itself, an amount that was just short of an overload. That was constant, the magical energy imbued in the device by its creator. She still didn't understand its purpose, but that wasn't important right now. What *was* important was that the device was draining every ounce of energy contained in Basil's body. Not only the magical energy of his sorcery, but his very life essence itself.

The danger was that very soon, the energy sucked up from Basil was going to force the Talisman beyond its energy capacity, at which point it would act to save itself from overload by releasing its energy on the world. That release would, in turn, set off a trigger effect, causing the Talisman to dump not just the overload, but *all* of its energy at once.

And from the way the terrified guy was clinging to the artifact, she had a pretty good idea that he literally *couldn't* let go, couldn't stop himself from becoming the trigger to one of the greatest disasters of modern times.

She sat back on her heels and studied the twofold problem, aware of the clock ticking in her head, reminding her that time was short. Her priority had to be deactivating the Talisman, but she had to at least try to save Basil. And she could think of only one way to do both of those things.

Flattening her lips, she slipped out of her leather jacket, which had a handy silk lining, then turned the jacket inside out just as Damian hunkered down next to her, his attention shifting between her hands, which were digging compulsively into the silk fabric of her jacket, and the green glow of the Talisman where it sat clutched in Basil's trembling hands.

"What are you doing, Cassandra?" Damian asked, his tone clearly saying, *"Don't even think about it."*

"I'm going to take that thing from Basil before it sucks him dry."

Damian shook his head slightly. "Not a good idea, sweetheart. Let me get Nico—"

"There's no time," she said calmly. "It's sucking up his energy, and he's a sorcerer, which makes the situation far more precarious. Am I right, Basil?" The man nodded wearily.

Damian growled. "Cassandra, do not—"

But before he could finish his sentence, the device began to emit a deep, buzzing hum, and Basil's eyes went wide in fresh terror.

"Too late," Casey whispered. She dropped her jacket over the Talisman and wrenched it from the man's hands, staring in shock as he shriveled to dust right before her eyes. A moment later, and the device's magical signature begin to hammer at her own control. "Damian," she whispered. "Get—"

"Nico!" Damian's roar filled the tight space and pounded in her eardrums, but she was too horrified to care. She was no sorcerer. They had minutes before she lost control, before the device triggered itself and thousands of people died.

NICO VAULTED INTO the truck, his eyes going first to Damian, who was hunkered down in front of Casey, hands fisted as he fought against the protective instinct that was almost certainly telling him to grab the thing she was holding. But that would have been a huge mistake, and Damian seemed to realize it.

"Nico," he growled, never taking his eyes off Casey.

Nick gripped Damian's shoulder as he crouched next to him. "Talk to me, Casey," he said, even as he scanned the thing beneath her jacket. It was the Talisman, no doubt about it. He'd only tasted its signature once, thousands of years ago, but it came back to him as if it had been yesterday.

Casey's dark gaze met his, her pupils so wide that there was almost no brown left to her eyes. "He—" Her tongue swept out to lick her lips, and she swallowed, as if she needed that tiny bit of moisture to keep talking. "Sotiris bound Basil to the device. But he knew it would be too much." A trace of horror filled her gaze as she stared at him. "It drained him dry," she whispered, and her gaze shifted briefly to a pile of dust and bones on the floor next to her.

Nick's mouth tightened in disgust. "He's trying to trigger the device by overloading it," he said.

She nodded. "I think so. But, Nick, it's—"

"It's about to blow," he said, before she could finish. He cupped her cheek gently, detecting the tremor of fear she was fighting to hide. "Don't worry, Case. I've got this one."

Sliding his hands underneath the jacket, he closed his fingers over the artifact, shocked at how soft the bronze setting had become, the metal practically melting as the big, central stone heated up, overwhelming it. It wasn't this physical heat that Nick had to deal with, though, it was the magical energy of the thing. It was full to bursting, like an overripe fruit. Or one rotted from the inside.

Taking the device completely away from Casey, he rested it on the floor of the truck with both hands surrounding it, and then he closed his eyes and focused. There was so little magic left in the world anymore, that it had been a while since he'd had to deal with such a concentrated and potent energy source. Simply put, he was a bit rusty. Sweat rolled from his temples, his lungs heaving with effort as he examined the artifact, searching for weakness, for a way to disrupt the destructive power roiling at its center. After what seemed like hours, but was probably no more than a few minutes, he felt the jewel's power begin to collapse, dissipating harmlessly until finally the light faded and died. He held it a moment longer, almost as if his fingers were stuck and he couldn't let go. But finally his grip eased, his eyes opened, and he looked down on a dull, green stone in an ancient bronze setting that looked slightly worse for wear.

He lifted his head to find Casey staring at him in question. He smiled slightly. "This stone is clean," he said, in parody of one of his favorite movies.

She smiled slightly. She got the reference, of course. She was a magic nerd at heart, just like he and all of his hunters.

"It's all yours, Case," he said, standing.

"What? Wait—" Damian objected, but Casey waved him away.

"It's okay, Damian. It's dead, or at least inert."

"You can use this," Nick said, producing a tightly packaged silk bag from his jacket pocket. "Just to be safe."

But Damian wasn't satisfied. "Why don't you take it yourself, Nico?"

He turned to grin at his oldest friend. "I'm hunting much bigger prey tonight, brother. I've placed a marker on Sotiris's trail, and if I can catch him before he realizes it, he's mine. Take care of my Casey, and I'll see you in Florida."

CASEY LISTENED TO the rumbling purr of Nick's Ferrari, as he tore out of the parking lot with the screech and smell of burning rubber.

"*His* Casey," Damian muttered. He took her hand and helped her to her feet, and then held the silk bag open so she could place the Talisman inside. The bag didn't seem substantial enough to hold such a ponderous device, or maybe it was that the Talisman didn't seem heavy enough for the danger it had created. Either way, she was happy to see it in the bag, happy to tighten the drawstring and tie it off. Happy not to be touching it with her bare skin anymore. She shivered, remembering.

"I have a warded box in my truck," she told him, with a private smile for his muttered comment. "It'll be safer in there for the trip to Florida."

He walked to the end of the truck box, and jumped down, then turned around and put his hands on her waist, lifting her to the ground in a totally unnecessary gesture. She could have climbed down perfectly well. But it made her girlish heart flutter nonetheless.

He didn't let go of her, but tightened his fingers around her waist, tugging her closer. "So we're taking the SUV, huh?"

She wanted to point out that, of course, *she'd* be the one behind the wheel, and that *he* hadn't been invited. But she wasn't that self-destructive. Or delusional. So she just smiled up at him and said, "I might even let you drive."

Chapter Eleven

Pompano Beach, Florida

"HE'S NOT THERE, right? And you're sure you don't expect him? I need to get rid of this thing, and I'd rather make it simple."

"Honestly, Casey," Lilia said, clearly exasperated. "You're going to have to talk to Nick eventually."

"I know, I know," Casey agreed. "But Damian and I just got in late last night. I'd like a few days of peace before I have to deal with his irritating lordship."

"Whatever. Just make sure you bring Damian along. I want to see if the body matches the voice."

"You don't concern yourself about that."

Lilia laughed. "When are you coming?"

"Oh, I already did that," Casey murmured, and hung up to find Damian watching her.

"You're blushing," he said, moving close enough to stroke the backs of his fingers over her heated cheek. "What were you two talking about?"

"Just, you know . . . details."

He laughed. "I can imagine. Are we going to Nico's then?"

She nodded. "But he's not there."

He made the same exasperated noise that Lily had. "You should talk to him, Cassandra. Nico is a good man."

Everyone assumed that she was still pissed that Nick had kept her in the dark for so long about his true nature. And in a way, that was true. But it was far more than that. Now that she knew what he was, knew the kind of power he possessed, she didn't know what *her* role was supposed to be. She'd always been different than the other hunters, her talent unique and necessary. But now . . . he was a sorcerer. And not just any old sorcerer, but one of the five most powerful in the whole fucking world. He didn't need her to tell him about magic flows. He'd *never* needed her. So, what was left? Could she be content as just one more hunter, haunting auction websites and estate sales, roaming crowded fan conventions for the occasional true artifact among the replicas?

She couldn't say any of that to Damian, though. Or to anyone else. They'd think she was acting like a spoiled princess, upset because she wasn't the favorite anymore. And, okay, that was kind of true. Still, she didn't want to hear them say it.

"But that's the problem," she said, predictably, playing into the idea that she was simply pissed at Nick. "He's not a man at all, is he?"

"Because he's a sorcerer?" Damian scoffed. "Believe me, Nico is very much a man."

"Yeah, yeah. He's a real stud." She laughed as Damian yanked her up against his chest.

"What do you know of it?" he growled playfully.

She patted his cheek. "Don't worry, baby. You're quite the stud, yourself."

He snorted dismissively. "I wasn't worried, but if you'd like a demonstration—"

"No, no," she protested, slapping away his hands. "I'm still feeling your last demonstration." And that was putting it mildly. What she could have said was that her pussy was still clenching with mini-climaxes every time she remembered what they'd done that morning, and she was getting wet all over again just thinking about it. Though she didn't say any of that out loud, she didn't need to. The smug smile on his face told her he knew exactly what she was thinking.

His hand rested possessively on the curve of her ass. "We should probably take time to recover from our journey once we return from Nico's," he suggested. "A day in bed will do wonders."

She recognized that wicked gleam in his eye. And so did her pussy, which throbbed in eager anticipation. Her pussy was such a slut, she thought, grinning.

"What are you thinking *now*?" he demanded.

"I'm thinking we need to get the hell out of here before we're stuck with that damn Talisman for another day."

"Right," he said, pulling her toward the door. "I'll even let you drive."

CASEY WAS STILL laughing at Damian's reaction to Miami traffic when they finally arrived at Nick's estate. Her townhouse was on the outskirts of the city, so their trip to Nick's was the first time Damian had experienced a full-blown traffic jam.

"It's lunchtime," she'd explained. "Everyone's in a hurry to get somewhere."

"I'd be in a hurry to leave," he'd muttered as they'd sat there, surrounded by cars that were barely moving. But now he was eyeing Nick's rather spectacular home, which had a huge length of deep-water frontage and stunning views, especially at night with the lighthouse in the distance. "Nico lives here?" he asked.

She nodded, trying to see it through his eyes. She was sure it looked even more beautiful to him. Hell, he was probably wondering why he was stuck in her little two-bedroom townhouse when he could be living here.

"He always did like his luxury," Damian said rather fondly. "The rest of us preferred more modest accommodations. Comfortable enough, but with fewer silk curtains." He laughed to himself, probably remembering some private joke. Something between him and *Nico*. Maybe the rest of the *brothers*, too, she thought sourly.

She parked her Yukon near the front door, trying to ignore the contrast between her very utilitarian truck and Nick's elegant house. She felt as if maybe she should park around back, near the servants' entrance. Did Nick even have a servants' entrance? She'd never worried about it before, but seeing it all through Damian's eyes was making her insecure.

"Come on," she said brusquely, suddenly eager to drop off the Talisman and get out of there.

Damian offered to carry the box with the Talisman in it, and she let him. The artifact weighed relatively little, but the damn box was heavy. She'd let him use all of those big muscles.

The front door buzzed open before they hit the top stair to the rounded porch. Lilia was watching, as always. It was worth noting that Damian didn't blink an eye when the door snapped open. He had completely adapted to much of the modern era already.

"This way," Casey said, leading him down the long hallway to the east wing of the huge house, which was where Nick and Lilia had their offices. This was the only part of the house she was really familiar with. She'd been to the west wing once or twice, for social gatherings with the other hunters. But those meetings were rare, since the whole team was hardly ever in one place at the same time.

They hit Lilia's office first, although it was probably more accurate to call it her domain. It wasn't one office, but rather an entire suite. When you walked in the door, all you saw was an antique receptionist desk, with spindly legs and a desk lamp to match. A couch and two chairs in what Casey guessed was the same style completed the look, with tasteful art on the walls.

Lilia wasn't there. She was never there, unless outsiders were expected, and that wasn't the case this morning.

"Back here," Casey told Damian, and led him past the desk and through a reinforced door, holding it open while he carried the Talisman in its box into the chilly heart of Lilia's domain.

The room wasn't that big, maybe twelve feet square, but every inch of it was filled with technology. Computers mostly, with big screens that did double duty as computer monitors and video displays of broadcast and satellite reception.

Lilia spun around on her chair when they entered, a broad smile creasing her face. She was very pretty, and deceptively delicate-looking, with long blond hair that hung nearly to her waist, and big blue eyes that made her look like Alice in Wonderland. Except that this Alice was skilled in several martial arts disciplines and was a sharpshooter with the FBI's favored .40 caliber Glock 23.

Those big blue eyes were dancing now as she stood on tiptoe to return Casey's hug. "You made it!" she said, as if there'd ever been any doubt. "And this must be . . ." Her voice trailed off as she stared up at Damian.

"Damian," Casey supplied. "Damian, this is Lilia Wilson."

Lilia gave Casey a surreptitious wink of approval, and offered Damian her hand. Instead of shaking, he took her hand and kissed the back of it gallantly enough. But for one brief instant, Casey was sure she caught a quizzical look on his face, as if Lilia wasn't what he'd expected. The look was there and gone so fast, that she thought she might have imagined it.

And then Lilia was reclaiming her hand and waving it in front of her face with a murmured, "Oh my," like some sort of southern belle, which she absolutely was not.

"Yeah, okay, fine," Casey said, breaking up the love fest. "Where can I leave this thing?"

"I'll take it," said a voice from behind her.

She fought not to groan as she turned to see Nick standing there. "Nick," she acknowledged then aimed a glare at Damian. "You didn't see the rays of sunshine this time?" she muttered, remembering his earlier description of what he experienced when Nick was near.

Damian only grinned at her, unrepentant. He wanted her to work out her problems with Nick, and clearly wasn't above a little subterfuge to get it done. He turned over the box with the Talisman to Nick, who said, "Casey, why don't you come with me to my office? There's something I want to show you."

She stifled a sigh. She didn't approve of Damian's methods, but he was right. She and Nick did need to talk it out, because she liked her job, and he was the only game in town if she wanted to keep doing it. Besides, he and the other hunters were the closest thing to family she had.

"Fine," she said ungraciously. "We'll talk later," she warned Damian, and then followed Nick out the door and down the hall to his office, which was considerably bigger and way more palatial than Lilia's setup. An entire wall of windows looked out over the water, behind a massive desk of some dark wood. A short couch and some chairs of deep brown leather formed a conversation group in the far corner, and there were expensive-looking collectibles scattered on shelves and tables all around. None of them gave off a magical vibe, but they all said money.

"In here," Nick said, continuing through his office to a hidden keypad. He entered the appropriate code and a concealed door popped open with a hiss that spoke of a tight seal.

How cool was that? No matter how many times she'd been here, Casey was always intrigued by the very idea of a secret room. She followed Nick into the hidden room, and then gazed around, amazed again at the extent of his collection. She'd seen a lot of magical collections. Hell, she'd just spent way more time than she'd have liked in one of Sotiris's treasure troves. But this . . . this was possibly the largest collection of magical artifacts on the planet. She'd certainly never seen or even heard of anything like it.

"Still pretty nice, even compared to Sotiris's, huh?" Nick asked in a massive understatement. He walked over, and set the Talisman on a narrow table in the center of the room.

"Sotiris's junk room doesn't even come close," she admitted, then asked casually, "So, what's up?"

Nick turned with a grin. Sorcerer or not, she had to admit he was a damn fine male specimen. "You know what's up, Casey. You're pissed because I didn't reveal all the bloody details of my past—"

"Your past, Nick? You mean like two *thousand years* ago?"

He shrugged. "What does it matter? You wouldn't blink an eye at a thousand-year-old vampire, would you? Magic exists. You know that. And for some, it bestows great gifts. You know that, too. As for my past . . . there's a lot riding on the decisions I make. I won't apologize for that."

"Okay," she said, wanting to be reasonable. "I don't like it, but I can understand that. I can even understand your obsession with secrecy. After all these years, it's probably second nature. But this was *my* mission, Nick. Damian took that box from Sotiris's collection without telling me about it, and then *you* wanted him to keep it a secret, even after he turned it over to you. I know what drives Damian. He'd walk through fire if you asked him to do it. But it's not right, Nick. I should know what's happening on my own fucking mission."

"You're right. But if you only knew how important it was. . . . You know what, Casey? Come here." He walked past her to the far corner of the room, with its softly lit alcove, and the four small statues she'd seen before . . . no wait, there were only three statues now, and what looked like a pile of sand. She stepped closer. The statues were crudely made, nothing like the sophisticated art in the other room, but the figures were still discernible. Three warriors, all very different, and yet with the same fierce aspect, the same determination in their expressions. And the fourth . . .

The truth took her breath away. She glanced over at Nick, who was regarding the statues with a look of such longing that she knew he hadn't intended for her to see it. She shifted her gaze back to the crude stone figures. "This is them, isn't it? And that one"—she pointed to the pile of sand—"that was Damian."

"Yes," he said roughly. "These are what I work for. The whole reason I accepted this position with the FBI. Because it gives me access to resources and information that I can use to find them."

She looked over at him and cocked her head. "It was total serendipity that I found Damian and lifted his curse."

He smiled slightly. "But you would never have been *on* that rooftop if I hadn't sent you to find the Talisman. And aren't you the one who suggested that Damian's release could weaken the hold of Sotiris's magic on the others?"

She nodded. "It makes sense. His spell hit them all at the same time, which means the curses are linked at least a little bit." She tilted her head quizzically. "Damian told me about what was in that box that he took."

Nick smiled. "Of course he did." He bent slightly to retrieve a small, but elaborately carved, wooden box from the bottom shelf of the alcove. The shelf wasn't lit, and the one above it was solid, which explained why she hadn't noticed it before. Still, the box was gorgeous, its beauty only highlighting the coarseness of the statues above.

"This is what Damian brought me." He opened it, and Casey peered inside. She frowned. It looked almost like a child's collection of memorabilia. A small book, ancient and frayed, handwritten in a language she didn't recognize. A wicked-looking claw, big enough to be from a huge animal, though she had no idea which one. A fired ceramic figurine of a black bear, fierce and, yet, almost delicate, with golden eyes that were small chips of what might be topaz. And one last item—a child's ring of some thin metal, but with a bronze sunburst on the wide, flat surface. That one snagged her attention. It was Damian's. He'd told her about it, but even if he hadn't, she'd have known. She reached out as if to touch it, pulling her hand back at the last moment.

"What do you feel, Casey?" Nick asked quietly.

"Magic," she whispered. But the energy surrounding the objects was so fragile that she feared it would shatter if she got too close. "How did Sotiris get hold of these? Damian said you were betrayed."

Nick nodded. "We had a valet, someone whose family had worked with mine for generations, someone we all trusted, and considered a friend. And he traded all of that—the generations of loyalty, the trust and friendship of those good and honorable men—for gold. I tortured him for weeks, pulled out every last screaming excuse from his miserable soul, and I still don't understand why he did it."

Casey shot Nick a startled look at his casual mention of torture. She tried to cover it by brushing a stray hair behind her ear, but he caught it. He gave her a knowing smile. "You're shocked at the idea of torture? You should talk to your boyfriend."

"He's not my boyfriend," she snapped, but almost immediately knew how stupid that sounded. So did Nick apparently, because he laughed.

"So you're what . . . just sleeping together? You don't do casual, babe."

"Whatever." The last thing she wanted to discuss with Nick was her love life, and especially not her sexual relationship with his best friend. Indicating the box and its contents, she asked, "Can you use these to reverse the spell?"

Nick shook his head. "It's too late for that, even if I knew precisely what he'd done, the elements he'd used. Which I don't. But these were the foci for his casting. You felt the magic yourself. I've already used them in a counterspell to weaken the fabric of Sotiris's spell even further, beyond what the lifting of Damian's curse has already done. Whereas before, the magic worked actively to conceal itself, and hence my brothers' stone prisons, it will now draw toward itself the very elements needed to break the specific curses."

Casey thought about that. "You mean like . . . a person? Like me?"

"Exactly. Damian's curse required a female warrior; that was you. Had you not already released him, the effect of this new counter-casting would be to draw you to his side. The curses will now *want* to be lifted."

She nodded, deep in thought. She'd always been fascinated by magical theory, and here she'd been working with a bona fide expert, a fucking ancient *sorcerer,* and never known it. She slanted a scowling look at Nick, still pissed about that.

"Give it up, Case," he teased. "You know I did the right thing."

"Give what up?" Damian's welcome voice intruded. "Are you tormenting my girlfriend, Nico?"

Nick gave her a smug look at Damian's use of "girlfriend," which she ignored.

"What are you—" Damian's question broke off when he spied the wooden box and its contents.

"Nick was telling me about the curse," she told him. "And how he hopes to counter it now that you've brought him these." She lifted her chin to indicate the ancient mementos.

Damian shot Nick a hopeful look. "You really think it will work?"

Nick clapped a hand on his shoulder, and his eyes were suspiciously moist when he said, "I do. We're bringing them home, brother."

Casey watched as the two of them embraced. Two beautiful men, energy radiating off of them that had little to do with their powerful physiques, and everything to do with sheer force of will. And magic. Their link went beyond blood, beyond love. And she felt suddenly alone. They belonged together in a way she could never be a part of. She took an involuntary step back, almost as if preparing herself for the pain to come. But as if he'd felt her sudden distance, or maybe the hollow ache in her heart, Damian reached out and pulled her into the circle of his arm, including her in their little group hug. She wanted to be cynical about that, but she didn't feel that way. She felt relieved. She felt loved. She slipped her hand under his arm and up over his shoulder, tipping her head against his cheek. He kissed the top of her head, and she flushed with happiness.

Nick winked at her. "I'm sorry to break up this little love fest, but I have work to do," he said, pulling out of the group hug, and hustling them out of his vault. Closing the door behind them, he said, "You two go ahead and do . . . whatever it is that young people do these days."

"Oh good grief," Lilia said, walking into the office. "Is he pulling that old-man routine again? Nick, your appointment is here."

"Oh, right. Thanks, Lili." He turned to face Casey and Damian. "Seriously, you guys take a week off, get settled, play in the sun. But then I need you back here. My counterspell will only go so far in finding the others. The rest will be up to us and old-fashioned investigation techniques. Casey, now that you know what's what, I can target your particular skills much more effectively."

She met his golden-brown gaze from across the room, and saw understanding there.

"You got it, boss," she said, putting into her response all of the feelings she could never say to him out loud. Things he probably didn't want her to. "'Bye, Lili!" she called, then grabbed Damian's hand and pulled him down the hall and out the front door. But when they reached her truck, she hesitated. She looked up at him. "You don't have to come with me, if you don't want. I mean, I'd understand—"

Damian silenced her with a kiss. Although "kiss" was such an insufficient word for the way his lips teased hers open, the way he seduced her tongue into dancing with his, sending sparks of desire shooting from the tips of her breasts to her belly and deep between her thighs. She melted against him, her arms around his waist.

"There's nowhere, no *when,* I'd rather be than with you, Cassandra. I love you."

"I love you, too," she whispered, tears filling her eyes. "So, I guess we're going home."

"Home," he repeated then gave her a wicked grin. "Can I drive?"

Epilogue

Los Angeles, California

GRACE VAN ALLEN peered at the ancient scroll beneath her illuminated magnifier, ignoring the ache in her back that said she'd been at her task too long. Again. Her friends had all but given up on her, knowing their attempts to get her out of the basement and into some semblance of a social life were doomed to failure. She loved her friends, and certainly didn't want to lose them, but the main reason they went out was to meet men, specifically *the* man who would become *the* husband with whom to create the proverbial white picket fence and 2.5 kids. Grace had nothing against picket fences or kids. She just didn't think she was going to find her perfect mate in a poorly lit club with too loud music.

"Good God, Grace," she muttered. "You've become your mother." She grinned at the thought, and didn't know who should be more horrified by the comparison—her or her mom. "Mom, definitely," she said, then realized she was doing it again. She had a tendency to talk to herself when she was working all alone in the museum where she'd been lucky enough to secure an internship while working on her PhD in Archaeology. More specifically, ancient scrolls and texts. A new collection had come in this week, an acquisition from an aging private collector who didn't think his heirs were smart enough to appreciate their value. Their historic value, that was. He was afraid they'd sell his treasures to the highest bidder after he died, and they'd end up in the vault of some soulless billionaire, never to be seen again.

She tended to agree with his assessment of the collection's likely fate, and was thrilled that he'd donated them to the museum instead. She'd been cataloguing the new acquisitions for days now, but tonight was the first time she'd found something unexpected. The thrill of finding something new, something no one had seen before, was making her heart pound and her stomach churn. The scroll was in horrible condition. It had obviously never been restored. But it wasn't the physical condition that made this scroll unique. It was the language it had been written in. She'd been at it for hours, and still hadn't found anything familiar. In fact, she wasn't certain this was a language at all. The lines of text looked more like symbols than letters.

Puzzled, she walked the length of the basement, from her small corner to the very opposite end where the more senior researchers worked. She was hoping someone else might be working late, maybe someone who knew ancient architecture rather than language, and would recognize what appeared to be mathematic symbols on the scroll. She wasn't convinced that's what they were. But if it wasn't language and it wasn't math, what did that leave?

When she reached the opposite end of the basement, no one was there, of course. No one but the warrior who'd been standing guard in the same dark corner for as long as she'd been studying at the university, and probably a lot longer than that. She didn't know his story, where he'd come from, or why he'd never been moved upstairs, and the few people she'd asked hadn't seemed to know either.

Holding the scroll, she stopped to talk to him as she always did when no one was around. He always looked a little sad to her, his eyes conveying a loneliness that spoke to the skill of the sculptor. It drove her to reach out to him, to break his terrible solitude when she could.

She paused now, holding up the scroll in one hand, her fingers resting on his powerful forearm with the other. "I bet *you* know what this is, don't you? I wish you could come to life. We'd have a nice cup of tea—or you'd like something stronger, wouldn't you?—and you could help me decipher this damn thing."

She peered up at him, frowning. Was there a spark in those stone eyes that hadn't been there before? She stared until her own eyes watered, then she blinked and shook her head. "Time to go home, Grace." She patted the warrior's arm. "I'll be back tomorrow," she told him. "You think about it and let me know."

She walked back to her cubicle and locked the scroll away with the others, then took her purse out of her desk drawer and left, turning out the lights behind her.

At the other end of the long room, a noise penetrated the darkness—the gritty sound of sand hitting the linoleum floor.

To be continued . . .

Acknowledgments

I want to thank my editor, Brenda Chin, for seeing the possibilities in this book, and helping me bring it to life. I'm a better writer for having worked with her. I also want to thank Debra Dixon for giving me the leeway to tell my stories, and for designing such a beautiful cover for Damian.

My fellow writers—Angela Addams, Steve McHugh, and Michelle Muto—are always generous with their friendship and their talent, and make the solitary task of writing a lot less lonely. I want to thank Karen Roma for everything she does to promote my books, and for doing a beta read on a very short schedule.

As always, I have to thank my family for their love and support, and especially my wonderful husband, who's shown me every day we've been together what makes a true hero.

About the Author

D. B. Reynolds arrived in sunny Southern California at an early age, having made the trek across the country from the Midwest in a station wagon with her parents, her many siblings, and the family dog. And while she has many (okay, some) fond memories of Midwestern farm life, she quickly discovered that LA was her kind of town and grew up happily sunning on the beaches of the South Bay.

D. B. holds graduate degrees in international relations and history from UCLA (go Bruins!) and was headed for a career in academia, but, in a moment of clarity, she left behind the politics of the hallowed halls for the better-paying politics of Hollywood, where she worked as a sound editor for several years, receiving two Emmy nominations, an MPSE Golden Reel, and multiple MPSE nominations for her work in television sound.

Book One of her Vampires in America series, RAPHAEL, launched her career as a writer in 2009, while JABRIL, Vampires in America Book Two, was awarded the RT Reviewers' Choice Award for Best Paranormal Romance (Small Press) in 2010. ADEN, Vampires in America Book Seven, was her first release under the new ImaJinn imprint at BelleBooks.

D. B. currently lives in a flammable canyon near the Malibu coast with her husband of many years, and when she's not writing her own books, she can usually be found reading someone else's. You can visit D. B. at her website, dbreynolds.com, for information on her latest books, contests, and giveaways.

Printed in Great Britain
by Amazon